AMBUSH

Little Wolf raised his arm and was about to signal Black Feather when, suddenly, a figure rose in front of him, directly between him and his Cheyenne friend. His whole nervous system suddenly went numb. The man had been kneeling between two small boulders no more than ten feet in front of him. Little Wolf realized that Black Feather did not see the man. He also realized that the man, an army scout by the look of his buckskin shirt and blue army-issue trousers, was not aware of Little Wolf's presence behind him. As he watched, the scout slowly raised his carbine and drew down on the unsuspecting Cheyenne.

There was no time for thought. Little Wolf, without consciously thinking about what he was about to do, pulled his stone club from his belt and brought it down across the back of the man's skull. . . .

Wind River

CHARLES G. WEST

A SIGNET BOOK

SIGNET
Published by New American Library, a division of
Penguin Putnam Inc., 375 Hudson Street,
New York, New York 10014, U.S.A.
Penguin Books Ltd, 27 Wrights Lane,
London W8 5TZ, England
Penguin Books Australia Ltd,
Ringwood, Victoria, Australia
Penguin Books Canada Ltd, 10 Alcorn Avenue,
Toronto, Ontario, Canada M4V 3B2
Penguin Books (N.Z.) Ltd, 182–190 Wairau Road,
Auckland 10, New Zealand

Penguin Books Ltd, Registered Offices:
Harmondsworth, Middlesex, England

First published by Signet, an imprint of New American Library,
a division of Penguin Putnam Inc.

First Printing, July 1999
10 9 8 7 6 5 4 3 2 1

 REGISTERED TRADEMARK—MARCA REGISTRADA

Printed in the United States of America

For Ronda

CHAPTER 1

"Now what the hell's ailing you, Sadie?" Squint Peterson dug his heels into the belly of his balky old mule.

The mule had been cranky all morning, more so than usual. She was naturally bad-tempered anyway, so much so that Squint had named her after an ill-mannered prostitute who had accommodated him at the rendezvous in the summer of '39. He grinned as the thought of that particular union came to mind. It was his first and last rendezvous. He wasn't much more than a kid, fifteen years old. He had spent the winter trapping on the Yellowstone with his Uncle Bris. In fact, it was his Uncle Bris who introduced him to Sadie, giving her instructions to "Rub the peach fuzz offen him." He laughed when he recalled his introduction to *"the sins of the flesh."* She rubbed it off all right, but not without a gracious plenty moaning. The poor woman had whined and complained the whole time he was trying to satisfy his needs.

"You'da thought she was the Queen of Sheba," he announced aloud. When he concentrated on it, he could still see her screwed-up expression when he removed his buckskin britches, revealing long underwear that had not seen the light of day for at least two months before that night. The abrupt physical release that followed cost him two prime beaver pelts. She wanted two more, since he hadn't washed before coming to her tent, but he lied that two were all he had left. He might have been green as a willow switch and rutty as a springtime buck, but he wasn't about to let go of his hard-earned plews for one go-round on a puffy-faced old whore. She reluctantly admitted him to what she referred to as her paradise, the memory of which lingered with him long after he had journeyed back down

the south fork of the Powder. As a matter of fact, he had
not been able to rid himself of the last of those memories
until that winter's first freeze when he submerged his buckskins, with him still in them, in an icy mountain stream. He
almost froze himself to death but it got rid of the stubborn
body lice.

"Matter of fact," he told the mule, "that was about the
last real rendezvous they had." He shook his head in
amazement when he thought about it. "Twenty-four . . .
no, twenty-six years ago . . . Damn! Has it been that long?"
It was hard to imagine he had spent that many years roam-
ing around these mountains, still retaining his scalp. There
had been a couple of times when the threat of Indian trouble had influenced him to head back to civilization for a
while, but it never lasted. The longest was a period of two
years when he tried his hand at being a lawman. Two years
of that was enough to drive any man back to the mountains.

He shifted in the saddle a little to ease the ache in his
back. It caused him to ponder his chosen way of life and
the future it offered. He liked it best in the mountains, but
he wondered if he wasn't approaching the age where his
senses might start to lose their keen edge. And he knew
that when you lost that edge, you usually lost your scalp
along with it. The thought of his hair decorating the lance
of some Sioux warrior didn't serve to overly frighten him.
He just didn't like the idea of being bested by anyone when
it came to surviving by one's wits. There were a few gray
hairs showing up in his beard already but he could still cut
sign quick as most Indians and shoot better than any man
he'd met so far. He had to admit, however, that it was
getting easier to thread a needle if he held it at arm's
length, a fact that accounted for several briar rips in his
buckskins that needed repair. Maybe he should give more
thought to moving out of hostile country. Maybe it was
time to move on to Oregon, a big territory. Squint needed
a big country. He was a big man and he required room to
stretch out. *Well,* he decided, *I reckon I got a few years yet
before I'm ready to turn toes-up.*

"Sadie, git!" he admonished and stuck his heels in her
again. She seemed reluctant to step across the narrow gully
that had been formed by the recent snow and runoff. Had
he not been thinking of a prostitute at rendezvous, he might

have been more alert to the mule's skittishness. As it was, he was taken completely by surprise.

He found himself in midair before he had time to realize what had happened. At first he thought he had been attacked by a mountain lion or a bear. He landed on his back, his assailant on top of him. The force of his contact with the hard ground knocked the wind out of him. By then he realized his attacker was a man and, in spite of the pain in his lungs, he struggled to defend himself from the thrust of the knife as it sought to evade his arms and find a vulnerable spot. There was no time for conscious thought. He fought totally by reflex, sparring with the arm that held the knife while pushing against the man's neck with his other hand. He could hear the man grunt as he strained to gain advantage. Finally his assailant tore himself from Squint's grasp and raised his knife hand for one desperate thrust. Squint managed to catch his wrist in his hand and block the assault. There was one final attempt to free himself and then the strength seemed to suddenly drain from the man's arm like water from a busted water bag and Squint realized that he was in complete control. His assailant had given up the fight.

Squint quickly rolled over on top of the man, pinning him to the ground while he fought to regain his breath. His initial thought, as soon as he could breathe again, was to dispatch the red-skinned son of a bitch, for he could now identify him as an Indian, straight to hell. As furious as he was at having been attacked, he was almost equally angry for letting himself be taken like that, like a damned green tenderfoot.

There seemed to be little resistance from his adversary as he shook the knife loose from the Indian's hand. When he stuck the point against his throat, the man made no effort to defend himself. This lack of resistance caused Squint to hesitate and, since the man no longer seemed an immediate threat, he paused to consider what manner of being he was about to send to the great beyond.

"Why, hell, you ain't no more than a boy." He sat back on his heels, still astraddle the Indian. "And a pretty damn scrawny one at that."

There was no response from the boy. His eyes, dull and lifeless, appeared to focus on some faraway object. It was obvious to Squint that he was prepared to die. In fact, he looked like he was two-thirds gone already. It was evident that he had mustered all his strength for that one desperate attack and, when it failed, it had drained him. Moments before, when they had struggled for possession of the knife, Squint could have killed him without thinking twice about it. Now, as the boy lay helpless beneath him, he was reluctant to dispatch him.

"What the hell did you jump me for?" Squint demanded, not expecting an answer for he spoke in English, even though he could converse a little in several Indian dialects. It was a little late for caution, but he stood up and looked around to make sure the boy had acted alone. At the same time he kept an eye on his assailant, still lying there. Satisfied that he was in no danger of attack from another quarter, he turned his full attention to his captive. It occurred to him that the boy wasn't dressed too well for the chilly weather that had descended upon the valley for the past few weeks, wearing only a buckskin shirt and leggings. It was then that he noticed the dark crusted spot in the shoulder of the shirt.

"Damn, boy, looks like you been shot or something." This might explain the boy's apparent weakness. "Better let me take a look at that."

When he started to open the shirt over the wound, the boy recoiled in pain and made one feeble effort to resist.

"If I was gonna hurt you, I'da done kilt you," Squint grunted as he brushed the boy's hand aside.

The wound was bad. From the looks of it, Squint guessed it was caused by a bullet, and from the way it was all inflamed and swollen, the slug was probably still in it.

"I tell you what," Squint decided, "that thing looks like it's festering and I'm gonna have to dig it out of there."

If he had any objection, the boy didn't register it. He didn't have any fight left in him and offered no resistance when Squint took his arms and pulled him up so he could heft him up on his shoulder.

"Boy, you ain't got no weight to you a'tall." He marveled that the lad had been able to summon enough force to knock him off his mule. When he realized how light he was, Squint couldn't help but feel a little sheepish that he had allowed himself to be taken so easily.

"Whoa, Sadie. Hold still." He spoke softly in an effort to calm the mule. Sadie still seemed a mite skittish, what with the smell of Indian still in her nostrils. Rolling back her eye in an effort to keep the man and his burden in view, she attempted to sidestep her hindquarters away from him. He began to wish he had ridden one of his horses and left the mule back in his tiny corral. "Hold still!" Impatience crept into his tone as he grew tired of following the retreating beast around in a circle, the wounded Indian boy on his shoulder and the mule's reins in his free hand. Finally he gave the reins a hard jerk to show the reluctant mule who was boss and she kicked her hind legs once in response. But, after registering that one complaint, she settled down and accepted the load Squint slid off his shoulder onto the saddle. She grunted once more in protest when Squint stepped up behind the boy. He gave her a couple of hard kicks with his heels and she broke into a trot for a few yards, then settled down to a slow walk. Squint knew he could kick her until her slats caved in and she would still give him no more than a few yards at a trot before falling back into a walk. She would run, but only when she was with his horses when they ran. So he resigned himself to a leisurely ride back to his camp. "I hope you don't bleed to death before we git back." The boy was drooped over Squint's arm, unconscious or dead, Squint wasn't sure.

As he settled his body into the rhythm of the mule's walk, he wondered what manner of creature he was bringing home with him. He wasn't accustomed to running into anyone this far up in the hills and he didn't particularly care to have anyone know he was even there, let alone take them to his camp. This was not the first time he had decided to winter in the mountains, instead of going down to one of the settlements until spring. He knew it wasn't a real good idea to winter in the same camp two years in a row. Somebody might discover it and lie in ambush for you the next year. But this one was so well hidden he figured the odds were good that he was still the only man who had set foot in the small ravine he had stumbled on while tracking a wounded deer, two years ago this spring.

His mind returned briefly to that chilly spring morning. He had jumped the deer accidentally while making his way down through a stand of lodgepole pine, on his way to the

river to water his horses. When the buck suddenly sprang
from a thicket, it took Squint completely by surprise. He
reacted quickly enough to grab his rifle and get off a shot,
even though the animal was running directly away from
him and didn't offer much of a target. Squint only had time
for one shot. He hit him but he didn't kill him. The shot
caught him in the shoulder. The impact was enough to
knock the deer down and roll him over but he was back
on his feet immediately and off again. Squint hated it when
he didn't get a clean kill shot at an animal. That meant
tracking him until he bled himself out and died.

He must have followed that deer for a mile or more
before he lost the trail just on the other side of an outcropping of rock overlooking a stream, swollen with winter's runoff. There was no sign of the wounded animal
anywhere. Beyond the stream, a clearing stretched for a
quarter of a mile. If the deer had crossed the stream, Squint
would have been able to see him long before he reached
the other side of the clearing. He was sure he had not lost
the trail up until he reached the rock outcropping. There
was no other place for the buck to go, unless he went
straight up the side of a cliff. If it had been a bighorn, that
would have been a possibility, but a deer? Squint didn't
think so. Still, there was no deer in sight.

Feeling as though he had been totally bamboozled by a
dumb animal, Squint dismounted, for his horse was having
difficulty maintaining sure footing on the rock. As he led
him back the way they had come, he stumbled and would
have fallen had he not caught himself with one hand. As
he was about to straighten up, he glanced to his side at
what he had thought was a little stand of pines in front of
a solid rock wall. From his position close to the ground, he
was surprised to find that he could see daylight between
the tree trunks. Instead of standing in front of a solid rock
wall, the trees were in fact standing in an opening into the
wall. The fact that there was a solid bridge of rock spanning
the opening made it appear there was a solid wall behind
them. Leading his horse through the trees, Squint found an
opening through the rocks big enough for two horses to
pass though side by side. Once through the opening, he
had found himself in a clearing, maybe half of an acre in
size. It was walled in by the mountain on three sides with

a small stream trickling through the northernmost point. The floor was carpeted with grass and there, under a clump of low-growing laurel, the deer lay dying.

A sudden groan from the Indian boy, as Sadie almost stumbled, brought Squint's mind back to the business at hand. Now, two years later, he was bringing a human being into his secret camp, although the wounded boy might be closer kin to the wounded deer he had originally followed here. He had to admit that he had some doubts about giving away the location of this place. If there ever was a perfect camp, this place had to be it. What with the trouble that was brewing all over between the army and the Indians, a man needed a good secure camp to hole up in.

To say he was overly worried about Indian trouble would not be accurate. He wasn't as unconcerned as he used to be, however. It used to be that, if a man wanted to trap some beaver, take some meat when he needed it . . . even buffalo . . . as long as he stayed to himself . . . why, hell, the Indians wouldn't bother him. As a matter of fact, he had quite a few friends among the Shoshone. Wounded Elk's winter camp on the Wind River had been one of his favorite visits the year before. It was different now. This year, he wasn't sure if he would be welcome or not. All the tribes seemed to be in a state of agitation. There had been some reports that the Cheyenne were getting stirred up south of here. The Blackfeet were getting set to start some real trouble up north. They never got along with many of the other tribes as it was and they sure didn't have any love for the white man. Squint could readily see for himself that the Sioux were getting ready to give somebody some grief. For some time now, he occasionally observed Sioux, Lakota as they called themselves, in war parties coming through the passes that led down to the basin country. He only saw them from a distance but they were close enough to tell that they were not hunting or horse-raiding parties. They were wearing paint and feathers. The fact that his policy was to keep them at a distance, where he could see them but not vice versa, was the key to his survival in this hostile country.

A man with half a gourd full of seeds would probably pack up what skins he had and get the hell out of here before the real trouble starts, he thought. *But what the hell would I do to make a living?* The last job he had held down in civilization was sheriff of a two-horse town on the Missouri. "And I'm damned if I'm going back to that," he muttered.

Another groan from the Indian boy caused him to wonder if he wasn't just toting a body a hell of a long way to bury it. *Probably should have just cut his throat back there and be done with it,* he thought. It was a useless thought because Squint couldn't bring himself to kill a defenseless boy, and that was what irritated him most. "Too damn softhearted for my own good," he mumbled.

A low snort from one of the horses, probably Joe, told him that they smelled the mule approaching. He carefully guided Sadie over the rock and onto the thick floor of pine needles so as not to leave a track leading up to the entrance of his camp. As a matter of habit, he stopped at the opening in the rock and waited, listening. Joe snorted again and the mule answered. Joe seemed to feel a fondness for the mule, even favored her over Squint's other horse, a little mare he called Britches. He named her that because of her markings. She was dappled all over except for her legs. They were black and it made her look like she was wearing britches on her front and hind legs. All seemed in order in his camp. Even so, he entered the clearing cautiously, looking first to the ledges over the opening and then toward the clump of laurel, behind which the horses were tethered. Long ago he inspected his little hideout from the perspective of someone who might have a notion to ambush him. He decided these two positions would be the most likely places to hide, so he always checked them first. Content that his camp was safe, he entered the clearing.

Squint didn't know a hell of a lot about doctoring, but he knew enough to recognize an infected bullet wound when he saw one. And he had seen more than a few of them when he had been a sheriff, what with all the drunken cowboys and half crazy mountain men that had stumbled through his town, fighting over just about everything from cards to women. For most of the years he was the law there, there wasn't any doctor as such. Most of the bullet wounds that were treated at all were tended to by one old woman, who was really a midwife. Usually, if the victim didn't die right away, and the wound bled freely, it healed well enough if left alone. More gunshot cases were walking around with the lead still in them than those that had the bullet removed. Sometimes, however, the bullet would be close to the surface and the wound would fester if it hadn't bled clean, like this Indian boy's, and it would be necessary to dig the lead out and cauterize the wound. It wasn't much fun for the person with the wound but Squint didn't know any other way to stop the festering. He had seen it go untreated before and the result was usually the loss of a limb, or worse.

After he had checked on the horses and unsaddled the mule, he went about building a fire and readying himself to take care of the boy. His patient didn't appear to be faring any too well and Squint wondered anew if he was just wasting his time. Maybe it would be more humane to simply leave the poor kid in peace and not complicate his dying. Still, he thought, the boy was obviously unconscious. The only sign of life was an occasional babble of some kind that Squint was unable to make out. It sounded like Cheyenne, but he couldn't say for sure. At any rate, the boy was out of his head so it didn't figure to make much difference whether Squint dug the bullet out or not. The boy wouldn't feel it anyway, so he might just as well operate on him.

He took his skinning knife and cut the boy's shirt away, leaving the wound exposed for him to work on. It looked bad, swollen to the point that it looked like it was ready to bust open on its own accord, like a huge boil. He could see a dark blue spot in the center that had to be the bullet. It appeared to be just beneath the surface. Squint's experience with bullet wounds told him that it would be a lot deeper than it looked. He watched the boy's face as he stoned a keen edge on the already sharp skinning knife. There was still no sign of consciousness.

"Let's get it done," he sighed and wiped the blade of the knife on his leggings. "You're damned lucky you ain't awake for this."

Once resigned to the task, Squint didn't waste any time on gentleness. Human hide was tough and he sank the knife deep into the boy's shoulder at the top of the wound and then cut straight down across the entire swollen area. The boy stiffened perceptibly but made no sound. Almost at once, thick, yellow pus oozed from the incision and Squint recoiled when the acrid smell of rotting flesh assaulted his nostrils.

"Damn!" he exclaimed and backed away for a moment before continuing. He cleaned the wound as best he could with a square of cloth, the remains of a shirt he had brought with him when he first came to the mountains. Squeezing the cloth out in a pan of water he had placed near the fire to warm, he wiped away the rest of the pus. The wound was still weeping, but now it was mostly blood. He probed in the wound for the bullet but found that he had to cut deeper to expose it. The problem now was the wound was becoming a bloody, pulpy mess and it was difficult to see the piece of lead he was groping for. Still, he was determined to dig it out. After inflicting this amount of damage on the boy's shoulder, he couldn't quit without retrieving the bullet. Finally he felt the blade tick the piece of metal and, with the knifepoint, he worked at it until he had gotten it free of the surrounding flesh. After rinsing it with water, he held it up to examine it.

"That shore ain't no musket ball," he announced. It was a slug from a breech-loading rifle. "Army Spencer, more likely." Squint's interest was one of idle speculation. He wasn't really concerned with how the boy had come to get himself shot. Now that he had extracted the bullet, he concerned himself with the wound.

From the look of it, and certainly from the smell of it, there was a great deal of rotten flesh around the edges of the wound. *Little wonder the boy's so sick,* he thought. *It can't do him much good to have all that rot around that open wound.* He pondered his next move for a moment or two before deciding to proceed with the cauterization. He remembered seeing a medicine man in Wounded Elk's camp treat a lance wound that had festered about as bad as this one. He had stuck a handful of maggots right on the wound and let them eat away the rotten flesh. Squint didn't have any maggots. Even if he did, he figured that burning it away with a hot knife was better than maggots anyway.

Again, there was little response from the wounded boy

when Squint applied the red-hot skinning knife, just a mild, convulsive tremor before falling limp again. Since the response was so slight, Squint took his time and thoroughly seared the flesh over the entire wound, the smell of the infection now masked by the odor of burning flesh. The surgery complete, he sat back on his haunches to examine his work. The boy was breathing steadily. The thought crossed Squint's mind that the boy might fool him and pull through. It was, after all, a shoulder wound. If he had been gut shot, his chances wouldn't be worth much. It would probably depend on the boy's constitution, on how bad he wanted to live. Time would tell—Squint had done all he knew to do for him.

He decided it best to leave the wound open to the air that night. He could put some grease on it and bandage it in the morning. The night air would probably do it some good and, this time of year, there wasn't any problem with flies getting into it. He rigged up a bed for the boy and covered him with a deer hide. Night was settling in over the mountains by then. If his patient woke up in the morning, he would see about feeding him. If he didn't, he would bury him.

The boy was strong. He was still among the living when the sun rose high enough for the first rays to filter over the mountain and illuminate the delicate crystals of frost that had formed on the grass floor of Squint's camp. Squint yawned and shivered involuntarily as he stood at the edge of the clearing and emptied his bladder, absentmindedly watching the steam formed by his warm urine on the frost.

Cold, I hate being cold, he thought.

He glanced back over his shoulder at the still form of the Indian boy. He had checked on him as soon as he was awake and, although the boy still seemed to be asleep, he appeared to be breathing easily. His fever might even be broken. Squint couldn't tell for sure. "I reckon I better put some wood on the fire and see about getting us something to eat."

As he picked a few sticks of wood from his pile, he pondered his options now that he had taken on an invalid. He was still not sure the boy was going to make it. If he did, then Squint would have some decisions to make as to what he should do with him. He wasn't even sure the boy wouldn't attack him again when he got strong enough. "Hell," he muttered as he balanced a stick of firewood across the load already on his arm, "I might have to nurse him back to health just so I can cut his throat."

He stirred up the coals, all that was left of the fire, until he worked up a flame. Then he laid some small sticks on it until they caught well enough to start up the larger pieces. He had a pretty good-size woodpile and, if the winter was not too severe, it should probably last him through. He didn't like to go out looking for firewood in the deep snow. As he stared into the growing flame, feeling its warmth on his face, he couldn't help but remember how he had sweated when he had cut the wood last summer. It had been quite a chore, and Squint was not one to appreciate chores. "But when you got yourself a year-round camp," he muttered, "you have to do things like cutting firewood and drying jerky." It was almost like homesteading. And the wood had to be hauled in by mule from the other side of the mountain because Squint was afraid he might give away the location of his camp by cutting wood close by.

A groan from the boy pulled his attention from the fire and he turned to look at his patient. The boy, still asleep apparently, muttered several words that Squint couldn't make out. They were words though, not just grunts, Squint was sure of that. He still thought it sounded like Cheyenne. He bent low over the boy in an effort to hear what he was mumbling about. As he did, the boy opened his eyes and he and Squint stared at each other for a long second. There was a strangeness in the boy's gaze that confounded Squint. Finally he sat back and announced, "Dang if you ain't the first blue-eyed Cheyenne I ever saw."

The boy answered, his voice weak but clear, "I ain't Cheyenne. I'm Arapaho."

This served to startle Squint more than a little, not because of the boy's apparent lucidity, but because he had answered in English.

"Well, I'll be . . ." Squint gazed at the wounded boy in disbelief, never finishing the statement. He simply stared at the boy for a long while. Finally he blurted, "Well, what the hell did you try to bushwhack me for?"

There followed a long pause, during which the boy gazed intently at the grizzled mountain man hovering over him like some great bear about to devour him. There had been a moment of alarm when he first opened his eyes to find the huge man staring down at him, a moment when he wasn't sure what was in store for him. But he quickly decided this bear intended no harm and he answered, "I thought you was a soldier."

Squint considered this for a moment before replying. "Well, any fool can see I ain't." He was trying to make up his mind about the boy. Based on his remark, he wasn't sure whether he was a good Indian or a bad one. He didn't know many Indians who did like soldiers and he couldn't blame him for that. He had to admit that, since living in the mountains for most of the last twenty years, he wasn't sure he liked soldiers himself, and that went for settlers and prospectors and railroads and everybody else who was so damn hell-bent on civilizing the territory. He couldn't help but get riled up whenever he thought about it. If the damn government would just live up to their own treaties and leave the Indians alone, he thought, then there wouldn't be all this trouble that's been heating up over the last two summers. Now it's gotten so the Sioux are out to get any white man they see, no matter whether he's done them harm or not. It didn't take a genius to figure out that the Cheyenne, the Arapaho . . . in fact, all the tribes on the plains were pushed about as far as they were going to be pushed. There was going to be all-out war and he was likely to be caught in the middle of it. Realizing his mind was wandering from the situation at hand, he brought his attention back to his patient.

"Can you eat somethin' now?"

The boy nodded. His eyes betrayed the fact that the offer was met with some enthusiasm. It was not lost on Squint.

"I bet you ain't et for a spell," he said, "from the look of you."

Squint sat back and watched as the boy devoured half of a cold, snow hare that he had cooked the day before. The other half had been Squint's supper. He had planned to eat it for breakfast himself but it was disappearing fast. Since one half of a rabbit wasn't much nourishment for a healthy young buck, much less one that was half dead, Squint dipped into his precious supply of baking soda and mixed up a little batter for pan bread. His pan bread wasn't the best in the territory but, by Squint's standards, it was passable. He poured the batter into a frying pan and set it on some coals at the edge of the fire to let it raise. When he thought it was ready, he pushed it closer to the fire to let it bake. The boy's eyes followed his every move. When the bread was done, he flipped it out and tore it in half. The boy didn't hesitate to accept the half extended toward him.

"You don't waste a lot of time chewing, do you? Just sort of choke it down like a dog."

The boy did not answer but continued to stare at his benefactor. When he was finished, he indicated that he needed to relieve himself and Squint helped him to his feet. He almost fell when the sudden movement sent a stab of pain through his shoulder and Squint had to grab him to keep him upright. He seemed none too steady and Squint offered to help him over to the edge of the clearing but the boy refused. He made it clear that he needed no help when taking care of nature's demands.

"You a mite modest, ain't you?" Squint teased. He stood back and watched the boy stagger toward the woodpile. "Hold on to the woodpile for support. If you fall in your business, holler and I'll come pick you up." The boy made no response. Squint's attempt at humor was lost on him.

While the boy went about his toilet, Squint busied himself getting some jerky from a knapsack. Since the boy had done away with the rabbit, he would have to satisfy his hunger with cold jerky. Busying himself with the knapsack, he pretended to take no notice of the boy but, in fact, he was studying him intently out of the corner of his eye. The kid looked Arapaho right enough but, when he dropped his leggings, he sure had a pale behind. And a pale behind and blue eyes sure as hell didn't add up to any Arapaho he'd ever seen. Squint returned to the fire and made himself comfortable. He watched the boy as he slowly made his way back to the fire and gingerly lowered himself to a sitting position. Once settled, he pulled his shirt away to examine his wound.

"It don't look too pretty but it ought to heal up right proper," Squint offered in the way of explanation. The boy continued to stare at the fair-sized hole in his shoulder, already beginning to form a thin film of scab.

"Did you have to use an axe?"

He blurted it out so suddenly that it startled Squint and he couldn't help but laugh at the boy's tone. He fished around in the pocket of his shirt and came up with a small lead slug. "Well, first I had to dig this out of you." He threw the bullet to the boy. "Then I had to burn the wound to keep it from going rotten. Like I said, it ain't pretty but it'll be all right."

"You damn sure made a mess of it."

"If I had'na, you'da been a one-armed Arapaho and that's a fact."

The boy stared at Squint for a long minute while he evaluated the huge man's statement. Deciding that Squint did what was best for him, he said, "I reckon I ought to thank you."

"You don't have to if it causes you pain," Squint replied sarcastically. The boy didn't reply but shrugged his shoulders, wincing with the pain the movement caused.

They sat in silence for a long while, the boy obviously uncomfortable with the situation he found himself in, until Squint decided it was long past time for some introductions as well as a general understanding as to what their relationship was going to be. He broke the silence.

"My name's Squint Peterson. What's yours?"

"Little Wolf."

Squint considered this momentarily. "Little Wolf," he repeated and paused again. "I mean, what's your real name? Your Christian name? Do you remember it?"

The boy hesitated, obviously reluctant to admit owning one. The intense expression on Squint's face told him that Squint knew he wasn't a blood Arapaho. A frown creased his face as he replied. "I remember," he said softly. "It was Robert . . . Robert Allred."

"Well, Robert, or Little Wolf, whatever you want to call yourself, where are your folks?" He didn't wait for an answer before adding, "How long you been Arapaho?"

The boy thought for a moment before answering. "I don't know. I lost track. I think this is the fourth winter, maybe the fifth, I ain't sure."

"You been living with the Arapaho for four or five years?"

"I been living with the Cheyenne. My father is Arapaho."

That would explain why Squint was certain the boy had been mumbling in Cheyenne when he was delirious the night before. The Cheyenne and Arapaho were longtime allies and quite often lived together. Squint continued to prod him for information. "Tell me how you come to get shot."

"Soldiers." The boy replied in Cheyenne, his eyes narrowed as he spat the word out.

"Soldiers?" Squint echoed. He knew that Cheyenne word well enough. He waited for further explanation but the boy offered no more.

It was apparent that his guest had no use for the military, but Squint still had no way of knowing what he might have done to get himself shot. In his years in the mountains, Squint had occasionally run into white men who had taken up with a tribe of Indians. Most of them were a pretty sorry lot, as far as he was concerned. Some were hiding out from the law back East. Some were just living with an Indian woman temporarily. A few simply preferred the Indian way of life. Squint himself had considered wintering with the Shoshones but decided he'd rather go it alone. He looked long and hard at the boy, trying to see inside his heart. He could see no meanness in the blue eyes that now gazed absently into the fire. For the second time, he asked, "Where are your folks? I don't mean your Injun folks. I mean your white folks."

"Dead."

Squint studied the boy's expressionless face for a moment. "How? How long?" It was obvious the boy wasn't much of a talker but Squint was determined to get the whole story out of him so he kept prodding him with questions until finally he wore him down and he began to talk. It was difficult at first and slow in coming, but once he started, the whole story came out.

CHAPTER 2

Robert's parents were not really dead. At least Robert had no way of knowing whether they were or not. As far as he was concerned, they might as well be. So when he thought of them at all, he considered them dead. He was born in St. Louis. That much he was sure of because he could remember a little about St. Louis and playing in the streets as a small child with the few friends he had. He couldn't remember a lot about his mother. She tolerated him at best. His father had absolutely no use for him. They made little effort to hide the fact that his birth had not come as a blessing to a family with five young'uns already fighting over what little food there was to eat.

It seemed to him that he was a constant irritant to his parents, causing them to fight a great deal more than they did already. His father resented the fact that his mother had gotten herself pregnant for the sixth time, a deed he swore was not done by him. In fact, most of the time he referred to Robert as *that bastard brat of yours.* His mother denied it of course and hated his father for impregnating her with another child to birth. So one night in a saloon, when a mule skinner bound for Oregon casually stated to Robert's father that he wished he had a son to work for him, it appeared to be the answer to his father's prayers. It didn't take much to persuade Robert's mother and a deal was struck that very night. Robert, asleep in his corner of the cubbyhole he shared with his two brothers and three sisters, was trussed up and carried out like a sack of flour. He was all of ten years old.

The mule skinner's name was Lige Talbot. At first he tried to get Robert to call him *Pa* but the lad rebelled at the notion. He knew the nasty old man with the rivulets of tobacco juice framing his chin was not his pa and he refused to call him anything but *sir*. Lige kept Robert tied to his wagon for two days until he figured they'd gotten far enough from St. Louis to take any thoughts of running away out of the lad's mind. His caution was well-founded because Robert did think about it, but he didn't have any-place to go. Lige told him that he had bought and paid for him so Robert knew he wouldn't be welcome if he showed up back home. Being with Lige Talbot was better than being alone so he decided to stick it out for a while.

Lige was bound for Oregon. He was always bound for Oregon and Robert soon came to believe that he would never get there. He didn't have the fortitude required for the long trek so, although he started many times, he could never stick to it for very long. Two weeks out of St. Louis they joined a wagon train on the Oregon Trail but Lige's powerful thirst for spirits caused them to leave the train in Kansas territory where Lige hired his mules out. There were many hauling jobs between the river and the settle-ment of Wyandotte and a man with a good team of mules could make some good money for himself. For a while, Lige prospered. He worked Robert hard but he treated him well enough. There was never any love lost between them, though. It was strictly business. Robert worked, and in re-turn, Lige fed him and gave him a pallet to sleep on. The boy didn't spend much time worrying about his existence. He just figured that all boys had to work sooner or later and he soon forgot his playmates and his brief exposure to childhood back in the streets of St. Louis.

Winter passed and spring came around and, with it, Lige's urge to move on again toward Oregon. He had tired of the work and had become bored with Wyandotte. Be-sides, he had a sizable grubstake built up. So, one morning he announced to Robert that it was time to pack up and go to Oregon. This time he made it as far as Nebraska before the itch for a bottle and a soft shoulder overpowered him and he settled in for a time at a small trading post near the Platte. It was here that Robert came to know firsthand about Indian trouble.

The trading post was run by a man named Johnson so it was known throughout the territory as Johnson's Crossing, built near one of the favorite crossings of the Platte. This location gave him access to the wagon trains heading west as well as trade with the Indians, mostly Pawnee and Ponca.

There were many hardworking, fair-minded men running trading posts across the country. Freeman Johnson was not one of them. He was a short stump of a man with a huge belly and a face full of hair, with not a single hair on the top of his head. When Robert first saw him, he thought the man looked as if his head was put on his neck upside down. Even a boy of Robert's age could sense that the man was not to be trusted.

Lige Talbot was a different story. Lige found a drinking companion and never seemed to catch on to the fact that Johnson would sell him a jug of cheap frontier whiskey at an exhorbitant price, then help him drink it up. Johnson had an enormous capacity for whiskey. Robert suspected this accounted for his huge belly. Lige proved to be such a good customer that Johnson let him and Robert sleep in the back of his stable. It wasn't long until Lige drank up most of the money he had managed to put aside while hauling freight in Kansas. The close comradery Lige shared with Johnson faded quickly when the last of his money disappeared. With the money gone, they found they were no longer welcome to free housing in the stable. Johnson told them they would have to move out. In a moment of desperation, Lige agreed to trade Johnson two of his six mules in exchange for ninety dollars of credit and the use of the stable until the credit ran out. It was enough to make Lige feel comfortable for a while. Johnson was shrewd enough to know that Lige would use up most of the credit on whiskey that didn't cost him a tenth of the total.

Freeman Johnson was a double-dealing, underhanded scoundrel anytime he could get away with it. But he was at his worst when it came to dealing with the Indians who came in to trade with him. Robert came to despise the man, not so much for skinning ole Lige for everything he owned, because Lige more or less deserved it. He knew better than to throw his money away on whiskey but he did it anyway. No, Robert felt little pity for Lige. But it made him feel ashamed when Johnson openly cheated the Pawnees out of prime fox or beaver pelts for a jug of rot-gut frontier whiskey.

The young Pawnee men were like children, trusting Johnson to treat them fairly. It seemed to Robert that Johnson's greatest delight was to introduce a young Indian to the evils of drink. It was a downright dirty thing to do because, for some reason Robert never understood, Indians never seemed to be able to handle liquor. It made them crazy. Johnson convinced them that it enabled them to get more powerful visions and the more they drank the more powerful the visions became. Whenever he got one of them hooked on it, he might as well have owned him because the poor devil would trade anything he owned for that damn jug. Visions were mighty important to an Indian. Usually a young buck would go off by himself for four or five days without food or water in hopes of inducing a vision that would reveal the path of his life for him. With Johnson's firewater, they could sometimes get one in a matter of hours. The trouble was, with too much firewater, they soon didn't want to do anything else. In the few months Robert was there, he had already seen more than a few bucks started on the road to oblivion, thanks to Freeman Johnson. Sometimes Robert would think about it at night, lying on his straw pallet in Johnson's stable, and he wondered why God let somebody like Johnson go on doing the things he did. As it happened, it wasn't God who decided to do something, but rather a band of war-painted savages.

He heard them, nothing more than a rustle of hay at the far end of the stable. Still half asleep, he raised up on one elbow and stared at the small glow of light where the stable wall joined the back of the trading post. He glanced over at the lump that was Lige Talbot to see if he had noticed the light but the steady drone of Lige's snoring told him he was too far gone to notice anything. As he watched the light, it suddenly seemed to become brighter and he realized at once that the light was a fire and the fire was rapidly growing into discernable flames. *The stable was on fire!*

He was now fully alert and was about to yell out an alarm when he saw two, three, then four Pawnee warriors dart by the flames, heading in the direction of the front of the trading post. They looked like devils as the glow of the flames illuminated their faces, painted for war, causing their dark features to gleam menacingly and sending a shiver of cold fear down the boy's spine. Their shadows, twisted and contorted, danced across the stable wall like dark imps as they filed by the fire. Instinctively, he lowered himself back down behind the straw and, as quietly as he could manage, crawled over to the sleeping form beside him.

"Mr. Talbot," he whispered. "Wake up, Mr. Talbot."

Lige Talbot was deep in sleep, aided as usual by the strong spirits of the night before, and he was not easily aroused. Robert had to shake him roughly, several times, before he stirred.

"What is it, boy?" he finally replied, his voice angry, irritated at having his rest interrupted.

"Indians," Robert whispered. "We got to get out of here! Indians is burning the stable!"

"What?" Lige replied, not able to comprehend as yet.

"Indians!" Robert insisted, still tugging at Lige's shoulder. "We got to get out of here!"

Lige recovered his senses enough to get his eyes open and what he saw was enough to bring him out of his blanket. The hay at the end of the stable was blazing by then, sending sparks drifting into the back part of the building where the two of them were sleeping. It would be only a matter of minutes before the whole stable would go up in flames. "The mules!" he yelled and scrambled to his feet.

Robert had already gathered up his scant possessions in preparation for flight and he didn't have to be told to follow Lige when he ran for the back door of the stable. There were no Indians to be seen inside the building. Robert guessed they were busy setting fire to the trading post. They had evidently not seen the two of them sleeping in the stable, or were simply not interested in them.

The mules were in the corral out behind the building with all the other animals—horses mostly, along with a couple of pigs in one corner and one milk cow. This late in the spring, Johnson didn't keep horses inside. Once outside, they could see the trading post catching up in flame. Lige was too worried about his mules to check on Johnson's welfare and he yelled to Robert to get around behind them while he ran to open the corral gate. It wasn't necessary to warn Johnson anyway because, while they were chasing the livestock toward the gate, they heard him shouting profanities at the savages on the other side of the building. The shouts were followed by gunshots, fired by Johnson no doubt, but Robert never found out for sure. There were only three or four shots fired and then the only sound they could hear were the war cries of the savages.

The entire structure was ablaze by then and it lit up the corral and smaller outbuildings. Robert was terrified but still managed to make his feet move toward the gate, waving his arms, trying to herd the animals out of the corral. They too were terrified by the flames and the noise and, at first, they simply ran around and around the small corral in panic. Lige was finally able to turn the lead animal, a large bay mare, toward the opening and freedom and the horses and mules jammed the small gate, almost stopping it up. Robert could see several Indians running in their direction from the front of the trading post in an effort to head them off. It was no doubt their intention to take the animals themselves. Beyond the illumination of the firelight, he could see dark figures in the shadows, closing in on him from both sides. On his right a shadow moved toward the corral. Off to his left, several shadows moved from the trees on a line to intercept him. In his terror, he looked to Lige for assistance but Lige was concerned only with his mules and his own hide. Robert did the only thing he could and that was to get into the middle of the stampeding animals and run with them. He grabbed the tail of a small, dappled gray horse and let the animal pull him through the mass of flying hooves and dirt clods.

He lost his footing and went down in the mud churned up by the many hooves but he held on to the gray's tail, dragged until he could manage to scramble to his feet. As soon as he was up and running again, he looked ahead for Lige, just in time to see the axe buried in Lige's neck. Lige had been too occupied with two of his mules to see the axe coming or the Indian who killed him. It didn't look real. It was so grotesque, the axe buried up to the handle in the side of Lige's neck and the utter shock registered on his face. Robert could not believe it was happening right before his eyes. He didn't have time to react. Things were happening too fast in that moment of confusion. The horses, slowed by the narrow opening in the fence they were all trying to pass through at the same time, squeezed in together. Robert was fearful that he might be crushed by the sheer weight of the horses, even if the Indians didn't kill him. But he still held on to the gray's tail, although he felt he was drowning in a sea of horseflesh.

There was too much confusion and noise. Robert couldn't keep up with the horses and still look around him to see what was going on. So he concentrated on the one thing, staying on his feet and holding on to the gray for dear life, half expecting to feel the sudden bite of a toma-hawk or the sting of an arrow at any moment. Once through the gate, the mob of horses and mules headed for the open country. The gray hesitated for just a moment as if she was waiting for Robert. That moment was all the time Robert needed. He didn't have to think about it. He quickly released the gray's tail and jumped on her back. As soon as the horse felt the boy's weight on her back, she bolted after the rest of the animals in full stride.

Robert had ridden a few horses and mules around the corral of the trading post and once or twice down to the river with Lige, but never at a full gallop. And on those occasions, even though he had no saddle, at least he had a bridle and reins to hold on to. His primary thought now was not to fall off and be trampled to death. So he clamped his knees as tight as he could on the gray's sides and wrapped his arms around her neck. He couldn't be con-cerned with who or what might be pursuing him. All he could do was hang on. The night was dark so he couldn't even see where he might be running to. He just had to trust that the gray wouldn't stumble or run him into any-thing while she was blindly following the mob of horses.

After what seemed to Robert like a long terrifying ride but, in actuality, was only about a half mile, the horses gradually began to slow down until all but a few of the wilder ones broke into a trot and finally a walk. The gray, along with the other horses close by him, stopped and began milling about a small creek. Their panic subsided, they now seemed uncertain of their purpose and appeared to wait for direction from some source. All was quiet be-hind them. The Pawnees were evidently in no hurry to re-cover the livestock. Robert guessed they figured there was no one close enough to come to Freeman Johnson's rescue. They could round up the horses at their leisure after having their fun with Johnson, or what was left of him anyway. Robert didn't want to think about that at the moment. The one thing he was absolutely certain about was that he would be long gone when they did get around to looking for the stock. He pulled the gray's head around and gently kicked her into a canter, letting her go pretty much in any direction she fancied. He didn't care as long as it was away from the trading post. The fact that the gray set out toward Colorado territory would have held no interest for Robert, even had he known.

CHAPTER 3

The next few days following that terrifying night were but a blur in the boy's memory. It had all happened so fast that the one dominant thought in his mind was to run, and run he did. He kicked the gray into a gallop for most of that first night, ever fearful that he might suddenly hear the sound of the Pawnee raiders overtaking him. The rolling hills offered scant cover from pursuers so he knew he had to purchase as much distance as possible before daylight exposed him on the open prairie. The course he set was a wandering one. In fact, he had set no course at all, merely hanging on to the gray, pulling on the horse's ear occasionally when she showed signs of turning back toward their back trail. Eventually the night passed and, when daylight brought no sign of pursuers anywhere on the horizon, Robert finally permitted the weary horse to rest.

For the better part of a week he rode in a generally southwesterly direction, for this seemed to be the easiest route toward the mountains on the distant horizon. He came across enough streams to keep him and his horse from dying of thirst and there was plenty of grass for the horse. But Robert was getting weaker and weaker from want of food. Once he found a bush loaded down with reddish-blue berries and he filled his stomach with the sour fruit. When he had eaten all he could hold, he filled his pockets with the rest of them. The stomachache that resulted almost made him vomit them back up but he realized he had to have nourishment of some kind or he would lose what little strength he had.

He was grateful that the horse had more or less adopted him because he knew that, with no reins or even a rope, he could be afoot at any time the gray decided to rid herself of her burden. Whoever owned the horse had evidently broken her properly. As he rocked along with the rhythm of the gray's walk, he thought about who might have previously owned the animal before she ended up in Johnson's corral. These thoughts led to thoughts of the night of the raid and to Lige Talbot. Poor Lige, he never knew what hit him. Robert guessed that if Lige had to die, it was best that he got struck down before he had a chance to think about it. The image of Lige with the Pawnee's axe buried in his neck would burn in Robert's mind for a long time. He wondered if Lige had felt any pain, or if life was just snuffed out like a candle. When he concentrated on the image long enough, it would make him shudder and he knew he didn't want to die that way, quickly or not.

The berries didn't last long and the growling in his stomach was a constant reminder that he needed to find sustenance. At one point he considered killing the horse to keep from dying of starvation but the thought of being on foot was more frightening than going without food. Occasionally he would spot a small animal, a prairie dog he supposed, but he never got close enough to catch it. He would not have hesitated to eat it raw for he had no means to build a fire. He had a knife, which he always wore strapped to his belt, and the clothes he had on when the Pawnees attacked. But that was all. His other belongings had been dropped in the panic to save his skin.

His nights were filled with dreams of food, always meat, usually thick slices of beef, roasted over an open fire. Sometimes it was simple jerky, but always it was meat. He would awaken with his empty stomach gnawing at his backbone and, unable to go back to sleep, he would get up on the gray and start again toward the mountains. He knew somehow that he would find food in the mountains but the mountains never seemed to get any closer. And then one morning, when the sunlight had just begun to dissolve the shroud of mist that blanketed the shallow river he had just forded, he found himself climbing upwards through a stand of tall pines. At once he realized that the gray had been working harder than usual to maintain the pace and he shook himself from the half slumber he had fallen into. Looking back the way he had come, he discovered that he was at a fairly high elevation above the river. Looking ahead now through the trees, he discovered that he had to tilt his head back to find the top of the hill the gray was toiling toward. He was in the mountains! He had made it! The realization of it was enough to start his blood pumping and clear the cobwebs from his brain.

He had been unconcerned about direction, letting the gray have her head. Now he looked around to decide on a course through the mountains before him. Tugging on the horse's ear, he turned her back toward the river. It would make more sense to follow the river through the hills, he figured. Besides, it wouldn't hurt to stay close to the water. He felt a small measure of elation and his spirits were lifted in anticipation of finding some source of food. He had been telling himself for days that there would be food in the mountains. He had been keeping himself alive on berries and roots he dug up along the banks of the streams he crossed but he knew he had to find some real food soon. He could relax a bit now that he had reached the cover of the timber covering the slopes. Even though he had seen no sign of another human being, he had felt totally exposed the whole time he was crossing the rolling hills. Now there was a feeling of safety in the tall trees and mountain laurel.

The gray, once Robert turned her back to the river, seemed to know where the boy wanted to go and she plodded steadily along, following the water, working her way around rock outcroppings and fallen trees and back again to the riverbank. It seemed to Robert that there were game trails everywhere he looked. His heart was beating rapidly with thoughts of catching some small game. He knew he would eat before night found him on this day. Had he not been so absorbed in his thoughts of food, he might have been more alert. And he might have paid more attention to the sudden skittishness of the gray.

He still didn't realize the horse sensed trouble until the stillness of the morning exploded with a roar that split the silence like a lightning bolt, causing the horse to fall back on her hindquarters, sending the boy sprawling end over end down an embankment and into the edge of the river. Terrified, he scrambled back up the rocks only to come face to face with a brown monster. Standing on his hind legs, the bear looked to be as tall as the pines behind him. Robert had never seen one before but he did not have to be told that it was a grizzly, evidently infuriated at having been surprised by the boy and his horse. Robert was almost paralyzed with fear. He had no idea whether he should run or stand his ground. The grizzly roared again, causing the pine needles on the trees to vibrate, and the echo reverberated up the narrow canyon. Then, still upright on his hind legs, the monster moved toward the gray.

"Run!" Robert yelled when he finally found his voice. He couldn't understand why the horse was still sitting there on her haunches, her forelegs straight. She looked to be half sitting, half standing, her eyes wide with fear. "Run! Git! Git!" Robert screamed but the horse made no move to escape as the bear advanced toward her. Robert stood helpless as he watched the great bear slowly stalk the horse. He could see the animal's claws, like long yellow spikes, and his teeth bared as he roared again. He was powerless to help the gray.

When the grizzly had closed to within a few yards of her, the gray finally showed signs of reacting but her response was slow, as if she was in a trance. She turned slowly away from the bear and only then did Robert realize why the gray had seemed in a stupor. For now he could see the long gash where the gray's neck had been laid open by a swipe from the giant beast's paw. The horse had been hit when she bolted, throwing him. Robert heard himself gasp involuntarily when he saw the flesh, ripped and hanging from his horse's neck. If the blow had caught him instead of the horse, he would surely be dead!

The gray was on her feet now but the bear had closed the distance between them and was ready to pounce on the hapless animal. There was nothing Robert could do to save his horse. His thoughts, distracted for a moment by the horrible drama taking place between the two animals, returned now to saving himself. For what would the great beast do when he had finished the horse? Come after him? He told himself to run while he had a chance but he seemed to be transfixed by the spectacle of the slaughter.

The gray surely realized that she was finished. Her eyes rolled back in a wild stare as the grizzly lunged to complete the kill. But the gray was not short of courage and, in a final act of defiance, kicked out with her hind legs, delivering a solid blow to the bear's skull. It made a sharp cracking sound like a rifle shot. The blow was enough to stun the great beast and it fell heavily to the ground. Without pausing to think about what he was doing, or the danger he was in, Robert immediately pulled out his knife and attacked the fallen bear. Afterward, when he was in a more rational state of mind, he would find it difficult to explain his actions and why he did such a foolish thing. At the time, he had one thought only and that was to kill the beast before it recovered its senses and came after him. He had only his knife for a weapon so he rushed to the fallen monster in an attempt to cut its throat.

Dodging back and forth to avoid the huge mouth, Robert stabbed at the animal's throat with all his strength. He was unable to penetrate the tough hide, only causing the stunned animal to roll back and forth slowly. It would be a matter of moments before the beast shook off the effects of the blow to its skull. Robert was frantic. Seeing a large rock near his feet, he picked it up. It took most of his strength to lift it with both hands. Lifting it as high as he could manage, he then slammed it down as hard as he could on the bear's skull. He would remember long after this day the dull thud it made. And still the animal thrashed about. Robert was terrified. Dodging the flailing paws, he set upon the bear once more with his knife. He stabbed again and again at the animal's belly, with all the strength he could muster, causing the bear to strike out blindly with one huge paw. It barely missed Robert's head. The wounds brought blood but were not serious enough to be mortal. The boy had no conscious thoughts beyond fighting for his life but, when it was over, he would never forget the strong stench of the beast and his mind's eye would always remember a confusion of dark fur, matted with mud and spattered with blood. He jabbed again and again before he at last found a vulnerable spot beneath the bear's neck and the knife went in up to the hilt. He withdrew the knife and struck at the wound over and over, desperately ripping at the hole he had caused. His face was suddenly spattered with blood when he struck a vital spot. Still he continued to stab the bear until he was forced to back away to escape the flailing paws. Had he known more about bears, and grizzlies in particular, he would have had better sense than to try to kill one with a knife.

Luck was with him on this day. The wounded animal

roared and stumbled to all fours, blowing bloody foam from
its nostrils and again barely missing the boy with a wild
swing of its forepaw. Robert scrambled over behind a large
rock and watched, his eyes wide with fear, expecting a
charge from the enraged beast. But the bear seemed confused, maybe from the kick in the head, or from the huge
rock he had tried to crush its skull with. There was a great
quantity of blood streaming from the wound in the bear's
neck. Robert thought he must have seriously wounded him.
The grizzly turned back to the horse, now lying still on the
ground, either dead or dying, Robert couldn't tell for sure.
The gray was not a big horse but she wasn't small either
and Robert was terrified when he saw the enraged grizzly
slash the horse's side open with one powerful forepaw. The
gray was swept from the riverbank as easily as a person
might kick a cat out the door. Robert knew his life was
about to end if he didn't do something quick.

Figuring he had mere seconds before the lumbering beast
located his hiding place, Robert left the cover of the rock
and sprinted for a tree that was growing right up against a
solid rock cliff. There was a ledge about twenty feet up and
he figured, if he was lucky, he could manage to scramble
up the tree and get up on the ledge before the grizzly saw
him. From a dead run, Robert jumped up into the limbs of
the tree and climbed as fast as he could pull himself up,
expecting to feel the bear's claws in his back at any
moment.

Robert's escape was detected by the bear but the grizzly
did not spring into chase, as Robert expected. Instead, he
merely watched the boy as he climbed, showing no interest
in pursuit. Robert's heart was beating wildly as he climbed
out on the ledge and looked down at the huge beast. There
was a great deal of dried blood matted in the animal's fur
but Robert could still see fresh blood oozing from the knife
wound. Evidently he had hit an artery and the bear's rage
had caused it to keep pumping instead of clotting. *Maybe
he's had enough,* Robert thought. *Maybe he'll just go away.*
As if the bear had read his thoughts, the beast suddenly
turned and loped toward the cliff and the boy on the ledge.

At the foot of the ledge, the bear reared up on his hind
legs, reaching with his front paws, but the boy was safe by
a good ten feet. Robert jumped back from the edge when

the bear made several fruitless attempts to jump up and gain enough foothold to climb the cliff. Still, Robert didn't feel very safe on his perch and he looked around him for any possible route of escape. There was none. The only way off the ledge was to go back the way he had come and, judging by the enraged roars of the wounded bear, it didn't appear that the beast was going to lose interest anytime soon. He worried that the bear might ultimately find a way up to him, maybe by the same tree he had climbed. He had hoped that, after a few futile attempts to scale the cliff, the bear would tire of the game and give it up. But as he watched the persistent animal below him, it occurred to him that the best thing that could happen would be if the bear kept losing blood. He was already showing signs of fatigue. Maybe, if he kept aggravating him, he would kill himself from loss of blood.

He's already madder'n hell. It can't get no worse, he thought. With that, he picked up a rock about the size of a cabbage and threw it at the raging grizzly below him. The rock hit the bear squarely between the eyes and served only to further infuriate the beast. Robert looked around for something larger, and picked up the biggest rock he could lift and struggled over to the edge with it. The bear was directly under him. This time there was a definite effect when the rock impacted with the top of the bear's skull, and the boy felt a triumphant surge when the animal staggered slightly and backed away a few feet. The grizzly sat down, dropping heavily to the ground. Getting weak from loss of blood, the bear slowly rocked his head back and forth, from side to side, the ferocious roar replaced now with a cry that was more bellow than roar. Robert continued to pelt the wounded animal with rocks but the bear's will to fight seemed to have drained. Robert found it hard to believe he could have mortally wounded the great beast with nothing more than a hunting knife. The kick from the horse must have done more damage than he had thought. Whatever the cause, the bear was definitely quitting the battle. With some effort, it got up on all fours and slowly padded from the clearing into the trees.

Robert watched until the animal could no longer be seen through the brush. He was aware of the beating of his heart now, pounding against his ribs. It had seemed to stop while the monster was raging below the ledge. He suddenly felt weak in the knees and had to sit down for a moment before carefully climbing back down the tree. He looked around him constantly, fearful that the bear might suddenly appear in a cloud of fury and strike him down. But all was quiet in the little clearing by the river. Convinced at last that he wasn't about to meet his maker, at least not in the next few minutes, he walked over to look at his unfortunate mount of the past several days.

"Damn," he uttered softly, looking at the still, gray mound that less than an hour before had been his salvation in this vast wilderness. Now he was on foot. The horse had saved his life, certainly when he escaped the Pawnees, but again in the forest when she kicked the bear in the head. A wave of compassion swept over him as he recalled how faithful the gray had been, sticking by him all the way across the prairie. "Damn," he repeated, a little more angry this time. The more he thought about the bear attack, the more angry and frustrated he became. He looked around until he found his knife, wiped it clean and returned it to the deerskin case strapped to his belt.

"That bear looked awful damned poor when he dragged his ass off through the trees," he said. He made up his mind to follow his trail to see if the bear was indeed dying. He felt more comfortable with the idea that he was stalking the bear instead of the other way around. Besides, bear meat was meat and he needed nourishment. His mind made up, he trotted off in the direction he had last seen the grizzly.

The bear was not hard to follow. A blind man could follow the trail of broken limbs and smashed bushes and Robert did not fail to notice the occasional smears of blood on the leaves in the thicker foliage. The animal was apparently headed for higher ground, possibly to some cave up the mountain somewhere. Robert hoped to find him before that happened. He had no desire to follow a wounded grizzly into a cave. His worries were needless, however, because after climbing for about a quarter of an hour, the trail suddenly led back down the slope toward the river again. Only now the bear seemed to be confused and uncertain because the trail led first one way and then another, wandering aimlessly. Robert guessed the bear must have lost too much blood by then to even know where he was heading. The trail steepened a bit and Robert had to hold on to the bushes to keep from going too fast. All at once his feet slipped out from under him and he went down on his backside. When he tried to scramble to his feet, he went head over heels, thrashing and grappling in a frantic effort to stop his tumble. He ended up at the bottom of a ravine in a thicket of mountain laurel.

"Damn!" he swore, afraid to move until he was certain he hadn't broken anything. Satisfied that he had suffered no more than a few bruises and one or two skinned places, he carefully began to extract himself from the laurel. Once out of the bushes and on his feet again, he glanced to his left. There, no more than ten feet from him, lay the body of the grizzly.

His heart leaped up into his throat and he ran for the side of the ravine, scrambling up the slope on his hands and knees. When he was halfway up the steep bank, he paused, for he realized the bear had not moved. He froze motionless, holding on to the root of a small bush to keep from sliding back down the bank. Gasping for breath, he stared down at the huge mound of fur for a full minute before he finally relaxed and let himself slide slowly back down to the bottom.

He still felt the need to exercise a great deal of caution as he carefully approached the motionless brown heap, stopping every few feet to listen, staring to detect any sign of even the slightest quiver. He didn't know if grizzly bears ever played possum or not and he wasn't going to take any chances that this one might be waiting to grab him. After two or three such pauses with no sign of life, the boy finally stood over the fallen animal.

The bear was lying on his side and Robert could see the wound, still weeping slightly, just under the beast's huge neck. It seemed odd to him that a wound that looked so small could have been that lethal. A little bolder now, he reached out and poked at the carcass with his knife. There was no doubt about it, the bear was dead. He suddenly felt a warm, almost primal, feeling of triumph. He had faced a mighty foe, a challenge of death, and he had emerged victorious! Now, he thought, he would eat bear meat for supper!

With that stimulating thought, he set about the task of skinning the bear.

This proved to be almost as big a challenge as killing the bear. Robert knew nothing about skinning any animal, much less a bear, and he wasn't sure where he should start. One thing he knew, though, he couldn't wait too long in doing whatever he was going to do. It wouldn't take long for wolves or vultures, or both, to detect the dead animal and he had nothing but his knife to fend off any scavengers. He stood looking at the carcass for a full minute, trying to decide where to start. He remembered how tough the hide was when he had first tried to plunge his knife into the stunned animal so he decided the underbelly would be the most likely place to start.

The knife went in more easily than he expected but he had to work hard to force it, slashing and ripping a long opening down the length of the bear's belly. As the flesh parted, a smelly mess of entrails began to push out of the animal's insides, causing Robert to step back for a second or two and get a clean breath. Determined, for he was hungry, he set in again and finished disemboweling the beast. When he found what he was sure must be the liver, he remembered hearing tales told by some of the trappers that had visited Freeman Johnson's trading post. They had told of killing elk and deer and eating the warm liver raw. They said that nothing beat it for gaining your strength back. He stared at the still-warm organ for a moment before taking his knife and slicing off a piece of it. Holding the piece up to his nose, he sniffed it. His stomach growled and seemed to be twisting itself into knots, telling him that it wanted the liver whether his nose did or not. He had to have food, he told himself, so he shoved the liver into his mouth and started chewing. He was surprised—it wasn't nearly as bad as he had expected.

After he had filled his stomach with bear's liver Robert sat back to decide what he should do. The bear had killed his horse and the thought of being on foot in the mountains caused him considerable worry. It would be handy to have the bear's hide if he could manage to skin him. True, it was already spring but the nights still had a chill and it would be good to have a warm fur robe to roll up in. He needed to take some of the bear meat for food as well, but there was only so much he could carry with him. Even if he could carry more, it wouldn't keep. "I wish to hell I could make a fire," he muttered. Then at least he could cook a little bit more of the meat to take with him.

As he sat staring at the mutilated carcass of the bear, he heard a horse snort softly. He barely gave it a thought at first but then his heart jumped up into his throat when he remembered his horse was dead! He turned in the direction the sound had come from. At first he saw nothing and then, as the gentle breeze stirred the pine needles, causing them to dance back and forth, he saw them. There were three of them. They sat on their horses, silently watching him. *Indians!* Robert felt cold fear spread all the way to his fingertips.

CHAPTER 4

The bear is a powerful symbol to the Arapaho and Cheyenne. One who killed a grizzly took its power for himself. It took great strength as well as cunning to kill the mighty grizzly and, for that reason, Spotted Pony and his two companions were stunned by the scene they had come upon. A mere boy cannot kill a bear. That much Spotted Pony knew for certain, not unless that boy held special powers. And this boy could not have been more than ten or twelve summers. Yet there was no sign of anyone else around who might have felled this most fearsome beast of the mountains. Even though his face was partially covered with the bear's blood, he could tell the boy was obviously white. As the boy stared up at them, Spotted Pony was reminded of a small wolf interrupted in his devouring of the animal's liver.

They had happened upon the dead horse back by the river and followed the obvious trail to the ravine. Since there was no bridle or saddle on the horse, they weren't sure what they would find. There were other puzzling clues to this mystery. The horse was shod, which told them it was certainly no Indian pony. Add to that the abundance of blood that had evidently come from something other than the horse. There was a definite danger in cornering a wounded bear, if that was what had killed the horse, as it appeared. But the prospect of gaining prestige from killing a grizzly was enough to excite the three of them to follow. The scene they looked down upon now was hardly what they had expected to find.

"So, little wolf, have we interrupted your dinner?"

Spotted Pony's question was met with the same blank stare that had captured the boy's face from the first mo-

ment he discovered the Indians' presence. It was obvious
he did not understand his words.

"Do you understand? How do you happen to be here?"
Spotted Pony waited but there was still no response from
the boy. Instead, the boy took a step back from the carcass,
holding his knife up as if ready to defend himself. Spotted
Pony made one more attempt to communicate with the
child with sign language, the universal medium for all tribes
of the plains. The boy still did not understand. They were
at a standstill.

Robert could not make heads or tails of the strange gut-
tural sounds the Indian directed toward him. He had no
way of knowing what their intentions were but at least they
did not immediately set upon him. In fact, they showed
little excitement in their emotions, seeming more curious
than anything else. Unable to think of anything else to do,
Robert held up a piece of the bear's liver, extending his
hand toward the Indians as an offering. This brought a
smile to Spotted Pony's face and he nudged his pony down
the bank of the ravine. His two companions followed.

Robert backed away as the three Indians gathered
around the carcass of the grizzly, chattering excitedly
among themselves. He couldn't understand what they said
but it was obvious to him that they were impressed as they
examined the bear's claws and teeth. Several times they
looked at the beast and then looked back at him in wonder.

Spotted Pony was especially impressed. The boy was too
small to have killed the bear but somehow he had managed
it. This told him that the boy had received special powers
from the Great Spirit and, after he had satisfied his curiosity about the bear, he turned his attention toward Robert.
It was a rare thing indeed to find a white boy in the land
of the Cheyenne and the Arapaho and the Ute. That he
was lost was a foregone conclusion, but how he got this far
away from the white man's forts and wagon trails was puzzling to Spotted Pony and he wondered if it was by design
for him to find this little wolf.

Spotted Pony, an Arapaho, lived with his Cheyenne
brothers in Black Kettle's village. From time to time they
had contact with the white soldier chief but very seldom
with white women and children. Black Kettle hoped to
have peace with the soldiers but he would not lead his

people to the reservation where the soldiers had directed
him to settle after the Treaty of Fort Laramie. The soldiers
had promised separate lands to the Cheyenne and Arapaho, as well as the Shoshone and Lakota. But the white
soldiers had made many promises that blew away like so
many clouds on a summer day. Spotted Pony had seen the
reservation intended for his people. It would not support
one hungry coyote and yet the white chief expected the
entire tribe to live there. The white chief promised that he
would provide food for the people and that no other whites
would infringe upon this land. Some of the tribes had gone
willingly to the reservation and found through their suffering the hollowness of the white man's promises.

Black Kettle had led his people north and west into the
mountains where there were deer, antelope and elk to hunt.
And now to find this young white boy, a child really, in
the heart of their hunting ground should have troubled him,
but he was more impressed by the courage of the lad and
could not help but admire his accomplishment. He stood
directly in front of the boy and gazed deep into his eyes,
looking for any sign of evil intent. But there was none and
Spotted Pony was glad. He smiled again at Robert and,
using gestures and hand signs, asked if the boy had killed
the bear. Robert understood and confirmed his kill. Spotted
Pony smiled and nodded, indicating his approval.

Robert could relax a little at last. The Indians meant him
no harm. Of that he felt sure. There was a genuine look of
kindness in the older one's eyes, obviously the leader of
the three. The other two were much younger and seemed
to be friendly enough. They showed more curiosity about
the bear than about the white boy and they eagerly ate
of the liver he had offered. In fact, it occurred to the boy
that this gesture had met with such success that he might
go a step further and maybe gain their real friendship.

"Sir," he said, talking as he made gestures to convey his
message, "you can have the whole dang bear." He repeated
the motions several times until he was sure the Indian understood his meaning.

At first Spotted Pony thought he must have misunder-
stood the boy's meaning. To kill a bear was a great thing.
There was powerful medicine in such a feat. He had never
killed a bear, not by himself anyway, and it astounded him

that the boy would offer it as a gift. He smiled at Robert, studying his face intently. After a long moment, he decided that although the boy had taken the power of the great bear, he was still just a boy and might not be aware of the significance of his deed. He thought for a moment longer and then made another decision.

"This little wolf is brave but he does not have much training," he declared to his two younger companions. "Look at the mess he has made of gutting the beast." This brought a laugh of agreement from the two young men. "He has shown his friendship by offering the bear so we will carry the meat back to the village so that our people can share his medicine. I will take the boy to live in my lodge. Buffalo Woman can make him a fine robe of the bear's hide and I will make him a necklace of the claws so that everyone will know he has taken the power of the great bear."

Robert could not understand what the man had said and there was very little he could do but stand and watch as the three Indians set about carving up his bear. In the tension of the preceding minutes, he had forgotten his hunger. Now that he was certain there was no danger for him, the gnawing returned to his stomach. So it was a welcome sight when one of the young men produced a wooden drill and sat down to make a fire, which he did in no time at all. Soon there was a bright flame and the young man kindled it with pine needles and small sticks until it was burning stoutly enough to add larger pieces of wood. Robert, not waiting to be told, scurried around gathering up more wood for the fire for he noticed that one of the men was cutting up strips of bear meat and skewering them on green branches he had just sharpened.

Robert was amazed by the quickness, as well as the thoroughness, of the skinning and butchering. He did little more than tend the fire while the three Indians did the work. He would learn later on that the men considered this women's work and would not have compromised their dignity if it had been convenient to leave the bear and send the women back for it. As it was, they worked steadily, chattering good-naturedly as they slit and carved, pausing occasionally to pull a hot, sizzling strip of bear meat from a skewer. Robert filled his belly with the dripping hot meat.

He had never sampled bear meat before but he decided on this day that it was his favorite. For the moment he was completely at ease. His stomach was full, the fire made him warm and he felt secure with his three dinner companions.

The boy watched, fascinated, as Spotted Pony removed the hide, along with the huge head and rolled it into a bundle. This he tied with strips of hide and sinew, then secured it on the back of his horse. The butchered portions of the animal were secured to the backs of the other two horses and then the job was finished. They had left very little for the wolves and vultures. One of the young men extinguished the fire and Spotted Pony took one last look around the ravine before leading his horse up the side. He motioned for the boy to follow. The two young men followed them.

They walked, following the river, for what must have been several hours, long enough for the boy to begin to weary. Still he trudged along, keeping pace with the lean, slightly stoop-shouldered Indian in front of him. The man was silent as he walked, the reins of his horse held loosely in his hand. Robert did not doubt the horse would follow even if the man dropped the reins. Behind him, the two younger men followed, also in silence.

As they walked, Robert had plenty of time to contemplate what had befallen him on that day and speculate on what might be in store for him when they reached wherever they were going. In truth, he didn't feel that he was captured. It was more like he had been invited along. His knowledge of Indians was scant, his only exposure being that which he had experienced at Johnson's Crossing. Most of the Indians he had seen there were drunken Pawnees, addicted to Freeman Johnson's firewater. Except for the night of the raid of course—that night they were painted demons. Most of his other knowledge of them came from conversation he overheard from Lige Talbot and Freeman Johnson. According to them, Indians were worthless and lazy. Somehow these Indians he had met this day did not seem to fit any of those descriptions. He wasn't sure why, but for some reason, he wanted to trust the silent figure he was now following.

Robert was not the only one speculating about his future. Spotted Pony considered what an extraordinary day this had been. He thought back upon the days preceding this day's hunt and he marveled at the miracle that had come to pass. The more he thought about it, the more he was amazed. At the same time he was a little embarrassed that he had not seen it when they had first come upon the boy. Spotted Pony had long wanted a son but it appeared that it was not to be. His first wife had died in childbirth, along with the infant. He grieved their loss for a long time before taking Buffalo Woman as his wife, only to find that she had no fertile womb to nurture his seed. He could have taken a second wife but he genuinely loved Buffalo Woman and had no desire to have two women in his tipi. Barely two moons before he had completed a four-day fast and cut off the first knuckle of his little finger in hopes Man Above would have pity on him and send him a son. And now this day had come to pass. And he had not even recognized the answer to his prayers when it had been so plainly laid out before him. Spotted Pony's heart soared.

At last the small party emerged from the cover of a thick stand of aspens and Robert got his first glimpse of their destination. They were descending now, having left the winding river some few miles back. The village was about a half mile below them, Robert guessed, in a grassy basin where the river formed a U-shaped bend. It looked to be no more than fifteen or twenty tipis, arranged almost in a circle, with an opening facing the east. From the look of it, it was a fairly busy little village. Robert could see people moving about and children running back and forth between the tipis. There were horses and dogs adding to the general confusion, much like any little town, he supposed. As they drew near the village, he began to feel a sinking feeling in his stomach. It had not been difficult to settle into a rather comfortable, secure feeling with the three men as they had walked most of the afternoon. But now, the thought occurred to him that he was to face an entire village of strange, maybe even hostile people. Suppose the general sentiment of the people there was not as compassionate as that of the lean old Indian he was following? The thought caused him to unconsciously draw closer to Spotted Pony.

Robert's fears were unfounded. There was a great deal of commotion upon the arrival of the small hunting party. Robert was indeed the object of great curiosity, as any white child would be in this part of the territory. For many of the inhabitants of the village, it was the first time they had ever seen a white child. The three men were greeted warmly when they approached the camp and with much excitement when the people saw the quantity of meat they had packed on their horses. Spotted Pony called out to his friends as they entered the circle of tipis. Robert could not understand what he said, of course, but he seemed to be telling everyone of the day's events. This caused a great deal of excitement and men, women and children ran to meet them. Soon they were completely surrounded by a small crowd of people, pushing in closer and closer to see the white boy. Seized by a stab of terror at first, Robert soon relaxed. He saw nothing other than curiosity in the faces thrust almost into his own, followed by warm smiles and words that he took for welcome, although he could not understand them.

Then the crowd parted to make way for a woman working her way through the men and women, gently pushing aside the young children in her path. Spotted Pony greeted her affectionately and then stood aside, his hand extended toward Robert as if presenting the boy to her. She stood silent, gazing intently at the boy for several long minutes. Finally her face broke into a smile and she said something in a low, gentle voice. Her remark evidently pleased Spotted Pony for he at once broke into a wide grin. The boy did not realize it until sometime later but, at that moment, Robert had found a home.

Spotted Pony spoke to his wife. "My prayers have been heard. We have a son at last. It is not for us to question the Great Spirit for sending us a white son. For, though he may be white, he has been given the power of the great bear and will be a worthy son for me."

Buffalo Woman, still smiling broadly, replied, "He looks strong enough, except for the sickly pale skin."

Spotted Pony laughed. "We will call him *Little Wolf.* With my guidance, he will be a great warrior, a warrior with the power of the great bear."

So began Robert's education as the son of an Arapaho warrior who was a respected member of a Cheyenne village and his transformation from Robert to Little Wolf. He was to be surprised by his seeming acceptance by everyone in the small band of Indians, especially Buffalo Woman. The fact that he was a white boy and, consequently, obviously different, almost seemed to go unnoticed. Buffalo Woman adopted him instantly, even fussed over him like the pampered child she was never able to conceive. Spotted Pony wasted no time in starting the boy's training, however, for there was little time left before the women would take down the tipis in preparation for the journey to the summer camp. Although Spotted Pony was Arapaho, the small band he led were actually members of the tribe of the Cheyenne chief, Black Kettle. Buffalo Woman was Cheyenne and it was the custom among the Arapaho to live with the wife's people.

It was already late spring and soon all the bands of Black Kettle's village would gather together for the great buffalo hunt and the dancing and ceremony, as well as to council on the future of the nation. Robert, or Little Wolf as he was now called, would learn that this was the usual lifestyle. The whole tribe only gathered during the summer when there was plenty of game on the rolling grassy hills of the plains. During the winter, the village could not survive if they did not break up into smaller groups. There was not enough food on the plains during the long cold winters to feed everyone. In the mountains it was easier to find enough game to feed a small band of people.

Robert half expected to have to lick two or three Indian boys before being accepted by the children in the village. This was the way it had been in St. Louis. But that was not the case for the son of Spotted Pony. Little Wolf was accepted, welcomed in fact, by everyone in the village. Adults and children alike were very much in awe of the boy who had slain the mighty grizzly with only a knife. Spotted Pony made a song about the heroic deed and sang it before the village council, also performing his creation of the "Bear Dance" to act out the song. On his head, he wore the head of the grizzly. He had fashioned it to wear as a ceremonial piece, leaving enough hide and fur attached to the head to provide a short cape that covered his shoulders. The rest of the pelt had gone to provide a warm bed for Little Wolf. Buffalo Woman took special care in constructing a sleeping platform, complete with backrest, for her son. This was the custom of her husband's people, the Arapaho, although her own bed was a pallet on the floor of the tipi, in the custom of the Cheyenne. As a badge of his power, Little Wolf wore a necklace made from the claws of the great bear. He was well established for a lad of his age by the time Spotted Pony's band broke their winter camp and headed for the summer rendezvous in the year of 1861.

CHAPTER 5

Little Wolf sat silently watching the sun settle into the distant hills on the horizon. Soon it would suddenly disappear and the light would be gone from the plains, replaced by a darkness so deep that objects a stone's throw away would melt into the blackness, becoming all but invisible to the untrained eye. He turned to glance at the encampment in the basin behind and below him. The cook fires were already burning outside the tipis. Soon, when the darkness came, they would glow like a blanket of stars on the prairie floor. This was Black Kettle's village, almost one hundred tipis. Little Wolf felt at ease with the darkness. He welcomed it. He liked to look at the encampment below him where he could see the figures moving about the fires and know they were his people and they felt secure knowing that he was on sentry duty.

He was not the only sentry, of course. There were eight others. Red Shirt always did things in nines. There were always nine sentries posted at night. Whenever scouting parties were sent out under his leadership, it was always nine. Red Shirt believed the number nine held a special power for him. When he was a young man, while fasting and purifying his body in quest of his power, he had a vision. In the vision he had seen nine hawks attack and devour nine sparrows. It was an unmistakable message for him.

Red Shirt was highly respected among the council members and his primary responsibility was the safety of the camp. When there was no immediate threat of danger, he would often use the young men of the Kit-fox Society as lookouts around the perimeter of the village. Little Wolf was proud to be a member of the Kit-foxes. His friend Black Feather was Red Shirt's son and the two of them

were looked upon as the leaders of the Kit-fox Society. In
recognition of their standing in the young warrior society,
Little Wolf and Black Feather had been permitted to go
on several scouting parties with the older warriors of the
village. These were training sessions for the two young boys
in preparation for the time when they would take their
places beside the veteran warriors of the tribe. The scouting
parties they were delegated to were usually for food for
the people of the village, tracking the buffalo herds or following the elk to find their summer ranges.

The more important scouting parties were usually the
exclusive responsibility of the Dog Society, a group of older
men, men who had proven themselves in battle or had done
some other brave deed, like saving the life of one of their
fellow tribesmen. They were charged with the responsibility
of knowing the whereabouts of the white soldiers and were
the village's first line of defense. Someday, Little Wolf
thought, he would be invited to be a member of the Dog
Society. But for now, watching over the village was an
important responsibility and only those members of the
Kit-foxes like himself and Black Feather were deemed
brave enough and mature enough to be awarded that
assignment.

The low, throaty call of a night bird caught his attention
and he immediately brought his concentration to bear on
it. It was still not dark although the sharp outline of the
distant mountains was already softened into gray. Soon
they would blend into the night and become lost in the
darkness. He was confident the sound he had heard was
indeed a bird and not a signal from an enemy raider. Still,
his responsibility was to be alert in the event it was the
latter. He smiled and silently congratulated himself when
his sharp eyes finally spotted the bird perched in a laurel
scrub.

He relaxed and let his mind wander back to the summer
just passed. The birdcall reminded him of the signals used
by the men of his tribe to communicate with each other
during the great buffalo hunts. He loved the hunts. There
would be medicine dances for several nights before the
hunt and, when the scouts had located the herd, all the
men in the village participated in the killing. Little Wolf
remembered the first hunt he had participated in. The men

had circled around to come upon the buffalo from downwind. Before the herd was in sight he could smell them. It was a strange pungent odor, one that would be unmistakable from that first time forever after. It was fully another half hour after first picking up their scent until the animals were actually seen.

The hunters slowly worked their way up to a ridge in the rolling hills. Beyond the crest, in a broad grassy basin, Little Wolf saw buffalo for the first time. There were hundreds of animals, filling the basin with a solid sea of dark brown and black shapes. Their movement caused the prairie to take on the appearance of a boiling body of muddy water. The men broke up into smaller groups of five or six and began to work their way down to the head of the basin where it funneled into a narrow pass. This was to be the killing site. Far to the south, at the mouth of the basin, a group of hunters on horseback, led by Black Feather's father, came into position to stampede the animals toward the waiting hunters.

Little Wolf was in a group with his friend, Black Feather, and three older men of the village. One of them, a short bull of a man called Owl Speaks, was wearing a buffalo robe with the head attached. The disguise seemed a cumbersome burden to Little Wolf but Owl Speaks was strong enough to manage it. It allowed him to slip in closer to the herd. Little Wolf thought it a useless attempt when the whole herd was stampeding toward the head of the narrow basin anyway. But Owl Speaks always wore it in the hunt. Spotted Pony laughed when Little Wolf told him about it, saying that Owl Speaks was such a poor shot with a bow that he had to get close. He couldn't hit a buffalo with his bow if the animal was in the tipi with him, Spotted Pony joked. Little Wolf found out later that day that Owl Speaks could account for himself as well as any of the other hunters at the close range they fired from. Little Wolf himself shot all his arrows in the span of no more than a few minutes' time. Caught up in the excitement of the massive flow of buffalo, amid the dust and the excited shouts of the hunters and the pounding hoofs, he felt he was a part of a mighty storm. The rolling tempest ended almost as suddenly as it had started as the last of the herd thundered through the draw and up through the hills beyond.

Afterwards, as the dust settled, there was much whooping and laughter as the hunters darted from carcass to carcass to finish off the dying animals with their knives. There was a lot of joking and bragging about who killed the most as the hunters identified their arrows in the carcasses. There were often as many as four arrows in the same animal, resulting in a loud good-natured argument over which shot had been the lethal one.

Within minutes after the killing was finished, the women appeared to begin the skinning. They chattered gaily among themselves, bragging about the performance of their respective husbands and sons. Buffalo Woman was particularly pleased to find Little Wolf's arrows in six carcasses, one more than her friend, Black Feather, had killed.

Little Wolf marveled at the efficiency with which the women prepared the meat and hides from the day's kill. They cut the meat from the carcasses in large thin strips and hung it over pole racks to dry. Everyone, hunters and women, ate as they worked, for the organs of the animal were considered great delicacies and were devoured immediately. The women worked hard for they had to prepare as much meat as possible to feed the village during the long cold winter. Once the meat was properly dried, it would be stored in secret caches, protected and hidden from predators as well as from enemies. Some of the meat would be pounded and ground with berries and mixed with hot tallow. It was called pemmican and would keep for a long, long time. Thinking back on that first hunt, Little Wolf could not remember a time when he had been happier.

Little Wolf called his thoughts back to the endless stretch of prairie before him and scanned the horizon for any irregular shape that might indicate something out of the ordinary. He knew every hill and gully around his section of patrol and he wanted to make sure everything looked as it should while there was still enough light to see. All looked peaceful. None of the elders of the village expected attack from the soldiers. There had been none sighted by the scouts for many days. Still, they thought it prudent to be alert even though the word received from other villages was that the soldiers had their hands full trying to combat raids from the Dakotas to the north and the Southern Cheyenne to the south.

The thought of battle with the soldiers brought on deeper thoughts. It had been several summers since Little Wolf came to his first summer encampment. Those years had been happy ones for him. He had grown to love and respect his Indian father, Spotted Pony, and a deep affection had developed for Buffalo Woman. In fact, he barely thought of his white parents anymore. It was a totally new experience, not only to be accepted, but wanted by his new family and Little Wolf had thrived in his adopted lifestyle.

At first it was fun to think of himself as an Indian boy. It was like playing make-believe with his friends back in St. Louis. Before very long it became a natural way of life for him and he didn't think of his former childhood. The language was easy to learn. It was almost as if he wasn't aware he was learning the tongue when, suddenly, he realized that he spoke fluently. Also, just as suddenly, he began to grow. Already he was as tall as most of the grown men in the village and he was still growing. Buffalo Woman laughed when she saw how his feet hung over the sleeping platform she had made for him when he was younger. Spotted Pony joked that if he kept growing, he would make an excellent lodge pole for the council tipi.

"Ahhh . . . I think I have found a dead Arapaho. Maybe I'll take his scalp and hang it from my lance."

Little Wolf was startled but he checked himself before showing any emotion, taking great care to conceal his surprise. Without bothering to look around, he answered, "Even a dead Arapaho could hear the plodding feet of Black Feather. I was waiting to see if a herd of buffalo were coming but I see it is only you."

In truth, Little Wolf had not heard Black Feather until he spoke but he would never admit this to his friend. No one in the village, not even any of the Dog Soldiers, could move as silently as Black Feather. It was a talent Little Wolf envied. He had seen his friend creep right up to a prairie hen and simply reach down and catch it in his hands.

"I just wanted to make sure you were not asleep," Black Feather joked as he knelt down beside his friend. He would only visit for a few minutes before getting back to his post. He took a piece of dried buffalo jerky from a pouch and offered it to Little Wolf. Little Wolf took it and bit off a chunk, then returned it. Black Feather tore off a bite with his teeth and the two of them chewed the tough leathery meat in silence for a few moments. When the jerky had softened enough to allow room for speech, Black Feather asked, "Is all well?" It was nothing more than polite conversation for he knew, if all had not been well, he would have heard a signal from Little Wolf.

"Yes."

"Do you think the soldiers will come?" The thought excited Black Feather for he was anxious to prove himself in battle. Not waiting for an answer, he added, "I don't think the elders expect it. If they really thought the soldiers would come, the Dog Society would be guarding the village tonight instead of us."

"I don't know," Little Wolf replied thoughtfully. "Spotted Pony says that the soldiers know that Black Kettle wants peace."

Black Feather looked worried. "I know. There has been much talk that Black Kettle will lead the whole village to the white man's fort instead of separating into our winter camps. If he does, I don't think I will follow him." His voice lifted in his excitement. "Red Shirt will never follow him. There is no honorable peace with the white man. They just want us to be their slaves." A long silence followed while both boys thought about the possibility of the tribe splitting up. When there was no response from his friend, Black Feather asked, "If it comes to fighting the soldiers, are you going to fight the whites?"

Little Wolf thought for a long moment before answering. This question had worried his mind many times before. This summer had been a troubled one for the Cheyenne. More and more wagon trains were rolling through the land of the Indian, land that had been guaranteed to be theirs exclusively, and there had been many raids by the Cheyenne Dog Soldiers to punish these trespassers. Then there had been more talks and treaties with the white man, resulting in an uneasy peace. The white governor of the Colorado territory, a man named John Evans, met with Black Kettle in Denver. White Antelope and Bull Bear made the journey with the chief and they informed the governor that the Cheyenne only wanted to be left in peace to hunt and live as they had always lived. The chief of the soldiers in Denver, Colonel John Chivington, was there also and he told Black Kettle that if he brought his people to Fort Lyons, they would be safe there. Black Kettle believed the white men to be sincere but not all the men agreed with their chief. Some, like Spotted Pony and Red Shirt, were talking about making their own winter camp as they had always done.

Black Feather pressed for an answer to his question. "You will fight. I know you will. You are a Cheyenne warrior!"

"Arapaho," Little Wolf corrected.

Black Feather laughed. "I know, Arapaho, but you will fight with your Cheyenne brothers."

Little Wolf paused. "I have thought about it and thought about it. You know I would love to fight beside you but I'm not sure I can kill whites. I will go with Spotted Pony. He is my father." Little Wolf had embraced the Indian way of his adopted father wholeheartedly. But could he go so far as to draw his bow on white men? It had only been a few years since he was Robert Allred. Life as a white child was still alive in his memory even though each passing month pushed that memory further and further from his conscious thought.

Black Feather was disappointed but this was not the first time they had discussed the matter. He shrugged. "I understand. Maybe you will change your mind."

"Maybe."

Living as an Indian for the past several years, there was no way he could keep up with the months. The Cheyenne noted the passing of a year by the moons. They knew nothing of months. Little Wolf knew that his birthday was September twenty-eighth. There was no way he could know when it was September or October but, when the women took down the tipis for the summer camp, the days were already getting chilly with some mornings greeting the tribe with frost. So he was sure he had passed his sixteenth birthday.

In spite of the talk in the council lodge that summer about going to the reservation, no decision was made to do so. There were too many of the village's leaders, like Red Shirt, who were against giving in to the white soldiers' demands. When the tribe broke up into the customary small bands to move to winter quarters, Black Kettle still talked of saving the peace and urged the leaders of the individual bands to meditate and seek wisdom from the spirits on the matter. He reminded them that the buffalo had not been as plentiful that summer as before and the white chiefs had promised to feed his people if they respected the treaties.

Little Wolf said his good-byes to Black Feather and his family just as he had done the summer before. But for some reason he could not explain, this summer he was a little more reluctant to see his friend leave. There was so much talk of troubled times on the horizon that he could not escape the nagging feeling that this might be the last he would see of Black Feather. Black Feather must have sensed the same reluctance although he attempted to maintain the air of confident casualness that had come to be his trademark.

"Don't let the coyotes eat you this winter," he tossed at his friend in an effort to make light of the parting.

"The coyote makes water on himself when he faces the power of the grizzly," Little Wolf yelled back and laughed as he walked away.

"Take care of yourself," Black Feather called out. "I'll see you in the summer."

"I will." Little Wolf hurried to catch up with Spotted Pony. As he broke into a comfortable trot, he began to feel the void left by the departure of his friend. He stopped and turned back toward Black Feather. "I'll come to visit you after Spotted Pony has made our camp. We'll hunt together."

Black Feather's face lit up with a smile. "I'll look for you." He couldn't resist adding a tease. "Are you sure you can find our camp? Maybe I should come to lead you."

Little Wolf laughed and waved good-bye to his friend.

After splitting off from Black Kettle's band on the second day of the trek, Spotted Pony led his small group of followers west and north. One more day's journey found them in the foothills of the great mountains and Little Wolf and another boy his age, Sleeps Standing, were sent on ahead of the main party to scout out possible winter campsites. There were favorite campsites that were often used but never in consecutive winters for that would soon kill off the available game in the area. This year, Spotted Pony had decided to winter further south than the year before. Little Wolf guessed that the reason was partly to be closer to the other segments of the tribe in case there would be a reason to unite. After scouting for the greater part of three days, a site was selected that offered water as well as some protection from the cold winds that swept through the mountains. They sighted no animals in the valley they had chosen but there were plenty of signs to indicate that meat was available. Little Wolf and Sleeps Standing agreed that it was a good place so they rode back to the main party to get Spotted Pony. Spotted Pony looked over the area thoroughly, riding up into the hills all around the valley, surveying it from every vantage point. His concern was not only food and protection from the weather, but also the defense of the camp. When he was satisfied with his inspection, he complimented the two boys on their selection and the band settled in for the winter.

The weeks that followed were busy ones for Little Wolf. Each day was spent hunting the elk and deer that could still be found in the valleys and high meadows. Sometimes he went with a larger hunting party of eight or ten men, which was most of the men in the little winter village. Other days he went out alone, or with one other, usually Sleeps Standing. These were the hunts he enjoyed most. He had become quite skillful in stalking his prey. The long hours spent at Spotted Pony's side had not been wasted on Little Wolf. When he hunted alone, he disciplined himself to be patient, taking hours sometimes to steal up to his prey so that one shot from his sinew-backed ashwood bow was all that was needed to ensure a kill. Sometimes, when it was not mandatory that he return to the village with some form of food, he played a game of stalking. The object was to get close enough to his prey, usually an antelope or small deer, to kill it with his knife. He had never accomplished it but the more he practiced the game, and the more he perfected his patience, the closer he came. His dedication to the perfection of this skill stood him in good stead with the older men of the village and he was always a welcome member of any hunting party. He, in turn, was very proud of his reputation as a tracker and was recognized as second only in this skill to his friend Black Feather in the entire tribe. Spotted Pony often pointed out that Little Wolf was a good bit taller than Black Feather which actually presented a disadvantage to his son. He maintained that if Little Wolf was as small as Black Feather he might be an even better tracker than his friend. For his part, Little Wolf genuinely liked Black Feather and felt no sense of competition with him. In fact, he was glad to have the opportunity to learn from his friend whenever possible. This, and the fact that he missed his friendship, were the prime reasons he decided one chilly morning to visit his friend.

A light dusting of snow had settled over the village during the night, leaving a thin, pale blanket on the ground. Little Wolf knew it would all be gone by midday and the weather would be quite comfortable for his journey. Spotted Pony had studied the sky the night before and predicted the snowfall but assured Little Wolf that the sky would be clear in the morning. Spotted Pony was seldom wrong about the weather so Little Wolf was not surprised at all when the sun rose the next day to reveal a cloudless sky.

The air was crisp and cold when he walked to the edge of camp to relieve himself and, just for a second, he wished that Indians wore long underwear like he remembered wearing as a child in St. Louis. He had adjusted to Indian winters but he still felt the chill in the mornings. The men in his tribe never wore shirts except in special ceremonies, preferring to remain bare from the waist up. Warmth was provided by heavy robes of buffalo hides, the fur turned inward. They wore leggings of buffalo or deer hides up to the groin, covered by a breechcloth.

He said good-bye to Spotted Pony and Buffalo Woman and climbed up on the little pinto his father had given him. Making sure his hide parfleche of food was secure, he arranged his bearskin robe around him and nudged the pinto across the tiny stream and down toward the river. His only essentials for his trip, in addition to the small packet of jerky, were his bow, ten arrows, his knife, his war club and a fire drill. This was all he would need, no matter how long his journey might prove to be.

Spotted Pony and Buffalo Woman stood and watched until he could no longer be seen through the pines. Buffalo Woman sensed a feeling of foreboding as she watched her son leave. For some reason, she wished that he had not gone, but she would never ask him to cancel his visit. If her son felt he should go to visit the village of Red Shirt, then it was for him to decide. She said nothing of her concern to her husband. He would mock her for acting like an old prairie hen over her young. In these times she could not be certain they would ever see Little Wolf again. Sometimes she could feel impending danger hanging over her people like a great invisible mist and she didn't feel secure when those closest to her were away.

Little Wolf guided the pinto up through the mountains, through tall green trees and grassy meadows strewn with small boulders and scattered deadwood left in the path of countless storms. He would intercept the winding river on the other side of the mountain range and follow it until he found Red Shirt's camp. The climb was hard on the pinto so Little Wolf walked most of the way. He could have elected to follow the river from his village, around the mountains, until it intersected the river Red Shirt was camped on. But that would have taken longer. Also, in the high country, he was not as likely to be spotted by an army patrol, should one happen by, or a raiding party of Shoshones out to steal horses. He knew Red Shirt would be camped somewhere on the river, but how far he could only guess. But he was confident that he would find his friend, Black Feather.

After climbing for most of the morning, he finally crested a small ridge and started down the far side. Halfway through a stand of aspen, he detected a movement out of the corner of his eye. Immediately alert, he froze, scanning the brush below and to his side. For a moment there was nothing and then he saw it again. It was a deer, a large doe. She had evidently sighted Little Wolf at the same moment the boy had seen her. For a long moment the boy and the deer stood transfixed, staring at each other. Then the animal bounded off into the brush. Little Wolf smiled and, at the same time, reprimanded himself for carelessly stumbling down the mountainside, his senses numb. "Good thing it was a deer and not a Crow scalping party," he muttered. "Too bad I wasn't close enough to get a shot at it. It would have been nice to ride into Red Shirt's camp with a fat doe across my saddle."

Nightfall found him at the river. He hobbled his horse and made a camp under a large pine within sight of the river but far enough up the ridge to be hidden from anyone traveling the water. He judged his cover adequate to allow a small campfire so he bundled up in his bearskin, close to the fire, and was soon asleep. The night passed without incident and he continued his journey downriver the next morning.

Another day's journey carried him far down the river with still no sign of his friend's village. In some places the terrain was too rugged to continue along the bank and he would detour for long distances before working his way back to the river again. After another night camp and another day's journey, he began to have some doubts. Maybe he was following the wrong river. True, he had not known for sure how far Red Shirt's camp was from his own. But he had expected it to be no more than two or three days' journey. He had no fear of being lost. He was more concerned with the embarrassment it would cause him if he had taken the wrong fork and couldn't find the camp. Black Feather would never let him live it down if such was the case. Still, he had to believe he was on the right path so he decided to continue until he found the camp or until the river ran out, even if it was a hundred miles. As it turned out, he was closer than he thought.

Warm and comfortable in his bearskin, Little Wolf urged the little pinto along. It was another chilly morning and the horse seemed reluctant to get started. Little Wolf suspected the animal had not been ridden enough lately and was starting to protest the daily journeys. As the pinto struggled up a steep creek bank, Little Wolf noticed the horse's ears flicking as if he heard something. Thinking that it could possibly be other horses the pinto heard, which would mean the village might be close, Little Wolf pulled the horse to a stop, pushed the bearskin back from his ears and listened. At first he heard nothing but the sound of the water rippling over the stones in the creek bed. Then, faintly, he made out a distant cracking sound. He strained to listen. There was no mistaking it. It was gunfire. That could mean only one thing, he thought. *Black Feather's village was under attack!* It could be soldiers or a war party from some raiding tribe, but it had to be Black Feather's village.

He kicked the pinto into a gallop and followed the sound of the gunfire down the river, stopping every few minutes to listen to make sure he was going in the right direction. After a short while, it was no longer necessary to stop to hear the sound of the rifles. It was getting louder and louder and, from the sound of it, it had to be an all-out attack by soldiers. There was too much gunfire to be anything else. Red Shirt probably had no more than one or two old muzzle loaders in his whole camp. The shooting was almost without pause and so loud now that the pinto began to balk when he urged him forward. Little Wolf had to rein him hard and kick him repeatedly to keep him from stopping.

Now he could see smoke rising above the trees, not the wisps of breakfast fires, but the smoke that dozens of burning tipis might make. His heart was racing with the apprehension of what was probably happening in Red Shirt's village. He thought at once of Black Feather. His friend had been so eager to fight. He wondered if he was already dead. He hoped that Black Feather had escaped and not tried to fight the army's rifles with his bow and lance.

When he judged the smoke to be about a mile away, he began to scan the ground before him more carefully. He didn't want to ride headlong right into an army scout. He slowed the pinto to a trot as he looked left and right. The shooting had almost subsided by the time he estimated he was less than a quarter mile away from the smoke. Only an occasional crack of a rifle could be heard now. Mopping up, he thought, and the mental image of such an operation caused the anger to rise in his throat. Not wishing to chance detection by the soldiers, he tied the pinto in a stand of aspen and made his way down through the trees on foot, his bow in hand, his stone war club in his belt.

Long before he reached the edge of the forest, he could see the carnage still underway. It was a terrible scene and one that would live in his memory for as long as he lived. At first it did not seem real. He had been correct in his initial assumption. It was the army—blue-coated troopers were everywhere, galloping back and forth through the burning village, wheeling to fire at a wounded brave, charging to cut off the escape of a fleeing woman. Little Wolf was paralyzed by the horrifying spectacle. There were bodies everywhere, brown lifeless lumps that were once his friends. For a moment, he stood transfixed by the carnage, his eyes unable to blink, his nostrils filled with the peculiar stench of death. Then he regained his senses enough to think about his own welfare. Making his way carefully to the edge of the clearing, he dropped down behind a fallen tree to survey the scene. He felt helpless at this point. There was little he could do to help his fallen friends, yet still he felt the need to do something. He decided to skirt the clearing to see if he might find some survivors who had managed to escape into the forest.

Alternately running and crawling, he managed to make his way around to the other side of the village to an outcropping of boulders. He paused for a moment to listen. He was about to move again when he caught a movement beyond the rocks, just ahead of him. He held his breath, fearing that he might be heard. Then he recognized the low whispering from the other side of the boulder as Cheyenne. Still he did not expose himself until he could see them. As he watched, a figure crept slowly from the far side of the rocks, looking in all directions before crawling toward a thicket of laurel. It was Black Feather! Little Wolf could scarcely believe his eyes. It was a miracle! He was so delighted to see his friend that he almost called out to him. He stood up. Black Feather was still unaware of his presence. He looked back toward the rocks and motioned. A girl quickly made her way up beside him. Little Wolf recognized her as Morning Sky, Black Feather's sister.

Little Wolf raised his arm and was about to signal his friend when, suddenly, a figure rose in front of him, directly between him and his two Cheyenne friends. His whole nervous system suddenly went numb. The man had been kneeling between two small boulders no more than ten feet in front of him. Little Wolf realized that Black Feather did not see the man. He also realized that the man, an army scout by the look of his buckskin shirt and blue army-issue trousers, was not aware of Little Wolf's presence. As he watched, the scout slowly raised his carbine and drew down on the unsuspecting boy and girl. There was no time for thought. Little Wolf, without consciously thinking about what he was about to do, pulled his stone club from his belt and brought it down across the back of the man's skull with all the strength he could put into it.

The club made a dull sound on the man's head, like hitting a hollow log, and the man crumpled in a heap. He uttered no cry but his finger closed on the trigger as he fell, causing the rifle to discharge, sending a bullet whistling harmlessly through the trees. The explosion of the rifle so close to him caused Black Feather to whirl around to face his attacker. Knife drawn, he stood ready to defend himself. His face, at first twisted with rage, relaxed into a mask of disbelief as he looked into the face of his closest friend.

"Little Wolf!" he exclaimed. Then he saw the fallen army scout on the ground between them and understood at once what had happened. Suddenly his broad face broke into a wide grin. "I knew you would come." He reached out to clasp his friend's extended arm. Immediately his mind leaped back to the danger at hand. "Come, we must leave this place!"

Little Wolf looked down at the man he had just clubbed. The blow had been fatal. The pointed edge of the war club had crushed a portion of the man's skull and it was obvious that he was no longer a threat to them. That he was probably dying seemed certain but he was still breathing at that moment. Little Wolf hesitated. The man was an Indian, probably a Pawnee, though he wore the blue uniform trousers of the army. Black Feather, seeing his friend's apparent confusion as to what to do about the dying man, casually reached down and calmly cut the man's throat.

"Take the rifle," Black Feather whispered and motioned for him to follow.

Little Wolf might have gone away without the weapon had it not been for Black Feather's presence of mind. Little Wolf quickly loosened a bandolier of ammunition from around the man's chest, picked up the rifle and ran into the trees after his two friends. Behind him, the sounds of the troopers mopping up went on but he seemed not to hear them. A new sensation had taken hold of him now as he realized that he had killed a man. The thought numbed his brain, as did the picture of the gaping hole in the man's throat where Black Feather sliced it open. The whole episode made him feel a bit queasy. He hoped Black Feather and his sister wouldn't notice.

High up into the tall pines they ran, stopping only when they could no longer hear any of the chaos behind them. Finally satisfied that they had escaped, Black Feather dropped to the ground and gasped for breath. His two companions dropped beside him.

"I knew you would come," Black Feather repeated. "I dreamed it two nights ago." Little Wolf did not reply as he strained to catch his breath. "In my dream, a deer was being devoured by a black bear. Suddenly a great grizzly appeared and the black bear vomited the deer up and fled before the grizzly. The deer got to his feet and ran away. I knew the grizzly was you. Now I know what you were trying to tell me."

"What happened? Why did the soldiers come?" Little Wolf asked.

"We didn't even know they were close until they rode across the river as the sun came up. Many of the women had not even started their cook fires. They gave no warning, rode into the village shooting and killing—women, children, everyone. Some tried to fight them but our arrows were no good against their guns. Red Shirt is dead. I saw the bullets when they tore into his flesh. He did not have time to shoot more than one or two arrows before they killed him. I knew I could do nothing against them. I shot at two of the soldiers when they rode through the council tipi. I may have hit one of them, I'm not sure. I had to think of Morning Sky, had to take her to safety. There was nothing I could do."

"You did the right thing," Little Wolf quickly responded. "It is one thing to die in battle, but it is foolish to sacrifice your life against impossible odds." He turned to look at Morning Sky, a shy girl of barely twelve or thirteen. "You were right. You had a responsibility to save your sister."

"There will be other times," Black Feather said, defiantly. "The white soldiers will pay for this."

"Come, you and Morning Sky must come with me to Spotted Pony's village. We'll be safe there."

Black Feather agreed but first he wanted to remain where they were until they were sure the soldiers had gone. Then they could go back to the village to search for survivors of the cowardly attack. Little Wolf agreed but, from what he had witnessed of the massacre, he doubted there were any left alive. Another troublesome thought entered his mind. If the army attacked Red Shirt's camp, how many other camps were in danger of the same fate? He must return to Spotted Pony's camp as soon as possible to warn his own people to be prepared.

As Little Wolf expected, there were no survivors to be found when they made their way back down the hillside later that afternoon. The village was in ruins. Nothing remained but charred tipi poles and smoldering lumps that were once the bodies of humans and ponies. It was not a pretty sight. Black Feather's face was stern, frozen with grief. Morning Sky cried and moaned in her agony for her family and friends. Little Wolf saw at once there was nothing they could do there and he felt the urgency to return to his village.

They found Red Shirt's body next to the burned out ashes of the council tipi. He had been riddled with bullet holes. His blood, already congealed, formed a dark pool around his body. His face, contorted into a mask of rage, was frozen to register his anger forever for the cowardly attack on his people.

Black Feather and Morning Sky moaned in their grief at the sight of their father. Little Wolf could feel their sorrow. Red Shirt had been such a strong image of leadership in the tribe. He had always seemed so powerful and, seeing his lifeless body before him now, Little Wolf was shocked to see how small and frail the mighty chief looked in death. He was to learn that all men shrank when death overtook them. Although impatient to leave there and warn Spotted Pony, he could not deny Black Feather's request to help him prepare his father for his journey to the great beyond. They could not wrap him in his ceremonial shirt but Black Feather was able to arm him with a bow and lance and they used some of the lodge poles to construct a burial platform for him. When it was done, they went to the place Little Wolf had tied his horse only to find the animal gone. So they set out for Spotted Pony's camp on foot.

CHAPTER 6

It had taken three and a half days to make the journey to Red Shirt's camp. On foot, it would take the three of them a day longer to make the return trip. It seemed even longer to Little Wolf. As each mountain crossed produced yet another one before them, he began to worry more and more about what might be happening to his village. The raid on Red Shirt's camp was, more than likely, an isolated raid by a random army patrol. Still, until he saw Spotted Pony and Buffalo Woman safe, he could not help but speculate about the possibility of a concerted effort by the army to force the tribe to move on to the reservation. There was no need to press his feelings of urgency upon his friends. They sensed it and wasted no time on the journey, never stopping to rest until it became too dark to sensibly find their way through the pitch black valleys and ravines. At night Morning Sky slept between Little Wolf and her brother to stay warm. The nights were cold and Little Wolf had lost his warm bearskin robe along with the pinto. Sleep, when it came, was fitful and shallow. Little Wolf would finally doze off from sheer exhaustion, only to awaken a short time after, shivering from the cold. The sequence would be repeated several times during the night until morning light when they would again start out.

Finally they reached the last ridge that stood between them and the village. Little Wolf climbed a huge boulder at the highest point in an effort to spot the little village although he knew the tipis would not be visible even from this vantage point. Spotted Pony had taken care to locate the camp on the far side of a large stand of trees so it would not be easily seen by an enemy. Still, Little Wolf thought he might be able to catch sight of a trace of smoke from a cook fire if he scanned the treetops carefully. What he saw sent a feeling of cold dread through his spine. Black Feather, climbing up behind him, sensed his friend's concern.

"What is it?" he asked, searching in the direction of Little Wolf's gaze.

Little Wolf did not answer. He didn't have to. Black Feather saw at once what had momentarily captured his friend's gaze. Far below them he could see the river as it wound its way around the base of the mountain and down through the valley. On the far side of the river the land began a gentle slope, covered by thick forests, a peaceful vista marred only by a thin gray cloud of smoke floating just above the treetops, too much smoke to have been caused by cook fires.

There was no need for comment. Little Wolf turned and scrambled down from the boulder. Without pausing to explain, he started down the mountain, going as fast as he could without losing his balance and taking a tumble. Black Feather followed, motioning to Morning Sky. It was fortunate for them that there was no need for caution for the three of them made their way straight down the mountainside as fast as they could, taking no pains to conceal their movements. Little Wolf had thoughts only of reaching his father's side as soon as possible. Black Feather would have exercised more caution had he and his sister been alone but he was caught up in his friend's panic to reach the camp and followed without hesitation, looking back only occasionally to make sure Morning Sky was keeping up.

When at last he reached the base of the mountain, Little Wolf dropped down behind a large tree on the bank of the river. While he caught his breath, he allowed some sense of reasoning to reenter his brain before crashing headlong into the river. The feeling of panic gave way to a sense of dread. As he knelt there, straining to see through the trees on the far riverbank that shielded the camp from sight, he knew what he would find in the village. Death seemed to hang in the air in the form of the thin cloud of smoke. In a matter of moments, Black Feather dropped down beside him. A few seconds more and Morning Sky joined them, gasping for air.

Little Wolf remained motionless for a while after he had calmed his breathing, scanning the trees on the other side of the river, listening. There was no sound other than the distant cry of a hawk and the worried murmur of the water as it fretted its course around the boulders in the riverbed. Minutes earlier, he could not wait to make his way down the mountainside in his haste to come to the aid of his family. Now he was reluctant to travel the few hundred yards left, dreading what he knew he would find. The picture of the carnage in Red Shirt's camp returned to his mind. Finally he rose to his feet and turned to his friends.

"Come. I hear no sounds of life. I fear the enemy has already been here. We are too late." With that he started across the river.

For the second time within a week's span, Little Wolf witnessed man's capability for wanton, senseless slaughter. The scene he and his two friends walked into left him sick inside, a sickness that would live within his heart for the rest of his life. At that moment his soul was snatched from the white man's world and he became Arapaho completely. He could not align himself with men who would commit such atrocities as this. The carnage was much the same as he had just left in Red Shirt's village. Lumps that were once human beings lay everywhere amid the charred remains of the tipis.

"The son of a bitches didn't even bother to bury anybody. Just left 'em for the damn buzzards."

Black Feather looked at him, astonished, for he had blurted it in English. Realizing his friend couldn't understand what he said, he simply shook his head. Saying nothing, he continued to search through the ruined village for the two bodies he dreaded to find. He searched the whole village but could not find Spotted Pony or Buffalo Woman. When they were certain the bodies were not there, Little Wolf's hopes lifted, if only slightly. Maybe they survived the attack. They must have escaped. Or were their bodies lying somewhere in the forest where they finally fell from their wounds? Little Wolf had to know. He would search the woods until he found them or found nothing. He could not leave without knowing for sure. His search was in vain. There was no sign of his parents so he clung to the hope that they had indeed escaped.

Before leaving, they felt they had to do something for the dead. They could not simply leave them sprawled around the clearing. Little Wolf's inclination was to bury them but he had no implement for digging. Besides, it would have been impossible to convince Black Feather that the dead souls could soar into the heavens if they were buried under the ground. As a compromise, they laid out some charred lodge poles in a makeshift platform and laid the dead in rows. This pacified Black Feather's sensibilities somewhat. Before they left, Little Wolf took a buckskin shirt from a man he had known as One Who Hears The Wind. He encouraged Black Feather to find something to keep him warm but his friend was appalled by the suggestion, thinking it almost sacrilegious. Little Wolf shrugged and said, "Suit yourself."

Little Wolf felt alone in the world for the first time since he had fled Johnson's Crossing when Lige Talbot had gone down with a Pawnee axe in his neck. In truth he was not actually alone, for he had Black Feather and Morning Sky, but the loss of his adoptive parents scarred him deeply. The time he had spent with them had been the best time of his young life and now he had no idea where they were, or even if they were still alive. He was at a loss as to what he should do. Black Feather and his sister looked to him for guidance and he didn't feel he could provide it.

"What are we going to do?" Black Feather finally asked, prompting Little Wolf to make some decision.

"I'm not sure. We'll have to think about it. There must be some survivors somewhere. We'll have to find them." He thought for a moment longer. "For now, we'll scout the area for any of our people who might be hiding."

As they were leaving the village, Little Wolf spotted a half burned buffalo robe near the ashes of what was once a tipi. There was still a good portion of it that had not caught fire, enough to cover Morning Sky. "Here, put this around you," he said, wrapping it around her slender shoulders. She smiled graciously and pulled the hide up close around her neck. Black Feather frowned but said nothing.

Together they traversed the forest around the clearing. There was plenty of sign that some had escaped but there was no one to be found anywhere, no horses or dogs even. It was as if the soldiers had left nothing alive. After an hour or so, they abandoned their search. Little Wolf, encouraged now that his parents might still be safe, decided to head south in hopes of finding Black Kettle's camp, thinking that possibly Spotted Pony and Buffalo Woman had fled to join up with their chief. That was as good a plan as any as far as Black Feather was concerned, so the three of them set out across the river and turned south.

They had barely crossed the shallow water when Little Wolf thought of one place he had not searched. He was amazed that he had not thought to look there before, so he led his friends downstream for a couple hundred yards to a place where the river forked and passed on both sides of a tiny island of boulders. The young boys of the village had found the little island a favorite place to play their imaginary war games against each other. It was a favorite place because of the concealment the boulders offered and the challenge to "assault" the fortress without being seen by the defenders.

Stepping from stone to stone, they made their way across the water to the little island and Little Wolf led the way through an opening in the boulders to a fortlike enclosure. Once inside, he stopped so abruptly that Black Feather, who was walking right behind him, stumbled into him.

"What is it?" he whispered and then he saw what had stopped Little Wolf so suddenly. Two burial platforms had been constructed in the center of the rocks, one a few feet higher than the other.

In reverence to the dead, they began to back slowly from the clearing when Black Feather noticed that one of the bodies was not completely sewn up in its buckskin covering. Whoever had prepared them for burial had evidently been interrupted before he finished. He quietly pointed this out to Little Wolf and they stopped to speculate on what had happened.

"Little Wolf!" The voice came from behind them.

Startled, Little Wolf whirled toward the source of the voice, his hand on the rifle, ready to fire. It was Sleeps Standing, the friend with whom he had so often hunted.

"Sleeps Standing!" he exclaimed, overjoyed at the sight of a friendly face. The two friends locked arms in greeting. Little Wolf's broad smile faded as he remembered the graves. "Your parents?" He nodded toward the bodies.

"Yes," Sleeps Standing said softly.

"Are you the only one left? Where are the others?

Where are Spotted Pony and Buffalo Woman? Are they alive?"

Sleeps Standing told them that a few of the camp escaped the pony soldiers. Little Wolf's parents were among them. There had been no chance to defend the camp. He had been away on an overnight hunting trip with three other warriors. They had heard the gunfire and the screams from a distance when they were returning to the village but were unable to get there until it was all over. A few of the tribe had made it to safety in the forest but most of the people were killed. Some of those who had survived had fled to warn Black Kettle. Spotted Pony and Buffalo Woman were among these. The three young warriors who had been hunting with him were against going to Black Kettle's village. The soldiers were bound to attack the village, they said. They thought it best to go off alone to fight the white man wherever and whenever possible. He had stayed to take care of his parents' bodies and then he planned to join the other three in the high mountains to the north.

Sleeps Standing offered to share a deer he had killed if Little Wolf and his friends would wait until morning to start out for Black Kettle's camp. Since they had eaten very little during the past few days—berries, a couple of rabbits and some pemmican Morning Sky had managed to save from their village—they eagerly accepted the invitation. He had made a camp near a fork in the river where a stand of tall pines offered protection from the cold. Morning Sky cooked the meat and they ate their fill for the first time in days. Afterward, they lay before the fire and talked. Sleeps Standing spoke with great emotion of his need to avenge his parents and encouraged his guests to join him and the others in the high mountains. Little Wolf declined. He knew what he had to do but he could see that the idea appealed to Black Feather and, before it was time to sleep, his friend had caught the fire of revenge in his own eyes. So it was no surprise to Little Wolf the next morning when Black Feather told him of his intention to accompany Sleeps Standing and make war on the white soldiers. He made a brief argument to persuade Little Wolf to come along also but did not persist when Little Wolf again declined.

"You understand," Little Wolf explained, "I have to make sure Spotted Pony and Buffalo Woman are safe."

"I understand."

The two friends stood looking into each other's eyes for a long moment before Little Wolf spoke again. "I would join you if I knew them to be dead. It's not the color of my skin that keeps me from warring on the whites. I am Arapaho." He searched Black Feather's face for understanding. "I must go to them."

Black Feather smiled at his friend. "I know. It's all right. I'll kill some for you and I'll sing of your kill of the army scout."

Little Wolf smiled. He had not thought of the man he had killed in Red Shirt's camp. A kill was big medicine, especially when it was accomplished at close range with a knife or club. The Cheyenne and Arapaho found it more honorable to count coup than to actually kill an enemy at long range. But when a warrior is close enough to kill an enemy hand to hand, that is indeed a great honor. He thanked Black Feather and wished him and Sleeps Standing a safe journey. Black Feather had one request before they parted.

"We must travel fast and it will be a hard winter in the mountains, too hard for a young girl. Will you take Morning Sky with you to Black Kettle's camp?"

Little Wolf had anticipated his request. It would indeed be a hard winter for one so young. He knew also that Black Feather preferred not to have his sister spend the winter with a band of young men. She would be married before the spring came.

"Yes," he answered, "I'll watch over her as I would my own sister."

When morning came, the young friends parted. Little Wolf and Morning Sky said their good-byes and watched Black Feather and Sleeps Standing until they disappeared around the bend in the river.

"Come, little sister, let's go find Black Kettle." Little Wolf smiled down at Morning Sky. The girl had made no protest when told that she was not to go with her brother. Had he any knowledge of girls, he might have been able to see that she preferred to go with him, no matter what the destination. So they began their search for Black Kettle.

As a gesture of his friendship and to show support for their quest, Little Wolf had made a gift of the rifle and ammunition to Black Feather. They would have need of the weapon if they were to make war on the soldiers. Little Wolf was not reluctant to part with it anyway. He had his bow, his knife and his war club. These were all he would need to kill game on their journey. Even if he had kept the rifle, he would have been reluctant to use it for fear the shots might be heard. He was quite confident in his skill with his bow. If there was game to be found, he would find it. Of that, he was also confident. Morning Sky proved to be quite resourceful in finding berries and wild turnips, which she would bake in the hot ashes of their campfire at night. When it was time to sleep, she would wrap herself in her charred buffalo robe and press her young body up tight against his.

As they made their way south, leaving the cover of the hills and tall trees and on to the rolling grassy plains, she never complained and always managed to keep up with his pace. After five days' traveling, they came upon the basin Sleeps Standing had told them to look for. Here, where the two rivers joined, Sleeps Standing said Black Kettle had made his winter camp. There had been a camp there all right, but it had been abandoned. For what reason they could only guess for there was no sign of violence. It appeared that the entire village had simply packed up and left. As they stood in the middle of the deserted campsite, Little Wolf was careful to hide his disappointment. When he looked down into Morning Sky's face, she only smiled and awaited his instructions. She felt safe with him and was content to go wherever he went. He could not help but be lifted by the girl's spunk.

"It seems our journey's not over," he said cheerfully. She nodded agreement and they set out again in the direction that Black Kettle's tribe had taken. The trail was not hard to follow. It appeared Black Kettle had taken no pains to conceal his direction of travel. Little Wolf and Morning Sky walked for two more days before sighting another human being.

*　　*　　*

He saw them when they were maybe two or three miles away. It was a small party, maybe six or seven riders. He couldn't be sure but he didn't think they had spotted the two of them as yet so he motioned for Morning Sky to stay low and follow him to a group of cottonwoods by a dry streambed. There they could stay out of sight until the party passed. Judging by their direction of travel, the party would pass within a few hundred yards of their hiding place. Little Wolf crawled up close to the top of a slope that fronted the trees to keep a close watch on the riders. It would be impossible to tell if they were friendly until they came quite a bit closer. Still he strained his eyes in an attempt to identify the travelers as soon as possible. Every few minutes he would glance back at the cottonwoods to make sure Morning Sky was all right. He need not have worried. Quite secure in the knowledge that Little Wolf would take care of her, she was content to rest quietly in the shade of the small grove.

Now they were close enough to see that there were six of them, all men and, to his relief, they were Arapaho. Still, before he left the cover of the ridge, he waited until they were close enough for him to hear an occasional word as they carried on their casual conversation. He wanted to be certain they were friendly. They looked to be Arapaho but they could also be a band of Commanches who had wandered this far north to hunt. There could be no doubt, however, that their speech was Arapaho. When they were at the closest point in passing, he stood up and called out to them.

There seemed to be no leader of the party, just six young braves traveling together. They all wheeled as one when they heard Little Wolf's call, and their ponies danced back and forth from side to side as the young men searched for the source of the voice. One of them pointed to the ridge where Little Wolf stood and then they talked excitedly among themselves, probably deciding whether it was a trap or not, Little Wolf figured.

"I am Little Wolf," he called out, "son of Spotted Pony of the Arapaho."

One of the warriors turned and said something to his companions and then they rode toward him. "Little Wolf, I know you. What are you doing alone in the prairie?"

Little Wolf recognized the man then. He was called Bloody Claw, a member of the Dog Society and, like Spotted Pony, one of the few Arapahos who lived with the Cheyennes. Confident now that he was among friends, he called Morning Sky out of the trees behind him and told the men of their journey to find Black Kettle.

Bloody Claw spoke. "Black Kettle has taken his village to the soldiers' fort on the Horse River, the place the white man calls Fort Lyons. The white chief there has told him they will protect his people and give them food and there will be no more killing." He gestured toward his companions, some of whom Little Wolf recognized from the summer rendezvous. "My brothers and I do not wish to live under the white man's law. Black Kettle is a man of peace and we respect that. But it is not our way. We go to join the others in the high mountains to live as a warrior should live. Why don't you come with us? It is no way to live, to grow old on a reservation."

Little Wolf was tempted to join them. He had no desire to live on a reservation either. He had learned to love the life he had adopted, where the tribe was free to hunt and live where they wished. Still, he felt he must find Spotted Pony and Buffalo Woman. Now, too, he had the responsibility of taking care of Morning Sky. He had promised Black Feather that he would see his sister safely back to her relatives with Black Kettle. He felt bound to that promise.

"No. Thank you for inviting me to join you but I must find Spotted Pony first. When I see him and take Morning Sky back to her people, then I may come to find you in the mountains."

They said good-bye to the party of warriors and continued their journey south. Little Wolf had made a decision, one that he felt was the proper one. Yet he didn't feel completely at peace with it. Many conflicting thoughts troubled his mind as he and Morning Sky covered the slow miles toward Fort Lyons. He felt in his mind that he was Arapaho even though his childhood memories, though not fresh, were still there. He wished that he had been found by Spotted Pony when he was a baby, too small to have any memories of being white. Then these troublesome thoughts would not be there to bother him. Part of his heart wanted to be with Black Feather in the mountains. But part of him

still harbored a reluctance to make war on the people of
his birth, his blood kin. He had no desire to live on the
reservation and yet he had never actually lived on a reservation so how was he to know if he would like it or not?
Maybe it would be as the government had originally promised and the tribe would be given their own land with game
and water, and left in peace. This would not be so bad. He
could again enjoy his life with Spotted Pony. He could hunt
and trap and live the life he had come to love. So, he
concluded, the decision was good. He would join Black
Kettle and stay with his parents.

Two more days found them at the south fork of the
Horse River. From there, they followed the river further
south and east until, on the evening of the third day, they
spotted distant campfires that Little Wolf was almost certain were those of Black Kettle's people. Since it was already dark and the village was still some distance away,
Little Wolf decided it would be prudent to wait until morning before riding in. There was an army post close by and
he did not think it wise to proceed in the darkness. He did
not want to come all this way only to be shot by a cavalry
patrol from Fort Lyons. Bloody Claw had said that Black
Kettle was under the protection of the commander of the
fort but that might not be the case. He wanted to make
sure the tribe was not being held captive. He would wait
until morning to see if there were soldiers in the village.

Morning Sky was content to make camp for Little Wolf
on the bank of the river. He thought she might complain
when told he had decided to wait another night before
taking her to her people but she seemed content with the
decision. She even hummed to herself as she went about
gathering some small branches to make a bed for them. He
watched her busying herself around their makeshift camp,
her movements fluid and purposeful. He caught himself ad-
miring her face, a rather pleasant face, he thought. She was
really a graceful girl for one so young. She was going to be
a handsome woman one day. Realizing that he was allowing
his mind to travel in dangerous directions, and feeling a
mite sheepish about having thoughts about his best friend's
little sister, he jerked his mind back to the business at hand.
After all, the girl couldn't be more than twelve or thirteen.

He decided to see if there were any fish in the river. Maybe he could catch a couple for their evening meal.

Any fishing skills he possessed, he learned as a small boy because neither Arapaho nor Cheyenne cared much for fishing. The only time the men of his tribe would fish was if there was no other food available and they were starving. He had no fishhooks or line but he thought if he could sight one, he would make a try at shooting one with his bow. As it turned out, he didn't get the opportunity to test his skill because he walked up and down the riverbank for at least a half mile in both directions without seeing any sign of anything alive in the muddy water. Finally he gave it up when pitch-black darkness made it too dark to see anything.

Morning Sky had already built a small fire and cooked what was left of the rabbit he had killed earlier that day. He smiled to himself as he noticed that she did not have to be told to dig a hole in the bank for her cook fire so the flames would not be visible for any distance. She smiled warmly as he approached, her eyes following his every move until he had settled himself by the fire.

"Were your fish too heavy to carry by yourself? Do you want me to go back and help you carry them?"

She had taken to teasing him quite a bit during the last few days. "No," he replied, pretending to be irritated by her taunting. "I decided that you wouldn't know how to cook them so I threw them back in the river for the turtles to eat."

She laughed and held out a piece of the rabbit to him, then sat back to watch him eat. He didn't eat it at once.

"Where is yours?" he asked. When she reached beside her and held up a piece of the scrawny meat, he accepted his portion. This was something else he had begun to notice. If he wasn't careful in watching her, she would go without, giving him her share. He had started out taking care of her but, by the time they reached the Horse River, she was more often than not taking care of him. *I hope they have something to eat in the village,* he thought. He was growing tired of the steady diet of rabbit they had endured for the past several days of their journey.

They talked for a while before going to sleep. There had not been a great deal of conversation between them during

the days before. Morning Sky was a quiet girl and most of
the time she simply followed along behind him, making no
unnecessary talk. Now, on the eve of their reunion with the
tribe, it was as if the journey they had taken together had
somehow established a special bond between them. For his
part, he felt more relaxed than he had on any night since
they had left Black Feather and Sleeps Standing. For one
thing, he felt the journey had been completed. He had
found Black Kettle. And, he reasoned, there shouldn't be
much danger from army patrols. When they first made
camp almost within sight of their destination, he felt the
need for caution. Now he reconsidered. Why would the
army be out looking for Indians when the whole tribe was
camped right outside their gate? So he relaxed and enjoyed
the idle chatter of his traveling companion. She was obviously excited about joining her uncle's family in the
morning.

After a while the conversation seemed to have run its
course and it was time to sleep. Little Wolf banked the
coals of their fire so it wouldn't go out during the night.
The nights were cold now and the thought of sleeping in a
warm tipi appealed strongly to him after so many nights in
the open. During their journey, Morning Sky would make
a bed of pine boughs and aspen leaves, whenever they were
available, to give them some separation from the cold
ground. Some nights had found them on the open prairie
with nothing to use for insulation. These were the nights
that began a practice of sleeping together for warmth.
Morning Sky wanted to share her buffalo robe with him
but it was too small to cover them both. So she wrapped
herself in the robe and snuggled up tightly against his back
to keep him warm. With Morning Sky at his back and the
fire in front of him, he was reasonably warm, at least warm
enough to fall into fitful periods of sleep.

But on this night, their camp was almost as warm as a
tipi. It was a shallow cave, sculpted out of the riverbank
by the rushing spring thaws, when the water was high.
Morning Sky had dug out a fire pit on one side and the
little cave was quite comfortable. Little Wolf thought to
himself that he could enjoy staying here for a while, at least
until the spring thaws filled the cave with water. He settled
down beside the fire and made himself comfortable. Morn-

ing Sky took a cloth down to the water's edge and wet it. She always did this whenever they camped near a stream or river. Usually she went from the camp to wash some of the dust and grime away, far enough away to ensure her privacy. This night she soaked the cloth and came back to the cave.

"It's cold outside tonight," she offered in explanation.

He shrugged, already drowsy. "Yes, it's cold," was his only reply.

"If it's all right, I'll clean myself here where it's warm." She waited for his response. There was none so she prodded, "Is it all right?"

"What? Oh . . . yes, it's all right." He was too drowsy to really care what she was saying; his eyelids were already heavy.

After a few moments of silence, something nudged his sleepy brain and he opened his eyes again. Without stirring from his position, he glanced back toward the mouth of the cave, his eyelids still barely half open. His gaze was immediately captured by a vision of soft, brown skin. She had removed her leggings and her skirt, now pulled up almost to her waist, revealed well-rounded thighs and buttocks. He found his eyes riveted to the soft curves of her upper thigh as she slowly rubbed the wet cloth over them. It was more a caress than a cleaning motion and he was at once fascinated by the ritual. He knew he should roll over and ignore the young girl's bathing but he found he could not.

His eyes followed the bare thigh up until it was again hidden by the folds of her gathered skirt. His gaze continued upward to her blouse. It was untied and open enough to expose two young breasts, not fully developed, but swollen with the promise of womanhood soon to come. He felt a definite stirring deep within him, the thought of sleep all but a memory. At the same time he felt a twinge of guilt, for here he was gazing wantonly at his friend's little sister, she no more than a child and he charged with her safety. Feeling ashamed, he glanced up into her face, only to find her eyes locked on his. He knew at once that she was aware of his visual fondling of her body. He flushed, feeling foolish at having been caught leering at a child, and attempted to appear oblivious to her. But she knew she had captured his eye. He pretended to go back to sleep.

She lay down next to him as she had done on nights past when there was no protection from the prairie wind. It was not necessary on this night in their snug little cave. The fire kept it warm enough to sleep even without the buffalo robe. Still she pressed her body up close against his back. But on this night he was aware of the feel of her for the first time. He didn't like the thoughts that were racing through his mind and he tried to dismiss them. She was little more than a baby, he told himself, and she was Black Feather's sister . . . and his responsibility. He prayed sleep would come quickly.

"Little Wolf," she whispered softly.

He felt thousands of tiny needles up his spine and at first he pretended to be asleep.

"Little Wolf," she persisted.

"What is it?"

She put her arm around his waist and pressed her body even tighter against his back. "What's going to happen when we get to the village in the morning?"

He didn't understand her question. "What do you mean?" he asked, then said, "It depends on Black Kettle. He is chief."

"I mean what is going to happen to us, you and me?"

He was beginning to understand what she was getting at and he was also aware of the slight movement of her hand up and down on his bare chest. "I am going to find Spotted Pony and Buffalo Woman and you are going to your uncle's lodge," he said.

"I could stay with you," she said, her voice low, the words spoken with a deliberate softness. "I would make you a good wife."

Her childish attempt to be seductive was probably the only thing that saved him from doing something he might have regretted later. For suddenly the thought that she was trying to seduce him amused him and it immediately drove all erotic thoughts of her from his mind. Now it became a game of tease with his friend's little sister. But he had come close, awfully close, to taking advantage of the situation.

"You are too young to even talk of such things," he teased. "Wait until you are no longer a baby. Then we'll think about it. I'm not ready to tie myself to a wife now anyway, especially one that's not old enough to wean."

His comment brought the reaction he expected. She sat upright, indignant in her response. "I am not too young," she protested. "Look at me!" She pulled her blouse apart, exposing her young breasts. "See! I am almost a woman already!" When he did not turn over to look at her, she grabbed his arm and placed his hand on her breast.

Little Wolf was in complete control of his emotions by then and he was enjoying the situation. He left his hand on her breast for a few moments, feigning serious concentration before remarking, "Yes, I think I can feel something. Maybe it's a bee sting. Maybe you should put some buffalo fat on it when we get to the village tomorrow."

"You are too stupid to marry!" she exclaimed in disgust, jerking his hand away from her. "When you think you are ready to take a wife, I won't want you!" With that, she lay back and turned her back to him. "Stupid boy!" she muttered as she pulled the buffalo robe up over her head.

"Good night, little one," he laughed. She did not answer.

Chapter 7

"Little Wolf." He uttered the words softly but the look of joy in Spotted Pony's eyes was one of sheer excitement as he glanced up and saw his son approaching. He did not rise as he watched Little Wolf striding toward him but his smile told of the pride that filled his heart when his tall young warrior son made straight for his father's tipi. Spotted Pony knew he would come even though there had been much talk of the raids by the soldiers on the winter camps. Five days after Little Wolf had left, a messenger brought them news of the attack on Red Shirt's village, a raid that had taken the lives of all but a few survivors. There had been no time to find out if Little Wolf was in danger, for the following day Spotted Pony's own camp was attacked by a company of cavalry and the few survivors had fled to join Black Kettle. Buffalo Woman had been concerned that their son might be drawn back to his white blood when the attacks began and he would be forced to side with the soldiers. But Spotted Pony had scolded her for doubting her son's loyalty to the people and he promised her that Little Wolf would return to them, wherever the tribe went. And now, here he was, just as Spotted Pony knew he would come.

"Father!" Little Wolf called out when he sighted Spotted Pony kneeling before the fire. He quickened his pace to a trot.

Spotted Pony rose to his feet, his arms spread to receive his son, his smile a wide splash of joy across his face. Father and son embraced and Spotted Pony called out to Buffalo Woman to come greet her son. His mother, hearing noises outside, was already coming out of the tipi when Spotted Pony called. She was so filled with elation at seeing Little Wolf that she almost knocked father and son down in her eagerness to join in the reunion. After a few minutes of hugs and pats, Buffalo Woman suddenly realized that the young girl standing there watching them was with Little Wolf.

"And who is this? Have you taken a wife?" Buffalo Woman teased.

Morning Sky flushed visibly and looked down at the ground, afraid to look at Buffalo Woman for fear she might read the truth in her eyes. Little Wolf laughed and replied, "This is Morning Sky, Black Feather's sister. She has an uncle here."

Spotted Pony seemed concerned. "Where are her mother and father? Were they . . . ?"

Little Wolf quickly nodded. "Yes. When the soldiers attacked their camp, her father barely had time to string his bow. They were shot down as they came out of their tipi." He glanced at Morning Sky to see if she showed any emotion as he spoke. If she did, she hid it well, her gaze still pinned to the ground.

"And your friend? Black Feather? Was he killed also?"

"No. Black Feather has gone to the high mountains with the others to fight the soldiers. He asked me to bring Morning Sky to her uncle."

Buffalo Woman reached out to the girl and pulled her up close to her ample body. Putting her arms around her, she said, "You must be exhausted. Come and sit by the fire. Rest and eat. We will find your uncle's tipi after you have rested."

Without thinking, Morning Sky looked to Little Wolf for permission. He nodded and gently pressed her arm. Buffalo Woman did not miss the look in the young girl's eyes. Secretly she smiled to herself.

After they had eaten, Little Wolf and Spotted Pony escorted Morning Sky to the tipi of her uncle, the brother of her father, Red Shirt. There she was welcomed even though it meant one more mouth to feed and food was not plentiful this time of year. Little Wolf bade her goodbye, not noticing the look of pain in her eyes as she watched him return to his father's campfire.

Someday, she promised herself, *I will be your wife.* Little Wolf, for his part, had already put the girl out of his mind.

*   *   *

Little Wolf sat down to talk to his father. He had an uneasy feeling about the camp. It was a sizable encampment, several hundred Cheyenne as well as quite a few Arapaho, all under the guidance of Black Kettle. They were camped at the bend of Sand Creek, just north of the fort. Was it safe to be so close to an enemy that had just recently destroyed two winter Cheyenne camps, perhaps even more? It did not seem like a typical Cheyenne village. It was more like a prison compound. There were no walls or fences around them but the men appeared subdued, almost docile. There were no hunters galloping through the village on their way to or from the hunt. And certainly there were no signs of raiding parties. In fact, it appeared to Little Wolf that the men of the village were doing little more than sitting around, keeping warm inside their tipis. He didn't like the look of it.

Spotted Pony tried to explain the feeling of malaise that seemed to permeate the village. "The white chiefs have said they will no longer tolerate the refusal of the Cheyenne to return to the reservation. You know that the people vowed to resist the soldiers at first but the soldiers are too many and have too many guns. Black Kettle has talked with the white chief at the fort about striking a peace between the soldiers and our people. He has promised that our young men will not raid the white squatters anymore if the soldiers will cease their attacks on our villages. That is why our men sit in their tipis."

"But what about food?" Little Wolf asked. "I don't see any hunting parties."

"The white soldier chief has sent some food and has promised to send more if we keep our braves in camp. Black Kettle thinks the man speaks the truth. He has invited us to camp here, near the fort, while our chiefs talk of peace together. We see the army patrols leave the fort every day but they offer no threat to us, leaving us in peace. Black Kettle will negotiate a treaty for us to return to our hunting grounds."

Little Wolf found no reassurance in his father's words. He could not shake the feeling that he had walked into a prison camp.

"Father," he pleaded, "let us leave this place. You and I and Buffalo Woman, we can go back to the mountains.

This is not the way of the Arapaho. Black Kettle is Cheyenne. If the Cheyenne want to lie around before the white man's fort like a lazy dog lies in front of the fire, then so be it. But we are Arapaho; let us go into the mountains and make our winter camp as we always have. There are plenty of antelope and elk there and the heavy snows have not fallen yet. There is still time to prepare for the winter."

Spotted Pony hesitated. He listened to the impassioned plea of his son and considered the wisdom in his proposition. For even though he felt secure in the judgment of Black Kettle, he could not honestly say that he had not felt some qualms about the tribe's present situation. Black Kettle was chief but Spotted Pony was a man who could think for himself and he had questioned the wisdom in trusting the soldiers to grant the people their own private hunting ground, free from interference. It would be good to do as Little Wolf suggested and go far up into the mountains, away from the soldiers. Still he hesitated for he had always been loyal to his chief and it was not an easy thing to do, for a man to leave his village.

"There is wisdom in your words, my young warrior. I will consider what you propose. I'll think on it for a while and then I will decide."

Little Wolf felt relieved at once. He knew if Spotted Pony had rejected the idea, he would have said so immediately. He also knew that Spotted Pony would not immediately agree to his suggestion to leave the camp, even though he accepted the idea. He would have to think on it for a period of time before making his final decision. That was his way. They would leave this place. Little Wolf was certain of that. If he had known of the messenger on his way to Major Scott Anthony, the commander of the small garrison at Fort Lyons, from Colonel John M. Chivington, in command of twelve hundred Colorado volunteers, he would have left the village at Sand Creek that very afternoon.

Later that day, a member of the tribe's Society of the Dog came to Spotted Pony's tipi with a message from Black Kettle. The chief had heard that Spotted Pony's son had arrived and he asked if Little Wolf would come to the council lodge to talk with him. Little Wolf, of course, responded immediately. It was not a common thing, to be summoned by the chief. True, he had spoken briefly to the chief on several occasions while the whole tribe was gathered during the summer hunt. But it was never more than a polite greeting. Black Kettle's messenger gave no hint as to the reason for the interview. Little Wolf could only wonder why the chief wanted council with a boy of sixteen years. He had told Spotted Pony about the army scout he had killed with his war club at Red Shirt's village. This was a big thing to his people. To kill an enemy at close range, hand to hand, was strong medicine indeed and Spotted Pony had visibly swelled with pride when told of it. Maybe Spotted Pony had sent the chief word of his son's accomplishment and the chief simply wanted to congratulate him. This was not the case, however, as Spotted Pony had sent no word of his bravery. His intention, he said was to dance and sing of it at the council lodge when the elders met that night. The thought of his accomplishment being sung before the elders buoyed his spirits to the point of forgetting the general disarray of the village and the urgency he had felt earlier about leaving. He was already building a reputation that was quite impressive for a grown man and even more so for a boy his age.

The council lodge was located, as custom decreed, in the center of the village. It was larger than the other tipis, the entrance facing the east, toward the rising sun. The buffalo skins which made up the outside walls of the tipi were painted with wide alternating bands of red and black. Little Wolf had never been inside the council tipi. This summons was tantamount to recognition as an adult. He glanced briefly at his father before raising the entrance flap and could not help but notice the look of pride on Spotted Pony's face as he stooped to precede his son into the lodge.

"Ah, Little Wolf," the old chief greeted them as they passed through the entrance. He was seated on a woven mat close to the fire. To Little Wolf, Black Kettle seemed to have aged perceptibly since the summer hunt, the raids of the winter having obviously taken their toll on the old man. At one time he might have been perceived as a war chief but now, with the ever increasing numbers of whites and the firepower of their many rifles, his main concern was peace for his people. Little Wolf could not help but feel a sense of compassion for him as he motioned for them to sit beside him. Since his adoption as a child, Little Wolf had always thought the chief was of almost superhuman stature, the mighty leader of the tribe. Now he more nearly resembled a worried old man, concerned for the future of his people. Little Wolf was not sure what had changed his image of the chief. Was it due to the fact that he was no longer a child and saw him as he really was? Or had the recent troubled times torn the man down to this present state?

"Old friend," the chief said to Spotted Pony, "this son of yours is no longer a boy."

Spotted Pony grinned broadly. "This is true. He is already a head taller than I. He has taken the power of the bear and now he has killed an enemy in hand to hand combat."

Black Kettle's eyes lit up at this. He, of course, knew of the story of Little Wolf and the bear when Spotted Pony first found the boy. This was general knowledge among the people. But the killing of an enemy obviously impressed him. He pressed Little Wolf for details. Little Wolf recounted the encounter at Red Shirt's camp, modestly admitting that he had struck the army scout from behind. Black Kettle insisted that he should not belittle his accomplishment. For a boy of his age to inflict a mortal wound on an enemy was big medicine indeed. And the fact that it was done to save the life of a brother made it even more commendable. Little Wolf was embarrassed by the crowing and boasting his father did over an action Little Wolf did simply as a reflex. He had lived long enough with the Cheyennes to know that it was an honorable thing to boast about one's accomplishments in battle. Even so, he was not comfortable with the idea of spouting off about how brave he was. He was glad when the subject was changed.

Black Kettle began, "Little Wolf, I have heard many good things about you." He glanced at Spotted Pony as he spoke. "When I was told that your father had found a white boy and took him to his tipi, I was happy for him and Buffalo Woman for they could make no seed of their own. But I had little hope for the union. I have seen other white children adopted by the Cheyenne and the Lakota. It never seemed to work out. They would run away, back to the whites, or they would be sold or traded. And, in the end, they were still white. But you have become one of us. No man in the tribe is against you. You brought with you the medicine of the bear and it has made you strong. You are truly Spotted Pony's son. Because you bring honor to your father's tipi, and to our tribe, I know I can trust you to help me."

Little Wolf was beside himself with excitement. He was afraid he was literally glowing from the praise just heaped upon him by the chief and he was trying hard not to show it. It didn't help to glance at Spotted Pony for he was fairly beaming with pride. So he kept his eyes focused on the flames of the fire as he said humbly, "I would be honored to help my chief in any way I can."

Black Kettle continued, "I have been negotiating with the soldier chiefs for the peaceful return of our people to our rightful hunting ground. The soldier chief Anthony has told me that the soldiers will not bother our village here but he insists that we must leave soon and live on a reservation to the south. I think the soldier chief Anthony is an honorable man and, if I can make him understand that it would not be a good thing to take the people to the reservation, he would see that we need to be where there is game to hunt and buffalo to make our clothes and cover our tipis. I have seen this land where they want us to go. It is a dead land. Nothing lives there but snakes and toads. But I can't make him understand, and the reason is because he does not speak our tongue. He uses a Crow scout to speak for me and I don't trust him to give the soldier chief my words. I have never met a Crow who was trustworthy anyway. I know that you speak the white man's tongue. Tomorrow, when I go to meet with the soldier chief, you will be at my side. You will talk for me and make the soldier chief understand."

So this was the reason Black Kettle had summoned him. He was to be the old chief's interpreter. He was to sit by Black Kettle's side in an official meeting with Major Anthony. As he and Spotted Pony walked back to their tipi, his head was buzzing with the importance of his mission. He wondered what Black Feather would think if he knew that he, a Kit-fox, was to sit at the side of Black Kettle. This was a post rightfully suited to an elder. He wondered if this Major Anthony would know that he was really a white boy. He pondered the thought for a moment or two before deciding that he would look like his tribesmen tomorrow. He would have Buffalo Woman apply plenty of grease to his usually unruly hair to make the braids dark and straight. His skin, at least that which was exposed to the elements, was dark enough. He must ask Man Above to give him wisdom and maturity for tomorrow. He had not yet undergone the ritual of fasting for four days and then going off alone to seek a medicine vision. The Arapaho did not practice this ritual until they reached manhood. Consequently, he did not wear a medicine bundle. But he didn't need one. He would wear his necklace of bear claws that Spotted Pony had made for him. That would be medicine enough. The thought struck him that he wanted to tell Morning Sky of this honor bestowed upon him but he just as quickly dismissed it. Why should he want to tell a child of this?

Buffalo Woman was proud almost to the point of bursting when told of the honor brought to her tipi by her son. Her face was radiant with the pride that only a mother could feel. She pressed Spotted Pony to repeat every word of praise that Black Kettle had bestowed upon her son. Little Wolf could not remember ever seeing her happier than she was at that moment. Her excitement was infectious. It would be difficult for him to sleep that night and he needed to be well rested for his mission the next day.

He awoke early the next morning, shivering with the cold. It had been almost too warm in the tipi that night and he had fallen asleep with no robe over his bare torso. During the night the fire died down and the late November chill finally began to penetrate the thick air of the tipi. It was not yet daylight so he reached for a robe to pull over him. After a few moments he remembered the responsibility he had been given for this day and his thoughts soon brought him to be wide awake. After a few moments more he decided that his mind was too alert to sleep any longer so he tossed the robe aside. He felt the need to relieve himself anyway, so he pulled a buckskin tunic over his head and stood up. The tipi was dark except for the faint red glow of what live coals were left of the fire. In the darkness he could just make out the sleeping forms of his mother and father, bundled under a mound of buffalo robes. He took great pains to move quietly so he would not disturb them as he took a few sticks of firewood from the stack against the side of the tipi. Using one of the sticks as a poker, he stirred the coals until he made a glowing bed to lay the wood on. After watching the coals until he was sure the wood had caught flame, he went outside.

As soon as he dropped the entrance flap and stood erect, the chill of the morning hit him like a splash of cold water. A heavy frost covered the ground, giving the gathering of tipis an icy look, and brought about an involuntary shiver. Looking toward the east, out across the narrow river, he saw the first rays of the new day probing the silver darkness. It would be daylight soon. As he stood there before the entrance of Buffalo Woman's tipi, he could see the fiery tip of the sun over the distant prairie. His breath rose before his face like smoke. Then his bladder reminded him why he had gotten up and he quietly moved through the row of tipis to the edge of the camp.

Even in the early hours of the morning, when there was little risk that anyone might see him relieving himself, Little Wolf went well beyond the perimeter of the village to do his business. Unlike most young men of the tribe, he had always retained a certain degree of modesty when it came to answering nature's calls. His friend Black Feather laughed at his modesty and would, as often as not, relieve himself by the side of the tipi. The thought caused Little Wolf to smile to himself as he stood there in the cold. He wondered where Black Feather was on this morning, high up in the mountain country. "Probably under a knee-high snowfall," he grunted to himself.

Finished with nature's business, he paused for a few minutes to look about him. There was light now, enough for the land around him to take shape. Since he had just arrived at this place, he had not really had time to look around the village. Had it been his decision, he decided, he would have found a better place to locate the camp. There seemed to be no regard for the traditional precautions usually observed when locating any Cheyenne camp. He recalled the initial feelings he had experienced the day before when he first saw the village, reminding him of a prison compound. Even though Black Kettle had told him that the tribe had settled there with Major Anthony's permission and his promise of protection, Little Wolf still found it unusual that there were no sentries posted around the camp. Maybe he would be more reassured after meeting with the fort commander this morning, he thought, and pushed it from his mind.

Fingers of sunlight were just touching on the narrow band of water below the village now. Little Wolf decided to walk down to the river, which was little more than a stream, to see if he might catch sight of a muskrat. Moving silently and crouching to keep from making a high silhouette on the riverbank, he moved close to the water's edge and sat motionless for a long time, watching and listening. Back in the village a dog barked. Soon it was joined by several others. Little Wolf crawled back up to the top of the bank to see what had caused the disturbance. He could see nothing. The village was still sleeping as far as he could tell. He had walked several hundred yards beyond the outermost tipis by this time so it was difficult to see into the village. He listened hard but could hear nothing above the barking of the dogs. The sun was now touching the tipis on the extreme eastern rim of the village but the only signs of life were a few random ribbons of smoke indicating that some of the women were stirring up their cook fires.

He turned his attention back to the stream briefly before deciding that he was ready to return to the tipi for something to eat. When he stood up, he heard it. At first he could not identify the noise and he stood stone still, listening. It was a curious sound, muffled like a herd of buffalo. Then he felt the slight tremble of the earth beneath his feet and he immediately recognized that to be the same vibration he had felt during the summer hunts when the tribe stalked the great herds on the plains. The sounds he heard in the next few moments told him it was not buffalo he heard. When buffalo ran, there was no jingling of bridle and harness and no clink of metal on metal. He scrambled back up to the lip of the bank just as he heard the bugle call and then chaos erupted upon the unsuspecting village.

He was stunned by the scene before him, some several hundred yards downstream. Row upon row of troopers crested the rise above the village and swept down through the shallow water and into the sleeping camp, firing into the tipis and at anything that moved. The ranks of soldiers

seemed to be endless. Like a great scythe, they cut through
the defenseless village wreaking total destruction as they
went to the other side, then wheeled and crisscrossed their
way back through. The screams of terror carried above the
almost constant roar of rifle fire. It was obvious that there
was no thought of capture. The army's mission was nothing
short of annihilation.

Little Wolf, paralyzed for a moment, finally sprang to
life. He must get to Spotted Pony and Buffalo Woman! He
scrambled to his feet and started running as fast as he could
toward the village. There was no thought of personal safety.
His only thought was to get to his parents. As he approached the outer ring of tipis, many of which were burning by then, he began to gather his senses. It would be
foolish, and of no help to his parents, to charge headlong
into the melee, getting himself killed in the process. He
immediately dropped to the ground to survey the situation
before proceeding.

The village was in complete chaos. All of the lodges in
the center of the circle were blazing. There were bodies
littered everywhere, sprawled in grotesque postures, killed
as they tried to run. The bodies were so many that the
troopers' horses could not avoid trampling them under
their hooves. The sound of the massacre was a steady roar
in his ears as the soldiers continued firing at living targets
as well as those already dead. Little Wolf could not understand why he had thus far escaped detection. He should
turn and escape while he could still go back to the river
but he could not. He still felt he had to try to help his
parents. He made his way through the burning tipis as best
he could, stopping to pretend to be dead whenever a
trooper came near. Then, crawling and running, he finally
reached the back of Buffalo Woman's tipi. Half of it was
already destroyed, the remains smoldering. But half was
still intact, the half that covered their beds. As he lay on
his belly, working away at the tough buffalo hide with his
knife, he glanced toward the council lodge. There, on a
pole, a white flag along with an American flag was fluttering
listlessly in the faint breeze. He was to learn later that,
when the attack first started, Black Kettle had put up the
white flag. When the soldiers ignored it, he also put up an

American flag to show that the village was peaceful. But nothing slowed the assault on his peaceful village.

When he had ripped a place large enough to slip through, Little Wolf crawled into the half burned tipi. He was not prepared for what he saw. Buffalo Woman was sprawled across the cook fire, her face broken apart by the bullet that had killed her. In what once was the entrance to the tipi, Spotted Pony lay facedown, his bone-handle hunting knife in his hand, his bare back riddled with bullet holes. Little Wolf felt as if his heart stopped beating. His rage filled his throat to the point of choking him. His anger overwhelmed him and, without realizing it, he began to roar with the pain of it, a primordial scream, born in his very soul. Hearing his cry of anguish, a trooper turned his horse toward the source of the sound and came face to face with him. In his fury, Little Wolf did not hesitate. He drew his knife and leaped toward the mounted soldier. The soldier had time to raise his carbine and get off one shot before Little Wolf's knife found his stomach. The shot hit Little Wolf in the shoulder and he slid to the ground. The young trooper, realizing he was wounded, wheeled his horse around in panic and galloped off for help. Because of this, Little Wolf's life was spared.

He lay dazed for a few moments, his shoulder rapidly becoming numb. The sound of attack had decreased from the steady roar of gunfire and now individual firing could be heard as the soldiers killed those who were still barely alive. Little Wolf knew he was wounded but he couldn't be sure how badly. He expected to feel the impact of the fatal bullet at any second but apparently the soldiers paid little attention to the body lying next to that of his father. His shoulder began to throb but, other than that, there seemed to be no serious impairment. He laid motionless and held his breath when a soldier rode by, no more than ten feet from him. The soldier stopped, looked at him, then rode on. Very deliberately he rolled over on his side so he could see the area around him. Right then there was no one near him and he knew there would probably be no better oppor-tunity to escape. So he slowly slid around until he was partially hidden by the body of his father. Then pushing himself backward through the ashes of the tipi, he man-aged to slide back through the opening he had first come

through. Even though he knew it didn't matter to Buffalo
Woman's spirit, he paused to roll her body from the ashes
of the cook fire.

There were soldiers everywhere and later, he felt sure
Man Above was watching over him because he was able to
snake his way through the burning village and down along
the riverbank. Once he reached the spot from which he
had first seen the soldiers that morning, he felt it was safe
enough to stop and examine his wound before going on.
There had been a great loss of blood, but the wound didn't
look too bad and, at this point, it didn't seem to impair the
use of his arm. The thought flashed briefly through his mind
that it would have been an honorable thing to have stayed
and fought. After all, to die young in battle was preferable
to an Arapaho warrior, more so than dying of old age. His
rational mind had rejected that fate in preference to surviving so that he would be able to take a greater measure of
revenge in the future. "I'll fight another day," he promised
his dead parents. "This is not the last of it." At this sorrow-
ful point in his young life he could not know that this cowardly raid on this peaceful village would be the primary
cause of the Cheyenne-Arapaho wars that followed in the
years to come. The only thing he was certain of was that
he was at war with the U.S. Army. His only thought now
was to make his way northwest and find Black Feather
and his brothers in the mountains. The sounds of the army
mopping up the remains of the village could still be heard
clearly when he crossed the river and set out to find his
friend.

Luck was still with him for, when he had gone no more
than a mile from the river, he found a horse. It was a small
paint, an Indian pony evidently wandering back toward the
village after having been frightened away during the attack.
Taking great care not to startle the horse, Little Wolf was
able to walk up to it and take hold of the reins. There was
no saddle, only an Indian bridle, and from the look of the
broken left rein, the horse had evidently been tied outside
someone's tipi when the shooting started. Someone's favorite horse, he thought as he climbed on and kicked the little
paint into a gallop. He wanted to put some distance between himself and the fort right away. The paint had an

easy gait—little wonder she was someone's favorite. Little Wolf recalled the first time he had jumped on someone else's horse and fled. That time it was the opposite situation—on a white man's horse, running from Indians. It seemed like a lifetime ago.

His journey took a good deal longer than he had anticipated. He stuck mainly to the east of the mountains, riding the plains. It was his intention to get as far north as he could, farther than any soldiers were stationed. And he could make better time, cover more miles, if he kept to the plains. He pushed the paint, riding as long as he could each day before darkness forced him to rest and find food. It proved easier to find food for the horse than for himself and, as the days passed, he began to weaken. Adding to his problems was the wound in his shoulder. While it didn't seem to be serious at first, it began to swell and get more and more painful as each day passed. After a while he developed a fever. Still he pushed on. At times he would suddenly awaken to find that he had fallen asleep while riding. In time, he got to the point where he lost track of distance and days. Because of the cold and the pain from his wound, he kept pushing the pony on and on until it was in danger of being ridden to death. Little Wolf was too far out of his mind with fever to realize this.

At night, when he did rest, Spotted Pony and Buffalo Woman, Black Feather, Morning Sky, Sleeps Standing, Red Shirt, Black Kettle all walked through his dreams. Upon waking, he would look around expecting to see them only to find that he was alone. When he reached the point where he knew he could no longer go on without food, he turned west into the mountains, in hopes of finding something.

Climbing up a steep rise toward a forest of pines, the horse balked. Little Wolf prodded her with his heels but the horse was too weak to go on. He had ridden her to death. The realization of it served to shock the boy back to his senses and he immediately regretted having abused the animal. It was a stupid thing to do and something he would never do again. By then his fever was so hot that he had to force himself to think. At least the horse saved his life one last time, giving him something to eat.

He stayed there and rested after he had eaten the warm liver of the horse and he seemed to regain at least some measure of strength, enough to enable him to think clearly about his survival. He couldn't stay there long. True, the horse represented food but how long would it be before he would have to fight wolves, buzzards and other scavengers for it? He had to move on. That was the thought he concentrated upon, to keep moving, choosing not to let his mind dwell on the truth of his plight—that he didn't know where he was going or how he could survive with nothing more than a knife in a rugged country. What if there was a big snowfall before he could find a place to rest? He forced himself up on his feet and started down the hillside toward a small stream.

He lay on his belly, drinking the cool water, when he heard something. Alert now, he listened. There! He heard it again, not a loud noise, but it was definitely the soft pad of a horse's hoof. Slowly he eased back into a pine thicket and cautiously rose to his feet, scanning the forest below him. After a moment, he saw him, a man riding a mule. It was difficult to make out the man's features but he was not an Indian. That much Little Wolf could tell. He never once considered approaching the man and asking for help. He was a white man, maybe a soldier, but definitely an enemy.

From the direction he was heading, Little Wolf could estimate approximately where the man would cross the creek so he moved to a position just above it. Drawing his knife, he could hear the man scolding his mule as he prodded it across the creek, unaware of the ambush awaiting him. He waited, and when the rider was exactly opposite the thicket, Little Wolf summoned all the strength he had left and launched his body at the man.

CHAPTER 8

Squint Peterson figured it was pure luck the wounded, half starved boy had picked him to ambush. Most any other white man would probably have shot him right off instead of patching him up. The boy healed rapidly. Squint found that a little rest and nourishment was really all that was needed once the bullet was removed and the infection staved off. He was lucky. The bullet had lodged in the fleshy part of his shoulder instead of smashing bone and costing him the use of his arm. Squint's clumsy surgery had left a huge hole that would in time heal but would leave one hell of a scar. The boy didn't seem to care about that as long as the arm was all right.

You could say the two of them hit it off right from the start. Yet Squint could still detect an air of mild distrust on the part of this white boy turned Injun. It was as if the boy appreciated what Squint had done for him but he was half expecting him to revert to the ways of the other whites he had recently come into contact with. Squint didn't blame him. The boy had nothing but hard times every time he had run into whites. There was little doubt where the lad's loyalties lay. Still they got along due to a certain amount of respect they held for each other. Of course some ground rules had to be established. Right off, the boy let Squint know that he was Arapaho and "not no damn white man" and his name was Little Wolf, not Robert. Squint allowed as how that was fine with him. He could be Pocahontas if he wanted to as long as he swore he would never tell anybody the location of his secret camp.

"I got to have your word on that," Squint demanded.

At first the boy thought he was joking, but one look at the mountain man's stern countenance convinced him he was dead serious. "I ain't gonna tell," he shrugged.

"I got to have more than that," Squint pressed. "I don't
know what you consider holy—God, the sun, Man Above
or what. But whatever it is, I want you to swear on it. I
saved your bacon when I brung you here and I don't want
nobody else knowing where this camp is."

"All right, dammit, I swear!" Little Wolf was getting
his hackles up a little. If he said he would do something,
he would do it. If he said he wouldn't tell something, he
wouldn't tell it. He didn't appreciate anybody doubting his
word. Arapaho warriors didn't lie. "I swear on the name
of my father, Spotted Pony," he added, still testy. "If that
ain't good enough for you, you can kiss my Arapaho ass."

They glared at each other for a long moment before
Squint burst out laughing. "I'm sorry, son, I forgot who I
was dealing with." From that moment forward, they got
along perfectly.

As each day passed, Little Wolf grew stronger. His shoulder soon healed to the point where he regained complete
use of it. Had it not been for the heavy snows that had
sealed up the river valley, he might have been on his way.
As it was, travel would have been extremely difficult, if not
impossible. So he had little choice but to remain as Squint's
guest for a while longer. After the first few days of bad
weather, Squint would track out through the snow to check
and reset his traps, leaving in the morning and returning
usually by early afternoon. He never invited Little Wolf to
accompany him. He figured if the boy wanted to go with
him, he would say so. He knew he was taking a chance on
losing his horses and everything else by leaving the boy
alone in his camp. But he figured it wasn't much of a risk.
For one thing, he kept all the weapons with him and the
boy would be easy enough to track in the deep snow.
Squint felt confident in his ability to catch him. More than
that, Squint sensed a definite quality of honesty and integ-
rity in the boy and he didn't really believe Little Wolf
would repay his kindness with treachery. After another
week, the snows had piled up so deep in the valley that
Squint found it to be too great an effort to go out at all so
they both settled in to wait out the winter.

When Squint fashioned his winter camp two summers
before, he hadn't counted on having a guest. So the half
cave, half lean-to was now a little crowded when the winter

snows drove them inside. To remedy this, Little Wolf and Squint worked to expand the lean-to, using some of the logs Squint had cut for firewood as walls, covering them with branches and hides. They moved the fire pit out of the cave and into a corner of the new addition. This proved to be quite satisfactory, with a hole to let the smoke out of the hide roof and the rock walls of the cave acting to reflect and retain the heat. But it was still confining. Little Wolf found himself longing for the room and comfort of Buffalo Woman's tipi, but at least their camp was warm and dry.

Snowed in as they were for a long period of time, and in such confined space, the two strangers were bound to end up either killing each other or becoming close friends. In this case it was the latter. During the long winter days Little Wolf's stern countenance gradually melted and he allowed his guard to relax. Squint was grateful for the company to help him while away the long days and nights. He had wintered alone the year before and had really had some thoughts about the possibility of going loco. He had known it to happen to other men who chose to wait out the winter alone in the mountains. Most of the ones who made it through without losing their minds had an Indian woman to keep them occupied. While Little Wolf couldn't provide some of the pleasures that a female might have, he at least provided conversation on a fairly intelligent level. In addition, Little Wolf helped take care of the animals and helped supplement their food stores.

Squint had stocked his camp well with jerky, pemmican and hardtack to carry him when the weather was too bad to get out of his little hideaway. But naturally, he didn't count on an extra mouth to feed. It turned out to be no problem, however, for he found Little Wolf to be a highly skilled hunter. The boy had spent some time after the first light snow searching the mountainside for a suitable young ash to fashion into a bow. When he found what he determined to be a good specimen, he shaped a sturdy limb into a bow of about four feet in length. Squint, an interested observer in the project, wasn't overly confident in the effectiveness that could be achieved with the rather crude-looking weapon. But, as he watched Little Wolf string his bow with antelope sinew and wrap hide thongs around the midpoint for a grip, he became more impressed. Arrows were fashioned from the same tree, shaped by passing them through a hole drilled in a piece of horn. After smoothing the shafts by rubbing them with a grooved stone, Little Wolf attached stone heads by wrapping them with sinew. As the final touch, to make the arrow spin in flight, he added feathers from a blackbird. When the weapon was completed to Little Wolf's satisfaction, he took it out to test it. Squint was amazed at the power and accuracy of the weapon. After only a short period of practice, Little Wolf was familiar enough with his new bow to become deadly accurate.

The winter was hard. Squint could not remember one that had been more severe, but there was never any shortage of meat. There were plenty of elk and deer in the mountains, even though most of the animals had moved down to winter pastures. They were easy enough to track in the deep snow. The only hard part was transporting the meat. Little Wolf proved to be quite skillful in stalking the animals and very seldom failed to bring one down when he could manuever into position for a legitimate shot with his bow. Squint liked the fact that this method of killing was silent. He didn't expect much activity in the mountains in the dead of winter but Indians had to hunt in the winter, same as him, and a rifle could be heard a long way.

The days were bitter cold and any prolonged exertion outside seemed to sap the strength right out of a man. So they tried to hunt only when they had to. Finally it got so cold that Squint became worried about his animals, afraid they might freeze in the shelter he had built for them. Had there been room, he would have considered bringing them inside with him and Little Wolf. The two of them spent the better part of one day trying to insulate the shelter with pine boughs. As a final precaution, Squint dug a fire pit in the stable and built a fire. He didn't like having to use up his supply of firewood on two fires, but he couldn't take a chance on losing the horses. He stayed out with them for a few hours that night until he was satisfied they were going to be all right and the fire was banked enough to keep it alive till morning.

"I was beginning to think you froze," Little Wolf commented when Squint returned to the lean-to.

"Hod damn!" Squint exclaimed, stamping his feet in an

effort to force some circulation back into them. "It's colder'n a widow's ass out there." He moved to the fire to warm his hands. "I figured I better stay with Joe and the ladies for a while," he said.

"You want me to stay out there tonight?"

"Nah, they'll be all right. It ain't too bad in there now. That fire will hold till morning. I don't think they'll get too cold."

Little Wolf shrugged. "Don't matter to me. If you want me to sleep out there, I don't mind."

"Nah, they'll be all right." He continued rubbing his hands briskly in front of the fire. "Besides," he added, joking, "I been noticing the way you been looking at that little mare lately. You better stay in here."

Little Wolf laughed. "I ain't about to step in and cut you out."

They both laughed. Squint sat down in the opposite corner and pulled his buffalo robe up around his shoulders. "I tell you what, it has been a damn long winter. If I don't see some signs of spring pretty soon, I might consider marrying that little mare . . . or tracking up to that Shoshone camp and findin' me a squaw." As soon as he said it, he glanced quickly at Little Wolf in case he might have taken offense at the remark. Indians never used the term "squaw." To them, it was an insult. The boy seemed not to think anything of it so Squint continued.

"Last spring I had to take a little trip up to them Shoshones." He paused to tear off some tobacco from a twist hanging from the ceiling. He offered the twist to Little Wolf but the lad declined. There was a long pause while Squint crumbled the tobacco and packed it down in the bowl of his cherrywood pipe. Little Wolf waited patiently for his friend to light his pipe and resume his story. Squint lit the pipe and drew on it deeply, filling the cramped lean-to with heavy blue smoke. With a small twig, he tamped the load down firmly and relit it. Content that it would now burn evenly all the way to the bottom, he removed it from his mouth long enough to spit on the dirt floor, then picked up the story where he had left off.

"It was hard last winter, I swear. You know, the trick is, you got to keep your mind off women. 'Cause when you're up in these mountains by yourself for that long a time, if you once get to thinking about it, you can drive yourself crazy. That dang near happened to me last winter. I swear, I got so rutty I was 'bout ready to rut around with the elks by the time the thaws started. As soon as the snow melted enough to get through the pass, I hightailed it up to ole Wounded Elk's camp." He laughed as he remembered the chief's reaction to his plight.

"Ole Wounded Elk, he thought it was pretty funny—I mean, me needing a woman so bad. He said he didn't think white men ever did it unless they was wanting to make a baby. I told him, Hell no. White men get just as stupid as any animal when they get the scent of a female in heat. Well, he was enjoying my predicament rightly enough, but he finally told me his wife's younger sister would be willing to take care of my needs. Well, she weren't very stout, not more than a slip of a thing, but she was spirited." He paused, took his pipe out of his mouth and winked at Little Wolf. "She weren't exactly pretty either, but then neither am I." He shook his head and laughed. "Like I said, she was spirited and it might have been quite a ride. Ole Wounded Elk said she wanted to see how it was to take on a man big as me, 'specially a white man. Oh, it would have been quite a ride all right. Problem was, ole Wounded Elk was just as curious as she was about how white men did it. He stayed right there in the tipi with us, made hisself comfortable over in the corner where he could watch the show."

Squint paused to tend his pipe again, re-tamping it and lighting up once more. "Well, I ain't never been bashful with the women. But I ain't never done it with no audience before either. That little ole gal was willing, no doubt about that. She dropped her skirt and leggings and threw that thing right up in my face. And I want to tell you, son, I couldn't do a damn thing with it. She was doing all kinds of things too, I mean, jumping around and pulling on my horn, and everything. But I couldn't do her no good a'tall. I mean, there weren't no starch a'tall in that thing. It was downright mortifying. And that ole son of a bitch setting over in the corner hollering, 'No good, got to make hard, no good.' I finally had to tell him I couldn't make the damn thing hard with him setting there gawking at it. Hell, it's got feelings too. He just finally got up and walked outside, still shaking his head and mumbling, 'White man no good, got to make hard.' "

Little Wolf sat fascinated while Squint went on with his story. He would not volunteer the fact that he had, as yet, never been with a woman. He and Black Feather had talked about it but neither of them had given much thought toward making love with any of the young girls in the tribe. When they did discuss it, they talked in terms of taking a mate, a wife, and there was plenty of time for that later. He was surprised that Squint discussed his pursuits and conquests so openly, placing no more importance on them than emptying his bladder. Still, Squint's talking was entertaining and set his thoughts in motion.

"So," he asked, "did the people laugh at you?"

"Nah," Squint replied. "Oh, they snickered a little at first when ole Wounded Elk went outside." He smiled to himself and gave Little Wolf another wink. "But after we got shed of that old son of a bitch, we got it right enough. I want to tell you, son, we got it right enough then. She was singing a different tune about white men by the time I let her go."

Little Wolf laughed with his friend. He was amazed, however, that Squint would tell embarrassing stories about himself. No Indian would. A Cheyenne brave would be far too ashamed to admit to something of that nature. And a Dakota might be inclined to kill the woman rather than risk losing face before the tribe. And yet Little Wolf could see no strain of weakness in this bear of a man who laughed at his own foolish blunders. Little Wolf decided that Squint undoubtedly possessed a confidence in himself that made it unimportant what others thought of him. Squint Peterson was a different breed of man, he decided.

They talked of many things during the long wait for the spring thaws. One subject that surfaced more than once was Little Wolf's future. At first Squint merely questioned him about his plans when the winter was done with. But more and more, the talk got around to whether he had given any thought toward going back to the settlement with Squint and living like a white man. While he would never admit it to Squint, Little Wolf did give it a passing thought. While he would never be able to bring himself to forgive the white man for the crimes against his people, hunting and trapping with Squint might not be a bad path to choose. When he thought back to the village on Sand Creek, it was sometimes hard to believe it had all happened. But then, the picture of Buffalo Woman's broken face as she lay dead in her own cook fire would burn its image into his mind and he would remember his vow that he was at war with the U.S. Army. Admittedly, it was difficult to maintain the venom toward all whites while sitting by the fire listening to Squint spin yarns. Spring was near. He would have to decide soon.

At last the long hard winter relaxed its frigid grip on the mountains and the first real signs of spring appeared. The breezes sweeping down the passes were still cold, but no longer icy and the streams began to flow freely once more. It had happened almost without their noticing. It seemed that one day it was winter and the next it was spring. The days were becoming longer. There were little patches of grass showing through the snow so the horses were able to graze again. All members of the little winter camp were ready to get out and stretch their legs, man and boy, horses and mule. The hibernation was long and hard so Little Wolf was readily agreeable when Squint proposed a trip up to the Shoshone village of Wounded Elk's.

There was little doubt in the boy's mind as to the purpose of Squint's visit to the village. Another tryst with Wounded Elk's sister-in-law was obviously on his mind and had been since he recounted the first visit to Little Wolf. As for his own reasons, aside from a serious case of cabin fever, he was hoping to hear news of his friend, Black Feather. Perhaps the Shoshones had heard something of the small band of Cheyennes that had fled the slaughter by the soldiers. So they packed some provisions on Squint's two horses and set out on the two-day trek up through the mountain passes to the tiny valley of the Shoshone. Squint let Little Wolf ride Britches, the little mare, while he threw his saddle on Joe. He had only the one saddle but it didn't matter to Little Wolf. He simply fashioned an Indian saddle from rawhide straps and a blanket. He was more accustomed to riding this way anyway. They started out one morning before the sun had climbed high enough to light the valley, wrapped in buffalo robes to protect them from the chilly morning air. Sadie, the mule, brayed in protest at being left behind when the two horses disappeared through the opening in the rock cliff.

"Hush, Sadie!" Squint admonished. "These horses is probably good and damn glad to take a vacation from your complaining."

Little Wolf pulled the robe back from his face so he could feel the brisk morning cold on his cheeks. It was cold, but not like the deep winter cold. Perhaps it was just a feeling he had, knowing that it was the beginning of spring, that made it seem fresh and rejuvenating. He had come to greet spring with a sense of excitement. Spring had meant the women would soon be packing up the tipis, readying the village for the summer rendezvous with the rest of the tribe. It had meant the whole summer season of the hunt was all before him, that he would soon see Black Feather and all the other friends he shared the summer with. Then he had to remind himself that things would be different now, after the massacre at Sand Creek had killed his parents and scattered his friends. Black Feather had been on his mind a great deal during the last several days. He wondered how he and his fellow warriors had fared during the winter and if he would be able to find them. The thought caused his brow to furrow into a worried frown. Did he want to search for them? Or should he accept Squint's invitation to throw in with him and do some trapping? He still didn't know. After a moment, he shook it from his mind. The morning was too pleasant to waste with worries.

Squint adjusted his sizable bulk in the saddle. It had been a while since he had ridden any distance and his body wanted to stiffen up on him. He turned to glance back at the silent figure behind him. The boy fit the mare perfectly, riding easily with her motion. He looked a hell of a lot better than he did the first day they met. He was little more than skin and bones then. But looking at him now, Squint could see a lean strength that signaled the beginning of manhood. He was still a boy by Squint's reckoning but he was soon going to be man enough. You could tell that by looking at the long, muscled arms and legs. And he was tall, too tall to be a Cheyenne Dog Soldier, Squint was thinking. The boy was good company. Squint hoped he would give up the notion of returning to the tribe and throw in with him.

CHAPTER 9

It was a two-day journey to Wounded Elk's village on the Wind River, two days that Little Wolf thoroughly enjoyed. It was good to get out in the open again after the confines of the cramped hovel that Squint called his camp. The wind whispered softly through the pines as they made their way leisurely along the slopes and down through streams swollen with melting snow and ice, climbing again through cottonwood and aspen on the lower slopes. Little Wolf could feel his senses regaining their sharpness. Long dulled by the smoke-filled cave he had shared with Squint, they seemed to return now that the cold mountain air flushed out his lungs. The sweet, almost spicy aroma of the fir trees lay heavy on the wind and he breathed it in deeply. The forest was so fresh and clean, purified by the long months of snow, that he could almost taste it. High above them, he heard the cry of a hawk piercing the soft murmur of the wind in the trees. It was good to be alive on this morning and he felt himself to be a part of the mountains and forests.

As they rode in silence, he wondered if Squint felt this same oneness with the mountains or if the sensation was strictly Indian. Spotted Pony had taught him to be one with the land as every Arapaho father taught his son. Looking at the solid bulk of Squint ahead of him, hunched over against the chilling spring air, he decided it was unlikely his friend had anything on his mind but Wounded Elk's sister-in-law.

Upon arriving in the Shoshone village, Squint and Little Wolf were greeted cordially. Old Wounded Elk came out of his lodge to welcome them himself. Squint was obviously regarded as a friend and, since the Shoshone were not enemies of the Arapaho or the Cheyenne, Little Wolf felt he would be treated courteously as well. Squint wasn't worried about it from the first because, although his hair was long and he still wore the buckskin shirt and leggings of his tribe, Little Wolf looked like just another trapper to the Indians. Besides, the winter months, as well as his recovery from his wound, had left him pale and looking very much like a white man again. These facts irritated Little Wolf, and he immediately spoke to Wounded Elk in the Cheyenne tongue, letting him know in no uncertain tones that he was an Arapaho brave, respected in his tribe. He had taken the power of the grizzly with his own hands, he had killed a Pawnee army scout with his war axe and a soldier with his knife. He was not to be regarded as a white trapper. Wounded Elk was impressed and invited Little Wolf to sit down and smoke the pipe with him, explaining that it was a natural mistake since he had come with Squint. He also explained, with some amusement, that it was somewhat unexpected to encounter an Arapaho brave with a face full of stubby whiskers. Squint couldn't help but chuckle at this. Little Wolf's hand immediately went up to rub his chin. It was obvious that, until the remark, he hadn't even considered the fact that he had a growth on his face. He was far from flustered, however, and replied at once that the mighty Cheyenne measured a warrior by his heart and deeds, not by the hair on his face. Squint knew enough Cheyenne to piece the conversation together. He learned something about his young friend that day. Little Wolf was not to be taken for a boy. There was a sense of self-confidence and pride that had not surfaced during the long months in Squint's camp. He made a mental note that he had best be careful how he stepped on his friend's toes in the future, now that the lad seemed to have regained his health.

It was a large village and, from all appearances, a permanent settlement. Squint told him these people were different from most of the plains tribes. They didn't break up into smaller bands in the winter and come together in one big tribe in the summer. The valley in which they had settled offered ample water and the surrounding mountains provided plenty of game. The men formed hunting parties in the summer and went to hunt buffalo but they were seldom away for more than a week at a time. Like their brothers, the Sioux, the Cheyenne, the Utes and the Arapaho, they went on raiding parties to steal horses or war parties to avenge some wrong. But they operated out of the one central village.

On this day there were but a few of the men in the village, only enough to defend it in the unlikely event of an attack by an enemy. Only crazy men made war in the winter snows. Even the Blackfeet were relatively peaceful in the winter. Most of the men of the village were gone on a hunting party. Wounded Elk explained that game was still pretty hard to find in the mountains, but soon the great herds of elk and antelope would return from their winter ranges. Then there would be much dancing and feasting. Little Wolf waited until the common courtesies had been observed and the pipe had been offered to the four corners of the earth. Then, after the three men had all taken the pipe and drawn deeply from it, he pressed Wounded Elk for the information he was most interested in.

"I am seeking word of my friend Black Feather and a small number of Cheyenne warriors. They should have made a winter camp somewhere near the Wind River. My people were camped under a flag of peace near the soldier fort on Sand Creek. My chief, Black Kettle, wanted only peace with the soldiers but they attacked the village without warning, killing women and children. My own father and mother were killed. These friends I seek came to the mountains after the cowardly attack on Red Shirt's camp."

Wounded Elk responded, "I have heard of the cowardly attack on Black Kettle's camp. It was a bad thing. I am sorry for your loss. Our scouting parties have not reported any contact with your Cheyenne friends but there was talk among a band of Utes visiting our village during the last full moon. They told of a band of Cheyenne warriors wintering in the Absaroka territory. But that is all I have heard."

This was welcome news to Little Wolf. Who else could it be but Black Feather and his comrades? This meant that at least they were still in the high mountains. Now he had to make the decision about which path his future was to lie in—Black Feather's or Squint's. It was not a simple decision to make. He would have to fast and seek spiritual guidance.

"My friends have vowed to make war on the soldiers," Little Wolf stated. "What will the mighty Shoshone do? Will you go to war with the army?"

Wounded Elk took a long, slow pull from the pipe before answering his young guest. The heavy smoke curled up around his face, framing the deep lines that furrowed his mouth and forehead, lines formed and deepened by many moons of war and harsh winters. He was accustomed to the impetuous prodding of young braves. His own young men were impatient for the answer to the same question. Even now, a few of the more aggressive braves questioned the old chief's wisdom in his decision to wait. To the east the great Oglala chief, Red Cloud, was warring with the white soldiers. He had sent an invitation to most of the important chiefs to join him in his battle with the army. Wounded Elk looked deep into Little Wolf's eyes. There was no blind impatience burning there, merely a desire for the answer to a simple question. So he was patient in his reply.

"Many of our young men want to join the Sioux in their battle with the soldiers. Red Cloud has many warriors but there is no end to the soldiers. Where one is cut down, two spring up in his place. Every soldier has a gun—some, the new gun that shoots many times. We have no guns. The Dakota have but a few old rifles. They will be useless against the soldiers. It is my feeling that we should stay in the mountains and let the Sioux fight the army if that is what Red Cloud wants." He shrugged his shoulders in a gesture of indifference. "His war is nothing more than raids on the small camps of workers building the trail for the iron horse"—he paused—"and on the settlers." He looked at Squint, seeking agreement from someone older than the boy and, presumably, wiser. "This is the land of the Shoshone. The soldiers will not come here in the mountains. I say, let us stay here and hunt and care for our people and defend what is ours."

Squint said nothing but in his heart he felt the old chief was more than a shade nearsighted in his reasoning. He knew what Wounded Elk was referring to. The army was trying to build a railroad up to the Montana territory and, if his memory served him, it was going to run smack-dab through the middle of Sioux hunting grounds—little wonder Red Cloud was upset. There were more Sioux than there were prairie dogs in the Big Horn country and Red Cloud ought to be able to raise a whole lot of hell. But what the Sioux didn't understand was the inexhaustible supply of blue coats the army could send against him. In the end, the Indian had to lose. It wasn't necessarily right, but it was the way it was gonna be. Wounded Elk figured the army wouldn't bother with him way off up in the mountains. But he was dead wrong. Before this thing was finished, the army would have every last Injun on a reservation somewhere. He also knew something else. His days of solitary trapping in these mountains were damn near at an end. It was going to get a trifle too hot for one lone white man in these parts when the real wars got heated up.

"Well"—Squint stretched and rubbed his belly—"I need to feed this old coyote inside me. I can hear him growling and getting riled already." The conversation about war had gone on long enough to suit him. If the old chief was going to get too occupied to remember his manners, then Squint would just have to remind him.

"Forgive me, my friend." Wounded Elk smiled. "Let us share some food and then you must go into my lodge to rest." There was a twinkle in his eye as he added, "Perhaps Broken Wing will lie down with you to see that you are not disturbed."

Squint grinned. This was what he had really come for in the first place. Wounded Elk proposed the same hospitality for Little Wolf but Little Wolf declined. He had more serious thoughts on his mind. The talk of war with the whites troubled him. He told Wounded Elk that he must find what was in his heart and he was going to fast and seek a vision, hoping Man Above would show him what he must do. Wounded Elk understood and suggested that he purify himself in the sweat lodge. He would have one of the women assist him in his preparation. When asked when he would like to start his fast, Little Wolf replied that he was ready then.

"Good," the old man responded. He knew the seeking of a vision was a good and necessary thing for a young man to do and he was eager to help Little Wolf get in touch with the spirits.

Squint, perplexed by the sudden request of his young friend, stepped aside as Little Wolf was led from the lodge by an old aunt of the chief's. "Well," he stammered, "I reckon I'll see you in a few days then."

Little Wolf only nodded in reply, already focused on the

ordeal ahead. Unlike some of the other tribes, Arapahos never sought visions until they were adults; consequently this was to be his first experience with this highly important and religious ceremony. Leaving Squint to satisfy his sexual needs, he followed the old woman to a small sweat lodge on the edge of a rocky stream. It was constructed of willow branches bent into a dome and covered with hides. The lodge was barely high enough for him to stand if he stooped over. A fire pit was dug in the middle of the lodge and large rocks were arranged within it. After a hot fire was built, using a stack of hardwood piled on one side of the small structure, the stones were rolled into place. Once they were heated enough, Little Wolf removed his clothes and the old woman poured icy water from the stream over the rocks to make steam. She seemed oblivious to his nakedness, apparently more interested in keeping the fire hot and continuing to bring water to make sure the small lodge was filled with steam.

Little Wolf crouched before the fire. Soon the heat brought little droplets of sweat to the surface of his skin. In a matter of minutes, rivulets of perspiration ran down the insides of his arms and legs. His breath became labored as he breathed the hot damp air into his lungs. When he could stand it no longer, he went outside and plunged into the icy waters of the stream. The sensation caused his head to spin and every nerve in his body came alive. At the coaxing of the old woman, he repeated the ritual several more times until he felt so weak he had difficulty standing. Satisfied that his body was purified, the old woman wrapped a blanket around him and helped him to Wounded Elk's lodge. After giving him a bowl of tea made with special herbs and purifiers, she directed him to lie down and rest. Tomorrow he would begin his fast.

With the first golden splinters of sunlight that filtered through the mountain pass above the Shoshone camp, Little Wolf emerged from Wounded Elk's tipi. Pausing only to note the direction of the rising sun, he began his journey into the mountains, a journey that would last at least three days, maybe four, depending upon what he might learn from within himself. He took nothing with him but his knife, a heavy buffalo robe and a small pouch of dried elk meat which was to be eaten only after he had attained his vision. He would be weak from hunger then and food would be scarce in the mountains this time of year. The robe would serve as his coat and his bed.

He was surprised that he had slept so soundly the night before. Perhaps it was the potion the old woman had given him. Whatever the reason, he felt rested and stong, considering he had not eaten since the previous afternoon. Passing silently among the sleeping tipis, he left the village at a trot, a pace he could keep up indefinitely. This journey was to be made solely on foot, the destination unknown to him, as was the direction he was to start in. Each brave had his own medicine, known only to him, and Little Wolf was confident his medicine would be revealed to him and guide him on the right path and he would know when to stop and wait for his vision.

As he climbed higher into the mountains, he felt a sharpening of his senses, as he had on the trip to the Shoshone camp two days before. Only this morning they seemed to be keener still and he thought that he was aware of Spotted Pony's spirit beside him. He smiled, for the thought pleased him. Could it be possible that his father had returned to guide and protect him on his quest? Little Wolf did not question it for he had listened to similar experiences around the campfire in Spotted Pony's camp.

"Father, if it is your spirit, I welcome you. We will go on this journey together. Help me to find my medicine and to see the path my soul must travel."

He was answered by the sudden chatter of a squirrel and he smiled. He took it as a sign that Spotted Pony had heard his prayer. His father's early lessons returned to his memory and he whispered to himself. "Become one with the forest. Feel the trees and the streams and the earth beneath your moccasins. They will tell you what you want to know, just as they tell the fox and the bear and the hawk. But first you must become one with them." He thought of the time when he was a young boy, stalking game with Black Feather, and the friendly competition they shared. His heart warmed when he thought of his boyhood friend and he had an urgent longing to see him again. As he made his way around the dark gray boulders, highlighted by the sun's

first brushstrokes, he carefully avoided the scattered
patches of snow that would display evidence of his passing.

All that first day he journeyed, never stopping to rest,
never thinking about food or water. When the sun disappeared behind the far peaks, turning the valleys into pools
of darkness, he stopped and spread his buffalo robe under
a giant fir, the low branches his only shelter. A handful of
snow was all he permitted himself to take into his mouth.
He slept fitfully and with many fragments of dreams but
nothing that he would remember the next morning.

The second day brought the first sensation of real hunger.
He expected it and ignored it, pressing on deeper into the
mountains. As he made his way among the trees and boulders, he searched for a sign. He didn't know what he was
looking to find but he was certain he would recognize it
when he saw it. Again, that night, he allowed himself no
sustenance other than one handful of snow.

By the time the sun was directly overhead on the third day,
the lack of food and water began to take its toll on his body,
and the exertion expended in the climb up the steep moun-
tainsides left him light-headed and dizzy. It became necessary
to stop periodically to rest. By twilight, he felt his strength
drain from his body and he almost staggered as he made his
way slowly along a ledge high above a valley floor. Suddenly
his feet seemed to take on a weight that strained him to lift
and he knew he could go no further. Directly before him a
huge boulder jutted out over the mountaintop and he decided
that he should rest there that night. With what seemed to be
the last few ounces of strength left in him, he pulled himself
up the side of the boulder to find a flat grassy patch on the
level top side of the rock. For a moment his mind left his
body and recalled a day Spotted Pony had taken him to
hunt for elk. When it was time to make a camp that night,
Spotted Pony had selected a place high on a hillside. Little
Wolf pictured his father's face when he said simply, "This
is a good place." He took the memory as a message from
his father, that this spot was where he was to meditate and
wait for his vision. He smiled and whispered, "This is a
good place." Then he fell, exhausted, into a deep sleep.

He was running. His lungs ached as they demanded more
air and he longed to stop and rest. But he could not. Some-

thing chased him but he could not determine what that
something was, only that he could not slow down or it
would overtake him. As he ran, he was aware of many
images and faces along his path. The faces watched him
dispassionately, seeming unconcerned with the urgency he
felt. Some of the faces he recognized—Black Feather, Buffalo Woman, Morning Sky. Spotted Pony sat beside a quiet
stream, talking with Squint Peterson. They both glanced up
at him and smiled as he trudged past. "I wouldn't slow
down if I was you, pardner," Squint called out to him. The
quiet creek bank looked so peaceful and serene that he
wanted to stop and sit down beside the two men. But he could
not. He had to keep running.

Glancing back over his shoulder, he caught sight of an
animal chasing him. He felt the panic in his heart as he
recognized the animal as a cougar. The cat was huge, its
coat a golden hue, and it obviously meant to kill him. He
tried to run faster but he could not. The beast was gaining
on him, close enough now that he could see its gleaming
white fangs, dripping with the blood of a prior kill. He felt
helpless. Thoughts raced through his head that he did not
want to die this way, running from a savage beast. He
wanted to die as an Arapaho or a Cheyenne brave should
die, in battle. He must stand and fight but his legs would
not stop. Suddenly a huge bear stood directly in his path.
The bear was as big as a mountain. Reared up on its hind
legs, its massive forepaws flashed razor-sharp claws. Its
teeth bared, it roared, filling the valley with a wave of thunder that caused icicles to form on his spine. Still he could
not stop running, even though he feared the giant bear
would send him to the Great Beyond.

However, when he approached the beast, the bear moved
out of his path and let him pass. He did not look back but
he could hear the sounds of mortal combat, and he sensed
that the cougar was no longer a threat to his life. He looked
down at his feet and was surprised to discover that he had
on only one moccasin. His other foot, the left one, was
bare but the stones in his path did not cause him any dis-
comfort as he raced on. Then he glanced down again to
find that the ground beneath his feet was far below him,
as if he was flying. Suddenly, he could see the land below
him in a wide vista of mountains and valleys. It was more

beautiful than any place he had ever seen before. He passed over a long stretch of rocky mountain ridges until they ended in one great white wall, beyond which a valley appeared with a rushing stream running through the floor of pines and firs. Though he continued running, he was aware that the fatigue had left him. His running was effortless and he felt at peace with himself.

He awoke. He had slept so soundly that his eyes were swollen and puffy and he was reluctant to open them to the morning light. Although he had been exhausted the night before, and he was aware of the hunger that was now gnawing at his belly, he still felt refreshed and alert. His dreams were still fresh in his mind and he sought to make some sense of them. Although they told him nothing initially, he was sure that it had been more than a mere dream, that it was in fact the vision he sought. He must meditate and search the vision for its meaning. He wasn't sure why, but something told him that his vision quest was over and it was now up to him to interpret the message sent to him.

Fully awake now, thoughts of food and water demanded his attention but he felt strongly that he must not think of those things until he searched his mind for the message he needed. The time to make his medicine was now, while the vision was fresh in his mind. Only then could he eat and drink. Sitting cross-legged in the center of the small patch of grass that had been his bed, he faced the rising sun and let his thoughts focus on the first rays lighting the tips of the green forest on the horizon. The floor of the valley was covered by a mist that lay over the stream like a great silent blanket. From his vantage point, high above the valley floor, he felt as one with the hawk and the eagle and he knew that he was as much a part of the mountains as the trees and rocks. He closed his eyes and let the vision come to him once more.

The full meaning of his vision did not come to him at once. Sitting there on the rocky outcropping, feeling the first warmth of the sun's rays on his closed eyelids, he puzzled over the fact that he was running in his dream. Running from what, he wondered. True, he had to run to escape the soldiers at Black Kettle's camp on Sand Creek.

But he was no longer running. He was safe for the time
being. He even had the choice of going with Squint, eventually returning to white man's civilization. No one would
know he was Little Wolf if he chose that path. One thing
that stuck in his mind, however, was the fact that other
than Squint's, there were only Indian faces in his dream.
There were no images of his real mother and father, of his
brothers and sisters, or any childhood playmates. This
seemed to be important to him because he felt certain it
indicated his choice to follow the path of the Arapaho and
Cheyenne to be the correct way for him. This in itself was
enough to ease his troubled mind, for this was the question
he sought most to answer.

But what was the significance of the battle between the
cougar and the great bear? And why was he being chased
by the cougar? Was there a message there? Or was it
merely the nonsensical impulses that penetrate many
dreams? In his heart he knew it was part of his vision for
the Arapaho felt all dreams were messages from the spirits.
He would think on it. Maybe, in time, it would become
clearer to him.

He opened his eyes again, convinced that there would be
no more explanation of his dream for the moment. One
decision had been made for him. He was Arapaho. He
would not go with Squint Peterson. Instead, he would seek
out his friend Black Feather. In his dream, Squint and Spotted Pony had both smiled at him as he passed them. This
indicated that they both approved of his decision. He recalled that, when he had been running and looked down at
his feet, he had but one moccasin. It was significant to him
that it was a moccasin and not a boot. He knew also that
the cougar and the bear held significance for him and he
would look for confirmation of this in the future. But for
now, it was time to leave this place and return to the village
of the Shoshone.

It had been nearly dark the night before when he
climbed the rock outcropping. In the morning light, he noticed another ledge beyond and slightly above the one he
had slept on. Out of curiosity, he decided to climb atop
that ledge to have a look around before making his way
back down into the valley. There was a small trail up from
the boulder he stood on, used no doubt by the large white

goats that abounded in the higher rocky elevations. As he made his way up into the rocks, he spotted an occasional hoofprint to confirm his speculation. At the top of the ledge he discovered a small patch of grass about the same size as the one on the boulder below. He discovered something more that caused his heartbeat to increase in alarm, the unmistakable paw print of a bear. By the size of the paw, it was a monstrous bear, a grizzly probably, and the tracks were recent, as recent as the night before, he guessed.

He was immediately alert. His body coiled in anticipation of danger and he quickly looked all around him. He was in no position to meet with a grizzly, weak from hunger and lack of water, with no weapon except a knife. But there was no living thing on the ledge but himself. When he was sure of that, he relaxed and studied the tracks more thoroughly. They indicated that the animal had paced all around the narrow ledge and, from the looks of the matted grass on one side, it had slept there. What, he wondered, would a grizzly be doing this high up above the tree line? This was too unusual to be coincidence. When he turned back to look in the direction he had come from, he realized that the boulder he had spent the night on was immediately below where he now stood. His spine tingled with the realization that he could have been under observation by a huge grizzly the whole time he slept helplessly below him. From this vantage point, the bear could not help but see him. The fact that he had not been attacked could only be explained by the medicine of the bear power he had carried since he was a boy when he had killed the grizzly. It had even been a part of his vision—the grizzly had protected him from the cougar. The excitement of the thought made his spirits soar. He had spent the night weak and exhausted and the power of the bear had watched over him! A white man could not know of such things. Before descending from the mountain, he scouted around in an effort to find signs of a cougar but there were none.

After descending from the mountain to the stream in the valley floor, he satisfied his thirst and ate the elk meat he had brought with him. Before starting on his return journey to the village of the Shoshone, he looked around him at the valley lying before him. Then he turned and looked back at the mountain from whence he had just come. He wanted to impress this place on his memory for it was an important place to him. It had told him where his heart belonged and that the power of the bear would always be his special medicine. Shielding his eyes from the morning sun with his hand, he searched the ledges high up near the top of the mountain. There! He was sure he could see the very place he had received his vision. As he stared at the dark boulder, protruding from the face of the cliff, he remembered the great white wall he had seen in his dream. It was not this place, of that he was certain. But something told him that if he ever found the white wall, he would recognize it immediately.

Back in Wounded Elk's village, Squint Peterson was beginning to worry about his young friend. It had been almost a week since Little Wolf had left the village in search of his vision. When Little Wolf said he was going to fast for four days, Squint expected him to be back in four days, not six. In the meantime, the men of the village had returned from their hunting party and Squint thought he could sense an uneasy atmosphere because of his presence. Some of these braves he knew, and had even hunted with them the year before. Now they were a mite reserved and cool toward him. It was not that they were impolite, for he was a guest of their chief. They were just not really cordial as they normally would be. Squint could see that they didn't feel too comfortable with him around. He was a little disappointed with their attitude but he couldn't blame them for not wanting to trust any white man anymore. He made up his mind that he wouldn't be spending the next winter in these mountains.

The visit had not been a total loss, however. Old Wounded Elk's sister-in-law, Broken Wing, had proved to be more than enough woman to catch Squint up on his sexual urges. The truth of the matter was she had just about worn him out. She had been without a husband for more than a year and she had some catching up to do herself. She would not have been a bad-looking woman had it not been for her nose. It had been broken by a Crow war club, the same club in fact that had done in her husband. She had been left for dead but she was tougher than they thought. The result was a flattened nose that restricted her breathing considerably, causing her to make a whistling noise when her passion was high and her heart was pumping hard. In the darkness of the tipi, it was not that noticeable at first. Toward the end of the third day, Squint began to notice it a little more, to the point of distraction.

When they made love, Squint wanted her to face him, like the whores back East. Broken Wing had never done it that way before, having always been mounted from behind by her husband, just like the horses and the dogs did it. But she wanted to please Squint so she lay on her back for him. The first time it was all right because Squint was so desperate for biological relief he could have gotten satisfaction from a knothole in a pine log. Broken Wing, on the other hand, thought it a rather strange way to mate and she couldn't help but stare in wide-eyed amazement at Squint's frantic fumbling and struggling. Pretty soon Squint began to notice her staring and it started to bother his concentration. Finally, he turned her around and mounted his assault from the rear. Now she was in a position with which she was familiar and she heated to the occasion. Squint found it less disturbing to his concentration anyway. He no longer had to avoid her wide-eyed stare and he didn't have to look at her flattened nose. He found, in fact, that he was in for a wild ride because, when Broken Wing's blood got overheated, she backed up to meet his thrusts, her nose whistling in rhythm, often backing him all the way across the floor of the tipi. He enjoyed the ride but his knees were getting sore from scraping the earthen floor. After a few days of love Injun style, he was glad to see Little Wolf stride back into camp one afternoon.

Squint welcomed his friend back. "Dang, pardner, you look like you been wrung out and hung up to dry."

Little Wolf smiled at him but made no reply. Wounded Elk, who was visibly curious to know the success of this white Arapaho's vision quest, stood silently by Squint. Most white men he had met did not have the intelligence to ask the spirits for guidance. They thought they knew everything already while it was plain to the Indian that they knew very little. He was pleased when Little Wolf looked first at him and requested food and rest so that he might complete his meditation. Wounded Elk looked deep into Little Wolf's eyes and he was pleased to discover no sign of confusion

there. He knew without being told that Little Wolf had
found the answers he had sought. He sent for the old squaw
who had assisted the young man with the purification of
his body. Little Wolf smiled briefly at Squint once again
and followed the old woman to Wounded Elk's tipi.

Squint was confounded by his friend's demeanor. "You
rest up, pardner," he offered as he watched Little Wolf
walk away. "We'll head on out as soon as you're ready."
Even then he was not at all sure he would have company
on his return trip. It was apparent to him that it was a
different Little Wolf who had returned to the Shoshone
village. Maybe he was just weak and dazed from lack of
food and water. He hoped so, but there was a different
look in the young man's eye, like he had aged some in the
few days he had been away. Something had happened to
him up in those mountains and it looked to Squint like he
might have lost his partner. All winter Squint thought Little
Wolf would eventually go back to his real people. Now he
was not so sure.

Squint did not see Little Wolf again until the following
morning and, when he did, he was taken aback somewhat
by the young man's appearance. His hair had been freshly
oiled and parted in the middle, in the style of the Cheyenne. This in itself was not so surprising. The sight that
startled Squint was the appearance of his face. He had
hacked away his whiskers with a hunting knife in an attempt to shave the stubble off smooth. The result was a
face that sported patches of stubble of uneven length, interrupted by areas of raw skin where the blade had nicked
him. Squint would have laughed out loud at the sight had
it not been for the seriousness of the occasion. Little Wolf's
decision seemed to have been made.

"You done a lot for me and I appreciate it," Little Wolf
started, obviously searching for the words to tell Squint
what Squint had already surmised. "I reckon I might have
died if you hadn't done for me." Squint said nothing, just
shrugged it off. Little Wolf continued, "I reckon I don't
have to tell you I'm going back to my people."

"I reckon," Squint answered. He studied the young man
standing before him, his stance and manner already pro-
jecting the confident air of a Cheyenne warrior. There was
no mistaking the look in his steady gaze, the look of a man

who was sure of himself. Squint knew then that it would be a waste of time to try to change the boy's mind. Still he made the effort. "Well, I reckon a man's gotta do what he's gotta do, but you know you would sure be welcome to throw in with me if you change your mind."

Little Wolf smiled. "I know."

Squint hesitated a few moments, then continued, "Son, I know you like the wild life with the Cheyenne. Don't blame you—I might like it myself. But it ain't gonna be the same around these parts for much longer. You sure you're gonna feel the same way six months or a year from now, when the real trouble gets stirred up? You might think you can stay clear of it up in these mountains but any fool can see there's gonna be a helluva war with the Cheyenne and the Sioux. Hell, it's already started. And ain't no place gonna be safe." He paused to see if his words had any effect on the boy. "And I wouldn't consider myself any kind of friend if'n I didn't warn you."

Little Wolf shrugged. "These are my people."

"What about when the soldiers come? What about then? You gonna be able to fight agin your own blood?"

"I will fight beside my people. I will fight my father's enemies; the soldiers who killed Spotted Pony and Buffalo Woman could never be of my blood." Little Wolf's face took on a hardened look, his eyes narrowed as the memory of his parents' slaughter returned to his mind. "I will live and fight with the Cheyenne, as my father did."

"Robert," Squint implored, using the boy's Christian name, "you can't win. There ain't no way the Injuns is ever gonna win against the army. Why don't you come on back with me? Hell, we'll head up to the north country, go to Oregon territory, do some trappin', lay around and get fat in the winter. Whaddaya say? Forget about the damn soldiers."

Little Wolf stared deep into Squint's eyes for a moment. Then his expression relaxed and he smiled as if he was patiently explaining to a child. "You have been a good friend to me. But I must go where my medicine tells me to go. I am Arapaho, no matter what I started out. My place is in the mountains with my Cheyenne brothers. If the army comes, then so be it. If they are too many, then it is better to die as a warrior than to sit around a campfire when I am so old I have no teeth to chew the pemmican."

There was a long silence that seemed to put the final punctuation on the young warrior's words. Finally Squint shrugged his shoulders and sighed. "Well, so be it then. I wish you well, son. I hope you find what you're looking for." His face broke into a quick smile and he added, "I can at least leave you my razor and strop so you don't have to torment your face no more."

Little Wolf laughed and ran a hand gingerly over his chin. "I'll take you up on that and be damn grateful. Cheyenne generally pull their whiskers out by the roots but I ain't too fond of that. I got too many of them."

This would be the last time they would see each other for a long time. Little Wolf had made his decision and would leave early the following morning to scout the north ridges in search of his Cheyenne friends. Squint, after one final stampede across the tipi floor with Wounded Elk's sister-in-law, would set out in the opposite direction for his camp two days east. He would be minus one horse on the trip back since he had insisted that Little Wolf take the little mare. He left with the definite feeling that things were not going to be the same in the Wind River country, and even though old Wounded Elk told him he was welcome to visit anytime, the sullen stares from the other men in the village told him differently. As he kicked Joe into a canter across the frosty meadow fronting the outside ring of lodges, he was already considering the wisdom in sticking to his secret camp the last two seasons. He sighed as he thought about it. It might be the last time he visited old Wounded Elk. It's a damn shame, he thought, that the soldiers and the gold miners and the settlers had to mess things up for mountain men like himself. In a way he couldn't blame Little Wolf for deciding to be Injun instead of going back to civilization. As for Squint, he preferred to line up on the winning side in most any scrap. And he had little doubt that the white man would win out over the Injun in the end.

"It ain't gonna come cheap though," he muttered aloud. "There's gonna be a helluva lot of dead soldier boys before they build the first church on the Wind River."

CHAPTER 10

"Gnats!" the soldier cursed softly under his breath. "What in hell did God have in mind when he made gnats?" He reached up for at least the fiftieth time since he had dove into the shallow ditch and fanned the bothersome insects from his eyes. "All they ever do is try to get in your eyes and ears and mouth, and up your damn nose." He snorted softly as if to punctuate his statement. His behind was beginning to itch from the wet mud soaking through his trousers so he shifted his position, being very deliberate in his movements so he wouldn't catch the eye of a Reb sniper.

The long sweltering Mississippi afternoon was gradually melting down into an early evening. An occasional errant breeze, having lost its way, blundered down the shallow ditch, teasing him with a moment's respite from the heat trapped inside his sweat-soaked shirt. He turned his head to glance down the ditch a dozen feet at the stiff bodies of two Johnny Rebs. They were there when he dove into the ditch. He didn't know if a rifle ball from his weapon had killed either of them. He didn't care. He had stopped caring a million years ago when he had come through his first infantry charge alive.

He shifted his gaze back to the cornfield before him, raising his head just enough to allow clear vision above the low embankment. It had been dead quiet now for the better part of an hour. Soon it would be twilight. He wondered where the rest of his company was. When they charged into the woods, he was in the middle of a line of his comrades. The Rebs had laid down a blistering fire. Rifle balls were snapping through the leaves like angry bees. It seemed impossible to avoid being hit but somehow he had made it through. When he emerged from the trees, there was no one on either side of him so he scrambled for the first bit of cover he saw, which was this muddy ditch.

The last Confederate stragglers disappeared in the rows of corn and it appeared they would probably re-form on a ridge on the far side where they would have the high ground. He had decided to sit tight right where he was until some more of his company showed up. He damn sure wasn't going to go charging into that cornfield by himself. As it turned out, he didn't have to wait long before the battle was rejoined. From the far end of the cornfield, a Union cavalry company suddenly appeared, sweeping through the rows of corn at full gallop. They were led by an officer on a spotted gray mount, sword raised high in front of him as he crouched forward in the saddle, yelling at the top of his lungs. The charge flushed out a dozen or more Rebel soldiers who had hidden between the rows. They scattered, fleeing for their lives before the charging horses. As he watched from the shallow ditch, he could not help but wonder about this enemy that had fought with such bloody obstinacy. At this moment, they did not even resemble a military unit, not a complete uniform among the handful he could see, looking more like a band of riffraff in flight. Yet this band of riffraff had proven in the last few days to be a force to be reckoned with, giving ground stubbornly to vastly superior Union forces. The mopping up of Vicksburg was supposed to be a fairly simple operation for General Grant. Overall, maybe it was. As for his own small piece of the operation, it had been damn bloody.

When the cavalry unit advanced to the far side of the cornfield, the Rebs on the ridge laid down a devastating volley of fire, taking a heavy toll on the troopers at the forefront of the charge. Among the first to go down was the officer on the spotted gray. Horse and rider tumbled under the hailstorm of miniballs. The horse soldiers retreated, regrouped and mounted a second sweep toward the ridge but were again turned back, suffering heavy losses. Finally, after one additional foray into the deadly field in an attempt to recover their wounded, the Union cavalry was forced to quit the fight. By then it was late afternoon and both sides apparently decided to withdraw for the night. The Confederate snipers on the ridge, however, continued to control all activity in the cornfield, firing at anything that moved. After an hour or so, there was no more sniper fire and the cornfield was quiet.

From his vantage point at the edge of the field, he could see the carnage that had resulted from the brief skirmish. He would wait until dark before exposing himself in the open pasture between him and the woods behind. The snipers were no doubt still watching from up on the ridge. There was no sense taking a chance. He would find his way back to his unit that night. So he lay there in the mud of the ditch and waited.

A slight movement toward the middle of the cornfield caught his eye and he strained to focus on the spot. For a long while there was nothing and then, suddenly, he saw it again. Someone was alive down there! As he continued to stare at the spot, a man struggled to pull himself between the corn rows, using only his arms to drag his body. His legs were apparently useless and he just barely managed to drag himself around the corpse of his horse in an attempt to put the dead animal between himself and the enemy on the ridge. It was the officer on the spotted gray and evidently it was all he could do to get that far because once he got behind his horse, he lay still again.

For the private watching from the cover of the ditch, there was no real decision to be made. One of his officers was lying wounded and he would have to go to his aid. But he wasn't stupid enough to go running out there in broad daylight. He would wait until darkness and then try to see if he could get the man out of the cornfield. If the officer died before then, he would probably have died anyway. No sense in both of them dying. So now he waited, fighting the gnats, until he felt it safe to leave the ditch.

At last the twilight deepened enough for him to leave his hiding place. He crawled up over the bank of the ditch and paused there, listening. There was no sound of enemy activity other than the muffled voices from the ridge, indicating a settling down for the night. He felt confident there would be no one venturing down into the cornfield before morning, so he ran, half crouched, across the field toward the wounded officer.

Although it was still twilight, once he entered the corn rows it was much darker, and he found it necessary to stop often to make sure he was still heading toward the spot where he had seen the wounded man. The dirt was still warm from the afternoon sun and the smoke and smells of the recent battle still lingered, trapped upon the cornstalks like a shroud. There were dead men everywhere it seemed, as he made his way toward the middle of the field. He began to think he had miscalculated his directions and was about to double back when he spied the corpse of the spotted gray, ghostlike in contrast with the dark rows of corn. Dropping to his hands and knees, he inched his way closer. There was no sign of the officer.

Damn! he thought. Then he called out in a loud whisper, "Sir, can you hear me?" There was no response. He decided he wasn't going to waste much more time in this field of death but he tried once more. "Sir, I'm a Union soldier, come to help you." As he called out, he continued to crawl in a circle around the carcass of the horse. Suddenly he heard the unmistakable click of a cavalry pistol cocking. It was off to his left and he froze in his tracks.

"I've got a pistol aimed right at your head," a low husky voice advised him.

"Well, dammit, don't pull the trigger!" His first reaction was one of disgust. After all, he was risking his neck to save the man. It wouldn't do for him to get shot for his trouble. "I coulda just left you out here to die."

"What's your name, soldier? How do I know you're not a damned Reb?"

"Well, if that don't beat all. You know I ain't a Reb because I said I ain't a Reb." His patience was wearing thin. "I'm Private Thomas Allred of the Second Missouri Volunteers and I don't aim to spend no more time jawing out here in this damn cornfield. You coming or not?"

He heard the officer chuckle softly before answering. "I'm ready, Private. Let's get the hell out of here."

The wounded man had taken miniballs in both legs so Tom had to get him up on piggyback. It was a struggle because the officer had some bulk to him and he was in a great deal of pain. Tom feared the man might cry out as he strained to pull him up on his back. After considerable effort, he managed to get him up with his arms around his neck and his legs locked around his hips.

The going was rough, trying to walk through the soft dirt of the dark cornfield, and soon Tom forgot all thoughts of being heard by the Rebs. It was all he could do to keep walking without stumbling under the weight of his burden. Once he almost fell over the body of a dead soldier, Union or Rebel, he couldn't tell in the dark. After that he kept his head down in an effort to see where he was placing each foot. So concerned was he in staying up under his load that he didn't see the other man until they almost collided in the dark. They both swore and excused themselves when they discovered that both were carrying a wounded man on their backs. It didn't occur to Tom until they had gone their opposite ways that the man was a Reb. It was ironic, he thought. There had been no thought of killing each other, just a polite "Excuse me," and on about their business. "Helluva war," he muttered to himself while shifting his load for a better hold. If the officer he was carrying thought anything about the encounter, he didn't comment.

He walked through half of that night, only stopping twice to rest his aching back, before reaching Union pickets and his regiment. The officer was rushed to a field hospital in the back of a wagon and Tom was given a hot meal and a place to sleep before returning to his company the next morning. He was told that the officer he had rescued was Captain Winston Thrasher, one of General Grant's favorite cavalry commanders, and the general had thought him lost for sure. Tom was not to know until months later that this single incident on the fourth of July, 1863, was a crossroads in his life and was to change the course of his destiny. Captain Winston Thrasher was not a man to let an act of gallantry go unrewarded. His wounds, suffered on that sweltering July afternoon, were painful but not debilitating, and allowed him to be returned to duty after two months in a Union hospital. One of the first orders he issued, after resuming command of his company with the new rank of major, was to find Private Thomas Allred.

"Well, I see that it's Sergeant Allred now."

"Yessir," Tom replied, aware that the new stripes stood out against the faded blue army-issue shirt. "Most of my squad got wiped out at Vicksburg, including Sergeant Weathers. So I guess they had to stick these stripes on somebody."

"So they stuck 'em on you."

"Yessir."

There was a moment of silence while the two men looked at each other, Major Thrasher pausing to choose his words, Tom waiting to receive the thanks he assumed was coming. There couldn't be any other reason for him to be summoned to report to an officer in a different branch of the army.

"I never really got the chance to thank you for risking your neck to pull my bacon out of the fire that night." He paused for a moment. "I want to do that now."

"No need for thanks, sir." Tom grinned. "You'd probably have done the same for me."

"Yes," he answered matter-of-factly, "I would have. But a lot of men wouldn't."

Tom shrugged, not knowing what more to say. "Well, you're welcome, sir," he finally stammered and prepared to leave. "Is that all, sir?"

"One more thing. How would you like to spend the rest of this war sitting down instead of walking?"

"Sir?"

"Let me put it this way," the major stated as he pushed his camp stool back to give him room to stretch his legs. "Damn legs still get stiff as hell," he explained before continuing. "You're a damn good soldier, Allred. You obviously don't scare easily. I've seen evidence of that firsthand and evidently somebody else thinks so too, or you wouldn't have those stripes on your arm." He interrupted his thoughts with a question, "How old are you, anyway?"

"Eighteen, sir."

"Jesus Christ! I thought you were older than that. You look older than that." He thought about it for a moment. "Hell, I guess in this damn war everybody looks older than they are. No matter, eighteen or eighty, like I said, you're a damn good soldier and I need good soldiers. How'd you like to transfer to the cavalry?"

Tom hadn't expected this. He had to think about it for a long moment. He was a city boy, and had never been on a horse in his life. Still, the thought of riding through the war instead of walking did have a certain amount of appeal. Deep down inside himself he had to admit that a memory still lingered, a slight shiver of emotion that traveled the length of his spine when he had witnessed the charge of

Major Thrasher's cavalry into that cornfield. True, they had been turned back. Still, even in defeat, they had seemed glorious to the young infantry private lying in the muddy ditch.

"Sir, I ain't ever been on a horse before."

The major looked surprised at this. He more or less took it for granted that every man had ridden a horse at some time in his life. But he gave it no more than a moment's concern before he shrugged and said, "Well, that won't be any problem. You can learn." He paused. "You aren't afraid of horses are you?"

"No sir. I just don't know nothing about 'em."

Major Thrasher looked relieved. "It's not important. You'll be riding like an old trooper in no time." He brushed it aside. "What's important is that you've got the makings of a damn good soldier, the kind of soldier I want riding with me." He drew his legs back up under him and leaned forward, looking Tom straight in the eye. "How about it, Allred? You ready to ride to glory and honor with me?"

"Well, yessir. I reckon I am," he blurted.

"Fine! Damn fine!" The major stood up, indicating an end to the interview. "I've already had orders cut on you. You can just go back and pick up your personal things and report back here in the morning to Lieutenant Matheson. You'll be in his company."

"Yessir," was all Tom could reply. He was overwhelmed by the suddenness with which he had been transferred from the infantry to the cavalry. He was to learn later on that any of General Grant's favorite cavalry officers could get pretty much anything they desired when it came to improving their units.

Right after reveille the following morning, a somewhat bewildered ex-infantry sergeant reported to Lieutenant Matheson. Feeling lost and out of place in the confusion of a full troop of cavalry preparing to move out on a campaign, it took Tom most of the morning just to find him. At first the lieutenant looked as bewildered as Tom felt when the young sergeant handed him a copy of his orders. It seemed that in the busy process of breaking camp, Major Thrasher had neglected to inform his lieutenant of the addition to his muster. Matheson, however, being a patient man and not one to confound easily, took it in stride and told

Tom to go down and pick out a mount for himself after getting his tack from the quartermaster. He wasn't even overly vexed when Tom admitted that he didn't know what tack was, let alone have any notion about how to pick out a horse. Matheson simply sighed, looked at his new man for a moment, then sent for a corporal to take Tom in hand. An hour later, Major Winston Thrasher's newest horse soldier sat nervously on a strawberry roan named Pokey, his knees trembling as they tried to grip the horse's sides, wondering what he would do if the animal suddenly decided to rid itself of its burden.

A lot of water had passed under a lot of bridges since that July day in Vicksburg. It seemed like eons to Tom. In fact, it was only two years. But the two years of war was like ten normal years. Friendships were made and forgotten. Men who were boys when they signed up were old men of twenty and twenty-one after two years of battles in little, seemingly insignificant churchyards and crossroads between Chattanooga and Atlanta. General Grant had been ordered to replace General Rosecrans in an effort to find someone who could chase Braxton Bragg out of Chattanooga. Naturally, Grant took Winston Thrasher with him on the campaign, so young Thomas Allred learned to ride a horse on his way to Tennessee.

Stretched out comfortably on a train headed for Fort Riley, Tom smiled to himself when he remembered that horse. Pokey—it was a good name for the animal. Whoever gave him that name must have known the beast well. He was slow, but at the time, Tom was thankful for Pokey's reluctance to get excited. The horse was too lazy to buck, which was probably the sole reason Tom was able to stick on him all the way to Chattanooga. No one had warned him about the sore behind and the other assorted aches and pains a greenhorn could expect after sitting on a horse for twelve hours a day, days on end. After the first two days, Tom thought he would never be able to straighten up again. He was too sore to ride and too stiff to walk. There was no choice but to gut it out, so gut it out he did . . . and in silence.

He knew the other men were amused by his ordeal, having suffered it themselves at one time or another, but he refused to give them the satisfaction of hearing him complain. So he and Pokey limped to Chattanooga, and by the time their journey was finished, Tom could manage him pretty well. He still found himself holding on to the saddle with one hand during a gallop but at least he didn't fall off when he participated in their first encounter with Confederate cavalry. He made it through that first skirmish unscathed, but Pokey didn't. The poor old nag was shot out from under him near Lookout Mountain when their patrol was ambushed while foraging for food. It was Tom's coolness under fire that caused him to be awarded another stripe on his sleeve when a rebel rifle ball created that vacancy. After his horse went down, Tom directed an attack on the line of Rebel riflemen forming the ambush and led the assault on foot until his mounted comrades overtook him and routed the Confederate troops.

The rythmic click, click, click of the wheels on the steel rails served to lull him into a near dreamlike state. His mind relaxed, permitting him to think back and reflect on the events that had so recently reshaped his life. In his brief military career, he had already earned a reputation as a fearless soldier who held no regard for his own personal safety. Thinking about it now, he really had no explanation as to why he felt no sense of fear when in the heat of battle. He harbored no notions that he was a hero. When the rifles were popping and the cannons were roaring, it was just too busy to think about anything but doing your job. There was just no time to be afraid.

He allowed his mind to drift back and take inventory of his accomplishments since transfering to the cavalry unit. A great deal had happened. Lieutenant Matheson took a rifle ball at Kennesaw Mountain and his command was taken over by a strapping man from Maryland named John Shirey. Lieutenant Shirey was an ex-schoolteacher from Baltimore. He may have been an able officer, Tom couldn't say. Shirey was lost to the company before they saw their first action under his command. He came down with dysentery and was sent back to a hospital in the rear. Major Thrasher appointed Tom temporary platoon leader.

By this time, General Grant had taken over command of the Army of the Potomac and General Sherman was directing the campaign against Atlanta. At Kennesaw Mountain,

Thrasher was promoted to colonel and, by his recommendation, Tom was awarded a battlefield commission to second lieutenant. His only regret, as he now sat on a westbound train, was that he never got to see Atlanta. There had been so much talk about the siege of that seat of Southern pride that he had built up a sizable curiosity to see the city. He never did, for after Kennesaw Mountain, Colonel Thrasher was transferred to General Grant's command at the general's request. In the short time Tom had served under Winston Thrasher, the colonel had come to appreciate the efficiency, as well as the bravery, with which the young lieutenant performed his duties. For that reason, and because Tom had carried him out of that cornfield, Thrasher did one last favor for Tom the night before leaving to join General Grant's staff. As he sat there with his eyes closed, he replayed the scene in his mind.

"You sent for me, sir?"

"Yes, Tom, come on in." He picked up a pile of papers resting on a camp stool and placed them on the floor of the tent. "Sit down, sit down."

Tom settled himself on the tiny stool. "You all ready to go, sir?"

"Just about. Listen, Tom, the reason I wanted to talk to you . . ." he started, then paused to reframe his words. "Let me put it this way." He paused again. "You've been a damn good officer and I'm sure you'll continue to be as this campaign goes on. I don't know what kind of future you have in mind for yourself after this damn war is over but I think you could do a damn sight worse than being a career soldier. I've never asked you your feelings on it before so I wasn't sure."

This was unexpected. Tom had never really given the subject much thought. He was only eighteen when he enlisted and, at the time, he enlisted simply to help fight a war. It seemed like the thing to do since he had no immediate prospects for an occupation. It never occurred to him to think of the military as his permanent employment. Now, since the question had been put to him, it didn't seem like a bad idea. At least, at the moment, he didn't have a better one. Army life wasn't that bad, even in wartime, and there was no one waiting at home for his return. So, he thought, why not?

"Well, sir . . ." He hesitated before expressing a definite commitment. "I reckon it wouldn't be a bad choice at that."

Thrasher smiled. "Can I take that to mean you are interested in staying in the army after the war?"

"Yessir, I guess so, sir."

"Good, I thought you might. I already had orders cut for your transfer." He could see Tom's eyes widen with surprise and he hastened to explain his statement before Tom got the wrong idea. "I don't mean you're going to Washington with me. You don't want to go there anyway, a young fighting man like yourself."

Tom was confused but he waited for the colonel's explanation.

"Tom, this war will be winding down before the year is out. And when it does, most of the young officers like you who got battlefield promotions will either be mustered out or, if they stay in, will revert back to their original grade. For you, that would be sergeant. But if you go ahead and reenlist in the Seventh Cavalry and take a transfer out there now, you most likely will keep your commission. And the chances for advancement ought to be a helluva lot better on the Western frontier. For one thing, you won't be butting heads with so many West Point men. And hell, you might go out there and build up some seniority and then transfer back East . . . if that's what you want."

Tom did not respond at once, but took a few moments to consider what Thrasher was telling him. He was smart enough to see that the colonel was trying to do him a favor. He was also smart enough to know that, with his lack of education and training, he would have too much competition from the regular army officers. He didn't know much about the Western frontier, except there was seemingly constant trouble with the Indians. And he had never heard of the Seventh Cavalry, which had recently been formed under General Alfred Terry. Finally he answered.

"I reckon it sounds like a good idea." He shrugged. "I reckon fighting is fighting—Rebs or Indians, don't make that much difference."

"Good man," Thrasher replied. "I think it's a good decision."

And so, barely two weeks later, Tom Allred was on a train bound for Kansas.

CHAPTER 11

Fort Riley was a hot, dusty assembly of stark buildings and scant fortifications in the summer of 1865. Tom had not seen a great deal of the surrounding countryside since his arrival three weeks before, but his fellow officers assured him that what he had seen on the two patrols he had accompanied was representative of the whole damn territory. He had at least seen enough to know that it was in stark contrast to the green, damp river bottoms of Mississippi or the rolling hills of Tennessee. It didn't really matter that much to him anyway. He could make do just about anyplace. There was no one at home waiting for his return to St. Louis. That city might have been the place of his birth but home was wherever he could count on a cot and three meals a day. It was fortunate for him that he was of that disposition because life was pretty dull for most of the officers at Fort Riley. It was miserable, monotonous duty for those who had families back East, a fact that turned out to be a piece of good fortune for Tom because otherwise he might have been assigned as mess officer. That was what the regimental commander, Colonel Watt Thompson, had in mind for him, since Tom had no experience on the Western frontier. Before orders were signed, however, B-Troop commander Captain Wesley Rogers Bluefield had requested that Tom be assigned to his troop as executive officer. Captain Bluefield's former exec was one of those who succumbed to the terrible monotony of garrison life at Riley and had deserted two days after Tom arrived. The general consensus was that he had said to hell with it and gone back to Ohio where his wife and parents lived.

Tom had made no protest when first told he was to be in charge of the post mess tent but he certainly felt no enthusiasm for the job. So it was with a great deal of relief that he learned he had been plucked from the kitchen to be a frontline cavalry officer again. He had ridden on one short patrol with Wes Bluefield and the man seemed to be a levelheaded officer. He didn't waste a lot of words on idle conversation. When he spoke at all, it was usually to give an order. This was all right by Tom. He didn't cotton much to a lot of jawing anyway. He was to find out later on that the only reason he had been ordered out on that first patrol was so Bluefield could look him over.

B-Troop had a scout assigned named Andy Coulter. Andy didn't look like much but he was reputed to be one of the best scouts in the territory. He was a short man with a barrel chest and arms that looked too short for his body, making him appear froglike when he wasn't seated on a horse. Andy took an almost immediate liking to Tom. Tom was green, that was obvious. But Andy saw a determination in the young lieutenant and he liked the way he used his eyes and ears on that first patrol, like he was memorizing everything he saw and heard that day. Andy offered his opinion to Bluefield even though it had not been solicited.

"Reckon he's a mite green but he shows backbone enough." He punctuated his observation with a long stream of tobacco juice that raised a tiny cloud of dust at his feet. "Cain't say fer shore but you might could do worse."

Bluefield glanced at his scout briefly. Without changing his blank expression, he replied, "Maybe." He turned his attention back toward the young lieutenant, seated on a rock, eating his ration of salt pork. "Fact is, the old man is sending us to Laramie and I need an officer. I reckon young Allred there would've had to fall off his horse before I rejected him."

This caught Andy's attention. "Laramie," he repeated. "I reckon we're really going then." It was a statement but it was offered in a questioning tone. He had suspected that Colonel Thompson was going to have to dispatch at least one company to Fort Laramie. Ever since he had heard that the army was sending Colonel Henry Carrington's Eighteenth Infantry out from Laramie to build three forts and protect the immigrants trying to get to the Montana goldfields, he'd known there was going to be big trouble. And he knew that sooner or later he would be in it with the rest of them.

"Yeah," Bluefield confirmed, his tone that of a regular army man who was accustomed to getting nasty details. "We're going. That damn Oglala Sioux is hell-bent on stopping the road." He didn't have to say Red Cloud. Andy knew who he meant.

Andy spat, then thought a minute before he spoke again. "Now, I'm gonna tell you, Cap'n, there's gonna be some trouble on this one. I hear tell Red Cloud's got so dang many of them red sons stirred up till it's gonna take more than two or three cavalry troops to whip him. That ole son of a bitch ain't no fool. He ain't gon' stand for the army to keep kicking him around. These damn fool immigrants have been stomping through his hunting ground like they don't give spit about no treaties. Get shot up and scalped, don't make no difference, they just keep on coming. Now that trail that Bozeman and Jacobs marked, it's a shortcut all right. But it's a shortcut right through the heart of the Injuns' best hunting ground. I wouldn't stand for it if I was him. Hell, we gon' be a while on this one."

Andy's gut feelings were to be proven accurate if not naively conservative. The Sioux chief Mahpiua Luta, known more commonly as Red Cloud, had gathered some sixteen thousand warriors to his cause. Most of these were Sioux but there were also many Cheyenne and Arapaho, all determined to stop the government from building a road through the heart of their most sacred hunting ground.

Captain Bluefield made no reply to his scout's comment, but in his own gut he experienced a gnawing suspicion that once again the higher brass back East had underestimated the fighting capabilities of the Indian. According to reports received by Colonel Thompson, Red Cloud captured the first contingent of army engineers dispatched to work on the road and held them for more than two weeks before releasing them. The mystery of it was why he let them go. Bluefield speculated that the chief was hoping to save a lot of bloodshed with a simple warning. Well, if it was a warning, it didn't work. The army pushed right along with the Bozeman Trail, as it was now called, and Red Cloud was raiding work parties and any immigrant trains that were brave enough to take the new shortcut to Montana. Like Andy, Bluefield figured they would be a while on this one.

*   *   *

What was scheduled to be a twenty-one-day march turned into a month in the saddle, what with the pace slowed down considerably by the fifteen supply wagons the troop was ordered to escort to Fort Laramie. It was a long, hard trip even for seasoned veterans. It seemed endlessly monotonous to Lieutenant Tom Allred, who was unaccustomed to such vast tedium. As each day passed, the boundless prairie stretched out before them, the distant horizon never changing from day to day, until Tom began to think the whole world had turned into prairie. They encountered no hostiles along the entire route. The only Indian activity they saw was an occasional band of half a dozen or so passing far off on the horizon. Andy said these were Pawnee hunting parties. They were supposed to be on the reservation but Captain Bluefield was unconcerned with police action along the way. His orders were to get the troop to Fort Laramie.

To break the monotony, Tom accompanied Andy on scouts away from the column anytime he could. Bluefield approved, even encouraged the practice. He figured time spent with the scout was as good as sending the young lieutenant to school. Andy liked to talk and he was more than willing to share his knowledge and experience with anyone who was willing to listen. Tom proved a good audience and quietly absorbed all the stories of Andy's campaigns against the red sons, as he called them, never blinking when some of the scout's escapades bordered on the heroic. In the process, Andy developed a fondness for Tom and Tom picked up a great deal of information about Indians that would do him in good stead later on.

By the time the column reached Fort Laramie, all the men were thoroughly trail-weary and starved for something to eat besides salt pork and boiled corn. On the march, Captain Bluefield had allowed Andy to hunt very little, not wishing to waste any more time than necessary. The march had already stretched into too many days and his men were looking pretty ragged and far from battle-ready. When at last Andy galloped back to the column and reported that he had sighted the lookout towers of the fort, Bluefield relaxed a bit in the saddle. He had hoped his luck would hold out and they would not run into any hostiles before he had a chance to rest his men. Fort Laramie was a welcome sight.

"All right, men," he ordered, "let's look alive." He turned to Tom. "Lieutenant Allred!"

"Sir!" Tom reined up beside him.

"Let's see if this bunch of ragtags can shake some of the dust off and look like soldiers. I don't intend to go dragging our behinds into the garrison."

"Yessir!" Tom wheeled his horse and galloped toward the rear.

Fort Laramie turned out to be a brief respite for the travel-weary troopers for there was hostile activity to the north, along the Powder River. Bluefield's company was allowed two days to rest and get supplies before joining some other units that had been waiting for his arrival. Combined, they formed a full regiment under Colonel Henry Lockley, and set out at dawn of the third day for Fort Phil Kearney, a small outpost near the foothills of the Big Horn Mountains. The march took them up the Platte River to Deer Creek Crossing, where a small train of twelve civilian freight wagons were waiting to combine with a larger train before being allowed to proceed into Indian territory. The freighters were mighty glad to see soldiers because they were getting weary from sitting there stranded at Deer Creek. They tagged along behind as Lockley headed north, along Sage Creek, toward the Powder. Patrols were sent out left and right of the column, as well as ahead. Lockley took no chances on being surprised by Red Cloud even though he felt it unlikely the hostiles would hazard an attack on a full regiment. It would be near impossible to hide the presence of a body of soldiers that size passing through Indian territory so there was no attempt at secrecy. To the contrary, part of the reason the soldiers were being sent was to impress the hostiles with the military might of the army. Lockley and the brass back East in Washington were to find that Red Cloud was not a man easily impressed.

From the time they left the North Platte and turned northward, they saw plenty of hostiles, usually in small bands far in the distance. Andy said they were just keeping an eye on the soldiers. They would parallel the column for a while then disappear. Before long another band would turn up on the horizon and follow their progress for several miles before disappearing like the band before them. And so it went. It seemed to Tom that they always had hostile observers with them. At first, there was excitement in the ranks when the first Indians were spotted. After several days, they were hardly noticed.

Plodding along beside Andy Coulter, Tom wondered aloud, "If we're supposed to be going out here to fight the Sioux, why don't we send out a patrol after that bunch?"

Andy glanced over his shoulder at the band of maybe a dozen or more hostiles who had been following the column since midday. "Lockley ain't gonna start splitting off parts of his men to go chasing after a few Injuns. He figures they ain't likely to tangle with a bunch this size. But let them get us split up in small bunches and then see how many of them red sons pop up. They'd make short work out of this regiment then."

By noon of the following day, the column reached Fort Reno. The fort consisted of little more than a log stockade around some warehouses and stables. The soldiers' quarters and the powder magazine were out in the open plain, high above the river. The men of the garrison were mighty glad to see the long column of blue coats and greeted them with loud shouts, discharging their pistols in the air. Tom learned that the engineers had been constantly harassed by Sioux and Cheyenne raiding parties, so much so that there had been little time to work on the road they were there to build. It was all they could do to stay alive. This was to be his station for some time for, after the main body had paused to rest for a day, they moved on north, leaving Captain Bluefield's men there to reinforce the garrison. And so began Tom's indoctrination into Indian fighting.

CHAPTER 12

Little Wolf shifted his position to ease the strain on his knees. His friend Black Feather glanced at him and smiled. Black Feather could squat on his haunches for hours at a time, never moving a muscle. So could most of the other young men in this band of Cheyenne warriors. Little Wolf's long legs were not built to withstand the strain on his kneecaps, and if he didn't change his position every ten minutes or so, he would soon be in pain.

"Soon now," Black Feather whispered and pointed to the last few soldiers mounting up, preparing to escort the work party out of the crude log fort.

Little Wolf nodded. Without consciously thinking about it, he checked his bow, feeling the sinew bowstring for worn places. They would wait until the column of soldiers and workers had cleared out of the fort and disappeared over the rise before leaving their positions in the deep draw that ran tangent to the easternmost corner of the stockade. He had scouted the fort for a few days before this and knew there would be no more than a dozen or so left to guard it. It was his guess that of those left behind, no more than half that number would actually be carrying weapons, the rest being cooks and grooms.

Sleeps Standing rose and made his way quickly and silently along the dry gulley to kneel at Little Wolf's side. "The soldiers are gone. They are no longer in sight."

"I know." Little Wolf smiled patiently. "Do not be so anxious to die." There were only twenty young men in his war party and they all looked toward Little Wolf to give the signal to attack. In the year since finding Black Feather in the mountains, Little Wolf had emerged as the leader of this small band of Cheyenne and Arapaho braves. Though they fought with their Lakota brothers in what the white man called Red Cloud's War, they maintained their autonomy and operated independently as a small band of raiders. Little Wolf was considered a bit young to be called a war chief but Red Cloud graciously treated him with the respect shown any tribal leader, especially one who undertook such daring raids upon the enemy while maintaining a reputation for bringing his warriors back safely.

Sleeps Standing began to fidget, causing Little Wolf to lay a steadying hand on his friend's shoulder. He gestured toward the low hills behind them. "In a little while the sun will come up over those hills. When it is high enough, we will move directly to the stockade wall. It will be harder for the sentry to see us if we have the sun at our backs."

Sleeps Standing nodded. He had come to trust Little Wolf completely. They had raided all summer up and down the Powder, keeping the army workers too busy to build their road. This day their mission was to raid the nearly empty fort to get rifles and ammunition. Little Wolf's little band of Cheyenne warriors had only a half dozen outdated muzzle loaders, extremely cumbersome and unreliable. He found his bow to be much more efficient in their style of hit-and-run tactics, where swiftness and surprise were the main elements of combat. As the summer wore on, however, there were more and more soldiers being sent to deal with "the Indian problem." Little Wolf was smart enough to realize the freedom he now enjoyed, to fight when and where and how he wanted, would not last. He and his braves had decided to operate independently. It was, they acknowledged, Red Cloud's war and they joined him in his fight with the army, but on their own terms. They were proud of their Cheyenne and Arapaho heritage, and while they did not deny the fierce fighting spirit of their brothers, the Dakota, they preferred to remain a separate force.

Red Cloud was winning his war. It was being waged on his terms. As long as he could choose when and where he struck and then escape on his fast Indian ponies, he exacted a heavy toll on the army. Because of their successes, Red Cloud's warriors were becoming more and more convinced of their invincibility, taking comfort in their greater numbers. It was true that the Sioux did indeed outnumber the soldiers in this battle along the Powder. But Little Wolf knew there was no limit to the number of soldiers the army could continue to send against them, and the next battle might have far different results. This was another reason to keep his small band independent, to move quickly if need be, to run if necessary in order to fight another day with better odds. Unlike the main body of Red Cloud's camp, they were not encumbered by women and children and the other trappings a whole village entailed. To give his braves further advantage, Little Wolf wanted weapons equal to the soldiers' breech-loading rifles. And those weapons were just on the other side of the rough log wall that was just now catching the first rays of the morning sun. His concern now was to scale that wall with enough of his braves to overwhelm the sentries.

"It is time." With that brief statement, Little Wolf motioned Bloody Claw and Black Feather close to him. Looking directly at Black Feather, he asked softly, "Are you ready, my brother?"

Black Feather smiled and nodded. On a signal, he and three others were to make their way across the open prairie grass that stretched between the draw and the fort, carrying a log that was to be used as a ladder to scale the wall.

Little Wolf turned to Bloody Claw. "You and Sleeps Standing take the two sentries at the front gate. I will silence the other one on the back guard post. There must be no sound before we get inside the fort. Once inside, we must kill the soldiers quickly before they can think to defend themselves."

He turned to Black Feather again. "When you are over the wall, you must open the gates quickly or you may have to kill all the soldiers by yourself."

Black Feather's smile broadened. "Maybe I should leave all of you outside so you don't get in my way."

"What if there are more soldiers than we thought?" This from Walks With A Limp, one of the Arapahos who came to the mountains with Bloody Claw.

"There won't be," Little Wolf stated. "Kill the guards first. Then watch for the soldiers coming out of the tent under the flag. They will have their weapons ready. Then the ones who cook and do the women's work will have no fight in them. They will surrender."

There were no further questions. Little Wolf had never been wrong before and he had led them on a dozen or more raids. Each man knew his responsibility and felt complete trust in Little Wolf's words. Silently, the small band of warriors slipped over the edge of the draw and dispersed.

It had been a long four hours for Private Will Johnson. He didn't have much love for guard duty but it was better than going out on escort detail again and getting shot at by hostiles. His guard tour was about up and he would be off for eight hours. The worst part about catching the last tour of the night was fighting off the overpowering attack of sleepiness just before sunup. He blinked hard a couple of times in an attempt to remain alert. A faint breeze drifted past the mess tent carrying the distinct aroma of bacon frying. This in itself was enough to make his mouth water. It had been more than two months since he had last eaten pork, having had nothing but wild game until the supply wagons from Laramie finally arrived. Now that the escort detail was up and out, the cooks were preparing a real breakfast for the few remaining men.

Daylight was coming fast now. The distant hills that were black moments before were now fading to gray and beginning to take on detail. He heard the call of a night bird off to the western edge of the grassy draw, answered moments later by another at the far eastern perimeter of the stockade. He often heard night birds calling on other nights. Still it was unusual to hear them this late in the morning. A golden half circle of light on the guard tower behind him told him that the sun had cleared the hills and he turned to view the daily ritual. Looking into the rising sun, he was forced to squint, it was so bright. Out of the corner of his eye he caught a moving shadow near the wall below him. A deer, he thought, and edged closer to the parapet to get a better look. At first he saw nothing but the bright image of the sun still dancing in his eyes. After a few moments, his vision cleared but his mind was confused, failing to comprehend the image before him. It was an Indian, taking careful aim with his bow. At almost the same instant, he felt the heavy blow beneath his rib cage, causing him to reel backward, almost knocking him off the guard walk. At first there was a numbness and he had no idea what had hit him with such force. As he stuggled to regain his balance, he looked down in disbelief to discover the shaft of

the arrow protruding from his tunic. In horror, he reached
down and clutched the arrow and attempted to pull it out.
When he did, he felt the searing pain and saw the rapidly
spreading bloodstain. He tried to turn and call for the sergeant of the guard but the pain doubled him over and the
fort began to swirl around inside his head and everything
went dark. His last conscious thought was that he had to
keep from falling. He was unconscious before he tumbled
off the guard walk onto the ground below.

Black Feather barely slowed down as he swerved to
avoid the body of the falling sentry and sprinted to the
front gate. It took but a moment to throw back the heavy
wooden bar and push the gate open. When he ran back to
the center of the stockade, followed by four Cheyenne
braves, Little Wolf was already there directing his small
force toward the troop tent area. When Black Feather approached, Little Wolf silently directed his friend toward the
mess tent and the cook fire glowing before it. Black Feather
knew what to do without being told. He and his four comrades quickly lit the fire arrows they had prepared. Little
Wolf watched unhurriedly until all arrows were burning
steadily. The stockade was still bathed in the half light of
dawn, the garrison unaware as yet that a hostile force was
inside the walls. When he was sure the arrows were burning, he directed his bowmen by hand signal, firing at one
target after another in the order of importance. First the
commander's tent. Little Wolf knew the commanding officer in this small outpost was not a high-ranking officer and
would be out with the main body protecting the workmen.
He knew there should be no more than one or two soldiers
inside now but they would probably be armed. So they
would deal with these men first. Next to be burned would
be the larger tents on either side of the command tent in
case a second in command was left behind in the commander's absence. Then the mess tent was to be fired to flush
out the guard detail that would surely be eating before
relieving the present sentries. Within minutes, the tents
were ablaze and the confused and panic-stricken soldiers,
sleep still in their eyes, emptied out into the compound,
cursing and yelling.

Little Wolf's raiding party was small but he had planned
his raid well, counting heavily on surprise and confusion on

the part of the soldiers. He suspected they would never anticipate an attack on their outpost. They had grown accustomed to the hostiles raiding like all the Sioux war parties they had fought before; with sudden attacks on the workers, out in the open, where they could strike swiftly and then withdraw. Little Wolf had ideas of his own about the most efficient way to battle the soldiers. Foremost in his planning was the safety of his fellow warriors. He would lose the confidence of his braves if he allowed heavy casualties when he led a raid. With this in mind, he had stationed his best bowmen to watch the soldiers bolting from the burning tents. He had instructed them to target those soldiers with weapons to eliminate any danger to the raiding party. They would deal with the unarmed after all those with rifles had been eliminated. Sleeps Standing and two others were positioned where they could watch the rows of tents where the troops slept in the event some had not gone with the main column.

As he had anticipated, the attack caught the small outpost completely by surprise. Not one shot was fired by the soldiers. In all, nine soldiers were killed and several more wounded. The few remaining soldiers, most of them cooks and the stable detail, put up no resistance, having been mesmerized by the suddenness and efficiency of the attack. Horrified, they watched as their captors moved among the dead, taking scalps and counting coup. At Little Wolf's command, the prisoners were tied up to the stockade walls while the Indians selected their best horses and loaded them with rifles, ammunition, food, clothing and anything else that might prove useful.

Bloody Claw approached Little Wolf, who was preparing to mount a tall bay mare that had caught his eye. "We are ready, Little Wolf. Let us kill these snakes and be gone."

Little Wolf hesitated. He knew his companions were anxious to kill all the soldiers. Their goal, after all, was to kill as many soldiers as possible and chase the white man from their hunting grounds. He tried to recall the image he had seared into his mind of Spotted Pony lying in a pool of his own blood and Buffalo Woman lying facedown across her cook fire. He had vowed to fight the army but still he did not like the idea of executing defenseless men, white or red. After a moment he spoke.

"Wait. Let these others live." Seeing the frown on Bloody Claw's face and the look of puzzlement on the faces of those braves who had heard his decision, he added, "These dogs are not fighting men. They are like women who cook and take care of the horses. We will leave them to tell the other soldiers that we have been merciful this day but they must take this as a warning. We will not allow the road to be built through these lands. They will also tell that this brave deed was done by the mighty Cheyenne and Arapaho so that they may know who their enemy is."

His statement was met with many blank stares as his men mulled over his suggestion. Little Wolf was not officially in command—as a war chief, he led by popular choice and his leadership was open for question at any time by any member of the band.

"This is a good thing." Black Feather spoke first, always in support of his friend. "We don't want the Dakota to take the credit for our bravery."

This seemed to receive favorable reactions from most of the warriors. Little Wolf was quick to take advantage of the moment. "We all have won the honor to count coup on all these that we leave behind." The young Indians accepted this. After all, it was more honorable to count coup on an enemy that still lives. "Good," he announced, "it is decided." As an afterthought, he added, "Strip them of their uniforms. We may have need of them."

They quickly went about stripping the clothing from the terrified prisoners and, when they had taken everything they could pack on the captured horses, Little Wolf shouted to the bewildered prisoners in English. "It is Little Wolf and the Cheyenne who have done this. When you tell of this, you must warn your people that Little Wolf will not be so merciful next time. Next time we may do as the cowardly soldiers who slaughtered our people at Sand Creek did!"

The warriors crossed the river and headed across the rolling plains toward the distant mountains. Little Wolf was intent upon gaining the protection of the mountain draws and valleys before the main body of soldiers had an opportunity to pursue them. The raid had been extremely successful. Although the total number of enemies killed had not been great, his band of warriors had inflicted great damage upon the tiny outpost. They would sorely feel the loss of horses, ammunition and food stores Little Wolf's companions now herded toward the mountains. And, most important to Little Wolf, he would return to Red Cloud's camp with every man who rode out with him.

Once they reached the protection of the hills, the raiding party relaxed their caution, secure in the knowledge that no army patrol would dare to venture this close to Red Cloud's camp. They knew the army had no concentration of troops large enough to mount an attack on the Sioux village. They were spread too thin, trying to protect the different groups of army workers and the many wagons that came up the Powder. Now Little Wolf allowed time to congratulate himself on selecting the mare. She had been well trained and cared for. Many of his band rode good army mounts now. Indian ponies were accustomed to the wild country and were more reliable but the army mounts were well-bred and strong. His choice would be envied.

Spirits were high in Red Cloud's camp when Little Wolf and his braves returned. Word had come to the chief that the army was pulling out of several outposts along the intended line of the road to the Montana goldfields. It was beginning to look like the constant harrassment by the Sioux war parties had not only taken effect, they had beaten the blue coats and driven them out of their sacred hunting grounds. Confidence was rising like a fever and spreading like wildfire through the encampment as Red Cloud's war chiefs hastily organized their war parties to pursue the departing soldiers. There was a general feeling that the army was in full retreat, which was not the case. In fact, they had only given up on most of the work sites, and were just withdrawing to the established forts. But this fuel added to the fire already burning in the hearts of every young warrior. Little Wolf's comrades joined in the dancing and singing and soon were pressing him to join the battle with their Dakota brothers. Little Wolf was hesitant. He was not sure why, but he preferred to fight as they had been fighting, as a small raiding force, operating independently of the main body of Sioux.

"We must finish the battle with the blue coats," Bloody Claw insisted.

Little Wolf could see that he was going to be outvoted

if he did not concur. "I agree, my brother. We will fight until the soldiers have all left this country." By the expressions on the faces of his young followers, he could see that this was what they had expected to hear. "We will go to fight the soldiers that were camped at the fort we have just attacked." He smiled and added, "Maybe they would like to see their horses again."

Black Feather grinned and threw back his head and offered a loud war whoop to the heavens.

Lieutenant Tom Allred shifted his weight in the saddle in an attempt to ease the ache now running the length of his backbone. It didn't seem to help, so he dismounted and walked a few yards away from his horse. The animal immediately started to graze on the buffalo grass that covered the hilltop. Tom stretched. Taking out his watch, he studied it for several seconds, as if he wanted to make sure it had not stopped. "Damn," he swore, gazing down across the grassland where the engineers were working. He hated escort duty. He felt like a guard over a group of convicts, waiting for the time to pass, and time was in no hurry when waited upon. At times he almost wished hostiles would attack, if only to break the monotony. Things had been pretty quiet since the fort had been attacked four days before. "Damn," he uttered again when he thought of the damage that raid had done on his men and supplies. It was not his decision to make, but had he been the ranking officer, he would not have left so small a detail to defend the fort. Captain Wes Bluefield was a competent officer, having proven himself as a first-rate Indian fighter and Tom wouldn't second-guess him. He just made an error in judgment and got caught. Tom knew that everybody made mistakes. This one cost nine lives plus horses and ammunition, not to mention the weapons that would now be used against them.

The sound of hooves below him broke into his thoughts and he turned to see Sergeant Erwin Hale coming up the hill at a gallop. "Sir, Lieutenant Perry says to form up the men. We're going back to the fort."

"It's a bit early, ain't it?" Tom looked at his watch again.

Sergeant Hale shrugged. "That's what he said, form 'em up."

"All right." Tom stretched once more and stepped up into the saddle. "Signal the outriders in." He watched for a moment as Hale galloped down from the hill. It suited him fine to go back early. It was getting too damn cold to sit around out on the prairie all day. Like as not, the winter snows would stop all work along the road before the month was out anyway. The last of the immigrant trains had gone through long ago and travel would not likely start again before late spring. Christmas was only four days away. They had been lucky the weather had held this long, with only a few light snows. Guiding his horse down the hill, he couldn't help but smile as he formed a picture in his mind of Lieutenant Perry, thin and shivering in the cold wind that was now sweeping across the prairie.

Lawson Perry and Tom were friends. Since Lawson was senior to him by a full year in grade, he was in command when Bluefield stayed at the post. Lawson made no bones about the fact that he had not gone through West Point just to fashion a career of chasing ragtag savages around the Western frontier, freezing his ass off in the winter and burning up in the summer. His every day was spent marking time, awaiting orders that he was sure would someday come to deliver him from this wilderness and transfer him to a post back East. He often expressed his amazement that Tom didn't expend any energy on regret. He even envied Tom's attitude, that one place was about as good as another. As far as Tom was concerned, he wasn't a West Pointer, he had come up through the ranks and he more than likely had no future in the army outside this duty station.

By the time he rode down into the basin, the column was already forming. The engineers and civilian workers, more than happy to call it a day, were loading the wagons and hitching the teams. Lawson Perry sat stiffly in the saddle, off to the side, watching the preparations with the bored expression of a man who had seen it a hundred times. Tom pulled up beside him.

"What's the matter, Lawson? Your backside get too cold?"

Lawson laughed. "I suppose yours isn't," he replied in his precise manner of speaking, a manner that offered evidence of his education and West Point background.

"Why, no, I was just thinking how pleasant it is out here."

Lawson's face sobered as he confided in his friend. "Look at this mess," he said, gesturing toward the half finished log bridge across a deep ravine, his tone laced with sarcasm. "You know damn well it's a waste of time and effort to build a bridge out here in the middle of nowhere. Even if the damn Indians let it stand, who's going to use it? Hell, anybody going to Montana has got the whole country in front of them. Why would they have to cross over this bridge over this little ravine?"

"I don't know, Lawson. Why would they?"

Lawson knew Tom was baiting him. "Ah, why am I wasting my time telling you? You don't clutter your mind with serious thoughts."

Tom laughed at his friend's exasperation. Lawson was right, however. Tom didn't clutter his mind with the why of things. Whether the bridge made sense or not was not his concern. His job was to guard the workers. He didn't worry about what the workers were doing. Seeing that the column was ready to move, he asked, "Want me to move 'em out?"

"Yeah, let's go get some hot food."

As the column topped the first line of hills, Tom saw Andy Coulter cutting across a grassy slope to join them. He soon pulled in beside the two officers and reined up next to Tom.

"Quittin' a mite early, ain't you?"

Tom laughed. "Yeah, Lieutenant Perry's backside is getting cold."

Lawson glared at them with mock disgust. "You know the brass will have to recall all of us off this silly damn detail anyway. It's a damn fool project and a waste of an officer's time."

To Tom, it was a waste of time debating the issue so he changed the subject. Turning to Andy, he asked, "See anything out there?"

Andy shook his head. "No, nary a sign. I scouted all the way to the river to the east, all the way back to them foothills to the west. I believe the Injuns took the day off."

"It's just getting too cold," Lawson offered. "They probably won't do too much more before spring."

"I don't know . . ." Andy took his hat off and thoughtfully scratched his head. "Some folks hold that Injuns don't like to go to war in the wintertime. And I reckon for the most part that's a fact. But I've seen 'em fight in the winter, seen 'em fight plenty. And this here Red Cloud is pretty dang serious about protecting his huntin' grounds."

Lawson shrugged, not wanting to recant completely. "Well, maybe some small raids, but I doubt they'll start anything major."

"Hard to say," Andy replied, after launching a stream of tobacco juice over his shoulder.

"S'pose we'll get another visit from that bunch that hit the post?" Tom wondered aloud.

"Doubt it," Andy answered. "They got what they was after, guns and ammunition. Besides, that was that bunch of Cheyennes that's been raidin' all summer. They don't usually hit the same place twice. That ain't their style."

"Little Wolf," Tom uttered, almost under his breath.

"What?" Andy asked.

"Little Wolf," Tom repeated. "Said his name was Little Wolf, said it in pretty good English according to the mess sergeant."

"Well, the bunch he's running with is Cheyenne all right." He paused to spit for punctuation. "Least the arrows I seen had Cheyenne markings."

The column was approximately halfway back to the post when the point man suddenly came back to them at a gallop.

"Hey-yooooo!" Lieutenant Perry halted the column and rode out with Andy and Tom to meet the rider.

"Lieutenant!" he called as soon as he was in voice range. "Gunfire! Over toward the river!"

"How many?" Lawson asked as the trooper pulled up and wheeled his mount around to parallel them.

"Hard to say, sir. I heard half a dozen shots, maybe more."

Both officers looked to Andy Coulter for a possible explanation but he was as puzzled as they were. There were no patrols out in that area. In fact, there were no patrols out anywhere since Bluefield insisted that the escort detail not be diluted. He had ordered that all engagements with the hostiles were to be defensive. They were vastly outnumbered if the savages decided to join forces in an assault on their little post. He felt his strength was in keeping his firepower in concentration.

"Want me to go have a look?" Tom offered. "Maybe some immigrants or prospectors run into some Indians."

"Yeah," Lawson quickly agreed. "Take Andy and a half dozen men." Tom started to leave. "And Tom, you be careful."

"Right." Tom reined his horse around and called out, "Sergeant Hale! Pick five men, on the double!"

With Andy in the lead, they galloped away from the column in the direction pointed out by the advance guard. After covering about a mile, Andy held up his hand to halt the detail. They could hear the gunfire distinctly and it appeared to come from the river, some seven hundred yards in front of them.

"Peers to me it's coming from just the other side of that bluff, where the river takes a turn around that clump of trees." Andy looked to Tom for agreement. When he got a nod in return, he kicked his horse into a canter, headed for a little hill before the river in order to find a place for a better look. Once they had reached the shelter of the hill, they dismounted and Andy, Tom and Sergeant Hale crawled up to the top to have a look.

"Damn!" Hale was the first to speak. "Where the hell did they come from?"

"Looks like we got some boys in trouble all right," Andy observed. "Wonder what they're doing out here in the first place."

Tom, anxious to size up the scene taking place on the opposite riverbank, was trying to decide what the best course of action was. A small army patrol of five or six troopers had obviously been ambushed by a band of twenty or more hostiles. From the look of it, they had taken a defensive position on the riverbank. The hostiles were armed with rifles and had the troopers ringed on three sides with the river at their backs. Tom's decision was not that hard to make. He had to come to their aid but he could see no way to get to them without crossing the river. And that would make his men sitting ducks. They would be picked off before they got halfway across. If he was to have a chance to rescue the soldiers, he would have to have more than the seven of them to charge across that stretch of open water.

"Whaddaya wanna do?" Andy asked calmly.

"You see any way to get to those men without crossing that open water?"

"Nope," was Andy's terse reply.

"Well then, we need more men."

"Glad to hear you say that, son."

Tom turned to Hale. "Sergeant, send one of the men back to the column. Tell Lieutenant Perry I need half of his detachment on the double." He turned back to Andy. "Maybe if they see us coming in strength, they'll run without a fight."

Upon receiving Tom's message, Lawson was inclined to lead the whole escort column to his aid, leaving the engineers and the workers to fend for themselves until he got back. He knew he would catch hell from Bluefield if he did, even if nothing happened while he was gone. So he did as Tom requested and sent approximately half of the escort, twenty-two troopers.

Tom anxiously awaited their arrival while watching the battle going on across the river. It was more than a quarter of an hour before his reinforcements pulled up at the base of the little hill, but the embattled soldiers on the opposite bank were still alive and apparently holding off their attackers.

"All right, men, we've got to move fast. Check your weapons." Upon noticing a bugler in the detachment, he signaled to him. "All right, let's let them know we're coming. Don't slow down until you reach the other side of the river!" He took one last look to see if everyone was ready then spurred his horse over the crest of the hill, leading his troops straight down the slope. With bugle blaring and rifles popping, they charged into the shallow river toward their beleaguered comrades.

His horse almost stumbled when its momentum was suddenly stopped by the chest-deep water and it began to struggle toward the opposite side. At once Tom was lost in the confusion of the fighting. Bullets were flying all around him and the almost constant roar of rifle fire was punctuated by the screams of horses and men. Something was wrong! In their confusion, the soldiers trapped by the hostiles were firing at his troopers as they attempted to come to their rescue. He began shouting, "Hold your fire! Hold your fire!" Then something heavy hit him in the back, knocking him from his horse. He remembered feeling the shock of the icy water, sucking the breath from his lungs, but he remembered nothing else after that.

It was dark when he finally came to. At first he thought he was drowning for he was up to his chin in the freezing water and, panic-stricken, he began to flail his arms in an effort to swim. He would have cried out but a hand immediately clamped over his mouth, choking off the sound. "Easy, son . . . easy. I gotcha. You're all right." He recognized the familiar voice of Andy Coulter. "Be real quiet. Don't worry, I got a'holt of you. We'll be all right, long as you don't make no noise." Tom let himself relax and Andy removed his hand from over his mouth. "Well now," he whispered, "glad to see you coming around. For a while there I thought you was a goner."

"Andy, what happened?" Tom whispered. He was gradually coming back to reality and he became aware of the feeling of numbness from his neck on down throughout his entire body, right down to his toes, which had no feeling in them at all. His head felt as if it would split and there was a throbbing in his chest. He didn't remember much about the events that caused him to be in the river so he repeated the question. "What happened?"

Before answering, Andy shifted his body around to get a better hold on his young friend. Tom's vision, which until that moment had been blurred, began to gradually focus and he could now see that they were up under a steep bank, behind a log. Softly, almost in a whisper, Andy told him what had taken place some two hours before when they had charged to the rescue of the embattled soldiers. "It was an ambush," Andy said. "Them weren't soldiers on the other bank. They was Cheyenne, dressed up in army uniforms. I seen you go down and, by the time I got to you, it was already too late. They was more of 'em dug in the riverbank behind us. They had us in a crossfire. There wasn't no place to go. They cut us down like wheatstraw."

Tom was stunned. "How many? How many wounded?"

Andy snorted in disgust. "Wounded? Hell, dead." He had to restrain himself from allowing his voice to raise. "You and me, Tom, we're the only ones left. And the only reason we ain't dead is we washed downstream behind your horse. I reckon they couldn't see us behind it. When we got 'round a little bend, I pulled us up under this bank. I weren't sure but what I was holding on to a dead man up till just now. But I figured I'd hold on to you till it got good and dark and then I'd get my ass out of here."

"Sweet Jesus," Tom moaned softly, the extent of the massacre just now becoming clear to him. The realization that he had led those men to their death hammered home to him. "Oh my God, Andy, I led them right into it."

"Hold on a minute, son," Andy quickly admonished. "Don't go putting thoughts like that in your head. It weren't no more your fault than it were mine. Hell, I didn't see it coming either and I sure as hell ain't taking on the guilt for them soldier boys getting killed. We got out-smarted. That's all there is to it."

"Little Wolf?"

"Yeah," Andy snorted, "Little Wolf all right. I heard his name called out a couple of times when we was floating downstream. I think I seen him. Leastways I seen a kinda tall buck that seemed to be giving the orders. I tell you, Tom, they just slickered us good on this one. They was dug in so good, I swear, we wouldn't have seen 'em if we had been squatting right on top of 'em. And once we got out in the middle of the river, it was Katie bar the door. We were goners."

They waited and listened for a while longer. Andy finally decided there were no hostiles left in the area and it was time to try to make their way back to the post. He knew Tom was wounded pretty badly even though the young lieutenant did not appear to be in serious pain. Andy knew that it was the icy water that numbed the pain. He figured Tom didn't know how bad he was hurt. He had to get him out of the water pretty soon though. He was afraid that if he didn't, Tom was going to freeze to death. Already his teeth were chattering uncontrollably. Much longer in the water and they would both be corpses.

"I'm gonna let you go for a few minutes. Hold on to the log. Can you hold on to it?"

"I think so." Tom struggled to pull his arms over the log.
Andy waited a moment until he was satisfied Tom could
manage to keep his head above water. Then he moved with
the current out from under the bank and slowly pulled
himself out of the water. The cold night air slapped his
wet buckskins up against his skin, chilling him to the bone.
Sopping wet, his boots squishing with every step, he quickly
scouted the trees up and down the riverbank. There was
no sign of anyone around. He was satisfied that the Indians
were gone. He was afraid to leave Tom for too long but
he knew he had to find a place to make a fire before he
pulled the wounded man out of the water. If he could get
Tom to a fire right away, he had a better chance of making
it back alive. A quick search turned up a big cottonwood
that was half hollowed out, making an acceptable backdrop
for a campfire. There was plenty of dried brush and small
limbs around to start a fire so he stacked them inside the
hollow of the tree. He would have ordinarily started the
fire the easy way, by striking a spark over a pinch of gunpowder. But his gunpowder was ruined by the water. At
least his flint and steel were still reasonably dry, wrapped
securely in the oilskin pouch inside his shirt. He labored
steadily over a handful of dried buffalo grass until finally a
spark caught fire. In a matter of minutes after that, he had
a blaze going inside the hollow of the tree. When he was
sure it was a serious fire, he left it and went back for Tom.

Andy had been correct in his assumption that the icy
water had numbed the pain of Tom's wound because Tom's
toes were almost frozen by the time Andy carried him to
the fire. The pain of his thawing extremities was as excruci-
ating as the throbbing pain of the wound in his back. Andy
stripped all of Tom's clothes off and covered him with
green branches pulled from the trees. He got him as close
to the fire as he deemed prudent without setting him on
fire. When he felt he had done all for Tom that he could,
he saw to warming himself.

When looking back on that night, Andy would always
marvel at the dumb luck and the good Lord for watching
over the two of them. Tom was in considerable pain and,
when he did fall into a fitful sleep, he moaned constantly
and cried out at regular intervals. Andy was afraid to let
the fire die down too low, afraid they would both freeze,

so they spent the night in hostile territory as obvious as a beacon in the darkness of the prairie. He would be forever grateful that there couldn't have been an Indian within ten miles, else their scalps would have been drying on Little Wolf's lodge pole by morning. One thought that kept coming back to trouble him was, where was Lieutenant Perry? When Tom did not return with his men, why didn't Lawson send a detail to find them? Andy didn't sleep at all that night, waiting for the sudden attack that, mercifully, never came.

Morning came with a heavy frost that coated the cottonwoods like a silver blanket. Andy greeted the new day with bleary eyes and a sense of relief and gratitude. He was reasonably sure they were alone in that part of the wilderness by the simple fact that they were still alive. Tom was feverish but lucid, enough so that he and Andy were able to talk their situation over. It was obvious that Andy would have to leave Tom there and go for help. There was nothing else they could do. They had lost horses, weapons, food, everything but their clothes. At least they were dry now. Tom understood that his only chance was if Andy could make his way back to the troop and get back to him with help. On foot, he should be able to make it in half a day if he didn't run into any hostile scouting parties. Since there was no sign of Indians during the night or again that morning, they felt reasonably sure that the Indians had not seen their escape downstream. As the sun began to paint gold tips on the uppermost branches of the trees, Andy carried Tom to a hiding place some one hundred yards further downstream. Tom was unarmed so Andy felt it safer to hide him away from the smoldering hollow tree that had served as their campfire during the night.

After Tom assured him that he would be all right, Andy took his leave, promising to be back for him come hell or high water. Before setting out straight toward the rising sun, he decided to scout upstream where the battle with the Cheyenne had taken place the day before. His hope was that the hostiles might have left something that could be of some use to him, a weapon or, better yet, possibly a frightened horse that might have returned after the noise of battle had subsided.

They had drifted further downstream than he had re-

membered for it took him almost half an hour to make his
way back along the bank to a clump of juniper overlooking
the spot where the troopers had made their ill-fated charge.
He felt his stomach twitch with a sudden feeling of nausea
when he cautiously peered through the branches at the
scene on the riverbank. There were over a dozen bodies
scattered across the sandy shore in various grotesque postures of death. All had been scalped. Other bodies must
have floated down past them during the night for there
were more soldiers to be accounted for than what he saw
before him. He could see the pits, dug in the sand, that hid
the ambush from them as they had galloped past in their
haste to meet death in the middle of the river. Andy shuddered at the scene, though not because of the carnage. He
had seen death before, as well as the aftermath of an Indian
massacre. He shuddered because they had charged so
blindly into that river and he might have been responsible.
He sure as hell didn't see it coming. Little Wolf staged a
perfect ambush. Andy decided that no one would have seen
it coming and, consequently, there was no blame to be
shouldered. Having acquitted himself of any act of care-
lessness, he put the matter behind him. Back to the business at hand, he decided there was nothing there that would
be of use to him so he set out toward the post.

He was accustomed to long hours in the saddle but he
wasn't much for walking, his legs being short, his body
barrel-shaped. For that reason he was mighty thankful to
sight the column of cavalry topping a rise in the prairie
after he had walked for the better part of three hours. At
first, he dove for cover until he was sure they were soldiers,
having been fooled the day before by Little Wolf's braves.
Once they were close enough for positive identification, he
climbed up on top of a knoll and yelled until he got their
attention. As they approached, he recognized the slender,
unmistakable features of Lieutenant Lawson Perry.

"Where the hell have *you* been?" Lawson demanded,
reining his mount to a halt in front of the squat figure now
awaiting him on the knoll.

"Where the hell have *you* been?" Andy returned.

In the accounting of the previous day's events Andy
learned that Lawson's body of men had been ambushed
themselves shortly after Tom had left the column. This ex-

plained why Lawson had not ridden to Tom's rescue. The bunch that attacked Lawson were Sioux but, after discussing it, it seemed obvious that they were fighting in collusion with the band of Cheyenne that Little Wolf led. It was obvious that the two-pronged attack was not only premeditated, but well planned and executed. Lawson, however, was more fortunate than Andy and Tom. He was able to fight his way through after a running battle that consumed the entire afternoon, finally gaining the safety of the fort after losing half a dozen men. He figured Tom was dug in somewhere, in a defensive position, waiting for relief. That was the mission he was leading when he found Andy. He was shocked by the devastating news that of the detail that rode into the river ambush, only Andy and Tom survived and Tom was still a question mark.

Lawson's patrol turned out to be a burial party that day but Tom was still alive when Andy led them back down the river. He was out of his head with fever for the most part and probably didn't even know what was going on but his constitution proved strong, and after a few days, he was well on the way toward recovery. The doctor said the freezing water probably was the only thing that kept him from bleeding to death.

Having lost a great number of his men in one day's fighting, Captain Bluefield decided that he would be forced to cancel all work parties on the road to Montana. His men would be stretched thin enough just escorting the woodcutters and water details from the fort. These were vital to their survival and he refused to reduce the number of troops necessary to guard the fort while the other details were away. To make matters worse, he received word a week later that his unit was not the only one to suffer defeat at the hands of the Indians. More than eighty troopers, led by Captain William J. Fetterman, had been massacred at another post. Bluefield had served with Fetterman and knew him to be an officer disposed to being somewhat cocksure. The word was he had allowed himself to be lured into ambush by a band of Sioux, led by Chief High Backbone on the same day Perry and Allred's men were attacked. It was not a very joyous holiday season for the army.

CHAPTER 13

While it was not a proud time for the U.S. Army, it was a time of honor and glory for the Red Man. The Indians were fighting for their very existence, fighting to retain their lands and their freedom from the steady stream of white men from the East. The army, as well as immigrants, were killing off the Indian's source of food and constantly threatening to push him from his sacred hunting grounds. Red Cloud called upon the Cheyenne and the Arapaho to join him in his fight to resist the invaders. Many of them answered his call. Some, like the Cheyenne chief Black Kettle, still hoped for a peaceful solution to the problem and declined to take the warpath. But the fierce Cheyenne Dog Soldiers, led by Chief Bull Bear, joined with their Dakota brothers in the fight.

Little Wolf and his band of Cheyenne warriors were being sung about around the campfires of not only their own tribesmen, but also of their allies, the Sioux. There was little argument among the tribes that the Sioux, principally the Teton Dakota, were the main force that stood between the Indian way of life and the reservation and it was a great honor for the young warrior chief to be held in such high regard. Although still very young when he led his warriors in the raid on Fort Reno, Little Wolf's name was being mentioned in the same breath with Crazy Horse and High Backbone, both of whom had participated in the annihilation of Fetterman's troop.

Little Wolf had little sympathy for the white man. The Sioux had been guaranteed their hunting grounds in the first Treaty of Fort Laramie. The white man had not honored that treaty. What could he expect? Did he really think that Red Cloud would turn tail and run? Instead, Red Cloud had taught the army a lesson about the fighting heart of the Dakota. And still the lesson was not learned. Still the army violated Sioux hunting grounds and still they lost battle after battle.

When the mighty chiefs sat in council, the one name that held more power than Red Cloud, Crazy Horse or Bull Bear was that of Tatanka Iyotake, Sitting Bull. Little Wolf had heard many stories about the great chief. He was a Hunkpapa Sioux and had been a leader of the powerful Strong Heart Warrior Society, a society much like the Cheyenne Dog Soldiers of his own tribe. During that winter, the chiefs decided to unite under his leadership. Sitting Bull had led his warriors in many battles with the army and now he was to command the entire Sioux nation. Black Feather said Sitting Bull's medicine was even more powerful than Red Cloud's. It would be a great honor to fight beside this great chief.

So they fought side by side with the Sioux throughout the rest of that year, raiding the army patrols and work parties until, finally, the army conceded defeat and work was halted on the Bozeman Trail. The army could not guarantee safe passage for the trains of immigrants coming out from the East. The pilgrims would have to take the longer way west of the Big Horn Mountains. The Sioux had prevailed. A second Treaty of Fort Laramie was signed, giving the Sioux exclusive rights to all of the territory west of the Missouri. The army agreed to remove all its troops from the Powder River country but Red Cloud refused to sign the treaty until he had seen the soldiers leave and his warriors had burned the three forts on the Powder and Big Horn. An unsteady peace settled over the mountains as another winter began to seep into the narrow valleys.

Little Wolf sat before the campfire, his legs crossed in front of him, a flap of deer hide spread over his lap to hold the bolt and trigger assembly of his rifle. Most of the Sioux who had rifles never cleaned or oiled them. They would simply fire them until the weapons fouled and then use them as clubs. Little Wolf had learned to clean a rifle as a boy when he was with Lige Talbot and he never forgot the importance of it. He encouraged his warriors to do the same but he knew his words were wasted. They looked upon a rifle as a somewhat magical thing. There was never any thought toward learning the mechanics of it. Little Wolf glanced up from his cleaning and smiled as a familiar figure came striding toward him.

"I see you finally decided to crawl out of your robe to see what the daylight looks like."

Black Feather smiled sheepishly and settled himself next to his friend by the fire. "I have been thinking, not sleeping."

Little Wolf laughed. "This is very serious," he joked, but he could see that his friend was in earnest.

"I have been thinking," he continued, "that it has been a long time since I have seen my uncle. It is getting cold. Before long the snows will come to the mountains."

Little Wolf nodded. Although Black Feather did not mention his sister, Little Wolf guessed his friend longed to see her as well. They had been very close as children but, as was the custom, he did not mention her name once they had both reached maturity. In fact, Black Feather had not mentioned Morning Sky's name since Little Wolf had found their camp after leaving Squint Peterson and the Shoshone village. On that day, Little Wolf's heart was heavy because he thought that Morning Sky and her uncle had been killed in the massacre at Sand Creek and he bore the burden of giving the news to Black Feather. When he attempted to explain to his friend that he had been unable to come to their aid, Black Feather interrupted him with the startling news that both Morning Sky and his uncle managed to escape, along with Black Kettle and several others. This one piece of news brought a sense of relief to Little Wolf's mind, for he had borne the guilt of not being able to help one he had promised to protect. It had been a long time, four winters in fact, since he had last seen Morning Sky. As Black Feather talked, he tried to form a picture of her in his mind and found that he could not.

"We have fought many battles. It is time we rested, I think." Black Feather hesitated. "I want to see my people again. Will you go with me?"

Little Wolf shrugged his shoulders. He considered the invitation. He had not given much thought toward the coming winter. Unlike their Sioux allies, his small band of Cheyennes had no women to ease the long winter nights. Perhaps they would have been welcome in Sitting Bull's winter encampment but Little Wolf preferred to maintain a certain degree of independence. For that reason, he and his warriors had moved back up into the mountains once the fighting had ceased. After thinking about Black Feather's request for a few moments, he shrugged again and spoke.

"We have been away for a long time. How do you know where to find Morning Sky and your uncle?"

"A man rode into Red Cloud's camp two days ago. He had come from Black Kettle's village on the Washita in the Oklahoma territory. He said that he knew my uncle. He saw him in Black Kettle's camp."

Little Wolf thought about this for a moment. He really had no reason not to go. Like Black Feather, he was somewhat weary of the recent raiding parties and the battles with the soldiers. And now that there was supposedly a new peace, there should be little danger in undertaking the journey. Still, he hesitated. He had come to enjoy the safety of the high mountains where he could rest from the war without the necessity for being constantly alert. On the other hand, it would be pleasant to visit a Cheyenne village again with women, children, old men and dogs, eating pemmican and corn mush. He smiled and said, "We will go then."

This brought a wide smile of gratitude to Black Feather's face. He wanted very much to visit his people but he was reluctant to leave Little Wolf's side. They had come to be very close after fighting side by side for the past several years and Black Feather had come to think of him as a brother. It would be a long journey to Black Kettle's village, maybe twenty or more sleeps, and he did not want to leave his brother that long. It was winter and peace was always uncertain in these times. No one could say what tomorrow would bring.

Morning Sky walked leisurely along the narrow path through the willows that lined the river. She carried a pail made of buffalo hide which she would fill with water to cook with the next morning. She enjoyed this walk at the end of each day. The river was peaceful in the fading light of the short winter days and it always filled her soul with its peace. She was never bothered by the chill in the late afternoon air, wearing no blanket over her deerskin dress. The leggings she wore under her skirt were enough to keep her legs warm and she was never overly uncomfortable. Her hair, long and dark as night, was worn parted in the middle from her forehead to the nape of her neck and braided, then tied together behind her ears. Some of the women in the village painted the part in their hair with red or yellow. She preferred to leave hers unpainted. In fact, she wore no decorations on her face at all since she was not interested in attracting the attention of any young suitors, a fact that caused her uncle some dismay. There had been several men of the tribe who would gladly have given her uncle as many as ten horses for her hand, for she was a handsome and virtuous girl. But she refused to consider any of them. She knew that she was a burden in some respects to her uncle as he felt she was well past the age to marry, but he remained patient with her. She, in turn, did more than her share to help Yellow Swallow. If her uncle's wife resented her presence in the tipi, she never demonstrated it.

Kneeling on the riverbank, she lowered the skin bucket into the clear water, holding it by a rawhide thong. She watched, not really concentrating on the bucket, as it slowly began to fill and sink beneath the surface of the slowly moving current. All at once she shivered for no apparent reason. She was not cold, yet a strange feeling penetrated her thoughts and she was suddenly aware of a foreign presence. At first she was alarmed and she quickly looked around her. Then her gaze was caught by a slight movement in the cottonwoods across the narrow river and held there. In a moment a young warrior emerged from the trees. He was walking, leading his horse. She recognized him at once.

"Black Feather!" she cried out, forgetting tribal custom that prohibited brother and sister from speaking after maturity. Even if she had remembered, she would have called out to him anyway, for Morning Sky was uncommonly independent for a Cheyenne girl. Those silly customs were for the old people anyway. She sprang to her feet and literally jumped up and down in her excitement at seeing her brother. Waving her arms, she called his name over and over, "Black Feather! Black Feather!"

Suddenly she stopped stone-still, her brother's name still on her tongue. For now, behind her brother, a tall figure appeared. The unadorned buckskin tunic he wore could not hide the wide shoulders it covered. His dark hair was tied in two braids and crowned by a single eagle feather. He stood a full head taller than Black Feather. It could be no other than Little Wolf.

"Little Wolf." She whispered the name to herself and could not help but be aware of the sudden pounding in her bosom. But this was not the boy she had thrown herself so wantonly at four years before at Sand Creek. Even at this distance, she could see that this was indeed Little Wolf, the young warrior chief whose bravery had been sung before the campfire of her own village. Although gone from her people for many moons, word had been brought by messengers over the years of the deeds of their young Cheyenne raiders. But most of all, the songs were sung about Little Wolf. She had prayed to Man Above that she be permitted to see him again, that he would not die in battle before she could at least see him once again. And now her prayers had been granted. Little Wolf had returned!

Little Wolf had not expected the welcome extended to them by Black Kettle and the village. He expected to be received courteously, even warmly, for these were his people. But he and Black Feather were treated as conquering heroes. A feast and ceremonial dance were immediately planned to honor the two young warriors for their daring raids against the soldiers. Little Wolf was unexplainably attacked by a siege of modesty and declined to participate in the dance, preferring to remain a spectator. Black Feather, however, was eager to dance and sing of Little Wolf's raid on the soldier fort and the ambush by the river, deeds that had prompted the mighty Sioux chief Red Cloud to award him the eagle feather he now wore.

The people were joyous to have an occasion to celebrate for this had not been the best of times for Black Kettle's village. Away from the Sioux wars, Black Kettle had continued to petition for peace. But since he was still unwilling to live on the reservation, his people were regarded as renegades and were still harrassed by the army. Their crime against the U.S. goverment was their desire to live free, as they had always lived. But this was no longer a choice that they could freely make. The winter was going to be hard, and the buffalo were disappearing from the plains. The Cheyenne had been forced to give up most of their hunting grounds to the north and this winter found them still farther south. With the heavy snows still facing them, Black Kettle grieved for the suffering of his people. There would be little to eat in this land.

Although proud and pleased by the attention he and Black Feather received, Little Wolf still felt embarrassed at the same time. He was glad when the celebrating was over and he retired to the tipi of Black Feather's uncle to rest. When he finally drifted off, his sleep was deep and he did not awaken until the sun had climbed halfway up the tall cottonwoods near the river.

"So, the mighty warrior chief has finally decided to climb out of his buffalo robe," Morning Sky teased when he came out of the tipi. Although it was getting colder day by day, the women still cooked outside the tipi. "I suppose now you want me to get you something to eat."

Little Wolf smiled, embarrassed. For a reason he could not explain, he didn't feel comfortable around Morning Sky. She had grown up so much. He found it difficult to talk to her and he felt clumsy when in her presence. "I'm not hungry," he lied and mumbled that he needed the privacy of the woods.

"I will leave some food for you by the fire. If you're hungry, eat it. Maybe the dogs won't find it first." She smiled as she gazed after the tall figure disappearing around the side of the tipi. Little Wolf had grown to be a man. But she could still recognize the bashful stumblings of a young boy who had just discovered the mysteries of the opposite sex. His reaction to her pleased her.

In the days that followed, Little Wolf gradually relaxed into the routine of the village. The principal activity of every man in the village, consisting of perhaps seventy-five tipis, was to hunt for food. Black Feather and Little Wolf joined in this pursuit but there was very little game to find. They would hunt from sunup to sunset, ranging far from camp, only to return with a rabbit or two. Still, at night, he would sleep easily. He had lived almost as an animal for so long in the mountains that it was difficult to sleep without one ear to the ground in case the enemy might find his camp. His small band of warriors often moved their camp to avoid surprise attacks. The army always had Indian scouts, usually the hated Pawnee or Crow, searching for their whereabouts. Now, temporarily safe, he feared he was getting lazy, maybe too comfortable with village life. He even began to think of taking a wife. These were thoughts that had never invaded his mind before and he tried to dismiss them. In fact, he was almost terrified by them. He was in no position to take on the responsibility of a wife. When these thoughts came creeping back, he knew it was the sight of Morning Sky that spawned them. His mind kept taking him back to that night near Sand Creek when she had attempted to seduce him. She was but a child and he had playfully rebuked her offer. Should he have given it more serious consideration? No, he told himself. She was but a child. Besides, there was no way he could have a wife while fighting in the Powder River country. That had been the secret of their mobility: no women or children to slow them down. But now, even though he tried to stay away from her most of the day in an effort to appear disinterested, he found that his mind was filled with her almost constantly.

Chief Black Kettle called the elders of the village into his lodge to discuss the dismal prospects that lay before them. Black Feather's uncle was among those who sat in council with the chief. The U.S. government had reopened an old army fort, Fort Cobb, as an Indian refuge. It was said that the white chief, Hazen, offered food and supplies to peaceful tribes who agreed to settle there. It was decided that Black Kettle and several of the leaders of the tribe should go to Fort Cobb and talk to this man, Hazen. Unlike the Dog Soldiers, Black Kettle's band of Cheyenne had always sought peace, even after the Sand Creek massacre. The elders of the village conceded that Black Kettle should agree to bring his people into Fort Cobb and submit to the white man's rule. The delegation would leave the next morning for Fort Cobb.

Later that evening, when Black Feather's uncle returned to the tipi, he related the decision to his nephew and his friend. The news was distressing to Little Wolf and Black Feather.

"Uncle, this delegation will bring no good to our people. Surely you do not expect the white soldiers to keep their word." Black Feather was clearly upset. "Old Black Kettle has lost his teeth and wants to sit around the white man's fire and eat flour cakes."

His uncle looked at him with eyes tired from searching for bright futures that never came. He patiently replied, "You and your friend have been away from our village for many winters. Look around you. Do you see fat women and healthy babies? You have been in the big mountains. There, in the land of the Sioux, there may be buffalo and antelope and elk. You have hunted with us every day. Did you see deer? Did you see buffalo?"

Black Feather was exasperated. "Why do you stay in this sorry land? Why don't you lead the people north to join our Dakota brothers?"

His uncle shook his head sadly. "It is too late." His eyes saddened as he explained, "The soldiers would not let us leave and we cannot fight our way out. Most of our young warriors left us long ago to fight with the Dog Soldiers, just as you did. We have many old men and women. Soon the snows will come. Many would die on the trail."

"It is better to die fighting than to be a beggar at the white man's fort," Black Feather snorted although he knew his uncle spoke the truth. He had to accept the fact that it would probably be better for the village to go to the reservation if only to survive the winter. Perhaps in the spring they could break from captivity again. He sighed and turned to his friend. "What do you say, Little Wolf?"

Little Wolf had been silent during the discussion, listening to both men. He shrugged his shoulders as if it was none of his affair. "I am a guest in this village and would not dispute the wisdom of the elders. Perhaps it is best for the people to go to the reservation. It is better than starving the women and children. For myself, I know this. The white man's word is like the thistle on the prairie. It bends with the direction of the wind and it changes as the wind changes. The soldiers said you would be safe at Sand Creek. The soldiers said that no wagon trains would come through our hunting grounds. The soldiers said there would be peace.

Now your people are camped in these hills, waiting for the winter snows to starve them because the white man wants our hunting grounds for himself. So I say, I do not trust the white man's word. I will not go to the fort."

"I go with Little Wolf!" Black Feather exclaimed.

There was no further discussion of the matter that night. Black Feather's uncle only shook his head sadly; the look in his eyes told of youth long lamented when he too would have gone with Little Wolf. On the other side of the fire, Morning Sky sat beside Yellow Swallow. The two women sat silently working on a fox skin that would become a warm headdress for her uncle. Though she did not comment, Morning Sky made up her mind that she too would go with Little Wolf, whether she was invited or not. She did not intend to wait another four years to see him again.

When Black Kettle's delegation returned from Fort Cobb, the news they brought back to their people was not good. They had met with Hazen. Black Kettle offered to bring his people into the reservation but Hazen rejected his offer. Hazen told the disheartened chief that he had no authority to let his people come in because Black Kettle's band was considered hostile and Hazen didn't have the authority to sign a peace treaty with the chief. In fact, he further advised Black Kettle that General Philip H. Sheridan was even then on his way to find his band and punish them for not coming into the reservation when they were first instructed to do so. Black Kettle pleaded in vain that he had always sought peace. Hazan dismissed the delegation, saying there was nothing he could do for them. The old chief's face and those of his party were etched in solemn lines of defeat when they rode into the circle of tipis on the Washita. A meeting was called in the council lodge that night.

Since this was a meeting of grave importance, a pipe was passed around the inner circle of elders. Younger members of the tribe, Black Feather and Little Wolf among them, were invited to sit behind the elders. After the pipe had been offered to the four points of the earth and smoked, Black Kettle spoke.

"My brothers, I have talked to the white chief Hazen. He has said that we are not welcome in the new fort." A low murmur of concern rose up from the circle of tribal members crowded inside the lodge. Black Kettle raised his hand to silence his people. "He says that he cannot sign the peace with us because we did not go to the reservation when the white father told us to go. Even now, a new army chief is riding against us with many blue coats to kill us and destroy our tipis. We must decide what we must do to defend our people."

An old warrior seated across the inner circle from the chief spoke. "The white man lies. The army blue coats don't like to fight in the snow. It is too cold for them."

A younger man called Four Legs jumped to his feet. "What you say is true but I talked with a Kiowa warrior two sleeps ago. He said he had seen many blue coats to the north on the big river called the Canadian. These could be the soldiers Hazen warned of."

The old warrior replied, "The soldiers have never liked to leave their warm fires when the snow is deep. The Kiowa most likely saw a scout party or a wood-cutting party."

"No," Four Legs insisted. "This man said there were many horses and two of the guns that shoot two times."

Another brave offered, "The Canadian is too far north for the soldiers to be coming to fight us. Our village is the farthest south. There are Arapaho and Kiowa villages north of us. The soldiers hold no danger for us."

The discussion continued for the better part of an hour. In the end it was decided that, as a precaution, the village should move further south in case the white chief Hazen spoke the truth and this new threat, headed by General Sheridan, was indeed searching for Black Kettle.

Just before the meeting was ended, Four Legs rose to his feet again and said, "I want to hear what the great warrior chief Little Wolf has to say on the matter."

Little Wolf said nothing for a few moments while all eyes around the council turned toward him. Up to that moment, he had been no more than an interested spectator, considering himself a guest and one who had already made up his mind to start back north before the sun in the morning. Now, considering Four Legs' request, he paused to decide what, in fact, he did think about the decision facing Black Kettle's village. He could not insult the old chief and his council by voicing his personal thoughts, that he thought the men of the village shamed themselves by going begging to the white man's fort. He thought a moment more then rose to his feet. There was a low murmur of approval when he stood erect before the circle. His tall, lean bearing alone commanded their attention.

"My brothers, I weep for your hungry children. It saddens my heart to see your hunters search the land for buffalo where there are none. I know that you must do what your hearts tell you is right. But I cannot speak for you. I can only speak for Little Wolf. Before the sun gets up in the morning, I will be on my way back to the high mountains. I am a warrior. I must go where I can better fight the white soldiers who killed my father, Spotted Pony, and my mother, Buffalo Woman. I will never live on the white man's reservation, begging the white man for food. It is not for me to say what you must do but I believe that it is better to go back to the old ways. The whole tribe never came together in the winter in the old days. We used to break up into our smaller bands and scatter into the hills, back toward the high mountains, where the soldiers cannot find us."

There was a long silence when he finished speaking. Then some of the younger men, Four Legs foremost among them, began to nod their heads in approval. "Little Wolf is right. We should strike the tipis and go to the north in smaller groups so the soldiers cannot follow all of us."

Black Kettle remained silent for a few minutes while the elders talked anxiously among themselves, some arguing for Little Wolf's advice, some against. When the discussion began to approach a state of general confusion, Black Kettle raised his hand and called for silence. When all had quieted, he spoke.

"Little Wolf speaks with the fire of youth. I think it is right for him to travel to the distant mountains but it is too late for the old men, the women and the children. There is not enough food to eat now. Our people will die in the snows even if the soldiers do not find us. No, it is better for the tribe to move farther south, away from the soldiers."

After discussing it for a while longer, the elders of the village sided with the old chief once again and voted to stay together. But all agreed that it might be prudent to move the village. So it was decided to start making preparations to leave the next morning, never suspecting the devastation about to descend upon them.

CHAPTER 14

First Lieutenant Tom Allred sat stiffly in the saddle, hunched against the biting cold of the November wind sweeping across the rolling prairie. The wound in his back had long since healed but the cold weather made it throb like a toothache. He had been lucky that day that Andy Coulter had been there to pull him out of the river. He missed Andy. When he was sent back to the hospital at Fort Laramie, Andy had remained with his old troop, which had gone on to Fort Lincoln after Fort Phil Kearny was abandoned to the Sioux. Now Tom wasn't sure he liked his new unit. He was back in the Seventh Cavalry, led by the flamboyant Colonel George Armstrong Custer. Tom's immediate superior was Captain Stewart Payne, a man who had seen service under Custer during the war between the states. Captain Payne's troop had joined other forces at Fort Dodge which were being assembled to mount an expedition against the hostiles believed to be camped in the Antelope Hills in Oklahoma territory.

He still felt like an outsider in his new regiment, though it didn't bother him unduly. It was a natural thing. Most of these men had been together for a couple of years, even before Payne assumed command. Payne seemed a fair enough officer, Tom had no complaints there. And, thank goodness, he had very little contact with Colonel Custer, or Longhair, as the Indians called him. From what he could see at long range, Custer was a mite too impressed with himself for Tom's taste. But as long as he didn't have to report directly to him, Tom didn't care how eccentric the man was. His thoughts were interrupted by a trooper galloping back toward him.

"Captain's compliments, sir. The captain says to walk 'em a spell."

Tom turned to the sergeant beside him. "You heard the man," he said.

"Yessir," the sergeant replied dryly and gave the order to dismount.

Tom welcomed the order; much longer in the saddle and he feared he would be frozen in that position. It felt like thousands of needles were pricking his feet as he took each step. Gradually some feeling returned to his toes as the blood began to circulate once more. He glanced down at the snow he was slogging through. No more than half a foot deep, it was trampled and dirty from the horses and men ahead of him. Damn! he thought. It's too damn cold to be stomping around out here in the middle of nowhere. Veterans of the Western campaign told him that in the old days, they only fought in the summertime. When the snows came, there was very little activity on either side, the army or the Indians. Tom could guess with a great deal of assurance why that was no longer the case. The army had had their rumps kicked too many times trying to fight the Plains Indians on the Indians' terms. The Cheyenne Dog Soldiers and the Sioux warriors on their fleet ponies could strike and disappear before the blue coats could regroup and pursue them. Then the Indians seemed to simply dissipate into the rocks and hills when the army searched for them. The generals had finally concluded that the only way to defeat the Red Man was to attack his villages when the tribes went into their winter camps. Tom didn't care much for this kind of warfare because more times than not it involved wanton massacre of women and children. Annihilation seemed to be the order of the day and this man Custer seemed to want to exterminate the Indian all by himself.

When they left Fort Supply, a temporary camp only recently set up, they had marched out into a howling snowstorm. Custer himself led the march. Their orders were simple; look for Indians and kill them, since all Indians not on the reservation were considered hostile. The column marched southwest along Wolf Creek before turning further south toward the Antelope Hills. When the storm let up, a scouting party was sent out ahead to look for sign. About midday the scouts returned with the news they had found an Indian trail across the prairie toward the Washita

River. This was the news Custer was waiting for and soon Tom heard the bugle sound officers' call.

While the column stood down for the noon meal, all officers assembled in a tent hastily set up in a grove of cottonwoods. In the center of a circle of his subordinates stood Colonel Custer. A man of average height, he appeared taller than he actually was because of his thin, chisled features. His face was clean-shaven except for a mustache that tapered to a fine point on either side of his chin. He wore a broad-brimmed campaign hat, cocked to one side, from under which his long tresses hung down to his shoulders. He remained silent for a long moment but, as he gazed around his circle of officers, his clear blue eyes almost sparkled. It was as if he knew a secret that no one else knew. He was by no means a handsome man but Tom had to admit he was impressive. When he was satisfied that he had every man's undivided attention, he spoke.

"Gentlemen, our scouts report a sizable hostile trail heading toward the Washita. It's my guess we'll find Black Kettle camped at the end of that trail. Our scouting reports indicate he is wintering somewhere in this area." He paused to gaze around the circle again, obviously looking for excitement in their faces. "We may have them catnapping!" Again he paused to test the reaction to this news. When some of the more astute of his staff realized that he was looking for a positive response, they displayed some emotion, even if it was less than genuine. This pleased their commander and he continued, "If we press on we can be upon them before they know we're even in the area."

"Sir," one of the officers pointed out, "the Washita is almost a day's ride from here."

"That is correct, Mr. Raintree. But if we leave our supply wagons here, we can cover the distance in a night march and be ready to attack the village at dawn."

Inwardly, Tom groaned. A night march meant a long, cold, sleepless night in the saddle. And there was the possibility that there was no village at the end of the Indian trail.

"Mr. Allred."

Tom jerked his head up in surprise to hear his name singled out.

"It may be of some interest to you to know there may be a certain Cheyenne war chief visiting in Black Kettle's camp.

One of my scouts is almost certain that the renegade Little Wolf is with Black Kettle." He smiled as he added, "I believe you had a little run-in with that gentleman, didn't you?"

This captured Tom's attention straightaway. "Little Wolf!" he blurted, then, "Yessir, I have met the gentleman." Without thinking, he reached up and rubbed his chest where the bullet had lodged after entering his back.

"Then I know you'll be keen to proceed after the bastard as soon as possible." Still smiling, he went on to outline the order of march and dismissed his officers to see to their men.

The colonel had suceeded in striking a deeper chord inside Lieutenant Tom Allred than he had imagined. In spite of Andy Coulter's argument that Tom was not to blame for leading his men into a crossfire in the middle of that river, Tom still felt responsible for the lives lost on that bleak afternoon. Little Wolf had set that trap and Tom had spent many a restless night at Little Wolf's expense. Now, far south of that river near Fort Reno, he was to cross paths with the Cheyenne war chief again. Tom could feel his heart pounding in the scar in his back. This time it would be different.

They marched straight through the night, following the trail across the snow-covered prairie. There had been no more than a few flurries of snow after the noon meal with a gradual clearing of the sky. By nightfall the puffy clouds had drifted away, leaving a deep starlit night. There was no moon but the stark white prairie reflected the starlight, giving the long dark column of soldiers a ghostly quality. There was very little conversation, just the soft plodding of the horses' hooves and an occasional clink of metal against the constant creaking of saddle leather. Sometime after midnight, the column halted at the foot of a low line of hills and the order to dismount was quietly passed along the line of cavalry. On the other side of the hills an Indian village lay in a bend of the Washita River. In the darkness, Custer deployed his troops before the unsuspecting village and waited for the dawn.

Little Wolf, awakened from a sound sleep, started to speak but a hand was gently placed across his lips and a voice whispered softly, "Shhh . . . Do not wake the others."

He blinked hard, trying to clear the sleep from his eyes. "Morning Sky?" he whispered, his still-sleepy brain trying to grasp the situation.

"Yes. Come, follow me. Do not wake the others."

"What is it? What is wrong?" he asked as he raised up on one elbow.

"Nothing is wrong. Just follow me. I must talk to you." She turned and moved silently past her sleeping uncle and his wife. Puzzled, he followed, taking up his buffalo robe to protect against the cold night outside. He glanced briefly at the sleeping lump next to him that was Black Feather to see if he too was awake, but there was no sign of life under the heavy skins.

Outside the tipi he found Morning Sky waiting for him. Before he could speak, she motioned to him to follow and then turned and walked briskly toward the river. *The woman has gone crazy,* he thought, but followed after her. The night sky was dark. There was no moon and the stars were so bright that they appeared to be just beyond the tops of the cottonwoods that lined the banks of the river. The air was cold and crisp when he breathed deeply to fill his lungs in an effort to awaken his senses. Just ahead of him, Morning Sky continued her brisk pace, taking a path she used every day to fetch water. Just before she came to the edge of the river, she turned and walked along the bank. When she reached a thicket of small trees and scrub, she paused briefly to make sure he was following then, bending low, she made her way into the middle of the thicket. He followed.

He found her kneeling on her heavy robe, which she had spread over the snow between the laurels. She motioned for him to sit down. "Morning Sky . . ." he started, but she stopped his question by placing her hand gently on his lips.

"Let me talk," she whispered softly. "I know that you leave when the sun comes again." She hesitated a moment, forming her thoughts. "I cannot bear the thought of seeing you leave me again." Amazed, he started to speak again. Again she silenced him. "Let me say this. I have been thinking about what I want to say ever since you returned." He settled back, dumbfounded, and heard her out. "I love you, Little Wolf. I have loved you for as long as I can remember, and in my heart, I have been your wife ever since we were together at Sand Creek. I think if you will listen to your heart, it will tell you that you love me too." She paused to let him speak.

His mind was reeling. He didn't know what to say. His brain was being bombarded with so many different emotions that he was unable to sort out his confusion. She had taken him so much by surprise that he had not had time to build a facade to maintain a sense of dignity. Instead, he fairly stammered, "Morning Sky, I . . ."

"You do love me?" she interrupted, seeing that he might never be able to finish his statement.

"What?" he stammered. "Morning Sky, you shouldn't ask me that. Have you no shame?"

"Don't talk to me about shame. I don't care about shame. You say you are going away again. I must know what your heart tells you. Do you love me or not?"

"Yes," he blurted, then, "I mean, no . . . I don't know." The girl's boldness mesmerized him.

"Then you do love me. Good. I knew you did if you would only listen to your heart."

"I didn't say I loved you." He didn't know why he was arguing the point. He had thought about her ever since he had returned. Still, her aggressiveness unnerved him and the fact that the matter was being handled backwards left him feeling defensive. After all, he reasoned, if he wanted to marry her, he should be the aggressive one and go to her uncle with gifts and horses—and it wouldn't be in the middle of the night when a man was half asleep.

"Then you don't love me?" she demanded and settled back on her heels, waiting for an answer.

He didn't know what to say. He looked at her, exasperated. He could no longer deny his feelings for her. He sighed and said, "Yes, I love you."

Again, her response confounded him. Instead of joy, she exhibited anger as she demanded, "Then why haven't you come to my uncle to ask for me?"

Again he was on the defensive. He didn't answer at first because he didn't know for sure that he loved her until this moment. "I could not take a wife with me. My warriors and I have been living like the wolf and the bear in the mountains, fighting the soldiers. It was no place for a woman. It is too dangerous. Besides, I did not own enough horses to offer your uncle.''

She did not answer at once. When she spoke, it was with a tenderness he had not seen before. "I am your wife, Little Wolf, no matter if you give not even one horse for me.''

He didn't know what to say. It didn't matter because she did not wait for his response. She reached up, taking his hands in hers, and pulled him down to her. "I was meant to be your wife. If you leave me in the morning, I want you to leave me with child. If the soldiers kill you, at least I will have part of you.'' Her lips were almost touching his as she whispered softly, "Come, we will marry each other tonight.''

He had no choice but to yield to the overpowering desire for her that suddenly engulfed him. It was dark in the thicket but the starlight sprinkled enough light to catch tantalizing glimpses of her firm, rounded breast as she lay back upon the outspread robe. She shivered slightly when his hand sought the smooth curve of her hips. As quickly as he could, he slipped out of his buckskins and pulled his robe over the two of them, making a warm tent for them. At first he was overanxious, fumbling to feel her breasts and thighs and in between her thighs, such was his inexperience. "Wait,'' she calmed him and guided his entry into her, slowly and tenderly, letting him feel the warmth of her body, loving him patiently until he could hold himself no longer. Then she rose to his passionate thrusts and met his with her own and they became one.

When his passion was spent, he lay beside her and let the natural urge to sleep take him. Before she slept, she gazed at him for a long while and smiled to herself. My mighty warrior, she thought. *Now he looks more like a little boy*. She was pleased. She did not have to be told that this was his first time, just as it was hers.

A little before sunrise, a light snow began to fall. Tom pulled his hat down to keep the flakes from landing on his chin. Bored and tired of waiting and, at the same time, apprehensive about the attack that would be ordered at dawn, he looked around him at his men. Silent now, they awaited the order to attack. A few of them, most of the older veterans, had managed to catch a few minutes' sleep and they were already covered by a thin blanket of new-fallen snow. *They look like graves,* he thought.

Restless, he pulled his Spencer carbine from its boot and checked it for at least the third time before slipping it back in the saddle boot. His assignment was to maintain the left flank of the assault, closing on the south side of the sleeping village, making sure there was no escape downriver. Custer had issued orders to kill *all* hostiles. He did not differentiate between male and female or, for that matter, adult and child. Tom was not comfortable with this. He thought of himself as a good soldier and a good soldier follows orders. But he could not see any threat coming from women and children. His was not necessarily a popular viewpoint so he kept his thoughts to himself. Still, he wished that the fighting took place on the open field of combat, not in the villages. Suddenly he shook his head as if to shake such thoughts from his mind. *Orders are orders,* he thought. *Thinking is for the high brass.*

First light in the eastern sky brought a messenger from Custer running down the line of stamping horses, their breath sending smoky clouds from their nostrils. The messenger found Tom and informed him that the colonel wished for him to arouse his troops and prepare to mount. The predawn stillness was broken by the sounds of groaning leather as the men stepped up into the saddle. Here and there a horse tried to shy away from its rider, its stamping hooves muffled by the snow, followed by the low sound of cursing from the rider. "Quiet!" someone whispered. A horse snorted and pranced as a trooper tried to hold his head down with the reins. Horses and men were ready to ride, tired of waiting in the cold, dark night. Tom instructed his sergeant.

"All right, Sergeant Porter, when you hear that bugle, I want you to wheel the troop around that bluff on the left. We're going to maintain our formation till we cross the river. Then I want a sweep right through the village."

"Yessir. Kill anything that moves?"

"That's the order," Tom replied with no emotion in his voice.

In the sleeping village, a dog barked. Soon it was joined by several others as the muffled noises of the regiment moving into position were transported on the wind. The snow stopped and the sun sent its first exploratory rays over the prairie. Custer, in the saddle and riding back and forth in front of his troops, realized the village would soon be aware of his presence so he gave the order to attack.

Tom, even though poised and waiting for the signal to charge, was startled by the blare of the bugle as it rent the cold November air. An explosion of men and horses immediately followed. His pistol raised, Tom kicked his horse into a gallop and led his troopers down the bluff, mud and snow flying from the churning hooves. The soldiers began firing into the village even before they had crossed the river, laying down a murderous rain of lead upon the hapless Cheyenne camp.

It happened so suddenly, with such impact on his sleeping brain, that Little Wolf reacted like an animal whose instinct tells it it is about to die. He tried to jump to his feet to defend himself but the heavy buffalo robe, now covered with a layer of fresh snow, caught in the branches and tripped him, making him stumble to his knees. By the time he cleared the fog of sleep from his brain and remembered where he was, the line of blue coats had already swept beyond him. The thicket where he and Morning Sky lay was too dense to gallop through, so the line of soldiers had parted and charged to either side. He looked back quickly to make sure Morning Sky was safe. She struggled to dress herself, her eyes wide with fright. The gunfire was a steady roar now; individual shots were not discernable. The terrible din of the slaughter was punctuated by the screams of the women and children.

"Black Feather!" he gasped. "I must go!" He looked again at Morning Sky. "You will be safe if you stay here." He got up to leave.

"Little Wolf! No!" She threw her arms around his legs. "You cannot help them! It is too late!"

He hesitated for a moment while he took inventory of his situation and his ability to help his brothers. He had no weapons except the skinning knife he always wore on the buckskin tunic he had hastily slipped over his head the night before. No rifle, not even a bow—what good could he do? Still, Black Feather was in the village. He must go to his aid. Even as he thought it, he could see wave after

wave of blue coats galloping through the helpless village.
Sabers flashed as the morning sun caught momentary re-
flections of their slashing arcs. A steady din of rifle and
pistol fire rumbled across the shallow river like thunder.
Already, many of the lodges were blazing. The screams of
the women and children pierced the din of the carnage as
they fled in panic, only to be met by another line of soldiers
sweeping in the opposite direction.

"Black Kettle!" he gasped when he saw the old chief
and his wife scramble up on a horse and attempt to escape
across the river. They made it to the center of the water
before a barrage of bullets cut them both down.

Little Wolf felt helpless. This was the second time he had
been forced to witness the massacre of his village while
happenstance prevented him from being a part of it. His
blood was hot with anger but his common sense told him
once again that it was useless to offer up his own life in
the hope of killing one or more of the soldiers before they
killed him. Morning Sky was right. It was too late. His
concern now must be to try to keep her safe and to escape
this massacre.

"You are right," he told her. "We must live to revenge
our brothers for this treachery." Although still trembling
with rage, he began to think calmly, deciding what his next
move should be. At the moment they were safe in the
thicket but his instincts told him that as soon as the slaughter was completed, the soldiers would ferret out every con-
ceivable hiding place along the riverbank. It would be best
to escape while the shooting was still at a fever pitch.

He moved on all fours through the thicket to the edge
of the river where he stopped to survey the bluffs on the
far side. He desperately needed a weapon and a horse, two
horses if he could find them, and his instincts told him that
there was probably a rear guard of some kind behind the
bluffs. The attack had come from that direction, so maybe
there was a supply wagon or some form of support for the
troopers there. If that was not the case, they would just
have to make it on foot. "Come," he whispered and
crawled out of the bushes and down into the shallow riverbank. She followed without hesitation.

There was cover in the trees on the opposite side of the
river if they could make it through the waist-deep water

without being observed by the soldiers upstream. Little
Wolf waded as rapidly as he could, ignoring the cold shock
of the water as it cut right to the bone. Quickly, he scrambled across the opposite sand shore and dived into the un-
derbrush. Once he was safely hidden, he turned to watch
Morning Sky. She had fallen behind in the icy current and
was still struggling to make the shore. *Hurry!* he thought
and was about to go back to help her when a movement
out of the corner of his eye stopped him. There, on the far
side of the thicket they had just come from, a soldier, an
officer by the look of his uniform, wheeled his horse as he
caught sight of the Indian girl struggling to crawl to the
brush on the other side of the river. The soldier stopped
and drew a rifle from his saddle boot. Little Wolf's heart
seemed to stop as the drama unfolded before his eyes. The
soldier was too far away. He could not reach him in time.
He looked back at Morning Sky. "Run! Run!" he called
out. She had no chance. The soldier could not miss from
that distance. Little Wolf held his breath and waited for
the shot to come. There was no shot. Little Wolf looked
back at the officer. He was not moving, seeming to be in
a trance. He raised the rifle halfway up to his shoulder then
stopped. Slowly, he lowered the rifle, wheeled his horse and
galloped off in the opposite direction, back toward the village. Little Wolf did not pause to contemplate the soldier's
actions. As soon as Morning Sky gained the protection of
the trees, he motioned for her to follow and ran toward the
bluffs. Their only hope was to run as far and as fast as
they could.

Tom reined his horse up hard to keep from running
down a bawling Indian child of perhaps three or four years
of age. He then spurred his mount back toward the lodges,
now engulfed in flames. This was not his idea of war, this
slaughter of women and children. He wasn't sure why he
had spared the Indian woman back at the river. She was
his enemy, a hostile, and she was escaping. He should have
shot her. But he had found that he just didn't have the
stomach for it. There had been enough slaughter. She
looked half drowned anyway, he told himself. She was not
alone, he knew that. He had heard someone call to her
from the trees on the far side. Still he chose to look the

other way. There were enough dead already. He galloped back to join his troop.

"Lieutenant!" He turned to see Sergeant Porter charging after him. "Up on the ridge!" Tom looked in the direction pointed out.

"Damn!" he uttered. Up above the burning village, hundreds of hostiles were assembling. He immediately looked to his rear on the other side of the river. More hostiles were gathering. He wondered where they came from. Soon they would be surrounded and it was apparent the Indians would greatly outnumber them. As he thought it, he heard the bugler recalling the regiment.

Porter pulled up beside him. "The colonel said to form up the column and prepare to march."

"March? March where?" As if in answer to Tom's question, the bugle sounded officers' call. He wheeled and made for the river where he could see Custer's white horse among a circle of his officers. The colonel was already giving orders to withdraw to the opposite riverbank, no doubt sizing up the gathering force of hostiles and realizing that their position would soon be untenable. Custer had been caught by surprise. The Indians now moving to surround the column of soldiers were evidently from villages downstream. They showed no signs of an immediate attack, even though they already outnumbered the soldiers. It was only a matter of time, however, for they were obviously out for revenge for the atrocities committed on the Cheyenne village. Tom could see the young braves, riding wildly back and forth beyond the bluffs, their ponies painted, feathers flying in the wind. He figured the only thing that was saving the troops was the fact that evidently the hostiles were not organized. They must have been several different bands from different villages, alerted by the sound of gunfire on the Cheyenne camp.

"Gentlemen," Custer announced, "we find ourselves surrounded and cut off from our supply wagons." Tom could swear there was a twinkle in the colonel's eye as he scanned the faces of his officers to test their reaction to such news. Then he grandly assured them that he would lead them out of this potential danger. "We will form up the column and march in an orderly fashion downstream. I want the hostiles to think we mean to advance upon their villages. When it is dark, we will double back and proceed to Camp Supply."

"Sir," Captain Payne said, "Major Elliott took a detachment after some of the hostiles escaping to the north."

Custer seemed perturbed. "I know. I ordered him to cut off their escape."

"Well, sir, he ain't back yet. Hadn't we better go look for him?"

"Captain Payne, it is my duty and responsibility to tend to the welfare of the regiment and that would deem it necessary to move the column out as soon as possible. Major Elliott is a seasoned officer. He'll make his way back to the column before dark." He raised his hand to indicate the conference was ended. "Let's get moving before somebody organizes that mob of savages on the bluffs. It is imperative that we move out at once and in an orderly fashion." He winked at Captain Payne and added, "Indians are like a pack of mongrel dogs. If they see you run, they'll chase after you. We'll show them our strength. They'll think twice before charging this column."

Tom glanced back at the burning village as the column started out downriver. The picture of that engagement, as Custer called it, would live in his mind for a long time. They had left no one alive in that camp. Bodies were strewn everywhere. The dead were left where they fell; men, women, children, horses, even dogs were not allowed to escape Custer's scythe. Black Kettle's band was no more. They had been annihilated. Custer would refer to that day's encounter as a dangerous battle and a glorious victory in the war against the hostiles. As for Tom, he thought himself a good soldier but he was not proud of that day's work. There was one disappointment for him, however. The information that the Cheyenne war chief, Little Wolf, was in the camp was evidently false. At least none of the bodies was identified as that of Little Wolf's. When Tom asked if anyone had seen the man before, Captain Payne said no, but the scouts said that Little Wolf was really a white man raised by the Cheyenne. Tom remarked that he had seen him at a distance and he didn't look like a white man to him.

Colonel Custer had been correct in guessing the column would not be attacked as long as they were on the march downriver. Many of the hostiles that surrounded them surmised that their villages might be the next target and departed to alert their people to the impending danger. When darkness descended, they doubled back to pick up their supply wagons in the Antelope Hills and then retreated to Camp Supply. Major Elliott's detachment never rejoined the column. Word came back some time later that the entire detachment had been cut off and surrounded by a large force of hostiles from one of the villages downriver. The troopers were forced to take up a position in a tall grassy draw where they were eventually slaughtered. Custer dismissed the unfortunate incident as the price of war but vowed to avenge every brave soul who gave his life that day.

CHAPTER 15

Trapping was only fair the spring after Squint and Little Wolf had parted company. Maybe the streams were getting trapped-out in his valley. Maybe his heart just wasn't in it anymore. Whatever the reason, Squint decided it was time to head back to civilization for a spell. It was getting too damn dangerous for a lone white man in these parts and he was getting tired of looking over his shoulder, half expecting to see some damn fool Injun coming for his scalp. Maybe part of the problem with his attitude was caused by just having had someone to winter with. He'd gotten out of the habit of living alone. Squint missed having Little Wolf to talk to.

"The damn army has got the Injuns all stirred up," he confided to his mule, Sadie, while he drew the rope down tight over the furs on her back. He had taken to talking to Sadie and Joe, his horse, more and more lately, another sign that told him it was time to come out of the mountains for a while. "We'll just head on back east a'ways, maybe to Laramie, see what's going on."

The packing done, he looked around his camp to make sure the fire had died and everything looked right. It was the best camp he had ever made and he expected to return someday to this secret hideout in the rocks. Satisfied that everything was tidy, he bade farewell to the tiny stream and the mountain fortress and thanked them for their hospitality, a custom he had picked up from the Indians. He stepped up on Joe, took one last look around and led Sadie through the opening in the rocks.

As it turned out, Squint didn't make it as far as Fort Laramie. After three days of cautious traveling, being careful not to cross paths with any Sioux scouting parties, he

struck the North Platte at Deer Creek Station. This was a
major crossing for folks heading west on the Emigrant Trail
to Oregon and Squint found that the number of log buildings had grown since he had last seen it. The trading post,
owned by a French Canadian named Bisonette, looked
about the same except for some telegraph wires strung up
on the side of the building. That would explain the small
detachment of soldiers Squint noticed camped down below
the corral. He had to admit to himself that he was surprised. He would have thought the Indians would have
burned Bisonette out by now. Off to the side, about fifty
yards from the building, a train of thirty or forty wagons
was circled up. From the looks of things, Squint estimated
the wagons had been waiting there for five or six days. The
livestock were bunched off toward the river, grazing, and
there were clothes hanging on lines strung up between the
wagons, like folks had camped for a while.

He sat for a moment while he took all this in. "Pilgrims,"
he muttered. Joe snorted in reply as if he shared his mas-
ter's disgust for the torrent of settlers cutting across the
prairie. He nudged Joe's ribs with his heels, guiding him
around the wagons and toward a large rough structure
bearing a hand-carved sign that proclaimed it as Mott's.
There were several horses tied up to the hitching rail and
Squint tied on, making sure Sadie was on the far side of
Joe at the end of the rail. Sadie was getting cranky and
Squint was afraid she might decide to take a nip out of a
strange horse if it got too close.

"Welcome, neighbor. What can I do for you?"

Squint stood in the doorway for a few moments before
his eyes adjusted to the dim light inside. He found himself
in one large room with a counter running the entire width.
The room was divided by some blankets hanging from the
ceiling. These served as curtains to separate the store from
the saloon so the womenfolk from the wagon trains could
come into the store part without feeling like they were
going into a saloon. He glanced back at the woman who
had greeted him. She was a large woman, dressed in a
man's shirt and pants tucked into a pair of mule skinner's
boots. Her hair, blonde at one time in her life, was streaked
with gray and piled up on her head in a knot. Her smile

was cheerful enough as her eyes sized up the large mountain man standing in the doorway.

"How do, ma'am. I got me some pelts I'd like to get rid of. I figured I might have to go back to Laramie to trade 'em. Tell you the truth, I didn't think Bisonette would still be standing. I didn't reckon on two trading posts at Deer Creek."

The woman's smile broadened. "Mister, you'll do better trading with us than toting them furs all the way back to Laramie. I reckon we're giving one or two cents a pound more than you could get back there and a penny a pound better than Bisonette. My husband does the trading. He'd be glad to take a look at 'em." She waited while Squint pondered the offer.

"Well, I reckon it wouldn't hurt to hear his price." He wanted to get rid of the furs as soon as he could because his bankroll was down to small change and he sorely needed some things. He didn't have much confidence in himself as a horse trader and he didn't want to get taken on the price of his winter's work, but it would be nice to have some cash.

"Mott!" she bellowed and, in a moment, a gnarly-looking little man pulled the blanket aside that separated the store from the saloon. Upon seeing Squint standing in front of the counter, he walked over beside his wife.

"Yessir?" He smiled up at Squint with stained teeth that told of long years of chewing tobacco. "What can I do for you?"

Mrs. Mott spoke up, "He's got some furs you need to look at. I told him you'd give him as good a price as he could get in Laramie."

The little man grinned and scratched his bald head. "I reckon I better." He winked at his wife. "He's a big'un, ain't he?" Turning back to Squint, he asked, "Where you got 'em?"

Squint motioned toward the door. "On a mule out yonder."

After a few minutes' dickering, the trade was made. The furs didn't bring as much as Squint had hoped for but, then again, he had already resigned himself to getting the short end of the stick from Mott. He didn't care as long as he got enough to take care of his needs for the time being.

He had a line of credit and a little bit of cash to buy a bath and a drink of whiskey.

After the trading was all done, Mott and Squint settled up and Mott returned to the saloon side of the building. "Bring some of that cash money over here," Mott called back over his shoulder before he slid through the blankets. "I got some honest-to-God drinking whiskey all the way from St. Louis. The first one's on the house, since you're a stranger here."

"I reckon I'll be over there soon enough but first I want to get me a hot bath and change into my clean clothes."

Mrs. Mott walked over to the back door of the store and called a boy of about ten or twelve who had been busy chopping firewood. "Lemuel, heat up some water and fill the bathtub for this gentleman here." Turning back to Squint, she said, "The bath is twenty-five cents. That includes use of the soap and towel. You can take your horse and mule around back by the bathhouse if it'd make you feel better. I don't reckon anybody'd bother 'em though."

Squint smiled. "Much obliged but I 'spect they'll be safe enough. That ole mule is a mite particular about who steps up on Joe." He paid the woman and went outside to get his saddle pack and rifle. Then he headed for the outbuilding the boy carried the water to. In the middle of the yard there was a huge iron pot sitting over a fire. The boy was dipping the hot water from it for Squint's bath. It appeared the pot served more than one function. Squint guessed it was used to wash clothes and probably as a catchall during hog killing too. "Don't get it too hot, son. I just want a bath. We ain't scraping no hog's hide." The boy didn't answer. Grinning shyly, he continued filling the bathtub, a huge wooden affair with metal bands around the staves. When the temperature suited the boy, he handed Squint a big brown bar of lye soap and showed him a towel hanging on a nail. That done, he left the big mountain man to his bath.

Squint scrubbed six months' worth of grime off his body. The soap was so strong his skin burned all over but it felt good to be rid of the dirt. He laid back and relaxed and enjoyed the soak. As large as the big wooden tub was, it wasn't built for the likes of Squint, but it did the job as far as he was concerned. He propped his feet up on the edge of the wooden staves and let the warm water soak in. He didn't realize he had dozed off until he was awakened by a voice behind him.

"I can throw these things in the wash pot if you want me to."

He was startled to find Mrs. Mott standing almost beside the tub, his dirty underclothes in her hand. She laughed at his embarrassment when he hurriedly tried to cover his nakedness. The bathwater was so gray, she really couldn't see anything anyway but he was still flustered to find her so oblivious to his privacy.

"Don't worry, it won't cost you nothing. I'm getting ready to do a load of Mott's and I'll just throw yours in with his." She walked around the tub to face him, as unconcerned as if she was making polite conversation with him on the front steps of the church.

"Why, I . . ." he started, stammering for words. "Why, thank you kindly. I reckon they could sure use it." He felt the flush in his face receding as she stood there smiling down at him. Hell, he thought to himself, if it don't bother her none, it don't bother me.

"You 'bout ready to get outta there?"

"I reckon."

Still smiling, she reached over and pulled the towel off the nail. He expected her to hold it out to him so he could cover himself but she just held it and waited for him to get up and reach for it himself. He began to feel the embarrassment creep back across his face. When she didn't make any effort to display discretion, he began to realize what was going on. As he slowly stood up and reached for the towel, she confirmed it.

"I reckon you been up in them mountains for quite a spell," she started, making no effort to disguise her interest in his physical inventory. "A man more than likely needs more than a bath and a drink of whiskey. Two dollars more will get you what you need."

There was little doubt about what she was referring to but he was still not sure whether she was soliciting business for herself or for some half-breed girl and he wasn't sure he would pay two dollars for an Indian unless he saw her first. Seeing his hesitation, she guessed what he was thinking.

"I don't make that offer to just anybody. I'm particular about that."

Damn, he thought, *so it is her own behind she's selling.* He said, "What about your husband? Ain't you a mite worried about doing it right under his nose?"

"Mott? . . . Nah. Mott don't mind. He knows I pick up some extra money ever now and then, when it suits me." She laughed at Squint's obvious expression of bewilderment. "Hell, he had to pay for it hisself the first time before we got married."

Well, if this ain't somethin', he thought as he considered the proposition. As he dried himself, conscious now of the shriveled state of his weapon from the long soaking in the bathtub, he attempted to cover his nakedness as much as possible. As he did so, he took a closer look at the formidable figure of Mrs. Mott. She was big, he decided, bigger than she was fat. It might be more like wrestling a man than making love to a woman. Still, her shirt seemed to be filled up around the chest and her hips were pretty tight in her skinner's pants. The idea was getting more appealing by the second.

"You'll dang sure get your money's worth, if that's what's bothering you." As she said it, she unbuttoned her shirt far enough to give him a glimpse of the merchandise she was offering. She was pleased to see that the gesture was not lost on the burly man cowering behind the towel. "Man like you ain't gonna get many chances to get on with a white woman."

"What the hell," he said, but even that was unnecessary. A noticeable stirring beneath the towel gave her evidence enough of his warming to the idea. She immediately went back to work on the rest of her buttons. At the same time, she reached back with one booted foot and kicked the door shut. He was amazed by the swiftness and efficiency with which she came out of her chothes. As was the case with her outer garments, she wore a suit of men's long underwear underneath. Over in a corner of the room, there was a rolled-up pallet that he had not noticed until that moment. She unrolled it and tossed it on the floor. He watched wide-eyed as she peeled off her underwear. She looked even bigger with her clothes off, but she was solid. There was no flab on the woman's body, he had to give her that.

Her skin was as white as a bucket of fresh milk except for her neck and arms, which were tanned from the prairie sun, indicating to Squint that all her time wasn't spent behind the counter in Mott's.

Squint had been with Indian women too long. He was amazed by Mrs. Mott's alabaster skin. But the thing that amazed him most was the size of her breasts. The last thing he had seen that size was a watermelon in St. Louis six or seven years ago.

"How you want it? On top or Indian style?"

"On top, I reckon."

"Good. I favor it that way myself." She took his hand and led him to the pallet. Still holding his hand, she laid down on her back and assumed the position. "Come on, honey," she cooed, her voice taking on a new, feminine softness. At this point, he was more than willing. Still, for some reason, he was reminded briefly of the last time he saddle-broke a green mustang.

Before diving completely into his work, he glanced over his shoulder toward the door. "What if somebody comes in? Your husband or the boy?"

"Don't fret yourself about that. Won't nobody come in when that door's shut. The boy knows better and, if Mott comes barging in here, he knows I'll kick his scrawny little ass for him. You just relax and give me all you got. I don't want you to think you didn't get your money's worth."

He did. And she was right, she gave him his two dollars' worth. At one point in the merger, she could have demanded more money and gotten it. When it was over and she had all but destroyed him, he lay in her arms like a sick puppy and she purred over him for a few minutes before announcing that she had chores to get done. Drained of energy, he sat and watched her as she quickly got back into her clothes and opened the door. "Lemuel!" she bellowed out the door. "Come empty this tub." Turning back to Squint, she winked and said, "Don't spend all your money on whiskey."

Now that he was all scrubbed down and properly relaxed, he decided it was time to have that drink of liquor. When he walked back through the store, Mrs. Mott greeted him from behind the counter as casually as you please. It was as if the session in the washhouse had never happened. He had halfway expected some little sign from her, a secret smile, a wink, something. But it appeared to him that she had put the business out of her mind.

"Your clean clothes will be done this evening, Mr. . . . I never did get your name . . ."

"Peterson."

"Mr. Peterson. Well, anyway, I'll leave 'em under the counter here. You can pick 'em up when you're ready."

"Yes, ma'am. Thank you, ma'am." He pulled the blanket aside and entered the saloon part of the building.

Two men stood at the bar. Squint immediately figured them to be from the wagon train camped nearby. The proprietor of Mott's was behind the bar and he favored Squint with a wide grin.

"Well, sir, I reckon you ought to be feeling a lot better."

"I reckon," Squint replied, watching the bony little man intently for any move that might seem suspicious. Maybe his wife was telling the truth when she said that Mott wouldn't object to her roll in the hay with any stranger she fancied. But then, maybe he wasn't as generous with her backside as she imagined. If he objected, he sure covered it well.

"Did the missus take care of you all right?"

The question caused Squint some amount of confusion. He didn't know quite how to answer. Surely Mott didn't know for a fact the extent to which his wife had seen to Squint's needs. "Why, yessir," he stammered, "I reckon she did."

"Ain't she something though?" Mott beamed proudly.

Squint, not wishing to pursue the matter any further, changed the subject. "Have you got any whiskey that's fitten to drink? I ain't talking about that stuff you sell the Injuns when you ain't dipping sheep in it."

One of the men at the bar laughed. He had been eyeing Squint intently since he came in. He had obviously seen mountain men before but not often one the size of Squint. Squint turned to study the two men. The one who had laughed looked harmless enough, a farmer was Squint's guess, probably on his way to find his paradise in the Oregon territory. His companion was a strange little man in an Eastern style beaver hat, one that had seen a great deal of prairie sun. His face, though pleasant enough, was red but not from the sun.

"Join me in a drink?" Squint offered when Mott, still grinning, produced a bottle from behind the counter.

The man who had laughed at Squint's earlier remark spoke up, "Thank you, sir, but I've had my limit. If I take another shot of that stuff, I might not be able to make it back to the wagon. Thank you just the same."

The one wearing the beaver hat moved over beside the big man, "Aye, I'll be happy to join ya, sir, but only if you'll permit me to buy your drink."

Squint looked at the little man for a moment. From the sound of his brogue, he figured him for an Irishman and one not long off the boat. He grinned and motioned for Mott to fill the glasses. "I tell you what, Mr. Mott here already told me the first drink was on the house. You can buy the second one. Then, if we're still standing, I'll buy the third."

"Spoken like a real gentleman," Beaver Hat replied and lifted his glass. "To your health, sir." He tossed the shot of whiskey down, closing his eyes tightly in order to contain the tears the fiery liquid spawned.

Squint hesitated but a moment while he held the glass up in front of his eyes. It had been a while, he thought, as he peered intently at the amber liquid. He wet his lips and anticipated the libation about to be enjoyed. Then he tossed it back. The wicked concoction hit the back of his throat like a hot coal, seeming to tear the lining from his esophagus as it went down. He stood there gasping for breath, tears welling in his eyes, fighting to keep from going blind. He tried to speak but could not utter a sound until some of the fire subsided in his throat. When finally he could, he simply exclaimed, "Damn!"

"Smooth, ain't it?" Mott asked expectantly.

Beaver Hat laughed, enjoying the huge man's reaction. When Squint looked to be recovered from his first drink, the little Irishman offered his sympathy. "It's the devil's own piss, I'm thinking. It takes a little getting used to, but after a few gallons of the stuff, it's like drinking your mother's milk." The Irishman almost giggled at Squint's obvious distress. He stuck out his hand. "Me name's Waddie Bodkin and I'm pleased to make your acquaintance, Mr. . . . ."

"Peterson," Squint managed to rasp. "Squint Peterson."

"Well then, Mr. Squint Peterson, are you ready for your second drink?" Squint would have sworn there was a twinkle in the little man's eye as he glanced at Mott, who held the bottle poised over the empty glasses.

"I reckon I am. I expect that first one has eat its way through my gizzard by now." He snorted and wiped his sleeve across his nose, which had begun to run after the first drink. "I got to have at least one more because I don't believe that first one burnt as bad as I remember."

Waddie Bodkin waved his hand over the glasses. "Mr. Mott, if you please. This one's on me."

It didn't seem possible but Squint would swear the second one burned deeper than the first. After a few moments to recover from the shock to his throat, he began to feel the warmth generated in his stomach. Realizing he was drinking on an empty stomach, he resolved to hold it to three drinks. Three drinks of that poison was enough anyway, he decided. He had no desire to see the contents of his stomach spew out of his mouth and a few more shots of that fiery brew were bound to lead him to that. It would have been impolite not to stand for the third round so he bought it but he nursed this one along slowly, only sipping it. His need for strong spirits satisfied for the moment, Squint settled into conversation.

"If you don't mind my asking, Squint, where are you headed for?" Waddie asked.

Squint scratched his beard, trying to remember. "Well, to tell you the truth, I ain't sure. Maybe Fort Laramie, might try to hire on with the army as a scout, I ain't decided. I've spent the last few years up in the Wind River country, trappin', and I know the country better'n most and the Injuns better'n some."

Waddie studied his new acquaintance carefully, plumbing the depth of the mountain man's character. They talked a while about the mountains and the Indians and then some about Waddie Bodkin's home in Ireland. Waddie had left there on a boat bound for Boston, two years ago. Like his father before him, Waddie was trained as a bookkeeper.

"What in hell is a bookkeeper doing out here?" Squint wanted to know.

Waddie shrugged his shoulders. "Like everybody else, I suppose, I'm just looking for something better."

By the time it got around to suppertime, the two had become pretty good friends and, at Waddie's suggestion, they collected Squint's belongings and went over to Waddie's wagon to rustle up some grub. Supper turned out to be some soup beans Waddie had boiled that afternoon. While they ate, Waddie explained that the wagon train was stalled there at the crossing, waiting for an army escort to see them through to Fort C. F. Smith.

"Fort Smith? Where's that?" Squint thought he knew where every fort in the territory was but he'd never heard of that one.

"It's just been there since this summer," Waddie explained. "Two fellows marked a trail that starts from this crossing, up through Indian territory to the goldfields in Montana territory. A fellow named Jacobs and a fellow named Bozeman, it was."

Squint interrupted, "Hell, man, you go north from here and you're goin' straight through the whole damn Sioux hunting grounds. Why, they catch a white near the Powder or the Big Horns, your hair'd come off quicker'n a fox can piss."

"No, no. It's not like that, Squint. You see, the army is here to protect the trains that take the shortcut to Montana. This Colonel Carrington, or something like that, left here just this summer with over two hundred wagons and I don't know how many soldiers, just to build forts along the trail. Dozens of trains have gone up that way already."

"Without no trouble from the Sioux?"

"Oh, I didn't say that. Sure, there's been trouble. Like you say, the Injuns don't take kindly to it. But if you have enough men to protect you, you can make it. That's why we have to wait here, for the army to escort us."

Squint shook his head thoughtfully. "Well, I still wouldn't feel too safe if I was you, Waddie. Them Sioux ain't got much sense of humor when it comes to traipsing across their hunting grounds. How far up is this Fort Smith?"

"There's three forts. Fort C. F. Smith isn't the only one. That's what makes it safer. There's Fort Reno on the Powder. Then there's Fort Phil Kearny on the Piney and Fort Smith on the Big Horn."

Squint shook his head again and slowly stirred the last of his beans around in the tin plate Waddie had filled for him. "I don't know, Waddie, it sounds risky to me. I sure wish you luck though."

Waddie got dead serious for a moment, looking Squint straight in the eye. "I need more than luck. I need me a partner and I'm thinking you're just the man I'd be looking for."

Squint was flabbergasted. "Me? Why in thunder would you want me? I ain't got no hankering to lose my hair. Hell, man, why do you think I left the mountains in the first place?"

"Just think on it a bit," Waddie insisted. "You said yourself you ain't heading anywhere in particular. Why not throw in with me and we'll head up the Powder to Montana territory and seek our fortunes. They've raised the color in Bannack City. Folks have been going up there for months. The word is now there's a bigger strike in Alder Gulch. The streams are full of gold, just waiting for folks to come get it."

Squint was still bewildered. He scratched his beard and laughed. "Damn, I don't know, Waddie, I ain't ever thought much about panning for gold . . . don't *know* much about it. Besides, I didn't raise much from my furs. I ain't got enough money to outfit for no prospecting even if I did want to go with you. I couldn't buy enough equipment to load up a frog."

"Hell, man, I know that. It's your back and your grit I'm needing. You've got plenty of both and I need a man I can trust to watch my backside. Whaddaya say?"

Squint had to think about it some more. He scratched his head and studied his new friend intensely. What a strange little man Waddie Bodkin was. He cut a right comical figure in his blousy shirt and his beaver hat.

"Let me show you something," Waddie said, walking around to the back of the wagon. "You see what I have loaded up in here? Nails and molasses, flour and dried apples, tea, coffee, picks. Do you have any notion what some of those folks in Bannack would give for a keg of nails? We can name our own price for this stuff in the goldfields. Hell, man, we'll sell the wagon and mules too. It'll bring plenty enough to stake us a claim. Whaddaya say, man? I need a partner."

Squint continued to look at Waddie in amazement, still saying nothing. He was thinking hard on the proposition and he could not come up with any good reasons why he should turn the offer down. After a few more moments of agonizing deliberation, he said, "Hell, all right, we'll give her a try. I been a fool all my life, ain't no call to do something sensible now." His expression sobered for a moment. "But I'm gonna tell you one thing. Army or no army, them Sioux ain't gonna take it lightly. That there country between the Black Hills and the Big Horns is their best hunting grounds and, the last I heard, they had a treaty that said the whites warn't supposed to go in there."

Waddie fairly beamed his pleasure, ignoring the warning. "It's done then, partner. I knew you were the man I was looking for the minute you walked in Mott's." They shook on it.

CHAPTER 16

Squint and his new partner waited around Deer Creek for eight more days before a detachment of thirty troopers arrived from Fort Reno to escort some army supply wagons back. While they waited, Squint spent the time hunting for fresh meat, some of which he shared with the folks in the other wagons. Most of them were immigrants, just in from back East, and fascinated with the opportunity to meet a real mountain man. Squint got real comfortable with the situation right away because some settler and his wife were always ready to offer coffee and a bite of something to eat in exchange for some genuine frontier stories. And Squint had plenty of stories to tell, most of which he fabricated from whole cloth. By the time the soldiers arrived, most of the people in the wagon train called him by name.

All of Squint's time wasn't spent hunting meat and spinning yarns, however. Most evenings found him and Waddie leaning on the bar at Mott's. When all was said and done, Squint really wasn't much of a drinking man. He'd have one or two just to feel the burn in his belly, but he never cared much for the sickness that usually followed a night of real hard drinking. In addition to that, he didn't like the idea of letting whiskey dull his senses to the point where he couldn't control his reflexes. In an untamed country, where a man's scalp was in peril half the time, he thought it best to keep his wits sharp all the time. Now, Waddie Bodkin was of a different religion. As long as he was on his feet and there was whiskey left in the bottle, he had room for one more drink. He had seen the bottom of his stomach many a morning and still it didn't dull his taste for the spirits. Squint wasn't a man to tell another what he should or shouldn't do, but he began to wonder if his role in their partnership was mainly to carry Waddie back to the wagon at night.

The day had been a hot one and about the middle of the afternoon the thunderclouds began piling up on top of each other. The clouds darkened and the wind picked up, cooling the sunbaked clay around Mott's. After seeing to the stock and making sure the wagon was closed up tight, Squint and Waddie stood outside Mott's store enjoying the freshness of the approaching storm. Off in the distance the first rumblings of thunder caused the leaves in the cottonwoods to tremble on the far bank of the river. Squint stood facing the breeze and smelling the damp sweetness of the coming rain. He always enjoyed a summer storm when there was shelter at hand and this one promised to be a stout one. In a matter of minutes, the storm walked across the prairie and the first huge drops of rain began pelting the bare ground around them.

The two men backed up against the side of the building under the eaves, reluctant to leave the sacrament of the storm until forced inside. As they watched, two riders emerged from the stand of cottonwoods on the far bank and forded the river. They were riding hard, trying to outrun the storm, judging by the way they whipped their horses. The lead horse stumbled and went to its knees trying to scramble up the riverbank. Its rider flogged the poor animal unmercifully until it regained its feet and galloped on into Mott's. This was enough to tell Squint that he had no use for the man. The two riders pulled up to the hitching rail and tied up, leaving the horses and the two pack mules they were leading standing in the rain. They barely glanced at the two men standing under the eaves as they stormed into Mott's store. Squint and Waddie decided it was time to go inside too. The rain was driving up against the building by then.

Even a blind man could tell the two riders were buffalo hunters. There was a stench that followed most of this breed that Squint learned to identify long ago, and the fact that they were soaking wet didn't help to ease their pungent aroma. They made no effort to step aside when Squint and Waddie entered the store. Squint had seen their kind before, half wild and mean as a grizzly. But they paid no attention to Squint and Waddie. Instead, they seemed intent on leering at Mrs. Mott who had just then come in from the storeroom. Not a word was said for a few minutes. The two hunters stood there, the dripping water from the fringes of their long buckskin coats forming puddles on the dirt floor. Squint heard only the first of the conversation as he and Waddie passed on through to the saloon.

"It's a right miserable day out there. I might have got me a chill." It was the big one who spoke. "I need me a little somethin' to warm me up."

His partner, a short, round man wearing a grimy bowler hat, piped up. "Yeah, I could use a little somethin' myself." He grinned and winked at the larger man.

"I told you before, I ain't got nothin' to help you, Kroll. If you want somethin' to warm you up, you can go buy some whiskey from Mott." Squint could tell by the tone of her voice that she didn't have any patience for the likes of them. He couldn't hear any more of the talk because he and Waddie were in the saloon and Mott's loud and cordial greeting drowned out the rest.

"Howdy, boys. What'll it be?"

They ordered a beer apiece and moved down to the far end of the bar. Squint took a long drink from the mug before speaking. "Looks like Mrs. Mott has got some mean-looking customers in there."

Mott walked over to the curtain and peered through at the two men in the store. "Kroll and Moody," he announced. "I was hoping the Injuns had got them two by now." He let the blanket fall back in place and turned back to Squint and Waddie. "They're ornery all right, and good for nothing too. The big ugly one is Kroll. He'll slit your throat just for something to do. The little fat one, that's Moody. He's pretty much harmless unless your back is turned. The missus can handle 'em though."

Since Mott didn't appear to be overly concerned about the two foul-smelling visitors, Squint figured he wasn't going to be worried about it either. He didn't like their looks and he figured he was obligated to alert Mott to their presence. Beyond that, it wasn't his business.

Waddie seemed not to be concerned about anything other than the glass of beer he had already finished. He shoved the empty glass across toward Mott and said,

"Weather like this makes a man thirsty." He watched as Mott filled the glass, then added, "Maybe you better pour me a shot of that coyote piss too. I don't want to catch me death of cold."

Squint laughed. Any kind of weather made Waddie thirsty. Mott held the bottle poised over the glass and looked quizzically at Squint. Squint shook his head no. His glass was still half full. "I reckon I'll just stay with this for a while yet." He didn't let on to Mott or Waddie, but he had a feeling that he needed to keep his head clear. The two buffalo hunters were still arguing in the other part of the store. Although he could not hear their words, he recognized the tone of their voices and he knew that whatever the conversation with Mrs. Mott, things were not going their way. He had a pretty good idea what they were trying to buy from her. Squint had spent almost twenty years around men like those two, part of that time as a lawman. Over the stench of buffalo guts and sweat, there was a distinct odor of trouble. As was his custom, Squint would try to avoid trouble. He'd just stay down at the end of the bar and mind his own business and wait to see what happened. He didn't have to wait long.

Kroll pulled a blanket aside and peered into the saloon. He fixed a cold eye on each of the three men in the room, coming back to the formidable figure in buckskins at the far end of the bar. Squint met his gaze and their eyes locked for a long moment as each measured the other. Squint noted the heavy cavalry pistol stuck in the man's belt, the handle right over his belly button, and the long skinning knife strapped to his side. He took just a half step out from the end of the bar so Kroll would be sure to note that he had a heavy pistol stuck in his own belt, just in case the man was already getting any ideas. The measuring over, Kroll suddenly ripped the blanket down as if it had somehow offended him. He threw it on the floor and roared at Mott behind the bar.

"Give me a bottle of whiskey, old man." He glanced back at Squint to see if there was any reaction from that corner. The man had evidently spent most of his life intimidating people. Refusing to be baited, Squint pretended not to notice and turned to talk to Waddie as if unaware of the presence of the two hunters.

Mott reached under the counter and produced a bottle. He glanced at Moody, standing behind Kroll, and asked coldly, "Will that be two glasses?"

"We don't need no damn glasses," Kroll roared and snatched the bottle from Mott's hand. He uncorked it and tilted it back, pouring a huge drink down his throat. Mott's whiskey didn't back down to any man, even a buffalo hunter as mean as Kroll. He swallowed twice but he couldn't take a third one and had to pull the bottle back down, banging it down hard on the counter. "Damn you, old man," he swore, trying hard to hold back the tears. "You been cutting that damn whiskey with kerosene!"

Moody laughed, reaching for the bottle. "Lemme give 'er a try." He tilted the bottle back and poured a mouthful down his throat. When he could speak again, he grinned from ear to ear and said, "Burns like fire but it's pretty good, Kroll."

Kroll, not about to be jollied up by his partner, snatched the bottle back and took another drink. This time he was ready for the fire and he held back the tears while the searing liquid seeped down into his gut. Then he turned and threw the bottle against the log wall of the saloon. It smashed, throwing whiskey all over the floor and the wall. "You old fart," he growled. "I ain't paying for no damn Injun whiskey."

Mott had remained stony calm throughout Kroll's tirade. His expression showed not the slightest hint of panic when he spoke. "I don't make it. I just sell it. And a bottle of whiskey's gonna cost you the same, whether you drink it or wash the wall with it. All the same to me."

"The hell you say . . ." Kroll started but was interrupted when Mott calmly pulled a hog-legg from under the bar and laid it on the counter, its muzzle looking right at Kroll's belly. Kroll backed away a step. "Why, you old son of a bitch," he growled, "you better mind who you pull a gun on." His face, twisted with anger, slowly transformed into an evil grin. "You pull that trigger and Moody here will put more holes in you than you got fingers to plug." Moody, recognizing his cue, stepped over away from Kroll and let his hand rest on the handle of his pistol, his face mirroring the nasty smile of his partner's.

"I reckon Mr. Moody might have a hard time pulling that damn pistol with his ass cut in half."

Startled, both men jerked their heads to the side to discover Squint's huge forty-four staring at them.

"This ain't none of your concern," Kroll countered. "You best keep your nose clear of it."

The two of them were beginning to get on Squint's nerves. This was his last night before starting on the trail and all he wanted was a quiet glass of beer before going to bed. He cocked the hammer back on the forty-four and spoke. "My nose has had enough of the stink of you two. Now I think it's time you two little darlin's said good night—as soon as you pay what you owe for that bottle."

Moody backed away toward the door but Kroll stiffened. "You're making one helluva big mistake, mister." Squint could see the fury welling up in the man. He glared at Squint for a long time, then he seemed to relax momentarily. "What are you gonna do if I don't wanna go? Shoot me?" He continued to glare at Squint. "I don't believe you got the sand."

Squint didn't believe in standoffs. His finger tightened on the trigger. In the tense atmosphere of the saloon, the explosion of the forty-four split the air and startled everyone else in the room. Kroll, almost deafened by the muzzle blast, stumbled backward into Moody, the two of them landing on the dirt floor. Unaware that he was hit at first, Kroll suddenly felt the pain on the side of his head and grabbed for his ear. He shrieked in horror when he felt the neat half moon where, moments before, a piece of ear had been. Furious, he made a move toward his pistol but thought better of it when Squint cocked his weapon again and stood with the barrel aimed right between Kroll's eyes.

"You got a choice." Squint almost whispered it, his voice cold as ice. "You and that other scum can drag your sorry behinds outta here or I can spill your blood all over the floor right now."

Kroll scowled defiantly but he wasn't fool enough to think he could get his pistol out before Squint's bullet spilled his brains. The tension in the little saloon was explosive as the two big men locked eyeballs. Finally Kroll conceded. "All right, you son of a bitch, you got the upper hand this time but there'll be other times."

Moody, having picked himself up and backed up to the blankets separating the two areas of the store, could not believe what he was witnessing. He had never seen anyone get the best of Kroll. And here was Kroll, down on the floor with a piece of his ear shot off. Now it appeared the man was going to get away with it and he and Kroll were supposed to slink off like whipped dogs. He couldn't believe it. As Moody stood there transfixed, seemingly not a part of what was taking place, he realized that all eyes were on Kroll on the floor. Nobody was watching him. Very slowly he reached his hand across his round belly to the butt of his pistol and gently began to ease it out of his belt.

"That'd be the dumbest thing you could do, Moody."

Moody's hand froze when he felt Mrs. Mott's double-barreled shotgun nudge the small of his back. As slowly as he had reached for the gun, he withdrew his hand. "All right, all right," he replied, his voice trembling. "Just be careful with that dang thing, lady." He reached down to give his partner a hand up. "Come on, Kroll, let's get out of here."

"You ain't paid for that bottle yet," Squint reminded him.

"No, and I ain't gonna," was Kroll's terse reply.

Moody took one look into Squint's eyes and was quick to blurt out, "Here, here's the money. I'll pay for the whiskey!" He grabbed Kroll's sleeve and pulled him toward the door.

The three of them, Mott, Squint and Mrs. Mott, all held their guns on Kroll and Moody as they walked them outside and onto their horses. Kroll remained silent until he was in the saddle but his eyes blazed with his rage. "This ain't the end of this, stranger." He directed this at Squint. "Next time it'll be different."

"I'll deal with that when the time comes," was Squint's only reply as he watched the two gallop off into the approaching night. When they had at last vanished from sight, he turned to Mott and said, "I should have shot him while I had the chance."

"I reckon," Mott replied.

Satisfied that they would see no more of Kroll and Moody that night, they returned to the saloon to find Waddie still standing at the end of the bar. He smiled at them and greeted Mott with, "Ahhh, Mr. Mott, I was wondering if I was going to die of thirst before you came back to save me."

Squint could only shake his head, amazed. "Waddie, I hope this little ruckus didn't disturb your drinking."

"Not a'tall, not a'tall," Waddie assured him. He turned to Mott, his empty glass outstretched. "Now, Mr. Mott, if you please."

Squint permitted his little friend to imbibe a few more rounds before he grabbed him by the back of the collar and pulled him out of the saloon. The wagons were pulling out in the morning at sunup and he wanted Waddie to be able to drive his mules without falling off the seat. They said good-bye to the Motts and as they walked out the door, Mott put his hand on Squint's arm and spoke.

"Squint, we're obliged to you for pitching in back there. You best watch your back, my friend. That Kroll's a mean one and he ain't the kind to take a besting like you give him and not look for a way to get even. You watch your back." He stood in the doorway as they walked toward the wagons. "And hang on to your scalps."

Chapter 17

Little Wolf lay with his eyes closed, listening to the barking of a squirrel high above his head. The constant murmuring of the busy stream as it rushed around the rocks and fallen timbers served to induce him to slumber. His bed was a sun-drenched boulder that jutted out into the stream. The sun felt good, like a balm that penetrated his shoulders and back. He felt its warmth gently probing the scar tissue on his left shoulder where the soldier's bullet had torn into the muscle. The wound was old now but it still ached occasionally when the wind was especially cold. He had to smile to himself when he thought about the huge scar it had left, due to Squint's clumsy probing to remove the bullet.

He had not thought about Squint for some time and probably no more than two or three times in all since they had parted company four years ago this spring. He allowed his thoughts to drift where they wished, choosing not to direct them. Soon he found himself thinking of that time, two years before, when he and Morning Sky escaped the massacre at Black Kettle's camp on the Washita. The man responsible for that attack was the Longhair, Custer, and Little Wolf had dreamed many times of avenging the death of his friend Black Feather and the wanton killing of the women and children. He dreamed how it would be. He would hunt down this arrogant devil and kill him. Then he would take his long scalp and tie it to his lance. The time would come when he would be given this opportunity to avenge his people. It had to. Man Above could not permit such an outrage to go unpunished. At the time, he thought that his opportunity would come right away. He and Morning Sky had been rescued by a band of Kiowas camped downstream from Black Kettle's camp. The men of that tribe were angry at Longhair's attack on the peaceful village. Soon there were warriors from other tribes gathered along the banks of the Washita. They were ready to fight but the soldiers had doubled back during the night and fled before the superior number of Indians. Much of the fight had been taken out of the Southern Cheyenne after Custer's cowardly attack. So Little Wolf brought Morning Sky back to the Wind River country, back to his small band of Cheyenne warriors. There they lived with the Dakotas as man and wife.

The shrill cry of a hawk somewhere in the distant treetops brought his mind back to his surroundings and he listened again, his eyes still closed. There was no danger here, deep in the mountains, yet still he listened intently to the noises of the forest, to the sounds of the living earth, and once again he felt as one with the mountains.

"Little Wolf." It was the voice of his old friend, Sleeps Standing.

"I am here, Sleeps Standing." He opened his eyes and rolled over to watch his friend make his way along the rocky stream bank, stepping gracefully from boulder to boulder.

"I knew you would be at this place." Sleeps Standing smiled as he pulled himself up on the flat boulder that had served as Little Wolf's bed. "I think maybe you are going to sleep the rest of your life away," he teased.

Little Wolf smiled. "I think that is not a bad thought. Maybe I will." It had been a hard winter in the mountains. They had been forced to hunt a greater distance from their camp due to the heavy snows that closed the mountain passes and drove the game down out of the hills. There had been very little fighting—a few raids, most of them by their Dakota brothers, on stagecoach stations or trading posts. The people had been too occupied with surviving the winter. Now that spring had finally come, there would be fighting again. Only this week a runner had come with word from Sitting Bull that wagon trains were already breaking the treaty and entering the sacred hunting grounds to find the useless yellow rocks the white man coveted. He asked that all Cheyenne and Dakota join together to chase the white man out.

Sleeps Standing drew his knife from the hide case at his

side and began to work on the edge. "Bloody Claw has called a council tonight to decide if we go to join Sitting Bull."

Little Wolf grunted. "I know." Bloody Claw was ambitious. He had been very busy campaigning for a following while Little Wolf and Black Feather were away at Black Kettle's camp. Two winters had passed since then but Bloody Claw was still actively seeking leadership of their small band of Cheyennes, a fact that didn't bother Little Wolf. Little Wolf did as he pleased. If the warriors chose to follow him, then so be it. It was every brave's choice and decision to make. Bloody Claw was constantly frustrated, for the other warriors trusted Little Wolf's cunning as well as his courage. He had led them on the raids against the soldiers and workers at the forts along the trail the white man called the Bozeman. And they had suffered very few losses of their own while killing and counting coup on many soldiers. Little Wolf had brought honor to all of them.

"Come, we will walk back to camp. The sun will soon be going to sleep." Little Wolf rose to his feet and stretched.

Morning Sky rose to greet Little Wolf when he entered their tipi. "And where has my husband been all day?" she teased. "Out looking for a younger wife?"

"One wife has taught me a lesson," he responded. "If I can rid myself of this one, I will never have another." Pretending to give the matter serious thought, he screwed his face into a frown and said, "I was going to sell you to Bloody Claw for two fat puppies but he said one puppy was too high a price."

Morning Sky could never play the game for very long. Giggling like a child, she suddenly jumped on her husband's back, causing him to lose his balance, and the two of them landed on the tipi floor. Laughing, they rolled over and over until he stopped them, permitting her to land on top.

"Aha!" she cried triumphantly. "So you would sell me to Bloody Claw, would you?" She pretended to pin his wrists to the floor as she straddled his stomach. "Little Wolf," she mocked, "the mighty warrior. What would your braves think if they could see you now, mighty warrior?"

"Maybe they would make you their war chief," he said.

"Go ahead," she taunted, gritting her teeth and squeezing his wrists as hard as she could. "Try to free yourself."

"I cannot," he laughed, "you are too powerful." He pretended to strain against her. After a few minutes, he said, "I tire of this game. It is time to feed your husband." With that, he easily lifted his arms straight up, picking her up in the process and holding her over him for a moment before gently lowering her to the floor. Laughing delightedly, she quickly scrambled back to lock her arms around his neck and hug him tightly. She was proud of her husband, of his stature and his strength. Among the Cheyenne and the Sioux, he stood tall and slender, almost a head taller than the tallest Sioux.

Morning Sky was perhaps, by her own reckoning, the luckiest wife in the entire Indian nation. Not only was she proud of her husband's reputation as a mighty war leader, she was secure in the knowledge that Little Wolf loved her. The years had dulled the memory of the tragic loss of her uncle and brother at the Washita camp and Morning Sky's was a happy life. The winter had been long and hard and game had been scarce but Little Wolf always found food for them. True, he was away for long periods of time, on the hunt or on a raiding party against the soldiers. But Morning Sky was a Cheyenne. This was a simple fact of life for her, just as death was. She knew that one day he might not return to her tipi, for the Cheyenne were a warlike people, like the Sioux. And he had told her that there would be more war. The white man continued to push further and further into the Indians' lands. Soon there would be no place else to go except the reservation and Little Wolf would not go there. She accepted it and worked hard to make the two of them happy while they had this time to share together.

"You will go to council tonight?"

"Yes," he answered. "Bloody Claw has called for it." He thought for a moment then added, "He is right. It is time. We must decide if we should leave these mountains and join with the others. Even though we are few, if we stay here, we will hunt off all the game. If we leave the mountains to hunt, it is not safe for so few to face the soldiers in the prairies."

A frown fixed on her face as she heard his words. She had been happiest here in all her young life and she was reluctant to leave. The soldiers seemed so far away from these mountains but she knew her husband was right. Then she relaxed her frown into a smile and said, cheerfully, "I will be happy as long as I am by your side."

Little Wolf sat and listened while Bloody Claw petitioned on behalf of Sitting Bull's invitation to join him in the Big Horn Mountains. As Bloody Claw expounded on the aggressive advances of the white man, Little Wolf studied the faces of the young warriors gathered around the council fire. He knew every man in this small band would defer to him to make their final decision even though they might agree with Bloody Claw. He also knew that he would vote to break camp and go to join Sitting Bull's Dakotas. The time had passed when he could hope to continue his war on the soldiers as a separate unit of raiders, having no women or children to slow them, moving constantly to strike and strike again before the soldiers could mount a counterattack. It was not a natural way of life for a Cheyenne warrior, who was accustomed to having a woman work for him and cook and provide a tipi for him to return to. The fact that there were no elders sitting at their council fire was unnatural. He knew his young braves were beginning to feel the absence of the old wise ones when there were important decisions to be made. They had been long enough on this path. He himself had taken a wife. How could he expect his warriors to forego the same comfort? Only two others in the camp had wives, Left Hand and Lame Otter. It was difficult for the rest to be alone.

After Bloody Claw finished his impassioned plea and sat down, there were a few moments of silence. Then Sleeps Standing spoke, "What say you, Little Wolf?"

Little Wolf rose slowly to his feet. "Bloody Claw speaks with wisdom. It is time to join our brothers in Sitting Bull's camp. Many of our people, Cheyenne and Arapaho, are with him now even as we speak. I have heard that many of our Cheyenne brothers from the south have fled the reservations and have come north to fight beside the Dakotas. The soldiers will be as many as the grass on the prairie. Sitting Bull will need many more warriors if he is to drive the white man out. I stand with Bloody Claw."

And so it was decided. They would break camp in the morning and start east toward the Big Horn country. The verdict was met with great excitement among the young warriors. Singing and dancing would go on until late that night as the braves boasted of the scalps they would take and the bravery they would exhibit as they drove the white man from their valleys and rivers. Of course Bloody Claw was especially pleased that his council was accepted, so and he led the dancing. Little Wolf joined in the ceremony for a while then quietly withdrew to his tipi and Morning Sky.

"So, we are leaving in the morning." It was not a question. Morning Sky knew what the decision would be before the council meeting was held. Already she had packed some of their things in anticipation of the morning march.

The journey to Sitting Bull's camp took five days, one day longer than planned, because a warrior named Lame Otter discovered a herd of antelope on the lower slopes and the men decided to take advantage of the opportunity to add to their food supply. A full day was taken to hunt and take the hides to be worked later. Enough meat was procured to feed the band of warriors for several days. Morning Sky was proud that her husband's arrows were found in three of the swift animals. As she quickly removed the hides, her deft hands skillfully cutting away the fore-locks and neatly splitting the soft white fur of the under-belly, she was already envisioning the fine ceremonial shirt it would make for Little Wolf. In her baggage, packed on one of the horses, she already had collected the porcupine quills and red beads she would decorate the shirt with. Her husband would be the most striking warrior in the camp!

When the journey was resumed, all the men were in a lighthearted mood. It was a good sign, finding the antelope. It indicated to them that they had made the right decision when they voted to join the main body of Sioux and it told them their medicine was strong. The only souls that were possibly disappointed were those of the pack animals whose loads had increased considerably. Two of these belonged to Little Wolf. Morning Sky rode a large bay that bore army brands. She led the two pack animals as well as three more that belonged to other braves in their band. Left Hand's wife did the same, as did the wife of Lame Otter.

Little Wolf rode ahead of Morning Sky on a roan horse with a white-spotted rump. The white man called this breed of horse Appaloosa. This was one of his favorite horses,

traded from the Nez Perces for one army carbine. He and
Sleeps Standing made the trip north the spring before and
both returned with one of the strange looking horses bred
by the Nez Perces. They were fast animals, larger than the
Cheyenne ponies, though not as large as the big muscular
horses the soldiers rode. Although he rode the Appaloosa,
Little Wolf led the little Medicine Hat stallion he preferred
to hunt and fight on. A Cheyenne's war pony was never
used as a pack animal. It had to be fresh and ready in the
event of attack by an enemy or, as was the case this time,
a herd of buffalo or deer were sighted. No horse was a
match for the Medicine Hat when speed and agility were
required. It could outrun the larger army mounts and continue to run long after they had faltered. And it could live
off the land, surviving on sagebrush, if that's all there was
to be had. Any warrior would envy Little Wolf's good fortune in owning the Medicine Hat. Some thought the little
horse had big medicine and that his rider was invincible in
battle because of the markings that made a bonnet over
the horse's head and ears, and a dark shield protecting its
chest. The Medicine Hat and the Appaloosa did not graze
with the other horses. They were always tied outside the
tipi.

The sun was almost setting on the distant hills when they
sighted the smoke of Sitting Bull's campfires. His messenger had said the great chief would be camped on the Crazy
Woman River. Little Wolf's band had struck the river at
midday and followed it north until they came upon the first
tipis near a bend in the river. A Sioux lookout spotted
them when they were still a good half mile away and rode
back to the village to alert the tribe of the arrival of Little
Wolf's Cheyenne warriors.

The Cheyenne prepared for the welcome. The young
men donned their most decorative shirts and feathers and
leaped astride their best war ponies for the entrance into
the camp. It seemed that everyone in the camp came out
to greet them. The air was filled with war whoops and animal calls and shouts of welcome.

Little Wolf called to his followers, "Let us show our Dakota brothers how a Cheyenne warrior rides!" With that,
he filled his lungs and released a bloodcurdling war whoop

and kicked the Medicine Hat into a gallop, leading his braves down into the camp. The response was deafening as men, women and children answered the call. Dogs joined in the melee, adding their vocal approval. Little Wolf looked down into a sea of smiling faces. The Sioux were greatly pleased to have his band of Cheyenne warriors in camp and they crowded around Little Wolf. It seemed that all the people wanted to touch him as he walked the Medicine Hat toward the council lodge in the center of the village. He had not realized his reputation had grown to such proportions among the Sioux. When he reached the council lodge, he stopped, for there, walking forward to greet him, was none other than Sitting Bull, principal chief and spiritual leader of the Sioux.

"Little Wolf," the chief smiled, "you and your warriors are welcome in our village. It is a great honor to have a warrior of your courage and cunning join us in our mutual fight against the white soldiers."

"Thank you for your welcome. We are honored. My braves and I know of no better place to taste the glory of battle than at the side of the mighty leader of the Lakotas."

There was a twinkle in Sitting Bull's eyes as he greeted the young war chief who had raided Fort Reno and made off with rifles and horses and then devised the ambush on the riverbank that wiped out a detachment of soldiers. As he clasped Little Wolf's arm in friendship, he studied his face intently. He saw courage and honesty in the young man's eyes. He was curious to know more about this tall young brave who was said to have killed a grizzly while still a mere child, with little more than a knife.

"Come and sit with me a while after you have seen to your people and taken care of your horses. We will smoke the pipe and talk."

"I am honored," Little Wolf replied humbly, surprised and pleased to be treated with such dignity. Such courtesy as this was usually reserved for a chief or an important elder. It was rare indeed for one so young as he.

He took his leave of the great chief and moved his band upstream a few hundred yards where he instructed Morning Sky to set up her tipi beside a group of Cheyenne lodges, already a part of Sitting Bull's camp. Left Hand and Lame Otter had their wives set up their tipis on either side of his. The rest of his band, being bachelors, were dispersed among the other Cheyenne and Arapaho lodges already there. It was a happy reunion because many of the warriors had relatives there. It was good to be back in a real village again.

Morning Sky set about her work quickly, unpacking the horses and setting the lodge poles that had served as a travois on the trip. Soon she had pulled the hides over the frame of the tipi and was busy building a fire to cook Little Wolf's supper. By the time Little Wolf had finished tethering the horses outside the flap of the tipi, she was almost ready to feed him. He marveled at her efficiency, not failing to notice that it would be some time yet before Left Hand or Lame Otter got anything to eat.

After he had eaten and rested with Morning Sky a while, he went back to the center of the Sioux camp to sit with Sitting Bull. He found him seated before the fire with three of the elders of the tribe. The old chief welcomed him and lit a long clay pipe. After he had drawn deeply three times on the pipe, he offered it to an old man on his left who was introduced to Little Wolf as Man Who Kills Horses. When the pipe came to Little Wolf, he pulled the smoke into his lungs and closed his eyes as he let it drift slowly from his nostrils. When he opened his eyes again, he was startled to find two women of Sitting Bull's tipi hovering over him. When they saw his eyelids open, they giggled and hurried away.

This seemed to amuse Sitting Bull, and when he saw the perplexed expression on the young man's face, he remarked, "They wanted to see your blue eyes."

The comment caught Little Wolf by surprise. It had been a long time since he had been reminded that he had white skin and blue eyes, so long that he had all but forgotten it himself. At first there was a slight feeling of irritation. He didn't like being reminded of his birthright. But there seemed to be no intent to insult. To the contrary, the smiling faces of the four Sioux before him were warm with friendship. Still, Sitting Bull wanted to satisfy his curiosity.

"You have fought bravely against the white soldiers, all here know this. Tell me, my son, do you ever regret making war on the people of your blood?"

"My father was Spotted Pony, Arapaho. My mother was

Buffalo Woman, Cheyenne. I know of no other family. The white soldiers killed them at Sand Creek. Longhair's soldiers killed my friend Black Feather at Black Kettle's camp on the Washita. There are not enough soldiers for me to kill to avenge the deaths of my family and my friend."

Sitting Bull nodded his understanding. The three elders all grunted and nodded sympathetically. "I am glad you are with us, Little Wolf," Sitting Bull said. "There will be much fighting and we'll need braves of your courage. The white man has found the yellow dirt in our lands, lands that were given to the Lakota long ago by the Great Spirit, long before the white man came to this land. Already our scouts have seen their wagons coming into the Black Hills, into our most sacred hunting ground. The white father has signed a treaty saying that no white man shall come into these lands but still they come. Soon they will kill all the buffalo and the white father does nothing. The treaty is worthless . . . Lies, like all the treaties before. They would send us to their reservations to rot and die. This we will not do. There will be a bloody war. They give us no choice."

Little Wolf rose to his feet. "Together we will drive the white man from our lands."

Pleased by Little Wolf's response, Sitting Bull embraced the young warrior as a proud grandfather might embrace his grandson. As Little Wolf turned to leave, the old chief stayed him with a hand on his arm. "I would ask a favor of you, my son."

Little Wolf paused.

"Do you still talk the white man's tongue?"

"Yes, though it has been a long while."

The chief hesitated as if still making a decision. "There is something you can do for me." Nodding at the man next to him, he continued, "Man Who Kills Horses tells me that two white men have been captured by one of our war parties. They have been brought here instead of being killed because they say they can get many of the army's new rifles for us if we let them live."

"Are they soldiers?"

"No. They say they worked for the soldiers but now the soldiers are chasing them. When our warriors found them, they were crossing the Powder River, heading for the Montana territory."

"Can they be trusted?"

Sitting Bull shrugged. "Can any white man be trusted? I think not, but still, it would be a good thing if we could get more rifles. Will you go with Man Who Kills Horses and talk to these men in the white tongue?"

Little Wolf followed Man Who Kills Horses through the village to a clearing near the banks of the river. In the center of the clearing the two white captives sat. Their arms tied behind their backs, they sat facing each other with their ankles bound together. A solemn young Sioux guarded them, his rifle cradled across his arms as he sat near a fire in front of them. At the sight of the old man and the tall young warrior, the men glanced anxiously at each other before raising their eyes to Man Who Kills Horses. Little Wolf could read the thin hope in the white men's eyes, no doubt wondering if they had bargained for their lives or whether their fate was to be a slow death.

One of them, the big, rawboned one, spoke in the Sioux tongue. "Friend." He nodded his head up and down vigorously. "Friend, friend."

Man Who Kills Horses said nothing but stepped aside in order to give Little Wolf a better view of the captives. The Sioux guard watched with but a slight display of curiosity. Little Wolf stood silently studying the two men. They were dirty and shaggy. Both wore long buffalo coats even though the weather was quite warm. The big one, the one who had spoken and was now watching Little Wolf like a camp dog waiting for a bone, had deep-set eyes that seemed to peer out of caves on either side of his long thin nose. His mouth, which seemed to naturally turn down at the corners, formed a crooked grin when he attempted to make a friendly smile. The rest of his face was covered by whiskers. Part of one ear was missing. Someone had shot it away or, possibly, some animal had bitten it off. Little Wolf barely glanced at the other man, a short little man with a round belly. It was easy to see which of the two was the more dangerous.

He had to think for a moment before he formed the words in English. "You are buffalo hunters." It was a statement, not a question.

"Oh, nossir," the big one hastened to reply. "We ain't buffler hunters. Nossir!"

"You smell like buffalo hunters," was Little Wolf's stoic reply.

"Oh, we mighta kilt one or two," he allowed, "jest to keep from starving." He looked at his companion for confirmation. "But we ain't done no real buffler hunting, not in these parts nohow."

Little Wolf remained expressionless as he studied the two of them. They were liars, of that he was certain. There was no doubt they were two of the scores of buffalo hunters who killed off thousands from the herds every year, taking only the hides and the heads and leaving the rest to rot on the prairie. The policy of the Cheyenne and the Sioux was the same when it came to dealing with vermin of this kind: kill them whenever and wherever they were caught. He turned to Man Who Kills Horses and spoke to him in the Indian tongue.

"These two are clearly buffalo hunters. Why is it they were not killed?"

"Guns. They say they can get many rifles, the new rifles that the soldiers carry." When Little Wolf did not respond right away, he added, "They were not killing buffalo when we found them. They were merely crossing through our lands."

Little Wolf considered this for a moment, then shrugged. "What is it you wish me to ask them?" He didn't like their looks and he questioned the wisdom in dealing with them at all. But, they were not his prisoners. It was not for him to make judgment.

"Guns," Man Who Kills Horses answered. "How many guns and what they want in return."

Little Wolf turned back to the two men before him. "How many rifles?"

"Oh, thirty or forty anyway," the big one answered.

"New rifles? Repeaters?"

"Yessir, brand-new army carbines, and maybe some other goods you might be interested in."

"What do you want in return?"

Kroll thought for a moment before answering, his confidence increasing when it began to look as if he might ride out with his hair after all. "Why, we'll take it out in hides'd be all right, I reckon. We jess wanna be friends with the Sioux, that's all."

Little Wolf turned again to Man Who Kills Horses, speaking once again in the Indian tongue, "They say they have many rifles they want to trade for buffalo hides. I think they are liars and not to be trusted but it is not for me to say. I think as soon as you release them, you will never see them again."

Man Who Kills Horses nodded soberly, weighing Little Wolf's words. He motioned for Little Wolf to walk with him and started back toward the council lodge. "I will talk to Sitting Bull. Then we will decide. Perhaps you are right and they want merely to save their scalps. On the other hand, it would be good to get the rifles."

Behind them, the two white men whispered together. "Gawdamn, Kroll, what the hell are you doing? We ain't got no gawdamn rifles."

"Shut up! That damn Injun might understand English too," he whispered, indicating the guard. "You wanna get out of here with your hair, don't you? 'Sides, it might be a good idea to trade with these red sons for hides instead of havin' to work fer 'em."

"But we ain't got no gawdamn guns!"

"Well, dammit, we can get some, maybe trade 'em some other stuff too. And I know where we can lay our hands on a whole wagon-load of goods. I'm gittin' damn tard of workin' them damn buffler anyhow. Maybe me and you'll just go into the tradin' business. We'll jess find us a spot in the shade this side of the Platte and wait till the next train comes along, cut us out a wagon and then we'll be in the tradin' business."

"But these damn Injuns want guns!"

"I know that, but hell, they'll trade for whatever we got."

The elders evidently decided that it was worth the risk to release the captives in hopes of gaining some rifles because early the next morning Little Wolf saw them riding out of camp. He watched them until they disappeared over the bluff, not really interested for it was of no concern to him whether they lived or died. His personal feeling was that they were not to be trusted and would probably hightail it for the goldfields where they were no doubt headed when captured by Sitting Bull's scouts.

CHAPTER 18

Squint nudged Joe gently with his heels when the horse hesitated on the bank of a small stream, unsure if they were crossing or just drinking. "Let's go, Joe. I'm tired too, but we ain't got more'n a couple of hours' ride. Then you might get a little grain tonight before you bed down." He had been making good time for the last two days since he had left Waddie Bodkin in the Black Hills and headed for Fort Lincoln. Waddie had done his best to talk him into staying on to prospect for gold but Squint had made up his mind that it was time to try something else.

Thoughts of Waddie made him laugh. "Damn crazy little Irishman," he chuckled. Two years in Montana and they didn't raise enough color to pay for the whiskey Waddie drank. *Well*, he thought, *I wanted to try my hand at panning for gold and I reckon I got that notion out of my head.* The work was too hard to suit him. After a year, he found himself staring at the mountains in the distance and wondering what was beyond them. He and Waddie had tried their luck at the Grasshopper Diggings before they moved on to Alder Gulch where they raised a little color, but not enough to make two men rich. So, when word came that there was gold discovered in the Black Hills, Waddie made up his mind to go there. Squint decided to go with him that far but then to continue on to Fort Lincoln and go back to scouting for the army. He'd had his fill of prospecting but he was also aware that the Black Hills were smack-dab in the middle of Sioux hunting grounds and that fact didn't appeal to his sense of self-preservation. So he took his share of the small amount of dust they had collected, bade farewell to Waddie and pointed Joe toward Lincoln.

*   *   *

"Hey, you old muskrat! Are you lost?"

Squint turned in the direction of the voice. There was a familiar ring to the voice but he couldn't identify it immediately. His face lit up with a wide smile when he spotted the short barrel-like body coming around the corner of the stable on legs so bowed he looked like a duck out of water. "Well, skin me if it ain't Andy Coulter!" He slid down off of Joe. "Hell, pardner, I thought you was kilt long ago."

"I thought your hair was decorating a lance up in the Wind River country," Andy returned. "What brung you into Lincoln?"

Squint tied Joe and his mule Sadie to the hitching post and walked around to shake Andy's hand. "I reckon I'm looking for a job," he said. "Thought I'd see if the army's hiring any scouts." He grinned and added, "But I reckon if they got you, they likely don't need any more."

Andy laughed. "I reckon I'm the only one they got. They got about fifty more on the payroll that calls theirselves scouts but I reckon if they hired you, then they'd have two. Come on, I'll take you to see Captain Benteen. I could dang shore use some help."

There was very little hesitation on Benteen's part after Andy's recommendation that Squint Peterson was probably the best dang scout in the whole territory with the possible exception of himself. He and Squint had trapped the Yellowstone country before the first prospector's wagon had made it to Montana so he was damn sure qualified to scout the area. Benteen seemed glad to have another experienced scout so Squint was welcomed to the regiment and turned over to Andy to get himself settled in.

"You can throw your bedroll in with me if you want to," Andy told him as they walked across the parade ground. "They let me have a little room next to the quartermaster. It's a little ways away from the soldier boys so it ain't so dang noisy."

"Who's the head man of this outfit?"

Andy chuckled before answering. "Colonel George Armstrong Custer," he announced.

"Custer? Hell, I thought he was shipped back East a while back for disobeying orders or something."

"He was. But he's back now, struttin' bigger'n ever. Says

he's gonna clean all the Injuns out of the Yellowstone country."

"He's a mite ambitious, ain't he?" The news was not especially pleasing to Squint. He had had no personal relations with the man, but he didn't like some of the things he had heard about him. Of course, he had to consider that some of the stories might be just that, stories, and he reckoned he would have to see for himself. "What's the job like?"

"Patrols mostly, chasing Sioux raiding parties"—he paused to spit a stream of chewing tobacco at a lizard scampering up a pole on the porch—"and burying prospectors."

Squint threw his pack up on the porch and turned to Andy. "Correct me if I'm wrong, 'cause I've been up in the mountains for a spell. But last I heard, there was a treaty that guaranteed all that country from the Black Hills to the Big Horns was Injun territory."

Andy snorted. "Hell, Squint, you know as well as I do them treaties don't mean nothin'. Besides, I reckon you heard there's some talk about finding gold up in that country—and where there's talk of gold, there's plenty of damn fools to risk their hair to git it."

"I can guarantee that. I just left a little Irishman back up in the hills."

After they had settled Squint's belongings, they walked back outside and sat down on the edge of the porch to have a smoke. Squint took out a well-worn cherrywood pipe he had carved four winters before in the Wind River Mountains. He watched as Andy tore off part of a twist of tobacco and stuffed it in his mouth then handed the twist to him. Taking his time, Squint tore off a piece of the twist and slowly ground it up in his hand. When it was right, he filled the pipe with it. He reached up and struck a match on a porch post and lit the pipe, drawing deeply until the tobacco was burning well. After a few puffs, he tamped the load down and relit it. Satisfied that it was working right, he leaned back against the post to talk.

"Andy, things might be fairly peaceful with the Injuns right now, but if the army don't quit letting settlers and prospectors go anywhere they damn please, it's gonna be more than a few killings here and there. It's gonna be all-out war. I'm satisfied the Sioux ain't gonna stand still for it much longer. Hell, look at what old Red Cloud did to the army. He damn sure closed up Bozeman's trail. And already old Sitting Bull is calling all the Sioux and Cheyenne together up in the Big Horns. Part of Red Cloud's people have joined up with him. At least that's the story I hear."

Andy shrugged his shoulders and launched a long stream of tobacco juice in the direction of a horsefly that landed on the step below him. "I reckon I can't argue with that. They's gonna be war all right but I think the army's made up its mind that it's gonna win this one. Hell, you know as well as I do they ain't gonna stop folks from moving in on that land."

There was a pause in their conversation while they watched a young officer walking in their direction.

"Here comes one of the few good officers in this whole damn outfit," Andy commented and punctuated the statement with a stream of brown juice.

"What are you doing, Andy, holding that porch down so the wind won't blow it away?" There was a wide friendly smile on the officer's face.

"Nah, I'm just settin' on my brains so the army don't see 'em and want to make me a lieutenant." They both laughed. "Say howdy to Squint Peterson. He's signed up to do some scouting for us. Me and Squint go way back. Squint, this here's Lieutenant Allred."

The young officer smiled and extended his hand. "Tom Allred, Mr. Peterson."

"Pleased to meet you, Lieutenant." Squint got up to shake hands.

"Damn!" Tom exclaimed. "You're a big one."

Squint simply shrugged his shoulders, not knowing how to respond. Finally he said, "I reckon."

Tom placed one foot up on the second step and leaned on his knee. "If it wasn't for ole Andy here, I wouldn't be around today. He pulled my fat out of the fire for sure."

Andy almost blushed. "Hell, Lieutenant, when them bastards caught us in that crossfire, I was grabbing for anything. It just happened to be you. Tell you the truth, I thought you was dead. I was just using you for cover while I floated downstream."

Tom and Squint glanced at each other. Both were grin-

ning broadly at Andy's modesty. Both knew he was lying.
Squint spoke up, "Why, I reckon the little ole runty var-
mint has saved my hide a time or two, like the time up on
the Yellowstone when them three Crow bucks jumped me.
I was up to my belly button in water with forty pounds of
beaver plews in one hand and trying to keep my possibles
dry in the other."

Andy laughed. "If you wasn't so damn tight, I would'na
had to help you." He turned to Tom and explained. "He
wasn't about to turn loose them pelts and he couldn't let
his powder and shot go, so he was just kicking at them
Injuns with both hands up in the air. He looked like a
moose trying to chase off a pack of coyotes. It was hard
for me to steady my aim, I was laughing so hard."

Tom laughed then straightened up and took his leave.
"Well, Squint, glad to have you with us. I've got to go see
if my horse is going to be ready to travel tomorrow. He
picked up a bad stone bruise on that last patrol and I'm
not sure he'll be fit."

Andy called out after him as he walked away toward the
stables. "We going out in the morning?"

"Yeah," Tom called back over his shoulder. "Captain
Benteen said to draw rations and ammunition for ten days.
He'll call for a briefing sometime this afternoon."

Andy was pleased to see that Squint and Tom had
seemed to hit it off pretty well. He had grown quite fond
of the young lieutenant and he felt the addition of Squint
would help keep them all out of trouble. He may have
saved Squint's hide a time or two but he knew that if the
account was balanced, he'd be the one owing.

CHAPTER 19

Four days out from Fort Lincoln the patrol halted in a grove of trees near the banks of the Little Missouri. It had been a long, tedious patrol and Tom decided the men could use a little rest and the opportunity to shake some of the dust out of their clothes. He was the ranking officer on this detail, Captain Benteen having remained in Lincoln with a slight case of the dropsy. It was one of the few opportunities Tom had to command a patrol of longer than three days and fifty miles. He usually rode second in command to the captain and he was enjoying the temporary freedom to make his own decisions. There was no real anticipation of trouble of a major nature since the Sioux had been relatively quiet over the summer with no hostile activity beyond scattered raids on settlers or freighters. With both Andy and Squint along as scouts, he had little fear of riding into ambush, at least not this close to Fort Lincoln. While the men and horses rested in the shade of the cottonwoods, both scouts were out on the western side of the river, Squint to the south and Andy to the north.

He settled himself with his back against a tree and removed his hat to wipe some of the perspiration from his forehead. From his position he could see out across the muddy river to the rolling plains and the distant mountains on the horizon. The mountains looked to be no more than a half day's ride from the tree he was leaning against, but he knew they were probably two full days away. "Everything is distorted in this damn country," he muttered. "It sure is a long sight from Mississippi." The memory passed through his mind of that hot summer day near Vicksburg when he lay in a muddy ditch and saw his first cavalry charge. That war was a million years removed from the war he was fighting now. Back then, it was a war with rules. A

man knew who and where the enemy was because most of
the time he was coming straight at you, firing volleys of
rifle fire. Cannon roared and foot soldiers charged, bayo-
nets fixed. And the cavalry was glorious, galloping into the
fray with swords drawn and brightly colored sashes flying.
With that thought in mind, he looked about him at the
weary troopers taking advantage of the short break in their
march. There was no glory to be won out here. Most of
the time they never caught sight of the savages they hunted,
only where they had been. It was like chasing spirits. On
the occasion when a war party was actually spotted, it was
usually because they wanted to be seen, hoping they could
lead you into an ambush in some blind draw. Or, if you
outnumbered them and gave chase, they would simply disappear in a country where you could see for miles all
around you. Maybe Custer was right. Maybe the only way
to fight the Indians was to attack them in their winter
camps. Then the memory of Washita came to mind and he
at once experienced a sour taste in his mouth. That engagement had sickened him with the aimless killing of women
and children. They had even shot the camp dogs. It would
be a long time indeed before he could rid his nostrils of
the stench of that burning village. He took a deep breath
and tried to shake the scene from his mind. He didn't like
to think too long on that *battle,* as Colonel Custer referred
to it. It was more like a slaughter in Tom's mind.

He stared at the tiny cloud of dust on the far side of the
river for a good thirty seconds before he brought his mind
back from its meandering and realized the dust cloud had
been kicked up by Squint Peterson's horse. Squint topped
a rise and headed for the river and Tom was forced to call
his attention back to the present. He was still a good distance away, but even at that distance, there was no mistaking the solid figure that was Squint Peterson. Joe was a
solidly built roan and big as most horses go. He had to be
to carry Squint's bulk. But Squint made him appear to be
no bigger than an Indian pony from a distance. He crossed
the river and headed toward the grove of trees where the
detachment was resting, Joe working at an easy gallop.
Tom guessed that whatever Squint had found, it wasn't
important enough to overwork Joe. Tom stood up and
walked to meet him.

"Lieutenant," Squint said calmly. "Might be somethin', I don't know, but I reckon you might want to take a look."

Tom reached for his horse's reins. He had been with Squint long enough now to know that as with Andy Coulter, if he suggested some action, there was usually cause to take action. "What is it, Squint?"

"Smoke, off to the northwest," he replied. "Could be a brush fire, too big for a smoke signal." He paused and Tom guessed that his next suggestion was what Squint really thought it was in the first place. "But it could be some settlers' wagons burning."

Tom was already in the saddle. "Sergeant Porter, mount 'em up!"

The detachment forded the river in a column of twos. Tom sighted Andy Coulter in the distance, angling across the prairie to intercept the column. Within a half mile's length, he reined in beside Squint and Tom.

"What do you make of it?" he asked Squint.

"Pilgrims, I reckon, or freighters," Squint replied. "Probably got hit by a Sioux war party."

"Yeah, that's what I figure. You can tell by the color of the smoke that it ain't no brush fire. That looks like folks' goods burning."

They rode four or more miles before they reached a horseshoe-shaped grassy draw that appeared to contain the origin of the smoke. Tom slowed the troop to a walk while Andy and Squint rode out ahead to scout the area. He didn't want to go charging into the draw just to find out he was badly outnumbered by hostiles who were eagerly awaiting him. Not more than ten or fifteen minutes passed before Andy reappeared on a knoll above the draw and signaled him to come on in.

The scene awaiting him was by no means unusual to Tom. He had witnessed the same scenario a few times before, only with different wagons, different bodies. This time there were two wagons burning, the livestock gone from one wagon. The other still had a team of horses hitched, all dead. This puzzled him somewhat. It wasn't like an Indian to leave good horses behind. The thought left him when he heard Andy behind him.

"I count six dead, five by the wagons and one more up the rise there." He pointed toward a lump halfway up the other side of the knoll. "All of 'ems been scalped. Three of 'em got arrows in their backs, Sioux markings."

"Poor bastards," Tom replied. "Looks like a typical raiding party." He stood looking at the smoking wagons for a long time before continuing. "But what in hell were they doing this far up in hostile territory? We aren't that far from the old Bozeman Trail. You don't reckon they were crazy enough to try to go through that way, do you?" His question went unanswered when Squint, who had been looking over the area pretty thoroughly, interrupted.

"Lieutenant, there was three wagons altogether. One wagon, loaded down, set off to the south, up yonder way." He pointed toward a range of low-lying hills. "I figure they took the team off that wagon and hitched it up with the team on the wagon they run off with."

"I wonder why they left these horses. You'da thought they'd have stole them too," Andy said.

Squint glanced at Andy. Andy nodded in agreement with what Squint was about to say even before Squint said it. "If it'a been Injuns, they most likely would have took the horses. But this weren't the work of no Injuns."

Tom looked surprised. "But what about the arrows and the scalps?"

Andy spoke up, "There ain't no tracks around this whole place but them that belongs to the wagon teams and whoever was riding the two shod horses that was flanking 'em. Ain't no sign of Injun ponies anywheres about."

"You mean you think they were murdered by some of their own people?"

Squint answered, "Looks like that, or somebody they met up with. And whoever done 'em in wanted to make it look like Injuns done it. But they sure as hell weren't very bright about it. Them men was kilt with guns and then whoever done it scalped 'em and stuck them arrows in their backs. Take a look at this." He motioned Tom over to one of the corpses. "This poor devil was shot right in the face. That's what kilt him. See that arrow stuck in his back? Hell, it ain't in deep enough to make him grunt. I'll bet you a plug of tobacca the bastard that done it drove it in with his hand." He stood up. "Look at them other two. The arrows is stuck in the same spot on their backs."

Tom stood looking down at the unfortunate teamster. "This is some dirty business here."

"I'd say," Andy answered. "And I'll tell you somethin' else. If they keep on the trail they lit out on, they're heading straight into Sioux country. They ain't thinking about taking that wagon back to Bannack or Virginia City."

"Could be gold from Montana," Tom speculated. "But the Sioux don't have any use for gold." He studied Andy's face. "You thinking rifles? You think they're taking rifles to the Indians?"

"Could be. Could be anything. But whatever it is, they got a wagon loaded down with it."

"Damn!" Tom swore. He was faced with a difficult decision. His orders were clear. He had provisions for a ten-day march. That meant five days out and five days back. He was to take note of and report any Indian activity he encountered. His was not an offensive mission, merely a patrol. Of course, if he encountered any small bands of hostiles, he was to use his discretion as to any action he deemed necessary, and he was to lend assistance to any civilians under attack. Had this piece of work been done by hostiles, he would have followed routine procedures and attempted to track the guilty band if possible and punish them if the hostile force was not superior in numbers to his own. Otherwise it was just another six fatalities in the war against the savages. But that wasn't the case. Now he might be dealing with renegade civilians who were selling guns to the Indians. What would Captain Benteen do? He always went by the book. Tom thought on it for a moment and then reluctantly decided. "Well, there isn't much we can do about it now. I haven't got the men or provisions to start out across hostile territory. We've been out four days. We can follow that wagon trail for another half day to see if they change their course. Then we'll have to abandon the search and head back. Sergeant Hale, get a burial detail and put these men in the ground."

The trail led south for a few miles and then turned due west for a couple of miles until it crossed a small stream. Then it turned south again and followed the stream. They were taking no pains to cover their trail. Since they were traveling in hostile territory, this further indicated their lack

of fear of attack by Indians. Tom could only guess how
much lead they had on the column but he pushed his troops
ahead at a canter. Darkness caught the column near a fork
in the stream and Tom ordered the march to halt there
and make camp. He informed his sergeant that the patrol
was to be ready to circle back toward Fort Lincoln the
following morning. The two scouts went out on reconnais-
sance to make sure there were no hostiles about. Pickets
were posted and the detachment settled in for the night.

Squint unsaddled Joe and gave him a ration of oats.
"You're gettin kinda spoiled, ain'tcha, boy? Eating army
grain for supper every night. I might need to take you back
in the hills before you forget to eat grass." He rubbed the
horse's neck for a few minutes before going over to the
small campfire to help himself to a cup of coffee. It would
be a while before the tin coffee cup would be cool enough
to touch it to his lips so, while he waited, he glanced around
to see where the lieutenant might be. He spotted him leaning back on his saddle, talking to Andy Coulter.

"My ass is sore as a new bride's," Squint confided as he
strolled over to the two men.

Andy laughed. "You jess gittin' too damn old. That's
your trouble."

"You know, you might be right. Why, I can feel my hand
just a'tremblin' trying to keep from spilling this hot coffee
on your sorry ass."

"Set down before you give us all a bath." Andy moved
over a little, offering him a portion of the small sapling he
was using as a backrest. Squint settled himself and tested
his coffee.

"Damn!" he cursed when the tin cup still proved a bit
too warm. Gingerly, he approached the offending vessel
with his lips pursed tightly until he managed to sip a small
portion of the hot liquid. Satisfied that he was at last making some progress, he spoke, "You know, it's a dirty damn
shame to let those bastards go. We're liable to be looking
at the business end of them damn rifles . . . if that's what
they're hauling."

Tom replied, "I know it, Squint, but dammit, I can't go
running off against the whole Sioux nation with a handful
of men. Besides, I've got my orders."

"Oh, I know that, Lieutenant. Hell, ain't no sense in

gittin these boys kilt over some no-account renegades." He paused to take another sip of the coffee. "But I was thinkin' you could send me out to follow 'em in the morning, just to see what they was up to."

"Have you gone loco?" Andy retorted.

"I couldn't do that," Tom said. "It's too dangerous. You'd more than likely lose your hair."

Squint shrugged. "Dangerous for a column of soldiers but not for one man. Hell, Lieutenant, I been traveling this country by myself for more years than you been in the army. I ain't got no intention of losing my hair."

Tom thought over the proposal for a minute. "It would be helpful to know who we were trailing and where they were going with that wagon. But hell, Squint, I don't know."

Andy studied his friend for a moment before asking, "Squint, what in hell do you want to go sneaking after that wagon for? Mind you, I know you can do it and I'll go with you if you want me to. But what do you want to do it for?"

"I'll tell you the truth, Andy, I just feel like doing it. I just feel an itch to see what them buzzards are up to." He turned back to Tom. "How 'bout it, Lieutenant? All right with you? I don't want the army to say I went on vacation and cut my rations."

"All right, if you want to do it. But Squint, be damn careful."

"Mister, you can count on that."

At sunup the next morning the troop broke camp and headed back east toward the Little Missouri. Squint rode out to the southwest, following the trail left by the renegades. Andy again volunteered to go with Squint but Tom didn't think it wise to return without at least one of his scouts. It didn't matter to Squint. Andy Coulter was a good man to have along on any occasion but Squint was just as glad to be on his own this time. "Unless you got an army with you, the fewer the better in Injun territory," he told Joe as he wheeled the horse around and took a last look at the departing column before crossing the stream and heading deeper into Sioux country.

Once the sun climbed a little higher in the sky, the morn-

ing chill disappeared and soon Squint pulled off his buckskin shirt and tied it behind his saddle. He had a feeling
he was gaining on the wagon, but since there had been no
rain for some time, it was still hard to tell how old the
tracks were. He had hoped to overtake them by nightfall,
but as mile after mile passed, he was not so sure. They
were making good time. Of course, with a double team
hitched to one wagon, they could have plowed their way
across the prairie by now, he thought.

It was necessary to be more cautious now, as late afternoon approached, because he was crossing through the rolling hills that lay at the feet of the Big Horns. *Smack in the
middle of Sioux hunting grounds,* Squint thought. He
couldn't avoid losing some of the ground he had gained
that morning due to the necessity of having to keep to the
low draws wherever possible, looking long and hard before
crossing any open flat stretch of ground. He knew his only
chance of coming out of this with his hair was to see any
hostiles long before they saw him.

He had been in this country many times before. It had
been a while but he remembered enough to know that he
was getting mighty close to the Powder River. By his reckoning, it couldn't be too far to the fork where the Crazy
Woman joined the Powder, a favorite camping place of the
Sioux. When night caught him still not within sight of the
men he followed, he decided to play a hunch. He was willing to bet that the destination of the renegades was indeed
the fork of the Crazy Woman and the Powder. They had
been heading straight for it all day long. The trail might be
hard to see at night but he was of a mind to keep going in
the same direction in hopes of making up some ground on
them. The odds were against their changing direction so he
pushed on in the darkness.

He rode on under a three-quarter moon that shone
brightly enough to form sharp shadows under the occasional patches of trees that lined the rims of the basin. He
kept as close to the tree line as he could, so as not to cast
a solitary silhouette under the moonlit sky. As he rode, he
strained to see as far ahead as he was able, and to each
side, watching for any shape in the shadows that didn't look
just right. Along about midnight, by his reckoning, he

topped a gently rising hill and suddenly there was a hazy glow on the horizon.

Campfire, he thought, *and a pretty good-sized one at that,* too big for the men he was trailing. He nudged Joe to pick up the pace a little while he kept his eyes on the glow, his mind busy calculating what he was riding toward. It had to be a village, and more than likely, it was Sitting Bull's village. From the size of the blaze, it had to be a council fire. He would know soon enough. If the glow spread out as he approached it, it would tell him he had found a village sure enough. This time of year, the squaws would be cooking outside the tipis. He guided Joe down a draw and up over another rise. Then he confirmed what he had suspected. It was a Sioux village all right, and a big one. There were hundreds of tiny cook fires stretching along the river. Squint felt a chill run down his spine and he suddenly felt very alone. He reined Joe to a halt and stepped down from the saddle. Leading his horse, he walked toward a stand of trees near the riverbank, his eyes darting constantly from the trees back to the glow of the cook fires across the river. Under cover of deep shadows, he stopped to listen and decide what his next move should be.

Well, he thought, they beat me to the camp. Ain't nothing I can do about that. I sure as hell ain't goin' in looking for 'em. His initial feeling was that he had lost, that they had gotten away with the dirty business back on the prairie. But he wasn't quite ready to give up that easily. Hell, I might as well find me a place to hole up and wait around for a spell. Maybe they'll come back this way, unless they mean to stay with the Injuns and my guess is they ain't. I reckon they'll be wanting to take payment and head north to Virginia City or south to Salt Lake. Either way, they'll most likely come back in this direction. Any other way, they got to go straight over the mountains. He thought about it for a moment more and it seemed to make sense. Another man might have simply turned tail while the getting was good and returned to Fort Lincoln. But Squint had a real strong desire to see the faces of the men who murdered those six freighters, and to see them hang for it.

Across the river from where Squint stood in the shadows, Kroll and Moody strutted triumphantly in the firelight of

the large council fire, holding a new Spencer rifle in the
air. About fifty yards away, a mob of Sioux warriors and
women crowded around their wagon, pulling one treasure
after another out for inspection.

"Empty it out!" Kroll called out, grinning first at his
sidekick then back at the Sioux chief Sitting Bull. "Just like
I told you, Chief. I told you we'd be back. Yessir, we got
a load of trade goods there too, and rifles, just like you
wanted."

The old chief stared unemotionally at the wild-talking
white man for a while before turning to Little Wolf, who
was acting as his translator. When he heard Little Wolf's
translation, his expression remained stolid and he instructed
Little Wolf to tell the man that there were only two cases
of rifles and twelve boxes of bullets in the wagon. He
needed more than this. Most of the items the white men
brought would be useful to the women but not to fight a
war. When Little Wolf relayed the chief's message, the
white men became concerned.

"Look here," Kroll said. "You tell the chief that this
here is all we could git this time but we know where there's
plenty more rifles . . . and ammunition too. You tell him
we'll bring him more next time if we git a good price for
this wagon. Tell him that." He attempted to force a friendly
smile in the direction of Sitting Bull.

Little Wolf scowled. He did not like these two and he
didn't like the fact that he had to be the chief's go-between
in negotiations with such vermin. Before he passed Kroll's
response to the chief, he moved a few steps to the wind-
ward to avoid the smell of them. Then he turned back to
Sitting Bull and said, "These buffalo hunters say they will
bring many more rifles if you give them a good trade for
this wagon-load of trinkets."

Although he had no way of knowing what Little Wolf
actually said, Kroll smiled broadly and nodded vigorously
as if in agreement. His sidekick, Moody, seemed a little
more nervous about the ring of Sioux and Cheyenne warriors that had gathered around the negotiations. It was
becoming obvious, even to one of Moody's limited intelligence, that the two of them were not exactly received as
welcome guests. He knew for sure the tall brave doing the
translating had no use for them at all and it wouldn't take

much to cause him to come after their scalps. At this point, both he and Kroll knew they would not be permitted to leave the village with the rifles. It was a question of whether or not the chief would permit them to trade the rest of the goods with the Indians standing around waiting for his decision.

Through Little Wolf, the chief asked, "You have firewater?"

"Yessir," Kroll was quick to reply, his face lit up measurably. "I shore do, four one-gallon jugs of genuine rye whiskey." He glanced at Moody as if to say, "Now we got 'em!" His enthusiasm was short-lived, however, when he heard the chief's response.

Little Wolf translated. "Sitting Bull says there will be none of the white man's firewater in his camp. He will not have his braves poisoned and he orders you to pour the jugs out on the ground. When you do this, you will be permitted to trade your trinkets with the people."

The trading went on for most of the night. Kroll and Moody didn't do as well as they had hoped, due mostly to the fact that the wagons they had stolen contained merchandise more suited to white prospectors than Sioux Indians. Still, they traded enough hides to load three pack mules. They didn't want the wagon anyway. Moody had managed to hold back a small jug of whiskey for the two of them and when the wagon was finally empty and the last of the mules were traded, they moved off to the edge of the village to have a drink before going to bed.

"I shore would like to have me a woman," Kroll said as they watched the men and women disappear into their tipis for the night. "I seen one or two of them squaws that looked pretty good."

"Hell," Moody replied, "I didn't see any of 'em that didn't look good."

"I'm gittin gawdamn rutty is all I know, with nothin' but your scabby ass to look at for the last month."

Moody changed the subject to one of more serious concern to him at the moment. "Kroll, we better git ourselves out of here. I don't cotton to hangin' around no damn Sioux camp for very long. They might git to thinkin' 'bout us being white men."

Kroll thought about it for a moment. Moody was probably right although he felt sure Sitting Bull wouldn't cut off a possible source for guns. Still it didn't make much sense to hang around too long. Maybe the best thing to do was take their pelts and skedaddle. "Hell, I'm tired. We'll lay up for a day and then light out for Virginia City and sell them hides."

It was apparent to the two traders that the people of the village were not too pleased to see the sun come up the following morning and find the two of them still in their midst. Men and women avoided the two white men as they lay next to their own campfire and, when Kroll approached a woman in hopes of striking a trade for some female companionship, she ran from him. Soon they were visited by Man Who Kills Horses. Kroll knew only a few words of Sioux but Man Who Kills Horses' message was unmistakable. They weren't welcome here.

"Well, that's a helluva way to treat friends," Kroll whined. "Why the hell ain't we welcome?" His dander was getting up at the thought of being treated as inferior to a bunch of savages. Man Who Kills Horses' expression remained blank; he was unable to understand Kroll's words.

"You are not welcome because our people do not welcome coyotes and vultures in our camp."

Both white men were startled by the words. They had not heard the tall Cheyenne warrior come up silently behind them. Kroll jerked his head around, his eyes flashing with anger as he started to respond violently, but thinking better of the notion when he met the steely gaze of Little Wolf. At once his expression softened and he forced a twisted smile across his face.

"Hell, pardner," he whined. "You got no call to talk like that. Why, me and Moody is friends. Didn't we bring you them rifles and stuff?"

Little Wolf's face was hard, his voice cold as iron. "You are enemies of my people. You kill off the buffalo we need to live. We have given you skins for the things you probably stole from your own people and now you will go back and kill more buffalo as long as the soldiers pay you. You think you traded for hides but what you traded for were your lives. Sitting Bull has allowed you to leave this village unharmed. Take your stench away from here while you can. Do not come back to this place." He paused to make sure his message was being received. "I go now with a hunting party. Remember my name. I am Little Wolf. If you are here when I return, it is Little Wolf who will kill you." He turned and walked away, leaving them speechless.

"Damn!" Moody exclaimed. "That buck means business. I reckon they don't want our company around here."

"That red-skinned son of a bitch," Kroll muttered. "Ain't nobody running me out before I'm damn good and ready to go." His hand dropped to the pistol stuck in his belt.

Man Who Kills Horses stood silently watching the two men. He had not understood a word Little Wolf had spoken to the two white men but he did not fail to understand the intent of the message. Now he watched Kroll, waiting to see his reaction. Moody looked around nervously, noticing that several warriors who stood silently watching now seemed interested in the conversation between the white men and Little Wolf.

"Look here, Kroll, you're fixin' to git us both kilt. Let's us just ease on out of here before the rest of them bucks git riled."

Kroll was mad but he cooled down enough to see that Moody was right. They couldn't fight them all. Better to take their pelts and go. "Yeah, all right. Don't piss your britches." He looked at Man Who Kills Horses who in turn made sign language for sundown. Kroll did not mistake the meaning. "Yeah," he grumbled, "sundown." He and Moody began gathering their belongings to leave.

Kroll was in one of his deepest black moods when the two of them led their mules out of the village and followed the river downstream. Moody didn't like to see Kroll in one of those moods. Usually it meant somebody was sure to get killed and he felt sorry for the poor bastard who got in his way. But this time there were too many Indians. If Kroll started something, they were both bound to get killed. This frustrated Kroll and only served to deepen his black mood. Moody decided it best to say as little as possible to him until he got it out of his system. The opportunity for Kroll to vent his rage came sooner than Moody expected. The mules were loaded down so they continued downstream for a while, looking for a shallow crossing. A hundred yards or so below a section of the village where some Cheyennes had put up their tipis, they came upon a group of women picking wild berries. Kroll pulled up and sat leering at the women for several minutes. Moody knew what was on his mind and kicked his horse up beside Kroll's.

"They's too many of 'em, Kroll, and we ain't hardly out of sight of the camp."

"I don't recollect asking you nuthin," Kroll shot back and continued to stare at the women who, by this time, had stopped their berry picking and watched the two white men warily. One of the women held her nose with her fingers in a gesture indicating a foul odor and the rest of the women laughed. "Gawdamn whores!" Kroll spat and kicked his horse hard. Moody followed, grateful that Kroll had not brought down the whole tribe on them.

Around a bend in the river they came to a shallow place and crossed. Once on the other side, they climbed the bank into a dense area of brush and trees. There was a path through the bushes and they followed it through the undergrowth, looking for a way out to the open country. Suddenly Kroll pulled up sharply. Moody, behind him on the narrow path, could not see what was ahead and called out, "What is it?"

Morning Sky was not aware of the two men until she heard Moody call out. Curious, but not alarmed, she left her berry pouch on the ground and straightened up to see who might be coming down the path. When she saw Kroll leering at her she was still not alarmed and, by the time she realized what he had in mind, it was too late. Instinctively, she tried to run into the bushes, out of the path of the horses, hoping to be able to make her way through the thicket where it might be too difficult for a man on horseback to follow. But Kroll was not to be denied this opportunity. He kicked his horse hard and crashed into the thicket, knocking Morning Sky to the ground. While Moody was still trying to see what was taking place in the thick brush ahead of him, Kroll was already out of the saddle and on top of the Indian girl. Although stunned, Morning Sky fought desperately, scratching and screaming until Kroll hit her several times with his fist, finally knocking her unconscious.

"Damn, Kroll!" Moody whined when finally he was able to see what had happened. "You're jest hell-bent on gittin' us kilt, ain't you?"

"Shut up and fetch them mules," he spat. The expression on his face told Moody that neither he nor anybody else was going to stop Kroll from doing what he had in mind. "I told you I was rutty, dammit, and I need to cut meat."

Moody was frantic. Kroll looked like a crazy man, like he had suddenly gone berserk, and they weren't that far away from the Sioux camp. "What if somebody else comes through this here path?" he asked, looking desperately in one direction then another.

Kroll dragged the unconscious girl farther into the bushes. Moody stared at her face, fascinated by the blood forming below her nose and under her eye. Kroll drew his long skinning knife and began hacking away at the girl's clothing until he revealed her naked body. He stood for a moment, leering at her young body. Moody, forgetting his fear, crowded in and peered over Kroll's shoulder. He reached down and put a dirty hand on Morning Sky's bare breast. Kroll took one hand and pushed him away, swearing.

"Git away, gawdammit, and give me some room." He hurriedly undid his trousers and pushed them down around his boot tops. "Git on back to that path and keep your eyes open. And watch them damn mules!"

"What about me? I'm jest as damn rutty as you."

"When I'm done." Kroll was losing his patience. "Now git on back there and take care of them mules!" Morning Sky started to regain consciousness just then and began to struggle under the weight of her attacker. "Listen, little girl," Kroll told her, "you're gonna give it to me one way or 'nother. You might as well jump in and enjoy it. How 'bout it?" In answer, she aimed a foot at his groin, which he easily avoided. At the same time, she wrenched one of her hands free from his grasp and clawed at his eyes. "Have it your way, honey," he hissed and struck his heavy pistol against the side of her head, one, two, three times until she finally went limp.

Moody waited nervously on the tiny path through the bushes, watching for any sign of someone approaching. Several feet away but hidden from his view, he could hear

Kroll's heavy grunting as he worked his fever out on the helpless Indian girl. He could feel his own excitement mounting as he listened. Moody only knew two emotions, fear and lust. Now he could hear the sound of the two bodies thrashing about in the brush then, finally, Kroll reappeared on the path, his face bleeding from the scratches under his eyes. He pulled his trousers up as he walked back to the horses.

"Did you let her go?" Moody was frantic.

Kroll scowled. "She ain't going nowhere. Hurry up if you aim to have your turn. I ain't staying around here long."

Moody scrambled down from his horse and disappeared into the bushes. After a brief time he reappeared, tying up his britches. "Damn, Kroll, you coulda waited to kill her till I had my turn."

"Quit your whining. You got some, didn't you?"

"I reckon. But it didn't seem right. I mean with her belly all laid open and bloody. I almost didn't shoot my wad."

Squint was beginning to think he had played the wrong hunch and the renegades were staying with the Indians after all. That, or maybe they had managed to slip out of the village and he missed them. He was just about to call himself a fool and give up the vigil when he spotted two men emerging from a thicket of bushes on the eastern side of the river. They were leading three pack mules. He climbed up into a tree for a better place to watch until they turned north.

"Virginia City, I reckon," he decided. "Ain't but two of 'em and they shore seem to be in a mighty big hurry."

He climbed down from the tree and took his time saddling Joe. Looking around to make sure he left no evidence of his presence there, he stepped up into the saddle and guided Joe out of the trees. He made a wide circle around the Sioux camp and cut the renegades' trail upriver. He was in no hurry to overtake them right away. Might as well wait until they got closer to a point directly west of Fort Lincoln before he jumped them and not have to bother with them until then.

He cut their trail easily enough but it was plain to see they were taking pains to cover it this time. Before, with the wagons, they acted as if they didn't care who knew where they were going. This time they crossed the river three times and once rode more than a mile up a rocky creek before doubling back and following the river again. "Mighty strange," Squint told Joe. "It's like they know somebody is trailing them. They must not trust their Injun friends, probably thinking them redskins is thinking about keeping the wagons and the hides too. Yessir, they shore are going to a heap of trouble to cover their tracks. And any fool can see they're following the Powder all the way to Montana."

The two men rode their horses hard, making about forty miles before stopping to camp in a large washout near the river. Squint was getting fairly tired of riding himself, and was glad when they finally tied their horses off and went about making a small campfire. He found a well hidden gully with an oak tree hanging over it and settled down to wait for dark. His would be a cold camp—it wasn't wise to risk showing a glow from a fire.

When it was dark enough, Squint moved silently up to the rim of the washout. If he hadn't been following them and seen them go in there, he wouldn't have been able to find them in the dark. From his vantage point, he could see the two of them settling themselves around the tiny fire, both men preparing to sleep. Obviously they didn't feel the necessity to stand guard, thinking they had covered their trail sufficiently. He waited until there was no longer a murmur of conversation and they appeared to be drifting into sleep. Then Squint got up and casually, but silently, walked into their camp.

"Evenin', boys."

Both men reacted as if he had thrown an angry rattlesnake in their midst. Moody almost rolled into the fire in an effort to get to his feet. Squint calmly kicked him over on his back again, keeping his pistol trained on Kroll, knowing this was where the more serious trouble was likely to come from.

"I wouldn't," Squint warned when Kroll started to reach for his rifle, which was laying next to his bedroll. "I don't know how fast you are, but if you want to see if your hand can beat this bullet to that there rifle, why, hell, give her a try."

Kroll was angry but he was alert enough to know that

the imposing figure standing across the fire from them had the advantage. He slowly drew his hand away from the rifle and sat up to face Squint. "What the hell do you want?" He spat the words defiantly, uncertain as to the nature of the attack on their camp.

"Why, I've come to be your personal escort to Fort Lincoln, make sure nothin' happens to you on the way. First though, we need to take a little inventory. Let's see how many guns we can find on you. You can start by taking that rifle by the barrel and sliding it over this way."

"Fort Lincoln?" Kroll growled. "We ain't going to Fort Lincoln. Who the hell are you, anyway?"

After he had relieved them of their weapons, Squint threw a couple of sticks on the fire and fanned the flames back to life. He had a feeling he had run across these two before and he wanted to get a better look at them. "Well, well," he said. "Now, I'm not surprised it's you two sweethearts." He recognized them as the scum he had the run-in with back at Deer Crossing.

Moody finally found his voice, "What you bothering us for, mister? Hell, if it's skins you're looking for, maybe we could cut you in for a share."

"Shut your mouth, Moody," Kroll warned. Looking back at Squint, he spat, "We ain't cuttin' you in for nothin'. We worked for these skins. You ain't gittin' shit."

Squint laughed. "I reckon I could cut myself in for all of 'em if I wanted to, since I'm the one holding the gun. You say you worked for 'em? I *saw* how you worked for 'em. I helped bury the six men you left back there in the hills. So I'll tell you what I'm gonna do. I'll take you back to Fort Lincoln where you can have a fair trial. Then I'm gonna set in the shade and watch while the army hangs your sorry carcasses."

Kroll did not answer immediately. He sat there and glared at the man he now remembered. After a long pause, he said, "We don't know nothin' about no six men. You got the wrong two."

Squint snorted. "We ain't gon' waste time talking about that. I tracked you to that Sioux camp. And I followed you here. You done it all right."

"It's a long ways to Fort Lincoln and they's two of us. I don't think you can make it before one of us gits you."

"Well now, I'm real sorry to hear you say that. I'd hoped we could go along like family. But I'm obliged to you for warning me." That said, he cocked the hammer back on his pistol and put a bullet into Kroll's right shoulder. The impact knocked Kroll over backward. "That'll give you something to think about on the trip besides jumping me."

The sudden explosion of the pistol startled Moody so badly that he thought he was shot too. "Gawd a'mighty, mister, don't kill us!" he screamed, fearful that the next bullet would surely be for him.

"Shut up. I ain't gonna shoot you if you behave yourself. Now take that rag off your neck and stuff it around his shoulder to stop the blood. I don't reckon he'll die before we can get him to his hanging."

After taking care of Kroll's wound, Squint held a gun on Moody while he had him tie up his wounded companion. Then Squint tied Moody up and settled in for a few hours' sleep before heading for Fort Lincoln at first light. He had it figured that Kroll was the real threat, and now that he was neutralized with a bullet wound, Moody would pose no problem. They started out with the first rays of the sun. Moody led, followed by the pack mules, then Kroll, cursing and groaning at every rough spot in the trail. Squint rode behind the procession. The trip to Lincoln took four days from the spot where Squint captured them, four days of hard riding with no more than a few hours of sleep for Squint. He was more than happy to see the gates of the fort just before dark on the fourth day.

"Well, good morning! Danged if you didn't sleep right through reveille." Andy Coulter set a cup of coffee and a mess tin down on the small table between the two cots. "I brung you some breakfast. Figured you'd be hungry if you ever did wake up."

Squint sat up on the edge of his cot. "Much obliged." He glanced out the open doorway. "Damn! It's past sunup. I reckon I did sleep, didn't I?"

"I reckon."

"I didn't get much the last four nights. Tell you the truth, I was a mite shy of closing my eyes very long around them two, even if they was tied up." He blew on the coffee and took a couple of careful sips of the boiling-hot liquid.

"Ain't nothing stronger than army coffee." He set the cup down and stumbled to the door. Looking right and left to be sure no one was around, he walked barefoot around the corner of the building to relieve himself. The colonel was mighty particular about pissing off the porch. Squint and Andy usually did it anyway when they got up. When he finished, he returned to the small room he and Andy shared and sat down to his plate of biscuit and gravy.

Andy tilted his chair back against the wall, cut himself a chew of tobacco and watched Squint eat. "Well, I see they got your two boys locked up in the guardhouse, waiting for trial."

Squint looked up from his plate. "Waiting for trial? Hell, I figured they'd just hang 'em and be done with it. If I'da knowed they was gonna go through all that horseshit, I'da just done the job myself."

Andy laughed. "Maybe you shoulda. You oughta know how the army operates by now. Tom Allred said the word was they would have a full investigation into the charges. Ain't no tellin' how long them boys'll be in the stockade."

"I reckon ole Custer just wants to have a big military trial to break up the monotony around here."

"I reckon." Andy lowered his chair back down on the floor and stood up. He walked to the door and spat. Wiping the brown tobacco residue from his chin, he said, "Soon as you're dressed, we got to go see Captain Benteen. He's taking the whole troop out on patrol in the morning."

CHAPTER 20

L ittle Wolf stood trembling. His body ached with sorrow and his brain screamed with despair. His very soul had been torn and wounded. His world, his happiness, lay before him lifeless and cold. The women of the village had found Morning Sky lying mutilated and bloody in the berry thicket. They had bathed her body and dressed her in a clean buckskin tunic. He had never before known such rage and he drew his knife and slashed his chest and stomach repeatedly in mourning, but nothing eased the pain from within. He was not sure he wanted to live this life without her. Morning Sky was dead. How could he accept it? He sobbed when he thought how she had met her fate, at the hands of the white vermin he had ordered from the village. Morning Sky gone? Surely this was a bad dream. Surely he would awaken and hear her soft singing as she went about her chores. He touched her hand, once warm and feeling, now cold and stiff. He would never again feel her warm caress. Then the weakness left him and he could feel the fiery hot venom of revenge filling his veins. He swore he would not rest until he had found the men who had done this.

Sitting Bull came to comfort him in his grief. They would organize a great war party to find the two buffalo hunters, he said, and to wreak revenge on all whites for this outrage. But Little Wolf refused the chief's offer of help. No, he told him. He alone must be allowed the right to punish the two white men. They must die by his own hand before Morning Sky's spirit could walk in peace in the other world. Sitting Bull understood and respected Little Wolf's wishes. It was his right.

A Sioux scout had ridden out after the men as soon as Morning Sky's body was discovered. He returned on the

same day Little Wolf returned from the hunt. The scout
reported that he had followed their trail, catching up with
the two men after nightfall. They were joined by a third
white man, who shot one of the buffalo hunters and tied
them both up. The next morning, the large giant of a man
tied them to their horses and took them away. They went
toward the white man's fort. Since the large man appeared
to be a formidable foe and seemed to be always alert, the
Sioux scout decided not to attack the three men, and returned to report his findings to Sitting Bull.

After Little Wolf had mourned for Morning Sky for
three days, he readied himself for his mission of vengence.
Word had been brought back to the village that the two
white men had been placed in the stockade at Fort Lincoln.
Little Wolf set out on a chilly fall morning, bound for the
fort. His mind was of one purpose—to kill Morning Sky's
murderers. Nothing else mattered. Sleeps Standing and
Lame Otter pleaded to accompany him but he refused. It
was for him and him alone to avenge his wife's death.

A light rain fell as Little Wolf rode, hunched over
slightly, a hood of antelope hide over his head for protection against the steady drizzle. The Appaloosa ate up the
miles with a steady gait that soon saw the Beaver River
and the Little Missouri behind them as he crossed the
harsh, rolling prairie toward Fort Lincoln. The high mountains were far behind him now. Near another river, he saw
the first signs of the white man's advances into the sacred
lands of the Sioux and Cheyenne. There was a roughly built
log hut with a horse corral and some planted crops growing
around it. He stopped at a distance and stared at the homestead for a long while before continuing on his journey.
After another day's ride he saw what could only be Fort
Lincoln on the horizon. He must be alert now for he was
surely in the land of the white man. The hatred that had
driven him on to this place must now give way to cunning—
he had devised no plan to find the two he hunted. First I
must sleep, he counseled himself, so that my senses will be
keen. After I have rested, I will think of a plan.

Skirting another settler's cabin, he rode until he crossed
a small stream south of the fort. Here he made his camp,
and after a supper of pemmican, he slept. His was the sleep
of the weary. He was tired and his heart was heavy under

its burden. He dreamed of his wife, preparing his food, sewing the hides he had taken, making love to him. And then he saw the faces of the two buffalo hunters, filthy and evil, and he was powerless to cast them out of his tipi. He fought with them but they became the mountain lion he had first dreamed of when he was still a boy searching for his vision. Then, as in that vision, the lion was overpowered by a great grizzly. When he awoke, he felt the strength of the grizzly from which he took his power and he knew that the dream was a good omen and his medicine was still strong.

Keeping a safe distance from the guard posts, he scouted the fort, searching for a way to steal into the encampment and find the two hunters. It became clear to him that if he was to find them, it would not be as he was, a Cheyenne warrior. In order to get close enough, he would have to be a white man again. He thought for a long time before he decided on a plan: he would go back to the first settler's cabin he had passed and wait for dark. Then he would go in and kill the occupants and take what clothing he needed. This decided, he got on the Appaloosa and retraced his trail.

He tied his horse to a small sapling and made his way through the trees that overlooked the rough cabin. From there he watched for a while. There was a cornfield between the woods and the cabin. The stalks were brown and barren but it would offer enough cover for him to get closer to the house. Looking beyond the cabin toward the river, he could see a man plowing a small patch of ground with one mule. There was one sorrel horse and a cow in a stable next to the cabin, and a large dog lying in the yard. Smoke from the chimney told him there was at least one person inside.

As he watched, a boy came out of the cabin. He was about the same age Little Wolf was when Spotted Pony found him, he guessed. The thought caused his mind to drift back to that time and he remembered how helpless and frightened he had been. It seemed a million summers ago. Though he could barely remember how it was to be a white boy, he could vividly remember the fear of being alone in the world. Suddenly he did not want to do what he had come to this cabin to do. The thought of leaving this young boy alone in the world caused a cold dread in his heart and he had to concentrate on the picture of his murdered wife in an effort to strengthen his resolve. The boy's father was stealing the land that belonged to the Indian. He must remember that. The white man was the enemy of his people. They had killed everyone he loved. He could not afford compassion at this point.

His attention was called from the boy playing in the yard to a movement beyond the cabin. When he glanced in that direction, he saw the father coming from the field. The afternoon sun was still high in the sky when the man put his mule in with the other stock. Little Wolf had anticipated a longer wait before the man returned to the cabin, but even in broad daylight, there was enough cover in the cornfield to work his way close to the cabin to do what must be done. He left the tree he had been watching from and made his way silently down between the rows of cornstalks. Moving cautiously and patiently, he worked his way to the edge of the field nearest the cabin. He had made sure he was downwind because of the dog. Now he could hear bits of conversation drifting on the wind.

The man took a pan and dipped water out of a rain barrel and began to wash his arms and face. The boy was standing beside him, talking to him. Little Wolf could hear the sound of their voices but was unable to make out the words. Keeping almost flat to the ground, he pulled himself a few rows closer. Now he was almost to the end of the field. He froze when a woman stood in the doorway holding a towel for her husband. Little Wolf reached back and drew an arrow from his quiver. His rifle would be too noisy, he decided. Little Wolf was certain now that there were only the three of them and he knew he could put an arrow into the man's back and a second one into the woman before she could run for a weapon. Slowly he raised up on one knee and, taking careful aim, drew the bowstring back. At this distance, he could not miss, but he hesitated. Something the boy said made him wait.

"Pa, remember, you said as soon as you got done plowing the back field. You promised."

"I remember," his father replied. "But I thought you'da

done forgot it by now. Wouldn't you druther do it tomorrow evening?"

"Ahhh, Pa, you said."

"The boy's right, Alvin. You promised him." His wife handed him the towel.

He paused a moment, looking as if he was treed. Finally he gave in. "All right, a promise is a promise. Go get the poles and we'll go catch us a couple." He turned to his wife and grinned. "That'd be all right, wouldn't it, Ma? You could fry a couple of fish to throw in with supper."

"I reckon so," she replied and smiled broadly.

Little Wolf sank slowly back between the corn rows, relieved that they were simplifying his task. Now there was only the woman to deal with. His heart was lifted of the dread he had suddenly felt over having to kill the family. If only the woman would go with them, he thought.

As if in answer to his wish, the man called back. "Why don't you come on with us, Ma? Supper can wait, can't it?"

"Me? Lord no, I'm almost ready to put supper on the table. I can't go traipsing off to the river with you two."

"Come on, Ma," her son pleaded. "Me and Pa'll show you how to catch a fish."

Lying in the dust of the cornfield, Little Wolf listened to the exchange and silently pleaded, *Go with them, woman. It may save your life.*

She stood smiling in the doorway, watching her husband and son walk away. Suddenly she called out, "Wait a minute and I'll cover the food. But don't complain to me if your cornbread is cold when we get back."

Little Wolf watched until they were out of sight before leaving the cover of the cornfield and walking unhurriedly into the cabin. Bloody Claw would have scoffed at his hesitation to kill the white family but Little Wolf refused to feel any guilt for his lack of aggressiveness. It was better this way. He could take what he needed and leave.

The aroma of hot cornbread filled his nostrils as soon as he entered the cabin. He walked over to the fireplace. The boy's mother had placed a big iron pot in the corner of the hearth to keep warm. A pan of cornbread was perched on top of the pot. Taking a rag from the table, he pulled the pot and pan out on the floor. The pot was filled with beans, cooked with some strips of fat pork. He took a large ladle from the table and ate from the pot until he was satisfied. Then he broke off half the cake of cornbread and ate it while he looked around the cabin for the things he needed.

One end of the cabin was divided into two rooms by blankets hanging from the ceiling. He found a shirt and trousers and a wide-brimmed hat in one room. There were boots in the other, but they were too small for his feet. He would have to get by with his moccasins. The one piece of furniture other than the bed was a chest of drawers. On top of it was a small mirror and Little Wolf stood staring into it for a few seconds, fascinated by the image looking back at him. The smooth, tan face looked Indian, especially with his long black hair. Maybe, if he piled his hair up under the hat, he would look more like a white man. He took the mirror with him along with the clothes.

Before leaving the cabin, he looked around to see if there was anything else he could find a use for. But there was nothing that interested him. Outside, he stood on the steps, looking in the direction of the river, and listened. There was no sound of the family returning. He looked at the horse and mule in the corral. If he stole the horse, the man would no doubt go to the fort to report it. It was not worth the risk. Satisfied, he strode off through the cornfield to the trees where he left his own horse. Before riding away, he wheeled and took one look back at the rough homestead. The boy would not be alone and he felt good about that.

Muley Rhymers straightened up from his work to stretch his back muscles for a few minutes. This was the third broken wagon wheel he had to fix this week. Sometimes he suspected the army's drivers of busting wheels on purpose, but it was no skin off his back as long as the army paid him to fix them. He took a red bandanna from his pocket and wiped the sweat from his forehead as he stood gazing out across the baked compound that served as a parade ground. He had been a blacksmith since he was thirteen, working with his father. That was thirty years ago. He had been the smith at Fort Lincoln for two years now and he was never surprised at the things he saw around an army post. For that reason, he was no more than slightly curious about the figure approaching him from the front gate. Another piece of trail fodder looking for work or a handout, he figured. Probably been up in the Black Hills looking for gold and lost everything but his horse and his hind end. This one looked half wild, riding a fine-looking horse but sitting an Indian saddle and bridle. Muley said nothing as the stranger pulled up and dismounted.

Little Wolf broke the silence. "Howdy."

"Howdy," Muley replied. There followed a long silence as the two men stood looking each other over. Finally Muley ran out of patience. "Somethin' I can do for you?"

It was still a moment before Little Wolf replied. He didn't want to make the man suspicious but his problem was that he didn't know what to say. He was out of place in the white man's world. He looked around him at the busy army post and the realization struck him that he was in the midst of his enemies. He looked back at the blacksmith. All he really wanted to do was look around until he found the two buffalo hunters. The longer he stood there saying nothing, the more suspicious, or stupid, he would look. Finally he blurted out, "All right with you if I tie my horse up here for a while?"

"Hell, man, you can tie your horse up anywheres, 'long as it ain't in the army's way . . . or mine for that matter." He studied the tall young man more closely. "You look like you run into a spell of bad luck. You been prospecting?"

"Yes, prospecting," Little Wolf agreed.

"Looks like you been up in the hills for a spell. You 'bout to grow outta them pants, ain'tcha?"

Little Wolf looked down at his stolen pants. The bottom of the trousers barely reached his ankles and the waistband was gathered up by a rawhide thong he had tied around them. "Yes," was his simple reply.

The stranger's Appaloosa had caught Muley's eye. He knew good horseflesh when he saw it and, never one to pass up an opportunity, he figured there might be a good chance to take advantage of the young man's desperate situation. "I don't reckon you're fixed too good for money, are you?"

"No."

"That there horse might be worth a little somethin' if you was of a mind to sell him. Looks like an Injun pony, but he might fetch enough to get you a grubstake." He paused when there was no immediate response to his suggestion. "You looking for work with the army?"

"Yes. I'm looking for work with the army."

"I thought as much. Well, I can tell you who to go see about it but I doubt they're hiring on right now." He assumed the young man would be seeking work as a scout. He carried a rifle but precious little else. "You work much with horses?"

"Some."

"I might could give you a few days' work around here if you don't mind cleaning out stables and doing rough chores." He watched the young man as he thought it over. "Give you somethin' to eat and a place to sleep." He waited for a reply. "Maybe grain for your horse."

"All right," Little Wolf accepted the offer. It would give him the opportunity to scout out the fort although he didn't care much for the thought of cleaning up after the army's horses. Though not dignified for a Cheyenne warrior, he supposed it would have to do for a white man with no money.

"Fine," Muley responded. "What's your name, anyway?"

Little Wolf had to check himself before answering. "Robert," he said.

"Robert? Robert what?"

"Just Robert," was the stoic reply.

Muley studied him for a moment then shrugged his shoulders. "All right, Robert. Folks call me Muley." He guessed the man had his reasons. Muley really didn't care that much. A lot of men showed up on the frontier with no last name. He was probably an army deserter from back East.

Little Wolf worked in the stable for the balance of that day, keeping his eyes and ears open. That night, when Muley was ready to go to his quarters, he told Little Wolf there would be a sentry walking a post around the stables at night but he would tell the sentry there would be somebody sleeping in the blacksmith shop. Otherwise he might be shot as an intruder. After they had eaten and Little Wolf was at last left alone in the stable, he took off his hat and let his long black hair fall around his shoulders. The hat made his head ache and it felt good to be free of it for a while. From inside the stable, he watched the guard detail mounted and made a mental note of where each sentry was posted. It was especially important to him where the guards for the stockade and the stables were posted and how often they made a circuit of their posts.

When it was fully dark, he went to the back fence of the corral and waited for the sentry to appear at the stockade. As soon as the sentry rounded the corner of the building and disappeared from view, he vaulted the fence and moved quickly across the deserted parade ground to the stockade and pressed his body against the side of the building. The building could not have been built very long before because the lumber was freshly hewn and smelled strongly of pine tar. Through the heavy iron bars in the windows, he could hear the murmur of voices. At any minute the sentry would complete his circuit. Little Wolf pulled himself up on the eaves of the building and rolled over onto the roof. There he waited until he saw the sentry pass below him and again disappear around the corner. Swinging back down to the ground, he made his way quickly along the back wall where barred windows indicated the location of prisoners. None of the cells were occupied except one and this was where he found them. There was no mistaking them, these were the two vermin who had ridden into Sitting Bull's camp and taken the life of his wife. As he peered in the corner of the window, Little Wolf could feel the bile rising inside him but he knew he must be patient. Quickly, he pulled himself up on the roof again while he waited for the sentry to pass once more. Afterward, he took a brief look at the bars on the windows. They appeared to be bolted through the new pine with large nuts on the outside. He would have to find a way to take them out. He would think on it.

"What was that?" Moody sat up straight on the small cot. "Did you hear somethin'?"

Kroll was unconcerned. "You're gittin' kinda spooked. I didn't hear nothin'."

Moody was adamant. "Didn't you hear it? I swear, it was a kind of bump or something on the roof."

Kroll was more interested in going to sleep. "Maybe it was an angel coming to git us outta here," he said sarcastically.

*   *   *

"Let's set a spell, Robert," Muley gasped when the wagon wheel was finally seated snugly on the axle. "Damned if I ain't gittin right short-winded. I must be gittin' old. Used to be I could hold up the wagon bed and fit the wheel on right by myself. No more. Damn, I'm panting like a dog."

Little Wolf said nothing but sat down next to his rotund employer. He accepted the outstretched dipper and drank deeply. The work was not hard but he still found it demeaning. It was his opinion that Muley didn't really need help with his work as much as he needed someone to talk to. The blacksmith was a lonely man. He lived alone and, while there were a few women on the post, they were soldiers' wives. Even had there been single women about, it was doubtful they would have shown interest in the portly figure of Muley Rhymers. Little Wolf studied the man carefully. Muley took frequent rest periods. He constantly complained about the work he had backed up but Little Wolf saw no cause for complaints. If only the man worked steadily, he could easily keep up with the demand for his services.

"God's truth, Robert, I don't know what they'd do around here if it weren't for me. I do ever'thin' that gits done." He took out his bandanna and wiped the sweat from his face.

Little Wolf did not respond at once. In a moment, he asked, "You build the stockade?"

"You mean the new guardhouse there? Nah, the carpenters built that. I made the cell doors and the bars on the windows."

Little Wolf pretended to notice the windows for the first time. "How did you nail those bars in?"

"They ain't nailed. They's bolted with six one-inch rods right through the window frame."

"What's to keep a feller from taking the bolts off and just pulling the bars off the window?" He attempted to sound as if he was merely making idle conversation.

Muley took another drink of water. "Well, for one thing, he'd have to have that there T-bar there to back the nuts off." He pointed to a heavy tool lying under his workbench. He took another drink of water then turned the dipper over his head, letting the cool water run down his neck. "And that won't do him any good after we get time to get over there and heat up some iron to braze them threads. I been meaning to get to that as soon as I get caught up with these damn wagons." He groaned as he forced his bulk off of the tiny stool he had been resting on. "Ain't no hurry. The bolts is on the outside. Ain't nobody likely to try to break in the jail, is there? Gittin' out is the problem."

"I reckon you're right," Little Wolf replied.

That night Little Wolf offered a prayer of thanks to Man Above for showing him the way to avenge Morning Sky's murder. As soon as Muley had retired to his room for the night, Little Wolf saddled the Appaloosa. Then he took two army saddles from the stable and cut out two of the sturdiest horses from the corral. When he had saddled them and thrown on a coil of stout hemp rope, he settled back and waited for the darkness to deepen.

He looked up into a motionless sky. The stars seemed to flicker as a gentle wind brushed the leaves of the one scrawny live oak that stood at the corner of the corral. The camp was quiet except for the murmur of voices from the sutler's store at the far end of the parade ground. Still he waited. He could see a few tents glowing from candle flames along the line of enlisted men's bivouac. He would wait until he was sure the post was asleep. Finally it was time and he climbed silently over the corral fence and ran across the parade ground.

Thoughts and images of Morning Sky flashed through his mind as he waited in the shadows, pressed close against the guardhouse wall. Then he heard the steady tread of the sentry approaching the corner of the building and he tensed his body for the attack. It must be done quietly, he reminded himself, and drew his knife. The sentry passed no more than three or four feet from him. Little Wolf waited until he was several steps past him then moved quickly up behind the unsuspecting guard. It was quick and it was silent. One hand over the startled soldier's mouth, pulling his neck back at the same time, and the blade of the knife opened the unfortunate man's throat. The sentry crumpled in a heap without uttering a sound. Little Wolf dragged the body back against the building and went quickly back to get the horses.

*   *   *

"Hey, what the hell . . . ?" It was Kroll's voice.

"Quiet!" Little Wolf whispered.

"Who is it?" Moody wanted to know.

"A friend," came the reply. "Now shut up if you want to get out of there."

Even with the leverage afforded by the T-bar, it was difficult to break the huge bolts loose. Muley had tightened them down pretty snug. Once he broke them free, it was short work backing them off the bolts. As he removed the final two, he pushed the rope through and told Kroll to secure it to the bars. Kroll wasted no time in complying but he was still baffled by the whole turn of events.

"How come you're busting us out?" he wanted to know as he worked feverishly to tie a secure knot in the rope, hindered somewhat by the bullet Squint Peterson had put in his right shoulder. "Who the hell are you? Who sent you?" Their mysterious benefactor's voice sounded remotely familiar. He had heard it before, but he couldn't place it.

"Does it matter? You want out, don't you?" He removed the last of the bolts. There was nothing holding the bars in now but the pine boards framed up around them. "Where is the other guard?"

Moody had been watching the lone guard, stationed in the front of the guardhouse while Kroll and the stranger were working at the bars. He answered Little Wolf's question. "Sleeping like a baby."

"All right, get ready, 'cause when this window comes out, you won't have much time before the whole fort wakes up." With that, he left the window and jumped up on the Appaloosa. The rope was tied to the saddle horn of one of the army mounts he had taken. He reached down and grabbed the reins and led the horse away from the building, taking the slack out of the rope. The horse hesitated briefly when he felt the resistance on the end of the rope but buckled down and pulled when Little Wolf brought the loose end of the rope down hard across his rump. The bars came out with a loud cracking sound of green pine.

Inside the cell, the two prisoners waited anxiously while this was going on. Kroll, still uneasy with the situation, harbored some misgivings at their seemingly good fortune. "Who the hell would be bustin' us out?" he demanded of Moody. "We ain't got no friends that I know of."

"I ain't worrying about it," Moody shot back. "Maybe he's got us mixed up with somebody else. I don't care. I sure don't cotton to stayin' in here and gittin' hung." Barely a moment after the bars were ripped from the wall, he was through the open window and headed for freedom. Kroll didn't waste time thinking about the matter further. He followed his partner.

Outside on the dark parade ground, they found the stranger, who was holding two horses for them. "Hurry!" he said. "Follow me!" He turned his horse and took off at a gallop around behind the stables and out the back of the compound. Without hesitating, they jumped on the horses and followed. Behind them, the sleepy guard was not yet aware of what had happened, having just been awakened by the sound of the breaking window frame.

Once they had put a safe distance between them and the fort, Little Wolf slowed to a canter for a short distance before finally letting the horses walk. Kroll and Moody pulled up beside him, both breathing a lot easier since making a successful escape from the hangman's noose.

"Whoeeee," Moody squealed, "that was slicker'n owl shit!"

"Yeah, that was slick all right," Kroll added, still suspicious of the tall dark form on the Appaloosa. The exertion had caused the wound in his shoulder to throb painfully, and his patience was running out. "Now I'd like to know what's in it for you. You ain't sprung me and ole Moody jest 'cause of our good looks. Who the hell are you, anyway?"

"I told you, a friend."

"We ain't got no friends." He reined his horse to a halt. "All right, friend, this is as far as me and Moody go." For the first time, he noticed the rifle cradled in the stranger's arms. "We thank you for busting us out but we'll go our own way now."

Little Wolf said nothing for a moment. He could shoot them both right there and be done with it, but he didn't want them to get off that easily. "The man who hired me told me to give you rifles and food. He has a job for you. He'll be here in the morning. If you want the job, there'll be money in it for you. If you don't, you can go your own way in the morning."

This tweaked Kroll's interest. "Is that so? What man?"

"I don't know his name. I'm just doing what he paid me to do."

Kroll thought about this for a moment. "Well, where's the rifles and food?"

"He'll bring them to my camp. That's where I was taking you."

"All right then, let's go."

Little Wolf led them back to the place in the trees where he had hidden his things before putting on the white man's clothes and riding into the fort. It was still dark although morning was not far away by this time. Kroll was impatient to get his hands on a weapon, but Little Wolf convinced him that there were no rifles there, they would be brought in the morning. Saying they might as well get some sleep, Little Wolf unsaddled his horse and pretended to settle down for the night. Kroll and Moody made beds with their saddle blankets and, after a great deal of grumbling, drifted off to sleep shortly before dawn. As soon as Little Wolf was certain they were asleep, he arose and went to the place where he had hidden his buckskins and his bow. He made not a sound as he returned to the camp, moving silently around the fire to a position facing the two sleeping men. The first rays of the sun began to creep into the trees where he stood and he waited for the screen of darkness to dissolve.

Moody was deep in sleep, dreaming of the hangman's noose, when he was abruptly jolted awake. At once he was aware of a heavy weight in his chest and a fiery rod through his belly. Totally disoriented, he floundered awake, trying to figure out where he was and what had happened. His heart almost stopped when he managed to focus his eyes and discovered the tall Cheyenne warrior standing over him, his long hair just touching his shoulders with one eagle feather braided into the dark locks, his face painted for war. Still befuddled by sleep, he tried to jump to his feet but the intense pain in his stomach stopped him cold and he looked down at his round belly. For a full moment he stared in disbelief at the arrow shaft protruding from his stomach. When he put his hand on it, he screamed with the pain caused by the movement. As he screamed, Little Wolf calmly let fly a second arrow. The arrow hit the rotund little man with a dull thump, shattering a rib and piercing his lung. Moody's scream increased in his agony.

Kroll, awakened by his partner's screams, rolled over on his side and lay there for a moment while he struggled to rid his brain of its slumber. "Jesus!" he yelled when at last he realized what he saw. He lunged to his feet but fell again in a heap, his ankles having been tied together. Aware now that he was fighting for his life, he attempted to crawl on his hands while dragging his feet. It was to no avail. Little Wolf caught him by the thong that bound his ankles and dragged him back into the clearing and dropped him in the middle of the campfire. Kroll roared like a grizzly and rolled out of the hot coals, landing on his back. He looked up to see the arrow aimed directly at him, the bow drawn fully. There was no time to react. The shaft of the arrow slammed into his midsection. He pulled frantically at the shaft but only caused himself more pain. Like Moody, he finally lay back, trying to be still in order to minimize the agony.

"Her name was Morning Sky," Little Wolf calmly stated. "She was my wife."

Kroll sank back against the ground. The horrible realization struck him fully then and he now recognized his assailant. "Little Wolf," he mumbled, knowing that it was futile to beg for mercy.

Little Wolf drew another arrow from his quiver and embedded it in Kroll's chest. "You will die slowly and, while you are waiting to die, you will think about the girl you killed. I will stay with you until I am sure you are dead." He fitted another arrow on his bowstring and sent it into Kroll's groin. The shaft pinned the man's testicles to the ground. The shock of it caused Kroll to lose consciousness. Little Wolf walked to the stream and brought back some water to revive his victim. Kroll jerked awake with a scream. While Little Wolf was at the stream, Moody attempted to escape, dragging himself away from the tree under which he had spent the night. Unconcerned, Little Wolf revived Kroll before going after Moody. He caught him before Moody had dragged himself ten yards. Taking out his knife, he reached down and scalped the helpless man and left him to die.

Kroll, realizing his life was running out on the ground in

the blood that had begun to puddle around him, cursed weakly at his executioner. "Damn you to hell, you son of a bitch. I didn't know that damn squaw was your wife."

Little Wolf stared at him, his expression almost blank. He had long before exhausted his rage for these two men. Now he was only intent on avenging Morning Sky's death in a meticulous manner, making sure the two of them understood the fate they had brought on themselves. "I will hang your scalps from my lance so that you will wander forever in the other world."

Kroll died shortly after Little Wolf took his scalp. To be certain, Little Wolf slit both men's throats and left them for the buzzards, along with the white man's clothes he had stolen from the cabin. A heavy burden lifted from his heart. He began his journey back to the mountains knowing they had paid with their own lives for the atrocity committed upon his beloved wife. But still there was no peace in his heart and there was no filling the emptiness Morning Sky's passing had left.

CHAPTER 21

There was a great deal of grumbling among the men unlucky enough to be picked to form the search party for the escaped prisoners. Tom wasn't too thrilled with the idea himself. He had just gotten back from patrol the day before. It was the normal routine to get at least one day off after an extensive patrol of troop strength. But that was the price B-Troop paid for having the two best Indian scouts in the regiment in Squint Peterson and Andy Coulter. Custer put the task of recapturing the escapees firmly on Captain Benteen's shoulders. Benteen, in turn, assigned the chore to Tom. So it was that Tom found himself back in the saddle on this chilly autumn morning.

The trail was easy enough to pick up. Three horses, hellbent for leather, lit out the back of the fort behind the stables. Squint found it interesting that only two of them were shod, the two stolen from the stable. The other was an Indian pony. It didn't take a detective to discover what had taken place. According to Muley Rhymers, a young fellow who worked for him had disappeared too. He obviously stole the two horses, pulled the window out of the guardhouse and made off with those two buzzards Squint had brought in. They had circled back south of the fort and appeared to be heading in a southeasterly direction.

"I don't remember Muley havin' anybody working in the stable with him," Andy said as he and Squint dismounted to check sign.

"He didn't when we went out on that patrol," Tom answered. "The fellow just walked in a couple of days ago. Ole Muley's not too popular with the colonel right now . . . Two army mounts stolen from right under his nose." He didn't need to mention that a young soldier had been killed during the escape, a fact that supplied all the motivation he needed to track down the three of them. He waited while his scouts mounted, then followed their lead down across a grassy bottom and along a skinny stream.

The sun was gaining on the morning sky when Andy stated, "Don't take much tracking to follow that trail." He pointed toward a group of scrub oaks on a creek bank about a mile away where half a dozen buzzards were circling.

Andy was right. It was the two buffalo hunters—at least, what was left of them. Tom looked at the grotesque figures of the two men for a few minutes and then turned away to get a breath of fresh air. The bodies had not been dead long enough to stink, but already the buzzards had found them and were circling closer and closer when the soldiers approached. Andy and Squint peered at the scalpless victims, their bloody wounds already crawling with flies.

"From the look of it," Squint decided, "I'd say the other feller sprung 'em just so's he could kill 'em hisself." He tugged at one of the arrows and, finding it deeply embedded in the man's chest, stood up and motioned to Tom. "Lieutenant, these arrows was shot at mighty close range. They're all in too deep to pull out without breaking 'em. Remember how them arrows was just barely stuck in them mule skinners we found . . . to make it look like the work of Injuns? Well, sir, these was shot with a pretty powerful bow, I'd say, and he must have been standin' right on top of 'em."

"Cheyenne," Andy pronounced. "See the way that scalp was slit? Across the front and partway back? That's the way a Cheyenne Dog Soldier lifts a scalp." He was talking more to Squint than he was to Tom. "Fer my money, I'd say that third feller is a damn Injun right enough and no foolin' at that."

"It shore looks it, don't it?" Squint agreed. "And from the looks of this here arrow pinning this one's balls to the ground, it had to do with violating somebody's squaw, I'd bet."

"I've seen a lot of bodies mutilated by Indians for no reason at all, just for the hell of it," Tom said.

"Yessir," Squint replied. "But usually they do all kinds of shit when they're just mutilating them for the hell of it . . . Cut their balls off and stuff 'em in the dead man's mouth, such trash as that, gouging out eyeballs and such. This ain't the case here. I ain't no detective but that's the way it looks to me. Anyway, them two coyotes, ain't no tellin' what they been up to. I don't reckon there'll be a whole lot of mournin' over their passing."

"You think this man's an Indian then?"

Both scouts nodded in the affirmative. "And I think he's got a pretty good start on us if you're thinking of going after him," Squint added.

"Why the hell would Muley hire an Indian? A Cheyenne at that?" Tom was still puzzled over the apparent execution. He ran it over in his mind for a few moments longer before bringing his attention back to his mission. "Hell yes, we're going after him, all right. The man killed a sentry." He paused for a moment before adding, "And he stole two army mounts."

"Well, sir, we damn shore better git goin' because I got a feelin' this son of a bitch ain't your ordinary ever'day Injun."

Tom decided there was little value in trying to send the bodies back to the fort, so he had them buried where they were, and then the detail started out after the Indian. The trail was not hard to follow for a few miles until they reached a point where the hoofprints divided. Tom halted the detachment while Squint and Andy circled and returned to report. It was obvious to them that the Indian turned the two army mounts loose.

"It'd be my guess you'll find them horses not too far away if you wanna send somebody after 'em." Andy scratched his head and aimed a stream of tobacco juice in the direction of a large black beetle scurrying out from under his horse's hoof. "Don't figure though, an Injun lettin' two good horses go."

"I reckon he don't want nobody trailing him. Three horses are hard to cover up," Squint said.

"I reckon."

"Follow the unshod one?" Tom asked.

"Follow the unshod one," Squint confirmed and they continued tracking the Indian pony.

The trail became more difficult to follow but Andy and Squint were able to stay with it. Eventually it led onto an outcropping of rock that hung out over a narrow creek. It was obvious the Indian felt it necessary to cover his trail, but had been waiting for the right place to start. "He picked a good one," Andy commented, and he and Squint combed the stream for a good half hour, trying to determine if he went north or south. It seemed impossible for a man to ride down a creek bed without leaving one single hoofprint. It was like he just rode up on the rocks and then started flying. Squint was beginning to think he had somehow doubled back on them when Andy sang out that he found a print. It led north.

Squint studied the single hoofprint for a long time. Something about it didn't look right. He walked a few steps farther back and found another one near the edge of the water, just barely into the sand. "Wait a minute, Lieutenant." He turned and splashed downstream, below the rock outcropping. Stepping very carefully, he made his way slowly downstream, searching the creek bed until he found what he was looking for. A handful of small pebbles had been disturbed, leaving a partial imprint of an unshod hoof. "Just as I figured," he announced triumphantly. "This ole boy is a sly one. He went in the water headin' north, just to throw us off. Then he backed his horse up to the rocks, probably right there,"—he pointed to a low shelf—"came out and went in the water again, headed downstream." Squint grinned like a schoolboy catching his first possum. "Yessir, this ol' boy is a sly one. We're gonna earn our money on this one, Andy."

It was slow going until they finally picked up the trail where Little Wolf left the stream and once again headed west across the prairie. They would stay with it for as long as the lieutenant said, but Squint was not overly optimistic about catching the man. Not only were they slowed down by the difficulty in following the trail, the army mounts were no match for the Indian pony in a flat-out chase, if it came to that. Joe might stay with the Indian for a while but, eventually, he would probably wear Joe out. As he saw it, their only chance to catch him was if he got careless and figured he had covered his trail. And somehow Squint didn't figure this Injun to get careless.

For the rest of that day they followed the Indian's trail, losing it occasionally, circling, then picking it up again. It was plain to see they had little chance of overtaking him at this rate for, even though it was obvious that he was in no hurry, they were unable to gain any ground on him. When they camped that night, Tom made a decision. From the direction of the Indian's trail, both Squint and Andy were confident their fugitive was making straight for Sitting Bull's camp. If they continued tracking him at the present pace, he would reach the village before they could catch him and they would have to turn back, or risk stirring up the entire Sioux nation. There was a slim chance, however, that they could overtake the Indian. Tom decided it was worth the risk.

The next morning only three of them—Tom, Squint and Andy—went on after the lone Indian. They each took two extra mounts. They planned to ride full gallop until a horse was worn out then cut him loose and switch to a fresh mount. By riding hard and switching mounts there was a chance they could get to the Little Missouri ahead of the Indian, especially since he still did not seem to be in a hurry. The rest of the troop was left with Sergeant Porter with instructions to follow along making the best time possible. A separate detail was dispatched to pick up the extra mounts the three of them cut loose.

Little Wolf sat cross-legged on top of a low hill and watched the horizon toward the east. As he watched, he cleaned the last bit of meat from the bones of a large hare he had killed that morning. His hunger satisfied, he threw the bones aside and continued to stare at the endless sea of prairie behind him. What he saw puzzled him. He knew the soldiers were tracking him, but he also knew they were not gaining on him. Now, to his surprise, he was seeing a small group of soldiers riding hard and rapidly closing the gap between himself and his pursuers. He found it difficult to believe the army's horses could reduce the distance that rapidly. He continued to watch because he had no fear of the soldiers and he was confident in his ability to lose them if he desired. Now, as they drew closer and he could see them more clearly, he discovered that they were three soldiers with three extra horses. As he watched, they halted abruptly, switched saddles and bridles onto the three extra horses and set off again at full gallop. He realized at once what their plan was. They were no longer tracking him. They were trying to get in front of him.

"So, if you are no longer tracking me, then I will track you." He rose and walked down the hill where the Appaloosa was waiting.

"There it is, there's the river," Squint sang out and reined his lathered mount to a halt. He was soon joined by Andy and Tom, their horses wheezing as they strained for air.

"You think we beat him here?" Tom asked.

"Don't know. I'd shore be surprised if we didn't," Squint replied. "We'd best be seeing about where he might cross. Right here is where them two buzzards came across before. From the looks of the tracks, I'd say more'n one Injun crosses here."

"He could cross anywhere," Andy pointed out.

"I reckon," Squint agreed. "But it'll have to be somewhere between here and the bends of the river. Ain't no other place for two miles. We'll be damn lucky if he ain't been here and gone. I reckon we better spread out and cover as much of this turn of the river as we can. Maybe one of us will be lucky enough to get a shot at him. Better water the horses first so's they'll be quiet."

"Our orders are to capture him if possible," Tom was quick to remind his two scouts.

"It ain't likely it'll be possible." Andy spat a brown stream that caught the lieutenant's horse on the forelock. He shook his head as if to apologize. " 'Specially since it'll likely be one agin' the other. More'n likely you'll have to kill him." He looked to Squint for confirmation and Squint nodded his agreement.

"I reckon he's right, Lieutenant."

Tom shrugged his shoulders. "Well, if he offers to surrender, let him. Now, we better get ourselves under cover or he'll find us first. Andy, why don't you spot from this big tree down around that bend. Squint can take this section of crossing and I'll ride upstream a couple hundred yards. That all right with everybody?" They both nodded agreement and dispersed to their assigned area of ambush. As an afterthought, Tom called after Andy, "How long do you think it'll be before he gets here?"

Andy looked back over his shoulder. "Not long, if he ain't already beat us here and crossed." He knew the odds were mighty slim they would even see the man, and once he got on the other side of the river, he'd be damn near impossible to catch.

Tom watched until both men were no longer visible then turned and rode upstream until he came to a clump of trees thick enough to hide him and his horse from anyone approaching the river. Drawing his carbine from his saddle pack, he checked to make sure it was ready to fire. Satisfied, he started to dismount, but decided to stay in the saddle in case he had to ride to support Squint or Andy in a hurry. He waited.

The afternoon sun began to settle into the trees on the hills across the river and Tom buttoned his jacket as the warmth of the afternoon started to dissipate into the chill of the autumn night. There was no sound save that of the river behind him and the occasional soft creaking of saddle leather whenever he shifted his weight, punctuated by the periodic swish of his horse's tail whenever a fly began to bite. He waited. Time passed as if on leaden wings. He looked at his watch and saw it was almost five o'clock. There was not much daylight left. He wondered if they were on a fool's vigil. The Indian might be miles away.

It was only a faint metallic click but it sliced the silence like a razor. Tom knew instantly what it was. Nothing else made a sound like that but the cocking of a rifle. He whirled around immediately and a cold shock numbed his body along the entire length of his spine. He was looking into the barrel of a rifle, aimed directly at his eyes, no farther away than ten feet. There was no time to raise his own carbine. He braced himself for death.

But death did not come at once. In the fraction of time following, when he could not understand why he was still alive, the image of the man who would be his executioner was burned into his brain. He was taller than most Sioux or Cheyenne. One eagle feather adorned his long black hair and the necklace of bear claws told him that the man who was holding him helpless was none other than *Little Wolf.*

He already carried one bullet from Little Wolf's rifle. Now the savage was back to finish the job! Why did he hesitate? Maybe he wanted Tom to make a move to save himself. Custer had said the man was really a white man gone renegade. Tom couldn't say—he looked Cheyenne enough to him. It mattered little at this point. Tom thought about making a try with his carbine, but knowing he didn't have a chance, he just sat there, almost in a trance. Finally he blurted, "Dammit, shoot if you're going to!"

Little Wolf's finger slowly tightened on the trigger but something made him hesitate. While the soldier sat stunned before him, he had recalled a picture in his mind of another river, on another day, and another young officer sitting a horse, his weapon drawn and aimed at a young Cheyenne girl. It was the same soldier.

In English, Little Wolf said, "Drop your rifle on the ground." When the rifle fell to the ground, he ordered, "Now the pistol, slowly." When the officer was disarmed, he spoke quickly and quietly. "I am giving you back your life in payment for sparing Morning Sky's life at Black Kettle's village on the Washita. You could have shot her but you did not. I know, too, that you saw me on the riverbank and you turned away. So I turn away now. But know this. The debt is paid. The next time we meet, I will kill you."

Tom, barely seconds from his grave just moments before, could scarcely believe his life had been spared. He was unable to react, sitting numbly in his saddle, his eyes held captive by the icy gaze of the savage. He watched, helpless, as the tall warrior quickly picked up his pistol and rifle and turned to leave. He was surprised himself when he heard his own voice. "Little Wolf?" he asked.

The Indian hesitated, surprised. "Yes, I am Little Wolf," he stated and stood there for a moment before he suddenly disappeared into the bushes and was gone, leaving the stunned lieutenant staring after the empty space where he had stood.

Tom did not move for a full minute. He had never been that stunned before. He couldn't explain it. He wasn't frightened by the face to face meeting with death as much as he was simply rendered helpless, like a fly in a spiderweb. The Indian, Little Wolf, wore the look of a predator, calm and deadly. He had caught Tom dead to rights. Tom was still shaken when he heard Squint's horse approach.

"Lieutenant! You all right?"

"Yeah . . . yeah, I'm all right." Tom shook himself out

of the near-trance he had been caught in. "It was him. I let him sneak right up behind me and get the drop on me, like a damn tenderfoot shavetail. He lit out across the river I think."

Squint turned momentarily as Andy reined up beside them, then looked back at Tom. "Yeah, I seen him when he come out on the other side. That's why I come a'runnin'. I was feared he might have cut your throat."

"What happened?" Andy asked. He had not heard or seen anything until Squint broke cover and galloped toward Tom.

"Little Wolf," Tom answered.

Squint's eyes went wide, the shock registering on his awestruck face.

"Little Wolf?" Andy responded. Then noticing that Tom had neither rifle nor pistol, he looked first at Squint and then back at Tom. "Are you shore it was Little Wolf?" He found it hard to believe Tom was still among the living if he had been jumped by Little Wolf.

Tom knew what he was thinking. "It was Little Wolf." Then he told them why his life had been spared. "But we're wasting time sitting here. He's getting too much of a start."

"Hold on, Tom." Andy usually called him Lieutenant except when he felt the need to give fatherly advice. Then it was always Tom. "We ain't got a chance in hell of catching that redskin now. For one thing, we done run these horses near to death already just gittin' here and his'n is pretty fresh. Even if our'n weren't wore out, we'd play hell trying to catch that pony he's riding."

"Andy's right, Lieutenant. We missed our chance. That one's gone." Squint had been listening to Tom's account of the incident on the Washita and he had been doing some thinking. Up to that point, they had been chasing a nameless Indian. It was a pretty sobering statement to Squint when Tom called the Indian Little Wolf. More than one Indian was named Little Wolf but this one sounded uncomfortably close to the Little Wolf he knew as a boy. He began to add up some facts in his head and the conclusions presented a bizarre situation, one he had to clear up in his mind.

"We might as well camp here tonight," Andy said. "This day's about done. We can ride back and meet the troop in the morning. That all right with you, Lieutenant?" The question came as an afterthought.

"Yeah, all right." Tom wanted to continue on after the renegade but he knew his scouts were right. His detachment wasn't prepared to go on an extended patrol deep into hostile territory and he didn't want to chance getting anybody killed.

After they took care of the horses and arranged their saddles into beds, they settled in for the night. Andy hustled up a fire in an attempt to make some coffee before Squint did. Whenever Squint made it, it was always so strong he was afraid it would melt his tin cup. While Andy busied himself at the fire, Squint sat down beside Tom.

"Lieutenant, how do you know that Injun's name was Little Wolf?"

"I ought to know. I've run across him before."

"Yessir, but how do you know his name is Little Wolf?"

Tom shrugged his shoulders. "Hell, I asked him."

"You asked him? In English? And he told you . . . in English?"

"He did. I forgot, you weren't with the company then, back at Fort Reno, when we got ambushed by his band. Yeah, he told me in English. The story is that he's not really an Indian, just raised by them. It's hard to say though, when you meet him."

Squint's mind was racing. "Tell me about him. I mean, you just saw him up close. What did he look like?"

"Like a damn Indian," Tom replied, but when he saw the intensity in Squint's face, he described the tall, dark-haired warrior who had spared his life that day. "Why are you so interested?"

Squint ignored the question. "Did he have on a shirt?"

"Not when he jumped me."

"Did you notice anything odd about him? Like a scar or something?"

Tom thought for a moment, trying to picture the man in his mind. He didn't want to tell Squint that he was too numb at the time to notice very many details. "Come to think of it, there was an odd-looking place on his shoulder. Could have been a scar . . . a big one."

This seemed to satisfy Squint's curiosity. He settled back against the tree they were seated under. "It was a scar all right. I put it there. Leastways, there was a bullet there and I put a big hole in him trying to git it out."

This sparked Tom's interest in a hurry. "You know Little Wolf? You never mentioned you knew Little Wolf!"

"It never come up."

Tom pulled a rock out from under his blanket and threw it aside. "If I ever get him in my sights again, I'll put a bigger hole than that in him."

Squint, sure of himself now but still scarcely believing what he had discovered, replied smugly, "Maybe, but maybe you wouldn't want to at that." When Tom responded with nothing more than a puzzled look, he continued, "Lieutenant, where are you from?"

"I was born in St. Louis."

"You had a brother, did you?"

"Well, I had one younger brother but he left us when he was just a little fellow, ten or so."

"Your brother, he went off with a mule skinner, right?"

Tom was astonished. "How the hell did you know that?"

"He told me. His name's Robert, ain't it?" He didn't have to wait for an answer—Tom's wide-eyed expression confirmed it. Squint went on, "I shoulda put two and two together I reckon but I never thought nothin' of it. I mean your name being Allred and his being Allred. Why, hell, Lieutenant, I wintered with your brother up in the Wind River country."

Tom could hardly believe what he was hearing. Little Robert had been taken from the family when he was just a tyke, no more than nine or ten years old as best he could remember. "Damn!" he exclaimed. "Squint, are you sure? Are you sure it's my brother?"

"Sure as spit."

When Squint did not elaborate, Tom pressed for more. "Well, where is he now? I'd like to see him. Where can I get in touch with him?"

Squint could not help but laugh. "You already have. You met up with him today."

At first Tom didn't understand but, after a moment, it dawned on him what Squint was telling him. For the second time that day, he was stunned. *"Little Wolf?"*

"Little Wolf," Squint confirmed.

CHAPTER 22

In the months that followed Tom's startling discovery on the sandy banks of the Little Missouri River, he began to almost doubt the incident had happened at all. The shock of Squint Peterson's revelation, that the savage he had sworn to kill was none other than his own lost brother, shook him more than the actual face-off with the murderous Cheyenne war chief. He had not thought about his brother for years. Their family was hardly a close one. For that exact reason he had escaped as soon as he was old enough. In fact, he considered himself lucky there was a war to give him a reason to go into the army.

When he left, he left for good. There was no contact with his mother or his sisters, and his father drank himself to death before Tom was fifteen. And now this. It was still inconceivable to him that his brother could be the notorious Little Wolf and he was not really sure how he felt about the turn of events. There was some degree of curiosity, he had to admit. The man was his brother after all. Still, he was, in fact, his enemy. Tom sought any information he could on the whereabouts of Little Wolf, but no one was able to supply any. None of the Indian scouts could offer any clue. It was as if the man had vanished from the earth. It became like a dream in his mind as winter set in, restricting troop movements for the most part.

Winter that year was a hard one and many of the scattered tribes wandered into the reservations to keep from starving to death. But Little Wolf was not among them. In fact, Little Wolf seemed to have vanished into the mountains, according to reports from Shoshone scouts friendly to the army. Sitting Bull's Sioux were not among those Indians retreating to the reservation. His winter camp near the Yellowstone was home to a great many Cheyenne but Little Wolf was not one of them. From information provided by the Shoshone scouts, Tom was able to find out that Little Wolf had not returned to the village after their encounter on the Little Missouri. No one there knew where he was. It was common belief that he was still grieving over the death of his wife and had chosen to become one with the spirits and live in solitary communion somewhere in the mountains. In his absence, one of the members of his band of Cheyenne warriors, Bloody Claw, had replaced him as war chief.

Gradually, as winter loosened its grip and spring reluctantly arrived, Tom's mind was less absorbed with the sudden appearance of a forgotten brother. The initial shock of it had been severe enough. But to be told that his brother was the same renegade who had killed and pillaged all over the territory was almost too much for the young lieutenant to accept. He became dismayed that fate had played such an ironic trick on him. As the days passed, Tom began to look at the situation with a somewhat more callous eye. At first, he had questioned Squint extensively about Little Wolf, seeking to learn everything he could about his brother. Little Wolf was his enemy but at least he could understand the man's motives. Squint never failed to stress that his brother was legitimate in his Indian leanings. Little Wolf was raised as a Cheyenne. But as the months passed and Tom moved farther away from that confrontation on the Little Missouri, compassion for his Cheyenne brother waned.

The army certainly harbored no feelings of lenience for the man they knew as a renegade white turned Indian. There was a price on his head and Custer in particular wanted him brought in. The colonel found it hard to believe an Indian, or any man, for that matter, could walk right into an army fort and bust two prisoners out of jail. The man's audacity infuriated Custer and he was determined to make an example of the renegade. When the weather permitted a more frequent routine of patrols, they still searched for information on the whereabouts of Little Wolf but to no avail. In truth, Little Wolf had vanished from the earth. In time, the subject of his brother receded to the back of Tom's thoughts and as weeks, months and finally years passed with no word of the hostile, Little Wolf became little more than a ghost in his memory. Even Custer conceded that he had most likely perished in that brutal winter three years past.

Custer had other projects on his mind, opportunities to further his image as a military leader, that pushed the desire to punish one renegade white Indian to the bottom of his list of priorities. In the summer of 1874 he persuaded his superiors to authorize a great expedition into the Black Hills. The purpose of this expedition was, supposedly, to explore the territory, make maps of the area, study geological formations, catalog the existence of different species of wildlife—things of a peaceful nature. Of course the presence of a couple of gold miners on the mission might have caused some folks to become a little suspicious. The fact of the matter was that there were dozens of prospectors camping in the Black Hills already, in spite of the fact there was a treaty with the Sioux that guaranteed no white man was to enter these hunting grounds. As far as Squint Peterson was concerned, the handwriting was on the wall. If there was gold in the Black Hills, there was no way to keep the prospectors out, treaty or no treaty. It wouldn't be the first time the government backed out of a treaty when they found something of the Indians' that they wanted. Custer had no business in that territory, peaceful or not, so Squint decided to sit this campaign out. He didn't like riding with Custer anyway. The man was obviously too fond of himself to suit Squint so he decided this would be a good time to take a little vacation.

"You shore you don't want to come along on this here party?"

Squint turned in his saddle to face a smiling Andy Coulter as he reined up beside him. "I reckon not. Reckon you can find your way to the Black Hills without me?"

Andy laughed. "Well, if I can't, I reckon I'll have help a'plenty. Ole Longhair is taking about thirty scouts, most of 'em Crows." He sent a stream of brown tobacco juice into the dust of the parade ground. Gesturing with his outstretched arm, he expounded, "Did you ever see a party as big as this one? Look at them supply wagons."

"No, I never," Squint allowed. "I just been setting here looking at all this fuss. There must be nigh to a hundred supply wagons lined up out there."

"Closer to a hundred and fifty," Andy corrected. "Hell, there's four columns of men. Ole Longhair ain't taking no chances." He pulled his battered campaign hat from his head and wiped the sweat from his forehead. "Already hot and the sun just barely up. Sorry you ain't goin' along for the fun. Where you goin' anyway?"

Squint shrugged off the question. "Oh, I don't know, up in the hills a piece. I been workin' an idea in my mind for a while and I just got curious enough to go check it out. I don't know. I might just lay up somewhere for a while, do some huntin' and fishin', a little trappin' maybe. I ain't sure."

Andy studied his friend for a moment. Squint obviously had a burr under his saddle about something but he didn't particularly want to talk about it, so Andy didn't pursue the subject. "Well, I reckon I better git on down there. I wouldn't want them to leave without me. I'll see you when we git back. You mind yourself up in them mountains. You'd look kind of silly without no hair." He gave Squint a little salute, wheeled his horse and headed for the front of the column.

Squint sat there a while longer and watched the expedition pull out. Custer was at the forefront, riding his big Morgan that he was so fond of, returning the sentries' salutes as he passed through the gates of Fort Lincoln. Benteen's battalion passed and Tom Allred nodded to Squint. Squint touched his forefinger to the brim of his hat as a form of salute. As he looked back along the column, he estimated that there must have been about a thousand cavalry, and at least that many more on foot. A multitude of wagons, driven by six-mule teams were followed by a herd of two or three hundred beef cattle. He was amazed by the size of the expedition. "Ole Sittin' Bull is really gonna love this," he thought out loud. Joe snorted in reply and Squint figured his horse was telling him it was time to go. He dug his heels in gently and Joe started for the mountains. The mule, Sadie, followed obediently behind. Squint didn't bother to tie a line on Sadie. The mule would follow Joe wherever he went.

The sun was warm on his shoulders and he pulled his shirt off to let the rays soak into his skin. Every once in a while he felt the need to absorb the sun into his body just as he felt the need to occasionally seek solitude. This was one of those times. He had stayed on at Fort Lincoln longer than he had imagined he could when he rode in almost four years ago. It wasn't usual for him to stay in one place that long. Were it not for the fact that he liked Andy Coulter and young Tom Allred, he would have been gone long before. Scouting for the army wasn't bad. It gave him grub and a place to sleep and a little bit of money for tobacco. But Fort Lincoln was getting too big and busy to suit him, and he was getting just a bit tired of being around the army anyway. Whatever the reasons, he needed to get away for a while, get back to the mountains in a place where he could have enough room to get acquainted with his own soul again. For him, that was Wind River country, so deep in the mountains that even the Indians couldn't find him.

He had something else on his mind this morning. For the past several days he had been thinking about the scrawny young boy he had patched up that winter long ago. He had developed a genuine fondness for the boy that winter and sincerely regretted the boy's decision to return to his Indian upbringing. His thoughts went back to the jailbreak of Kroll and Moody and how stunned he was when he found out that the Indian he was chasing was his onetime friend, Little Wolf. At the time he was glad they were unable to catch up with him. Kroll and Moody sure as hell deserved killing if anybody did and, more than likely, Little Wolf had a prior claim on that privilege.

He wasn't sure about Tom Allred's feelings toward the brother he never knew. Tom was hot to find him when he found out who Little Wolf really was, but Squint wasn't certain what Tom's reaction might be if he ever came face to face with Little Wolf again. Tom was army through and through. He had worn the uniform too long by now to be anything else. Tom might view Little Wolf more as an enemy of the army than as his own flesh and blood. At any rate, he was relieved when Little Wolf seemed to simply disappear. Squint was not ordinarily a sentimental man, but he was fond of both brothers and he didn't want to see one of them dead at the hands of the other. Maybe Little Wolf was already dead, he wasn't sure. But if Little Wolf had only decided to live a solitary life, Squint had a notion as to where he might have holed up. And that was where he was heading as he struck out west, across the Little Missouri and into the plains.

Since he had no desire to run into any Indians, he kept to the north of Sitting Bull's usual hunting grounds, crossing the Powder well above the fork of the Crazy Woman, one of the chief's favorite camps. There was no apprehension on his part at being in the midst of hostile territory. Squint was confident in his ability to take care of himself. He traveled cautiously, being in no particular hurry, keeping a watchful eye about him as he rode, and he chose his campsites carefully.

He crossed the Tongue River, keeping the Big Horns to the south, and then down across the Big Horn basin toward the Rockies. During the entire journey, he saw no other human being, but twice he crossed trails left by large bands of Indians on the move. From their direction, Squint guessed they were probably Cheyenne going to join up with the Sioux spiritual chief, Sitting Bull. Ever since the number of white prospectors had increased in the Black Hills, there had been more and more reports of Indians leaving the reservations and joining the Sioux. Even Southern Cheyennes from down around the Oklahoma territory were leaving the reservation and traveling north to fight the white invasion. In light of all this, Squint could guess what effect Custer's massive expedition into the Black Hills would have on the situation. "Probably about like throwing kerosene on a fire," he mumbled to Joe.

Two more days' riding brought him to the Wind River Mountains. He had forgotten how beautiful the mountains were in this part of the wilderness. It had been several years since he had trapped beaver in most of the streams that etched their way through the valleys and basins but, as he looked around him, it seemed that he had never been away. The only thing that'll never change, he thought, the high mountains. The rolling plains and the foothills might someday be chewed up into little patches by the settlers and opportunists but the mountains were too rugged to be changed. The mountains would always belong to the grizzlies, the sheep and the Indians.

He climbed high up into the pines and traversed a long

rocky ridge before descending into a narrow valley, green with summer grass. Sign was everywhere; deer, elk, even bear. The thought struck his mind that a man was a fool for ever leaving an Eden such as this. He pushed on across the valley and crossed another short ridge until he came to the stream. Joe snorted as if he remembered the place and picked up his pace without encouragement from Squint. He followed the stream for about a quarter of a mile until he came upon an outcropping of rock that overhung the busy water. He couldn't help but notice the accelerated beating of his heart as he approached his old secret camp. He dismounted and tied the animals to a tree. It would be wiser to go on foot from here. He was sure Joe knew where he was, and even the mule was showing signs of skittishness. It wouldn't do for them to start making noise to warn whoever might have taken over his camp.

After quietly making his way over the rocks at the base of the mountain, he stopped for a moment to listen and look around him. Far off in the distance, a hawk called out to his mate. A gentle breeze softly whispered through the needles of the fir trees. There was no other sound. He looked toward the base of the rock wall, trying to find the opening to the camp. The trees and brush had grown considerably since he had last been there, and he didn't remember right away which trees flanked the opening through the rock. There was no sign that anyone had approached the wall of the cliff but still he was cautious. He made his way through the pines, being careful not to break any branches or bend any twigs that might give away the hidden entrance. When he stood before the opening through the stone wall, he stopped and listened. There was nothing. He made his way slowly through the opening, keeping an eye on the rock ledge above the entrance. As soon as he emerged onto the grassy floor of the enclosure, he knew his hunch was right—someone was using the camp. A gentle snort caused him to spin to his right, his rifle ready to fire. He saw the Appaloosa he and Andy had tracked from Fort Lincoln, tethered behind the clump of laurel that he used to tie Joe and Sadie behind. Another horse was hobbled beside the Appaloosa, a white Indian pony with dark markings around his head and ears. White men called them War Bonnets. Most Indians called them

Medicine Hat ponies. Satisfied that there was no one in the camp, Squint backed slowly out of the entrance in the wall, placing each foot carefully so as not to break a stick or make a sound. He had a feeling the owner of the horses would not be far away.

"It's a wonder you have kept your hair as long as you have."

The voice came from behind him. He whirled, his rifle raised, to face the tall menacing figure of a Cheyenne warrior, painted for war. Even though he recognized Little Wolf, he was still shaken by the figure before him.

"Gawdamn!" Squint exclaimed. "You scared the bejesus outta me!" He lowered his rifle and drew a breath. "I knowed you'd be up here! I knowed it!"

Little Wolf remained expressionless, soberly eyeing the huge mountain man as if he was seeing him for the first time. "Why have you come here?" His voice was cool and even.

For a moment, Squint thought his onetime friend did not recognize him. "Little Wolf, it's me, Squint Peterson. Don't you know me?"

"I know you. If I didn't, you'd be dead right now. Why have you come here?"

"Why, to find you, dammit!" Squint was beginning to get a little exasperated. He had expected a somewhat warmer reception from the boy he had doctored back to health and wintered with. He searched Little Wolf's stony countenance for some sign of softening, but there was none. It was plain to see that there was little, if any, of the boy left in the lean and powerful figure before him. The years had hardened the man and dissolved all remnants of the boy, Robert Allred.

"So, you have found me."

"Yeah, reckon I have." Squint was perturbed. Now that he had found the man, he wondered if it was worth the bother. "I reckon I just wanted to see for myself if you was holed up here in my old camp." Little Wolf made no reply. "I wanted to see if you really did go wild like folks say you have. A lot of folks think you're dead." He stared into the unblinking gaze that continued to capture his own. Then, as if just then remembering, "How the hell did you sneak up behind me anyway?"

This brought a faint trace of a smile to Little Wolf's hardened face. "I watched you come across the basin and the ridge. I saw you tie your horse and mule in the trees and try to sneak into my camp. A herd of buffalo would not have been more obvious."

"Huh!" Squint snorted. "I wasn't of a mind to surprise you. I thought I was just coming for a little visit." It was a lie and he knew Little Wolf knew it was too, but he would never admit that his friend had gotten the jump on him. They looked at each other for a few moments longer in silence before Squint decided they had sized each other up long enough. "Well, I can see one thing. Your manners ain't improved any since you went plumb wild. You ain't invited me to your campfire for something to eat and I'm plumb starved. You got any fresh meat?" He didn't give Little Wolf time to answer. "I got some coffee in my pack. I bet you ain't had no coffee for a spell."

Little Wolf's expression softened a little. If he had intended to remain indifferent toward his guest, it was apparent Squint was not going to give him the option. "Son, you got any fresh meat?" he persisted.

"Yes." Little Wolf smiled.

"Well, git it then. I'm 'bout to starve to death. I'm goin' to get my animals." He turned and walked through the opening in the wall.

Squint could see that Little Wolf was not exactly comfortable sitting across the campfire from a white man, even if it was Squint Peterson. But before long, he relaxed some of the stiffness he had endeavored to maintain. Squint was confident that he would. There was something medicinal about coffee. It was just impossible to sit down and drink a cup of hot black coffee with an enemy. The high walls of their mountain camp soon blocked the rays of the afternoon sun and the warm July day cooled toward early evening, making the coffee even more cordial. By the time they had emptied the pot and eaten the last strips of meat, Little Wolf had apparently lowered his guard and appeared to be at ease with his old friend.

"Why did you come to this place? It's foolish for a white man to come here."

Squint licked the last of the thin grease from his fingers

and wiped them on his shirt. Sitting cross-legged in front of the fire, he leaned over to one side to release a fart. Feeling more comfortable, he began, "Well, to tell you the truth, I was kind of curious to see you, for one thing. You know, you've got a pretty big reputation with the army for being a bad renegade." Little Wolf registered some surprise at this but said nothing. Squint went on, "I guess I wanted to see if the Cheyenne Little Wolf was the same Little Wolf I wintered with in this same camp. Word is you left Sitting Bull's camp and turned into a loner. I thought you might have took yourself a wife by now." He saw at once that this struck a nerve.

"I did," Little Wolf said softly. "I had a wife. She is dead." After some prodding from Squint, he told him about Morning Sky and how she had been killed by the two buffalo hunters.

"I had a suspicion that might have happened," Squint said, after offering his condolences over the loss of Morning Sky. "I figured it had to be somethin' like that to make a man go to all the trouble to bust them two out of jail. When I seen them two where you left 'em, one of 'em with his balls pinned to the ground, I figured as much." Squint's face took on a frown. "I should'a kilt them two when I had the chance instead of just puttin' that nick in Kroll's ear. If I had, you wouldn't have been at Fort Lincoln and we wouldn't of been chasing you."

"It was you then? You were with the other two who came after me? The soldier and the other scout?"

"Yeah, it was me. Only I didn't have no idea it was you we was chasin' at the time." He paused to stir up the fire a little. "That's another reason I come up here. That soldier—you could have killed him but you didn't. How come?" Squint knew the reason because Tom had told him, but he wanted to hear Little Wolf's version of the story.

Little Wolf shrugged, an expression of boredom on his face as if to imply the incident was of no real importance. "It was a debt. That day on the Washita when Longhair came riding into the camp like a cowardly coyote, the soldier could have killed Morning Sky, and he could have killed me. But he didn't, so I spared his life. The debt is paid."

Squint studied his friend carefully as he asked, "Anything

about that particular lieutenant that struck you as odd, or familiar?"

"No. Why should it?"

"God, or Man Above if you druther, must have been lookin' out for you that day when you decided not to kill that soldier."

Little Wolf was puzzled. "Why do you say that?"

"Well, you wouldn't cotton to killin' your own brother, would you?"

Little Wolf was still confused. He didn't understand what Squint was telling him. He made no reply, waiting for Squint to explain. Squint, enjoying the opportunity to enlighten, let Little Wolf puzzle over it for a few moments longer before continuing. "That there soldier's name is Lieutenant Tom Allred . . . your brother."

If Little Wolf reacted to this shocking bit of news, he gave no outward sign of it. His face remained as stony as before. Squint could not know that the news had actually stunned the young warrior to his core. Little Wolf had not heard that name for so long that he had forgotten the existence of his white brother. And now, to have it suddenly thrust upon him, he did not know what to think or even how to feel. I have no brother," he mumbled softly, the words dropping from his lips with no thought behind them.

"The hell you don't. That feller's name is shore as hell Tom Allred and he shore as hell comes from St. Louis, and he shore as hell had a little brother named Robert that went off with a mule skinner when he was no more'n a tad."

Again there was a long silence while Little Wolf tried to sort out his feelings. He remembered his older brother vaguely. They had not been especially close, but there was never any trouble between them. Finally, he reminded himself that there was no past before the time Spotted Pony found him. "I have no brother," he repeated. This time it was a definitive statement.

"If you say so. It ain't for me to say but I just figured it was my place to let you know about that soldier you run into."

Little Wolf nodded his head and held up his hand, signaling an end to that topic of conversation. Squint knew that whatever the young warrior felt about the situation, he was not going to share it with him. He moved on to another topic.

"If you've done turned into a loner, living up here all by yourself, how come you're wearing that paint on your face?"

"It is true that I wish to live in solitude but I must end my solitude to help my brothers in our fight to keep the white soldiers out of our sacred hunting grounds. Many, many Cheyenne braves are already in the camp of Sitting Bull. The white men are infesting the Black Hills and the Yellowstone like fleas on a dog. Sitting Bull has called for all warriors to come to the aid of the Sioux. We must stop the white man now. I go to fight beside my brothers."

"Agin' your own kind?"

"No," Little Wolf replied sternly, "with my brothers, against the people who killed my father and mother and my wife."

There was no uncertainty in Little Wolf's tone. Squint realized that if he had come to find him a few days later than he did, Little Wolf would probably have been gone from this camp. It was obvious that he was not going to dissuade his young friend from joining the hordes of hostiles now flocking to the valleys of the Yellowstone. He thought of the huge expedition he had watched leaving Fort Lincoln some days before and what repercussions they would cause. At once he felt sad for his idealistic young friend. That he would die or be captured and sent to prison was almost a certainty, and he didn't like the thought of such a free spirit shackled to a jail cell. Little Wolf was a wanted man but, in his mind, he had done no wrong, at least nothing any self-respecting Cheyenne warrior would not have done. And he was a true Cheyenne, no matter the color of his skin.

"You're a wanted man, partner. I guess you know that." Squint's voice was low and deadly serious. "If they catch you, they're gonna hang you shore as hell. There ain't gonna be no prison for you."

Little Wolf looked surprised. "Why? Why do they want me any more than any other Cheyenne or Dakota?"

" 'Cause you're white. You're a renegade, a white man turned Injun. They're gonna want to make an example outta you."

"I don't understand why."

"Cause you're white," he repeated. "The army don't take kindly to white men that turns agin' their own kind."

Little Wolf was immediately indignant. "I am Cheyenne. Before that I was Arapaho. Before that, there was nothing. I fight the enemies of my people. I have killed no women or children, only soldiers."

"Hell, I know that. But the army don't look at it that way. They figure if you look like a wolf and you run with a pack of wolves, chances are you're a wolf too. Anyway, don't get riled up at me. I'm just telling you what's what so's maybe you'll be a little more careful. Maybe even think a while before running off to join up with Sitting Bull's bunch."

"I must do what my heart tells me to do."

"Yeah, I reckon," Squint answered, resigned to the inevitability of it. If he had hoped to persuade his young friend to reconsider his future, he now knew that it was useless to try. There was too much bitterness in the young man, rage that had to be tempered with revenge. They sat in silence for several minutes. Finally Squint spoke again, "Well, I'll never think of you as an enemy of mine. I hope you feel the same."

Little Wolf smiled and laid his hand on Squint's shoulder. "You will always be my friend. Just don't ride against Sitting Bull and you have nothing to fear from my bow."

"Hell, what would keep us from packin' up right now and headin' for Oregon? Whaddaya say? Ain't you had enough killin' for one lifetime? I know I ain't got nothin' I got to git back to Fort Lincoln for. Why, I hear tell that a man can make a livin' off one acre of ground out there, there's so much game. We can just hunt and trap and fish till we git so old we can't pull a trigger no more. Whaddaya say?"

Little Wolf did not answer but his smile was enough to tell Squint that the die was already cast. The war paint that formed two distinct vees of red and white from the bridge of his nose down across both cheeks could not merely be wiped off. They signified a commitment to a people, a commitment that ran deeper than the skin upon which they were painted. If he could have seen inside Little Wolf's heart, he would have realized the pain that had been suffered at the hands of the army. And the one image that had come to symbolize that pain was the image of the Cheyenne's hated enemy, *Longhair*. As long as Custer lived, there would be no peace in Little Wolf's heart.

"Well, it was just a thought," Squint sighed and reached over to stir up the fire. After a moment, he said, "It shore would be something to see that Oregon territory though."

They talked until the fire died out and both were too sleepy to get more wood, eventually falling asleep beside the glowing coals. When Squint awoke the next morning, Little Wolf was gone. The Appaloosa was tied next to Joe and Sadie. There had been no mention of it in their conversation the night before but Squint knew the horse was left in payment for the little mare, Britches, that he had given Little Wolf when they parted company years before in the Shoshone village.

"Won't be beholden to nobody," Squint muttered as he stretched and scratched. He looked around the empty camp. "Don't owe your brother nothin'. Don't owe me nothin'. Just owe them damn Injuns." He shook his head, exasperated. "We could have made a good life in Oregon." He got up to see to his horses and inspect his gift. "Dang, Joe, why didn't you warn me when he left in the middle of the night?" The thought that Little Wolf could get up and steal out of the camp without waking him bothered him more than a little. "I'm gittin' too damn old for this life." He looked at the Appaloosa, his white-spotted coat shimmering in the first fingers of sunlight filtering through the trees. "Boy, you shore paid off with interest. That little mare weren't half the horse you are." He took one last look at his favorite of all campsites, the perfect spot. Reluctantly, he climbed up on Joe. Leading the Appaloosa and Sadie, he headed back to Fort Lincoln and the army.

CHAPTER 23

There was a great deal of anger and heated discussion among the leaders in the Sioux camp over Custer's so-called peaceful expedition into the Black Hills. Gall, one of the most feared of the Sioux war chiefs, called the trail that Custer took the Road of Thieves, and demanded that the whites be punished for entering their sacred lands. The summer was not yet over and already there were hundreds of prospectors camping in the Black Hills. Not only had the army stopped enforcing the treaty, now the hated Longhair had actually led a huge armed force into the area.

After reading Custer's report on his expedition, the white chiefs in Washington decided that the Indian should give up the Black Hills so the white man could go in search of the yellow dirt. Washington called for a council with the Sioux to propose a new settlement with the Indians. It was to be held on the White River and many of the Sioux, Gall among them, argued against attending such a council. They felt there was nothing to discuss. Others, such as Snow Walker, felt it best to meet with the men from Washington to hear them out. It was rumored that the white man wanted not only the Black Hills, but the Indians' lands along the Yellowstone and the Powder. They would offer the Indians money for these lands. If, Sitting Bull insisted, they sold these lands to the white man, there would be nothing left for the Indian but the reservation. The white man had stolen everything else. The land was all the Indian had left. The discussion among the Sioux leaders was not over whether they should sell their lands, rather it was over whether they should honor the invitation to council with the whites . . . or simply go to war. This was the atmosphere into which Little Wolf rode one clear afternoon, just as the sun was beginning to nestle into the far hills beyond the circle of tipis of Two Moon's band of Cheyennes who had come from north and south to join Sitting Bull in his fight against the white invaders.

"Little Wolf!"

The voice was familiar. He turned to see Sleeps Standing striding toward him, a smile spread across the width of his face in warm welcome. Little Wolf smiled in return. It had been some time now since he had last seen his old friend and he walked to meet him. They embraced like two bears might, with strong hugs and a lot of pounding on each other's back.

"I knew you would come to fight with your brothers. Bloody Claw said you would not ride against the whites again, that your Cheyenne heart had gone cold." He beamed as he added, "But I said Little Wolf would return when the people needed him and here you are."

Little Wolf was touched by the warm reception. "Yes, I am here." He smiled. "I sought to live alone with my soul, maybe forever, but my soul was not yet at peace while the man responsible for the death of my mother and father and our friend Black Feather still lives."

"Come," Sleeps Standing insisted. "You must stay in my tipi. I have taken a wife since I last saw you. She is a good woman. Her younger sister lives with us. She is young and will keep you warm at night."

"I thank you, my brother. It will be an honor to accept your hospitality. I will stay in your tipi but I still sleep with Morning Sky."

Sleeps Standing nodded his understanding. It was not uncommon for a man to live with the spirit of a departed loved one. "Come. We will eat and rest and tomorrow I will take you to see Two Moon."

"It is an honor to have the brave and cunning Little Wolf join us in our battle." Two Moon placed his hand on Little Wolf's shoulder. "We are many here. Northern and Southern Cheyenne are pledged together to fight beside our brothers, the Lakotas. You are welcome. I have heard songs of your deeds in battle."

Little Wolf thanked the chief for his warm welcome and expressed his desire to fight with any group of braves who made war on Custer. He and Sleeps Standing smoked the pipe with Two Moon and talked with the chief about the possibility of all-out war against the army. Two Moon told them of the discussion at the council meeting and that the elders had decided to go to the council at White River to talk to the white men. They would hear them out and then they would list their own grievances but they would not give up their lands to the white man.

"There will be war," Two Moon said solemnly. "The white man will not accept our decision. He hungers for the yellow dirt and he will try to drive us from our hunting grounds, just as he has always done. But this time it will not be so easy. This time he will face many, many warriors united to turn the soldiers back. This time the soldiers will face the Cheyenne, the Sioux and the Arapaho."

When Little Wolf and Sleeps Standing returned to the tipi, they found Bloody Claw waiting for them. He eyed Little Wolf cautiously as he approached. "So it is true what I hear. Little Wolf has returned to the village of the Cheyenne."

"It is good to see you, my brother." Little Wolf extended his arm in greeting.

Bloody Claw clasped it. "Welcome."

Although they observed the polite formalities that courtesy required, Little Wolf knew he was anything but a welcome sight to Bloody Claw. They had fought side by side in many battles and should have regarded each other as comrades in arms, but Little Wolf knew that Bloody Claw did not wish to see him return. Bloody Claw had always felt a sense of jealousy that the younger man had commanded the respect of the small band of Cheyenne warriors from Black Kettle's old tribe. When Little Wolf left to go into the mountains alone, Bloody Claw assumed the leadership role. Now, he was concerned that Little Wolf had returned to regain his position. Little Wolf felt the need to reassure Bloody Claw.

"I have heard that you are a respected leader of our warriors. I would be proud to follow you in battle."

Bloody Claw appeared to puff up with this compliment, somewhat relieved but not altogether satisfied. "I would be proud to have Little Wolf fight beside us again."

The formalities over, Bloody Claw departed. When he

had gone, Sleeps Standing laughed. "Bloody Claw looks worried. He has been a war chief since you have been gone. I think he is afraid of your power."

Little Wolf brushed the comment aside. "He has nothing to fear from me. I come to fight the soldiers. I care not who leads who into battle."

"Maybe so, but I think the warriors will follow you when the fighting starts."

Two weeks after Little Wolf arrived in the village, the people set out to meet with the council from Washington. A tent had been set up near the banks of the White River for the committee of white officials to confer with the Sioux chiefs. The Indians were angry and, to show their anger, they showed up in force. Some fifteen to twenty thousand in all, warriors, women and children filled the bluffs along the river. While the chiefs met with the delegation from Washington, Sioux and Cheyenne braves raced back and forth along the bluffs on painted ponies, feathers flying as they galloped, brandishing their lances. Little Wolf sat quietly on his horse, his eyes on the tent across the river, amazed at the absurdity of the situation. The delegation of civilian government representatives were escorted by a small detachment of mounted cavalry which, if called upon for protection, would be swarmed in a matter of seconds should the multitude of Indians decide to attack.

He would learn later that the government offered the Sioux money for the use of their lands. When the chiefs refused the offer, the government offered to buy the Black Hills outright. Again the offer was refused. They were told that the Sioux would never sell their sacred lands and that the white man must leave immediately. Any white man found in the territory would be killed. Little Wolf wondered why the chiefs had agreed to meet with the delegation in the first place. He suspected it was to take the opportunity to impress upon the white men the sheer strength aligned against an invasion of the Indians' hunting grounds. The meeting ended with no progress on the government's proposal and the Indians returned to their villages confident that the white man had at last realized that the Indians would give no more ground.

In the weeks that followed, the government pulled army

troops out of the Black Hills. At first Sitting Bull assumed this a sign that the government had at last given up on the idea of invading the sacred Sioux hunting ground. But it soon became apparent that this was not the case. Sioux and Cheyenne scouts reported that more and more prospectors were streaming into the territory, unhampered by the army. From the Indians' point of view, and from the treaty signed at Laramie, the only reason for the army's presence there had been to keep the miners out. Now they were making no attempt to restrain the rush of prospectors looking for gold in the Black Hills.

Sitting Bull was angry. After fasting for three days and nights and cleansing his mind and body in the sweat lodge, he went up into the mountains to meditate. When he returned to the village, he told the people that he had seen a vision. Man Above had appeared to him, riding a white horse. He had told him that the Black Hills were sacred and that he must drive the white man out. The time for councils and peace talks was past. The time now was for the lance and bow. There must be no mercy for any white man found in the territory.

Waddie Bodkin straightened up from his sluice, both hands filled with the gravel he had been sifting through. "You hear it?"

His partner, a squarely built half-breed Crow named Sam Two Kills, nodded in agreement. They both stood silent, knee-deep in the chilly waters of Blind Man's Creek, their ears turned into the wind to catch the sounds of rifle shots far upstream. There it was again, maybe a dozen or so shots, barely audible.

"Damn!" Waddie swore. "That's the second time in a week. It's getting too damn close to suit me."

"Damn close," Sam agreed.

Sam didn't say very much, a trait that was sometimes aggravating to Waddie since the little Irishman enjoyed a good conversation as much, if not more, than any man. On the other hand, Sam wasn't blessed with a great deal of common sense and damn few opinions on any subject. In light of that, Waddie figured it was better if the half-breed kept his mouth shut most of the time. As they both stood motionless, listening for more shots, Waddie studied his partner as if seeing him for the first time. Sam was half-breed all right, but there was very little of his French father showing in his appearance. Although he could not have been much more than thirty years of age, he had lost all of his front teeth, giving him a somewhat vacant smile on the few occasions he found humor in something. His hair was long and wild. He never wore a headband so his dull black hair seemed to spew out of the top of his head like a dirty fountain, falling all around his face and neck. And he was bowlegged, more than any man Waddie had ever seen. Standing in water up to his knees, his legs appeared to be spread wide apart. Waddie would bet that the man's feet were close to touching. *Some partner,* he thought to himself. *Shows how desperate a man can get for company after a few years alone in the wilderness.*

It had been fully five years since he had parted company with Squint Peterson and packed off up into the Black Hills. He had tried his luck at several spots before finding this little creek. Sam had wandered in two years ago looking for something to eat. Waddie needed help and was hoping for some companionship so he offered Sam a share in the diggings. Sam had no place else to go so he accepted the offer. Waddie got the help he needed but failed to get much in the way of companionship. Still, Sam was a little better than a dog, Waddie figured. In fact, Sam was almost like having a dog around, a dog that could say a few words in English and could use a shovel and pan.

"Some poor devils are catching hell." Waddie finally broke the silence. He knew full well what the gunfire meant. Sioux and Cheyenne war parties had been raiding and killing all through the territory. He had been lucky so far, but he knew it was just a matter of time before his little claim was discovered by the scouting parties. He knew that he was living on borrowed time. But he had finally struck a little color that looked worthwhile, so he kept gambling one more day at a time in an effort to accumulate enough dust to at least show something for the years invested in this wilderness. He had long ago given up hope of returning to civilization a wealthy man. Now he was working day after day to go back to the settlements with enough to keep from being a beggar. Now, as he stood chilled to the bone in the icy waters of Blind Man's Creek, he decided it was time to pull up stakes and get out before either the Indians caught him or the heavy snows trapped him.

"Sam, it's time to cut bait while we still have some bait to cut."

Sam only grunted in response but Waddie could see by the expression on the half-breed's face that he was in full accord. Sam was only half Indian, but that half was Crow, and neither the Sioux or Cheyenne were overly fond of Crows.

They spent the rest of that day preparing to leave their claim. The Indian war parties might have caused them to quit their diggings a little sooner than they wanted, but Waddie was satisfied that they had gotten the better part of any dust there. It wasn't a fortune, but it was enough to split and provide a start at something else down in one of the settlements. He might even head toward Fort Lincoln to see if his friend Squint Peterson was still there. He wasn't figuring on Sam going with him. He didn't know or care where the half-breed was going. He'd probably just go drink it all up anyway. As far as Waddie was concerned, their partnership was at an end.

They packed up everything they planned to carry out with them and loaded the mules with everything but the gold dust. They decided to keep it in its hiding place until first light, when they would abandon the camp. The first year Waddie made this camp on Blind Man's Creek, he dug a cave up under a high bank of the stream to stash his gold dust. He wasn't about to work his hind end off for that gold only to have some outlaw steal it from the tiny cabin while he was down at the stream working the sluice. The entrance to his treasure cave was well disguised. In fact, it was necessary to wade into the creek to approach it.

That night a glow could be seen in the northern sky. Waddie figured it was the stockade a group of fourteen prospectors built on the fork of French Creek. There was no doubt the shots they had heard that afternoon had come from there. That glow indicated to Waddie that the miners at French Creek had gotten the short end of the fighting. It would be the second time the fort had been burned. Waddie had a feeling it would be the last. It also meant the war party that attacked the stockade was a sizable one.

Chances were they would be content to dance around the fire and celebrate their victory for a while which would assure him and Sam plenty of time to get a head start in the morning. He couldn't be positive the war party would head this way but, on the chance it did, he was damn sure he wasn't going to be there to greet them.

"Sam, you take the rest of that dried jerky. You might need it with winter setting in and game getting scarce. I'll be in Fort Lincoln in four or five days. I got enough to last me till then." Sam grunted his thanks and got up from the fire and wrapped the dried meat in a skin pouch. He walked over to his mule and stuffed the pouch into his pack. Waddie watched with amusement. "Well, partner, one thing I'll say for you, you sure as hell haven't worn out the language in the last two years, but you're a damn good worker." Sam grunted in response. "You haven't said where you're heading in the morning."

"Canada," Sam replied. If Waddie expected any elaboration on that, he was to be disappointed.

"Well, I guess that's as good as any. Me, I'm ready to see some white folks for a while, some stores and saloons and"—he paused to emphasize the last—"some women." The word triggered his memory and he recalled some of the towns he had seen and the people he had met, especially the women. He told Sam about places the half-breed could barely imagine, places like New Orleans and St. Louis, where a man with as much dust as he had could have a right entertaining time of it before it ran out. The half-breed listened for a while but fell asleep long before Waddie finished talking.

It wasn't quite daylight when Waddie was awakened by Sam. "Morning," he stated without emotion.

A light sprinkling of snow had fallen during the night, giving the woods around the creek a cold, colorless appearance, causing Waddie to shiver when he walked out of the tiny cabin to relieve his bladder. When he was comfortable again, he spent a few moments looking around the camp for signs of anything out of the ordinary. Everything looked in order. "I reckon we'd best get on with it," he decided and he and Sam walked down to the creek bank.

"Want me to git it?" Sam asked when they were directly over the cave.

"No use you getting wet. I'll get it." He waded into the icy water and pulled the stones and driftwood away from the opening. He would have let Sam go in after the dust but it represented all the sweat he had lost for the past five years and he had to make sure all of it was brought out. He trusted Sam. He had lived with the man for two years. But when it came to gold, it didn't make sense to trust a half-breed to bring out all the sacks. There might be too much temptation to leave a couple there to be collected at a later date.

Sam handed him a torch from the fire to use as a light. The cave was a good place to hide gold, but it might also be a good place for some kind of critter to hole up for the winter too, so Waddie took a good look around before crawling up inside. There were thirteen sacks in all. Five of these contained dust that he had panned before Sam joined him. The other eight were to be divided evenly between the two of them. Waddie handed them out one by one to make sure he didn't drop any in the rushing water. Sam took each one and placed it safely on the creek bank. Then he extended his hand and helped Waddie pull himself up from the cave.

"Well, I reckon that about does it up fair and square," Waddie said, as he divided up the sacks. "You satisfied?"

Sam nodded.

"Well then, I reckon we better get going." He extended his hand. "It's been nice knowing you, Sam. Good luck to you."

Sam smiled his toothless smile and took the outstretched hand. Waddie never saw the ten-inch skinning knife in the half-breed's other hand as it struck the little Irishman under the rib cage. At first he didn't know what happened, the knife had struck with such force. It felt like a log had been lodged in his insides. When he staggered backwards a few steps, still holding Sam's outstretched right hand, only then did he realize what had happened. As he stood there, reeling in shock, the half-breed pulled the knife from his gut. The fiery pain that resulted caused Waddie to scream in agony. He started to fall but Sam caught him with a second vicious thrust that buried the knife again in his gut, right up to the hilt. He held Waddie up on his feet, using the knife as support, until the poor little Irishman went limp.

Then, withdrawing the blade, he stepped back and let Waddie fall to the ground.

Sam stood over the body for a few minutes, watching for any movement that might indicate the necessity for another thrust of the knife. Waddie was moaning as his lifeblood ran into the sand of the creek bank. It would be only a matter of minutes before he would be still. Sam felt no animosity toward the little man who had taken him in as a partner. It was simply that, with him dead, there would be more gold for himself, so he waited patiently, without remorse, for Waddie to die. When the body quivered, then jerked once and was finally still, Sam began to gather up the thirteen sacks of gold dust.

With both arms filled with the sacks, he turned to face three mounted Cheyenne warriors, calmly watching him. He had been so preoccupied with Waddie's death throes that he had not heard them come up behind him. At once his eyes opened wide in alarm and he dropped his armful of gold dust to the ground.

"Peace!" he screamed and held up his arms.

"Peace, Crow dog," the tall warrior on the Medicine Hat pony spat back at him. In almost the same instant, three arrows struck the half-breed in his chest, knocking him backward into the stream. He was still barely alive when one of the warriors waded into the creek and took his scalp.

The tall warrior watched the scalping with only mild interest then picked up the sacks of yellow dust. One by one he emptied them into the water. "For this dust the white man chooses to drive a whole nation from their hunting grounds . . . Nothing more than dirt."

"Damn, it's cold out there!" Andy Coulter stomped into the Sutler's store, followed by a wintry blast of cold air.

"Well, shut the damn door before we all freeze!" Squint yelled at him from his chair propped against the wall behind the potbelly stove. "A body would think you ain't enjoying the season."

Andy snorted, ignoring the attempt at humor. He wiped his running nose with the back of his hand and hurried to warm himself by the stove. He stood close for as long as he could stand it before turning around to warm his backside. When the wet buckskin of his coat began to smoke, he took a step away from the stove and turned to face it again. "I'm shore glad as hell I ain't goin' out on no patrol today. A man would freeze to his saddle in thirty minutes."

"Hell, Andy, you're gittin' plumb girlish in your old age. Why, the cold weather ain't hardly hit yet. It's still a few days to Christmas. Winter won't hardly start for a month or two."

"That right? Well, why don't you go out and take a swim in the horse trough if the weather's too warm for you?"

Squint laughed. "I ain't the one complaining."

"I just come from the colonel's office. A dispatch rider just rode in half froze to death."

"In this weather?" Squint snorted. "Why didn't they telegraph it? Dang if I'd ride all day in weather like this. I'd tell them damn soldier boys to wait till spring and send a pigeon. Must be mighty important. Hell, you could kill a man in weather like this."

Andy peeled off his heavy fur gloves and threw back the hood on his coat. The heat from the laboring potbelly stove finally began to penetrate the layers of clothing. "I swear, your belly burns up while your backside freezes over." He turned to toast his behind again. "Wires cut again, south of the fort, second time this month."

Squint lowered his chair to the floor and held his hands up to the stove. "Well, what was so all-fired important that they couldn't wait till the line was fixed?"

"I'm fixin' to tell you if you'll give me a minute," Andy replied. "Naturally the colonel didn't discuss it with me but Tom told me it was from the commissioner of Injun Affairs. He said they was sending out orders that all Injuns have to report to their agencies by January."

Squint didn't understand at first. "He wants all Injuns to go back to the reservation? By January? Hell, that don't make a whole lot of sense."

Andy shrugged. "It didn't to me, neither. Tom said the government has had enough of the raidin' and killin' in the Black Hills and all Injuns that wasn't back on the reservation by January would be considered hostile and would be dealt with by the army."

"Andy, you know as well as I do that ain't gonna happen. In the first place, how you gonna get the word to all the tribes? They're all in winter camps now, scattered all over hell's half acre. Even if you could get the word to 'em, they can't hardly move a whole village of people that far in this kind of weather." His hands warm again, he tilted his chair back against the wall. "I'll tell you one thing, that ole buck Sittin' Bull ain't gonna take his warriors to no reservation anyway. Hell, he ain't got no reservation. He ain't never signed no peace treaty in the first place."

Andy scratched his matted hair and spat a brown stream onto the hot stove. He watched it sizzle for a moment before he spoke. "Looks to me like the politicians back East decided they want that gold in the Black Hills. The Injuns won't sell it to 'em, so they're just gonna take it. I fear there's gonna be some killin' in the spring. This ain't gonna be like last summer. That ole coyote has got every wild-ass buck in the territory running to join up with him."

CHAPTER 24

The winter of 1875 was a long one for Lieutenant Tom Allred. Garrison life at Fort Lincoln was designed, he suspected, to test a man's ability to withstand monotony. There had been very little action. The hostiles were holed up in their winter camps. The snows were so heavy and frequent that most of the fighting was confined to an occasional sortie to rescue an isolated settler attacked by some roving band of Indians. For the most part, the garrison simply waited for spring to come. Once in a while, Squint would get so antsy he couldn't stand it any longer and he would ride out to hunt. Game was hard to find, but he always managed to come up with something, and at least he would get away from the fort for a couple of days. Tom sometimes accompanied him if he wasn't scheduled for guard mount or some other detail. The conversation on these occasions generally got around to the coming spring and the prospects of a serious Indian war. This inevitably brought up the subject of Little Wolf. Tom was still unsure about his feelings toward a brother who had abandoned his own race and elected to become a savage. Squint reminded him that the boy had little choice. Still Tom found it hard to sympathize with a man who was regarded as one of the most fearsome savages in the territory. He had not merely taken up Indian ways, he had become one of the Cheyennes' most infamous warriors.

"You got to remember," Squint said one day when they had stopped by an ice-covered stream to build a fire to warm by while they ate their midday meal. " 'Bout the only thing Little Wolf remembers 'bout being white is that your folks sold him to a mule skinner."

"Granted, and he was only nine or ten, but that's old

enough to know that he's white and that he has a brother and sisters. I can't understand how he could forget that."

"From what I can tell, them Injuns that adopted him was mighty kind to him, better'n your folks I expect. They're the only real family he had."

Tom wasn't comfortable with the topic. He shrugged. "Yeah, I expect so. Still, he didn't have to turn out to be such a damn savage. Hell, Custer's put a price on his head. I wonder what he'd think if he knew he was my brother?"

Squint grunted. "I doubt he'd think highly of it. I don't think I'd let on if I was you."

"I don't intend to."

Squint cocked his head to the side and eyed Tom curiously, a thought just occurring to him. "What do you intend to do if you come face to face with Little Wolf in a fight?"

Tom's face lost all expression, a faraway gaze in his eyes. "I've been giving that a lot of thought," he said. "I guess I'd kill him."

"Your own brother?"

"A damn Cheyenne," he retorted. "I'd kill him."

Squint looked long and hard at his young friend. "You seem mighty damn sure of that."

"Brother or not, I'm a soldier, and if he's decided to side with the hostiles, then I guess I have no choice."

The spring of '76 brought an increase in Indian attacks on the stubborn prospectors still holding out in Sioux territory. Scouts brought back reports that more and more Indians were leaving the reservations now that the winter was over and fleeing to join Sitting Bull. There were reports of large concentrations of Cheyenne and Arapaho in the Sioux camp and there was much talk among the warriors of joining Sitting Bull to make a last great stand against the army.

At Fort Lincoln, preparations were being made for a large-scale expedition into the field. Supplies were brought in from the East as well as fresh horses and ammunition. Captain Benteen had Tom drilling the men every day to smooth off the rust that accumulated after a winter in garrison. At last, orders came down, and Benteen passed the word along to Tom. The plans called for a major campaign to settle the Indian problem for good and all, punishing all the tribes that lived along the Yellowstone. General Terry himself was going to lead a thousand men west from Fort Lincoln. This included Colonel Custer's Seventh Cavalry. The attack would be three-pronged. They would be joined in the campaign by troops from Fort Fetterman in Wyoming under the leadership of General George Crook, who was pretty well known as an old Indian fighter. From Montana, General John Gibbon was leading a force down the Yellowstone to meet them.

It was going to be a long time spent in the field. Squint was undecided until the last minute about whether he wanted to go on another campaign. He didn't mind the prospect of fighting Indians—it was the long marches that tired him out. Had it not been for Andy's persistent badgering, he might have chosen to pack his mule and head for Oregon. Peace and quiet were more on his mind of late, and the thought of a rippling mountain stream far back in the quiet mountains with plenty of fish and game was almost too much to resist. But on that frosty spring morning when the troops moved out toward the west, Squint found himself riding the Appaloosa with Joe on a lead line, Andy on one side and Tom on the other. Once again he was going to war.

It was slow going until they reached the Yellowstone. There, General Terry loaded himself and his infantry on a steamboat named the *Far West* and steamed up the river. Custer's cavalry was sent overland with orders to scout along the way. This suited Custer just fine. He preferred to be out from under the general's command, so the Seventh continued west to rendezvous with General Terry at the mouth of the Rosebud River.

The weather was getting warmer as the Seventh made its way westward. There was little sign of hostile activity along the way. Squint and Andy stayed away from the column most of the day, but their scouting resulted in nothing worth noting so the column moved along at a rapid pace. All told, Custer employed about forty scouts, many of them Pawnee and Poncas. Some were civilian like Andy and Squint. Custer liked Andy and he often sent for him to scout out in advance of the column. Squint, on the other hand, wasn't overly fond of the cocky little colonel whose devoted underlings still insisted on addressing their leader as General Custer, his brevet rank in the War Between the States. He was too vain to suit Squint and vanity wasn't a quality Squint looked for when picking a man to follow into battle. Consequently, he stayed close to Captain Benteen's troops and away from the front of the column. This way, he was also close to his friend Tom Allred.

Captain Benteen was a rather astute commander with experience in the field. He knew a good scout when he saw one. He also knew of Squint's opinion of their commanding officer, an opinion not so distant from his own. So, when scouts were discussed or evaluated, Benteen said very little about Squint, preferring to keep his talents anonymous. The result was a happy situation for all involved, including Custer. Squint cared very little for recognition and none at all for promotion. He was secure in the knowledge that he could take care of himself and that all he owed his employers was an honest day's work. As far as he was concerned, he worked for Benteen. Let somebody else scout for Custer.

On a warm afternoon in the latter part of June, Andy rode back to the column at a gallop. He pulled up and wheeled in beside Custer. "General"—Andy was not above a little bootlicking now and then—"the Rosebud is about a mile on the other side of that there rise." He pointed in the direction of a low line of trees in the distance.

"Did you see any sign of General Terry's forces?"

"Yessir. They's there all right, camped on the banks. The steamboat's there too."

Custer was irritated. Maybe, Andy thought, he wanted to get to the Rosebud first and he was a little agitated because the boat beat his cavalry. The colonel spoke, "Very good, Coulter," and dismissed him. To his bugler, he ordered, "My compliments to Major Reno and Captain Benteen."

"Yessir!" the bugler snapped and was off at a gallop to summon the two battalion commanders.

When Benteen rode off to the head of the column, Tom steered his mount over beside Squint's Appaloosa. They rode along in silence for a few minutes. Up ahead, Andy was waiting. When they caught up to him, he pulled in beside them.

"Won't be long before supper," he said. "The Rosebud's up ahead."

"That's why Custer sent for Captain Benteen, I reckon," Squint said.

"Yep," Andy replied. "Maybe General Terry will invite us to take supper with him on that there steamboat."

Tom and Squint laughed. "He might," Squint said. "Maybe we should bring a bottle of wine for the occasion."

They made camp on the banks of the Yellowstone, across from the "walk-a-heaps," as the Indians called the infantry, and soon the night was dotted with small cook fires. The following day they were allowed to relax while Custer went aboard the *Far West* to receive his orders from General Terry. Tom took advantage of the opportunity to peel off his uniform and take a bath in the river. Squint joined him, but Andy was satisfied to splash a little water on his face and neck, saying that his buckskins fit him about perfect now. If he took them off and got all wet, they might not go back on as comfortably.

The next morning the regiment was ordered to prepare to march again. The scouts had discovered a large Indian trail that led along the Rosebud. From the looks of it, Squint guessed that maybe an entire village had traveled that way. Custer was ordered to take the Seventh and follow the trail. It was the general consensus among the commanders that the end of the trail would, in all likelihood, be a sizable Indian village, maybe even Sitting Bull's camp. So, at about noon on the twenty-second of June as recorded in Tom's diary, the Seventh started out along the Rosebud.

For two days the column followed the trail along the river until it abruptly left the Rosebud, leading west toward the Little Big Horn valley. After a brief rest period, Colonel Custer signaled the troop to move out. Squint, at Andy's insistence, was scouting far in advance of the column. Andy had a strange feeling in his gut about the trail. For one thing, it was evident that a lot of Indians had passed that way. Add to that the fact that they didn't seem to care that they were leaving a broad trail to follow. Finally, the trail was leading straight to the Little Big Horn valley where there were reports that Sitting Bull might be encamped. For these reasons, he borrowed Squint from Captain Benteen. He had a feeling he didn't like about this expedition, and he wanted Squint's experience and savvy to help him scout.

The two of them rode ahead, keeping a distance of two to three miles between themselves and the column behind. There was a quiet between them that they both felt. Squint couldn't put his finger on it, but something told him that big trouble waited ahead of them. There was no physical sign. It was more like catching a faint aroma of sulphur just before lightning strikes.

"If I recollect, the Little Big Horn oughta be on the other side of that ridge," Squint said, as they crossed a little saddle of land with a small stream cutting across it.

"I think you're right," Andy agreed. He glanced up at the late afternoon sun, which was sinking lower now. "Looks like maybe that ridge might be a good place to camp for the night. Whaddaya think?"

"Good a place as any. We got time enough to look around a little to make sure."

When they were satisfied the ridge would provide a safe area to make camp, they rode back to meet the column and advise Colonel Custer of their recommendation for a campsite. The column settled in for the night, pickets were set and orders were given for a cold camp. This brought the usual groans and complaints. The men had ridden hard for two days and a hot meal would have gone a long way toward lifting morale.

On another river, some distance from Squint and Andy, Little Wolf watched a long blue line of soldiers in the distance, threading its way along the banks of the Tongue River. Their progress was slow due to the walk-a-heaps in the column. There were many mounted soldiers, but they could go no faster than those on foot could walk. This concept of war was puzzling to the Cheyenne. Did the army have so many soldiers but not enough horses? It made no sense to the Cheyenne Dog Soldier to go into battle on foot when a man on a horse could strike with the swiftness of the wind and cover more ground in a day than a man on foot could cover in three. As the column moved closer, Sleeps Standing moved quietly in beside Little Wolf and knelt behind the low bushes that shielded them from the army's sight.

"There are many soldiers. These must be the soldiers the messenger warned us of, from the south."

"Yes," Little Wolf replied. "They follow the river but I don't believe they know where the great Sioux village is. I think they are just searching for any band of Indians to kill."

Bloody Claw left his position near the rim of a deep gully and made his way over to them. "There are too many. We are few. We must go back to the village and tell the others. We will need many braves to fight the soldiers." As he spoke, he looked around him at the thirty or so Cheyenne warriors scattered in ambush, awaiting the soldiers. "We must report the presence of the soldiers to Two Moon." He looked directly at Little Wolf as though he expected him to question his decision.

It amused Little Wolf that Bloody Claw still felt he was in competition with him for the position of leadership of the small band of Cheyenne warriors. "You are right, Bloody Claw. A battle with that many soldiers would be foolish for the few of us."

"We must warn Two Moon," Bloody Claw repeated.

Little Wolf watched the line of soldiers intently for a few minutes longer. Then he spoke again, "Perhaps Bloody Claw would like to give these blue coats a welcome to our hunting grounds before we leave to tell Two Moon."

Thinking that Little Wolf was challenging his bravery, Bloody Claw quickly responded, "Yes, we can hide ourselves on both sides of the river and ambush them." He thought for a moment then added, "We will have to send a messenger back to warn Two Moon since the soldiers are so many—they will surely kill us." His eyes flashed with the fierce intensity of a man willing to give up his life for his people.

"Yes, it is a good day to die but there will be other good days. Would it not be better to kill some of the soldiers and then all of us will go back to warn Two Moon? Then we can return with our brothers and kill more soldiers."

"You have a plan?"

Little Wolf rose to his feet, still sheltered by the clump of laurel he had crouched behind. He pointed toward the column of soldiers, now close enough that he could see the end of the long line. "Look, see how the horse soldiers and the wagons ride in front of the soldiers on foot? The walk-a-heaps look tired from eating the dust of the horses. If we keep all our warriors on this side of the river and wait until the horse soldiers and the wagons pass, then we could strike the walk-a-heaps from the side, before the horse soldiers at the rear could come to their aid. We will strike swiftly and then be gone before the horse soldiers can react. Then, when we tell Two Moon of the soldiers, we can also tell him that we have spilled blood and counted coup." He paused while he waited for Bloody Claw's reaction. "Do you approve?"

Bloody Claw could hardly disapprove unless he could offer a better plan. "Yes, I think it is a good plan. Where do you think we should wait for them?"

Little Wolf looked down toward the river. The ideal place would be at the bend of the river where the steep bluffs would dictate a change of direction away from the river in order to traverse them. Judging from the distance between the cavalry and the infantry, there would be several minutes' time when the foot soldiers would be out of sight from those ahead. They could do a lot of damage in that several minutes' span. "There," he said.

Bloody Claw looked toward the spot pointed out by Little Wolf. "Yes," he said. "That is the place I would have picked. Come. We must be ready." He signaled the warriors. Little Wolf turned to go to his horse and found Sleeps Standing smiling at him. As they exchanged glances, Sleeps Standing nodded and winked.

The attack was swift and took the marching soldiers completely by surprise. Bloody Claw's Cheyennes struck at the belly of the column of infantry, killing several soldiers and wounding many others before the cavalry was aware of the action. Upon Little Wolf's suggestion, rifles were not used in the initial assault so the first casualties went down before a single shot was heard. When the soldiers began firing in defense, then the Indians used their rifles to return fire. By the time the rear guard galloped up to join the battle, the Cheyennes were already disappearing beyond the bluffs.

When they returned to the village, Bloody Claw and Little Wolf went to the tipi of Two Moon to report their encounter with the army troops. Two Moon listened intently as the two warriors reported the army strength and line of march.

"So it has begun," Two Moon stated softly when Bloody Claw had finished with his account of the battle. "This is the great war that has been coming for a long time. I think this war will be the one that turns the white man back from our lands forever. Our warriors are ready to fight. We will show the soldiers that we will die before we give another grain of sand to them." He looked at Little Wolf as he added, "If the soldiers are as many as you say, we will need many warriors to fight them."

That night, Two Moon sat in council with Crazy Horse, the war chief of their allies, the Sioux. Crazy Horse was inflamed when told of the soldiers marching up the Tongue River. "I will bring my warriors and we will fight the soldiers together. We will flood the river with their blood!" After a long discussion, it was decided to meet the advancing army at the head of the Rosebud where the lay of the land would favor the expert Cheyenne and Dakota horsemen on their fleet and nimble ponies.

The next day was spent in preparation for battle. Little Wolf carefully applied bands of red and black paint on the Medicine Hat pony. In the morning, he would paint his own face with the same colors in the striped design he favored, a pattern that started on the bridge of his nose and ran across his cheeks to the tip of his earlobes. This day he cleaned and oiled his rifle and inspected his bow and arrows to make sure everything was in order. This done, he felt ready to go into battle. He would rest to preserve his strength after he had offered a prayer to Man Above and asked that he should be strong and fight well.

"Come, my friend. We will go to my tipi and rest and eat." Sleeps Standing placed his arm on Little Wolf's shoulder. "Perhaps you might sleep apart from Morning Sky tonight. My wife's sister wishes you would let her keep you warm."

Little Wolf smiled. He knew Sleeps Standing worried about his physical needs, needs he himself had denied since his wife's death. "The days are warm. I have felt no need to keep warm at night."

Sleeps Standing was exasperated. "The summer nights may warm the outside of your body. A man must also warm the inside. This is not good that you deny your body of its needs."

Little Wolf waved his friend's protests aside. "Come, we will eat and rest. Do not worry about the inside of my soul."

After they had eaten the meat and corn cakes that Sleeps Standing's wife, Lark, and her young sister, Rain Song, had prepared for them, the two warriors sat before the fire and talked for a while. Inside the tipi, the women put away the cooking utensils and prepared the beds for sleeping. The sky had almost shed the last flickers of daylight and soon the camp would be clothed in darkness.

Little Wolf stared into the dying flames of the fire and it made him sad. He remembered sitting in front of Morning Sky's cook fire as she cleaned up after the meal and prepared their bed for sleep. It had been a long time since she shared his bed and his life but it didn't seem like that long. Maybe it was because whenever his thoughts were not occupied with fighting or hunting, they were almost always filled with memories of his wife. She was just a girl really, no more than a few years older than Rain Song when she was taken from him. As he thought of her, he could feel the rage building up inside him again, and he could visualize the images of the two murdering buffalo hunters who took her life. Their execution at his hand had not been enough to satisfy his desire for revenge. No matter how many raids he made against the white man, nothing seemed to dull the fire that burned to punish them for the wrongs committed against him and those he loved. Then his thoughts turned to the cavalry officer who had spared Morning Sky's life and whom he, in turn, had spared on the riverbank that day. Squint Peterson claimed the lieutenant was his brother Tom. Maybe it was true. The memory of his brother was no more than a foggy image of a child. Try as he might, he could not bring the child's face into focus. The thought of having a brother in the other world, before Spotted Pony adopted him, troubled his mind. He was glad that the soldiers he would fight the next day were coming from a fort in the south and not from Fort Lincoln. He would not have to worry about coming face to face with the officer tomorrow.

"It is time to sleep," Sleeps Standing announced and

stood up. Little Wolf got to his feet also and the two friends walked to the edge of the clearing to empty their bladders before retiring. When they returned to the tipi, the women had spread the soft buffalo robes along the perimeter of the tipi, Sleeps Standing and Lark's on one side and two separate robes on the other side, as usual.

Sleeps Standing pulled his buckskins off and crawled in beside his wife. They whispered softly to each other and Little Wolf heard a soft giggle from Lark. Her sister was already in her bed. Little Wolf made himself comfortable and turned his back on his friend and his wife as a courtesy to them. He felt a sadness on this night, more so than usual, and he felt his loneliness. Soon, however, he drifted off to sleep.

Deep in sleep, he felt Morning Sky come to him. He could feel the warmth of her young body as she slipped gracefully under the light fur cover of his bed and pressed close up against his back. He turned to face her and she came eagerly into his arms. He felt the smooth curves of her back and hips and he could feel the surge of fire ignited deep within him. He pulled her close to him, pressing the length of her body tight against his until it seemed her body melted into his. She kissed his neck and chest and he could smell the smoke of the cook fire in her hair. Suddenly he stiffened. This was not a dream! It was not Morning Sky but Rain Song who had come to him in the darkness of the tipi. Rain Song, feeling his hesitation, sensed the cause of it.

"Please, let me love you," she whispered. Had it not been dark, he would have noticed the tears in her eyes. "Please, tomorrow you go into battle. Let me love you tonight."

The thought flashed through his mind that this was wrong. But it was extinguished in an instant, overpowered by the stronger flame of desire. He pulled her to him again and they became as one. There were a few moments of awkwardness, since this was her first time, but he was patient and gentle in his passion, and they soon found fulfillment in each other's arms. Before the sun rose, she slipped quietly from his bed and returned to her own.

*   *   *

The Medicine Hat fairly danced in the bright sunlight of the morning. Little Wolf had to hold the pony hard as the combined forces of Two Moon's Cheyennes and Crazy Horse's Lakotas rode out to meet the advancing soldiers. Riders and horses were painted for war and the blood was running high for the prospect of battle. It was a little more than a half day's ride to the place where they would wait for the blue coats and the young braves were anxious, darting about the line of riders like honeybees. Little Wolf and Sleeps Standing, having fought many times before, rode patiently behind Two Moon. They would contain their excitement until the time it was needed. In the meantime they rode side by side, silent for a long while because Little Wolf was deep in thought. Finally he broke the silence.

"My friend, I feel I have brought shame to your tipi."

Sleeps Standing smiled for he knew what was troubling his friend. "Do not speak of shame. I do not care to hear any confessions today. Today is a day of honor. We will talk of shame and other things tomorrow."

"No. I must tell you this now. Who can say who will be here tomorrow to talk of these things."

"I know what troubles you. Rain Song came to your bed last night." He laughed as he added, "I know this because I told her to."

"You sent her?" Little Wolf was appalled. "But I violated her. She was a virgin and I have shamed you for she is in your care."

"You bring nothing but honor to my tipi." Sleeps Standing was more than a little amused at the genuine contriteness of his friend. "It is time for you to take another wife and Rain Song is a strong young girl. She will be good for you." He grinned widely at Little Wolf, who was evidently too stunned to reply. "Besides, if I wait for you to do something, she may be too old to give you sons."

Little Wolf's brain was under assault by the many confused thoughts this shocking turn of events had loosed. He didn't trust himself to speak for a long time until he had sorted some of his own feelings out. "I do not want a wife," he finally pronounced although with some hint of doubt in his tone.

"You need a wife and now you have found one. Cheer

up. Now we will be more than friends. We will be brothers!"

Little Wolf did not appreciate the humor Sleeps Standing found in the situation. He felt he had been tricked. He let the matter go for the moment but they would talk more on the subject after the battle.

Once in place, they waited. Two Moon sent Little Wolf and Sleeps Standing downriver to scout with a small party of Dakota braves. They were to establish a position several miles distant and wait there for the soldiers to appear. Once they spotted the advancing troops, they were to ride back and alert the main body of warriors.

Their vigil was not a lengthy one, for the advanced scout for the cavalry came into view within an hour after they had tethered their horses and began their wait. The Sioux scouts rode back to tell the others to get ready while Little Wolf and Sleeps Standing stayed long enough to make sure the column was intact and had not split forces. It would not do for their warriors to set up an ambush only to find that half of the troops had detoured and attacked them from another direction. The advance guard was within five hundred yards of the two Cheyenne warriors when they slipped along the river and spurred their ponies back to their waiting comrades.

Little Wolf watched as the army scout reined his horse to a halt and sat looking around him, first to the left and then back to the right. *A Shoshone*, Little Wolf thought. *He should be fighting the soldiers instead of helping them.* The Shoshone took his time, trying to see everything in the area around him. He sniffed the air as if trying to pick up a scent. Then he walked his horse slowly down to the water's edge and sat looking at the river for a long time. There was nothing to be heard but the distant cry of a lone hawk and the rustle of a slight breeze in the treetops along the riverbank. In a short time the first line of soldiers appeared, in a column of twos, their horses at a walk. The scout signaled to them to come ahead and he pushed his horse into the river and started across. Little Wolf slid back further into the bushes and waited. As he had guessed, the scout's path would bring him to pass within a few feet of the bushes he hid behind. He waited until the scout had passed his hiding place and then, like a great cat, he sprang to his feet and, running as fast as he could, hurled himself upon the scout's horse behind the unsuspecting Shoshone. The scout never had a chance to utter more than a hoarse grunt as Little Wolf's hand clamped tight over his mouth while the other hand slit his throat. He let the dead man slide to the ground. A young Sioux brave was there at once to roll the body out of sight. Little Wolf jumped to the ground and handed the reins to the young Sioux who quickly led the horse down behind the bluffs where their own horses were being watched by the boys of the tribe.

As the first soldiers splashed across the shallow river, Little Wolf ran, crouching to keep from being seen, along the ridge of the bluff to a position beside his friend Sleeps Standing. On either side of them, the Cheyenne warriors of Two Moon lined the ridge, waiting for the soldiers to cross the river. On the other side of the crossing, Crazy Horse's Lakotas lay in wait. The first of the column had reached dry land when Crazy Horse stood up and screamed his war cry. It was followed immediately by the sound of the riverbanks exploding in a hail of gunfire. The forward troopers were cut down, some as they tried to retreat to the river, their horses screaming as they were hit by the rifle slugs, sending them tumbling headlong and sliding along the sandy shore. The blue coats caught in the middle of the river struggled to control their hysterical mounts while trying to draw and fire their carbines.

Little Wolf fired again and again until his rifle jammed and he was forced to put it aside and use his bow. By this time, the troopers had managed to withdraw and fall back to a low bluff on the far side of the river where they established a defensive position. From there they returned fire and, after the initial minutes of the battle, effected a stand-off with the combined Indian forces. There were many soldiers and they attempted to re-form and advance upon the Indians. But on this day, the Indians were as great in number as their enemy, and each advance was met with such resistance that the army was finally forced to fall back along the way they had come in order to regroup.

When the soldiers pulled back, Crazy Horse again stood up on the top of the ridge and raised his war whoop. This time his cry was followed by the yells and whoops of his

excited warriors and they shouted insults after the retreating troopers. Even though neither side had conquered
the other, this day was clearly won by the Cheyenne and
the Sioux. They had stopped the invasion of the troops
from Fort Fetterman. Feeling victorious, they returned to
their villages on the Little Big Horn. There would be singing and dancing that night.

CHAPTER 25

Little Wolf did not want to insult his close friend but he did not want to face Sleeps Standing's sister-in-law when they returned from the battle at the Rosebud. He tried to explain that which he could not. He was confused in his mind whenever he tried to examine his feelings about Rain Song. It was useless to try to explain his confusion to Sleeps Standing. His friend was not burdened with deep emotional and complicated thinking. The issue was very simple to him—Little Wolf had no wife and Rain Song would make a fine wife. That to him was all that need be considered. He could not understand Little Wolf's reluctance to take a wife. So it was with a great deal of disappointment that Sleeps Standing finally shrugged his shoulders in a sign of exasperation and bade his friend good-bye as Little Wolf gathered his belongings from the tipi.

"So, you will not even stay the night?"

Little Wolf avoided the soulful eyes of his friend and busied himself with his horse. "No, there is no time. I have promised Two Moon that I will leave to scout the soldiers right away." When there was no response, he hastened to add, "It is important that we know where the soldiers have retreated to."

Sleeps Standing was not convinced. "The soldiers have run away. Why do we care where they run to? They would be fools to try to attack this camp. We are too many."

Little Wolf would not be swayed. "I promised Two Moon," he stated. He did not lie to his friend. Two Moon agreed that it might be helpful to keep an eye on the soldiers, but it was Little Wolf who volunteered to go. He would not admit to Sleeps Standing that the real reason he was leaving was to avoid Rain Song. The night of passion they had shared had happened because he was in a dream state, and it was not meant to be. Now he had to escape to be with his own thoughts and to ask Morning Sky' forgiveness.

"You will not even stay for the dancing and feasting in honor of our victory?"

"No." Little Wolf's answer was curt as he began to be irritated by Sleeps Standing's insistence. Lark and Rain Song were busy helping the other women of the camp prepare the food for the celebration and he wished to get his belongings and leave before they returned. When he and Sleeps Standing had returned from the Rosebud, it was all he could do to avoid Rain Song's glances.

"Very well," Sleeps Standing said and stood aside, giving his friend room to pass. "I wish you success on your journey and welcome you to my tipi on your return."

"Thank you, my friend," Little Wolf responded and walked past him to his horse. He did not look directly into Sleeps Standing's eyes for he was afraid he would see the hurt there. Sleeps Standing might be a simple man, but he was not a stupid man.

He climbed upon the Medicine Hat and walked the pony slowly toward the edge of the camp. Already there was a great deal of activity in the Cheyenne camp on the northern end of the Sioux village. The victory over the troops at the Rosebud had strengthened the resolve of the Cheyenne and fortified their confidence that they could fight the army and beat them. For a reason unknown to him, Little Wolf could not experience the feeling of jubilation his Cheyenne brothers felt. Instead, there came to reside in him a feeling of melancholy, almost a dreading of the future, and he realized that he had never before given a thought toward the future. For him there was no future, just as he felt there was no future for the Cheyenne, or the mighty Sioux for that matter. He wasn't sure why he felt this way. Perhaps it was something Squint had said when they had wintered together near the Wind River, that the white man would keep coming and the soldiers would multiply until they would strangle the Indians. Maybe he had known it from the time he was a boy, when Lige Talbot talked about the thousands of settlers that would make their way west Whatever the reason, he would just greet each morning sun

nd do what must be done on that day and never worry if
would be his last. But now, Rain Song had thrust herself
nto his life. If he allowed himself to have thoughts of her,
nen he would be forced to think about the future, a future
or her and for their sons. And he did not want to have
nose thoughts. Thoughts like those could make a man hesi-
ate in battle, and he had sworn to seek revenge against
ne army and especially Longhair. He could permit no
noughts of a woman to enter his mind.

He walked his pony slowly around the outer row of tipis,
kirting the bustling camp, and headed down through the
ong grass that bordered the river. So deep in thought was
e that he didn't notice the slight figure standing by a
wisted tree trunk near the water's edge. He was directly
eside her when she stepped from the shadows. His pony
topped and took a nervous step backward. She took the
ridle in her hand and quieted the startled animal, her
oice soft and calming. Little Wolf felt as if his heart had
topped beating.

"I see you are leaving," Rain Song said softly, still rub-
ing the horse's forelock. "You do not stay to celebrate
our great victory."

"Rain Song," he blurted. "Ah, no, I must go." He stum-
led weakly over his words. He could feel the blood rising
n his face and neck.

Rain Song continued to stroke the pony's forelock and
eck. "I love your pony. He is so strong and swift." With-
ut pausing, she changed the subject. "Your eyes have
voided me since your return from the battle. And now
ou are leaving our tipi."

"I must go to scout the soldiers," he interrupted.

"So you say. This may be so but I think you are running
way because you do not want to see me."

"Rain Song . . ." he started but she would not let him
nish.

"No. Let me speak. I only want to tell you that you do
ot have to run. I will not bind you to me. I came to your
ed because I wanted to. Do not fear that I want to be
our wife." Not waiting for his reply, she turned and ran
ack toward the camp, leaving a startled and dejected
oung man.

He had never known a feeling like this before, like he

had tortured an innocent and harmless animal. He tried
analyze his emotions but he had nothing to compare the
to. He simply felt miserable and he could not erase th
vision of the fragile Cheyenne girl seeming small and hel
less as he looked down at her. He did not know what
do other than spur his pony into a gallop and ride awa
from there.

He rode hard, hoping the wind would blow the worr
some thoughts of Rain Song from his brain. It was not
be, however, for with every motion of his pony's gallop,
seemed to feel the rhythm of her name. He tried to foc
his mind on Morning Sky's face but found that he could n
remember it in detail. Instead, the plaintive countenance
the fragile little Cheyenne girl in Sleeps Standing's tipi m
his mind's eye. He forced himself to look for signs th
might have been made by the enemy, reminding himse
that he had come to scout the area. He could alert h
senses for a time and then, before he realized it, he wou
find himself thinking about her. Exasperated, he moane
his frustration aloud and cursed the day he had accepte
Sleeps Standing's invitation to come to his tipi. In time
must forget her. This he told himself for he had made
promise to himself that he would hold no other woman
his heart but Morning Sky.

When night came, he made his bed under a canopy
oak trees near the scene of the battle at the Rosebu
There were no soldiers anywhere about, nor did he expe
to find any. He would have made a fire, but he felt
desire to eat. He only wanted to meditate and seek a visic
if possible, and visions came more easily in a fasting stat
Maybe the answer to his misery would come to him
a dream.

He slept and he dreamed. But no answers came to hir
Instead, they were dreams of Rain Song's slender boc
pressed warmly against his and the fire that consumed the
that night. He awoke the next morning in more of a qua
dry than he had been in the previous day. Breaking cam
he went on to the Rosebud. He ate nothing.

The trail left by the retreating army was easily rea
Whatever their intent, it was obvious their leaders had d
cided to withdraw and return along the route they had tra
eled up the Tongue River. He knew this information w

f no particular value to Two Moon, but he had promised
o scout the territory to make sure the soldiers had not
oubled back, so he followed their trail for several miles
efore giving up the mission. No longer concerned with the
rmy force that had confronted them, he decided to con-
nue to scout in the country around the Rosebud for a
hile longer. The real reason was to search his soul for
nswers, and to stay away from the Cheyenne camp long
nough to clear Rain Song from his thoughts.

He had still not eaten anything on the fourth day out
om the village and he could feel the strength being sapped
om his body as each hour passed. When the sun settled
ow in the western sky, he made his bed under a lone pine
hat stood like a sentinel over a bend of the river. He laid
here, waiting for sleep, his eyes open toward the sky where
Man Above resided. The sky gradually darkened as the last
eluctant rays of light withdrew from the day until, finally,
e was gazing at the stars before sleep claimed him.

He dreamed but, when he awoke the next morning, the
ream was not clear to him. There were many of his friends
nd family in the dream, but there seemed to be no particu-
r message that he could discern. The one thing that stood
ut in his mind was that Morning Sky and Rain Song had
ppeared in his dream and they were working together,
eaning a buffalo hide. He lay there for a long time, con-
dering the signficance of this, wondering if it meant that
e should take Rain Song as his wife. What else could it
ean? They were working together on the same hide. As
e thought about it, he realized that this was the way he
anted to intrepret the dream, for he had been unable to
d his thoughts of Sleeps Standing's young sister-in-law.
ut was this the real meaning of the dream? His thoughts
ere suddenly interrupted by a soft scratching sound on
e bark of the pine tree behind him. He turned to discover
large squirrel, halfway down the trunk of the huge tree,
aring at him in open curiosity. Little Wolf knew at once
hat this was a sign. He had received his vision. Morning
ky was telling him that she wanted him to take Rain Song
o wed, as the dream seemed to indicate, for she had sent
im food to end his fast. In one lightning-fast motion, his
nife flashed through the air, pinning the squirrel to the
ee.

He thanked Man Above and began his journey back
the village on the Little Big Horn. Sleeps Standing wou
be very pleased to know that his friend would soon l
planning to visit the Crow country to the north. Little Wo
had paid nothing for Morning Sky. Her family had all bee
massacred by the army. There was no one to buy her fror
He did not intend to ask for Rain Song empty-handed. Tl
Crows had always been his enemy. He would steal hors
from them to pay Sleeps Standing.

For the first time in quite a some time Little Wolf w
in a light-hearted mood as he guided the Medicine H
along the bank of the Rosebud. He had ridden north f
half a day before turning back toward the camp. Now tl
sun had already disappeared below the ridge in front of hi
and it would soon be dark. Suddenly he stopped, hearir
something on the wind. He sat stone still for a long tim
listening. There it was again and this time he could identi
it. It was the whinny of a horse, answered shortly after l
another. The sounds came from the far side of the ridg
It could be a hunting party, possibly. It could not be tl
soldiers they had turned back several days before, and we
far to the south. He thought it probably was a band
Sitting Bull's Sioux, returning from a raid. He decided
find out. If it was a hunting party, they might have me
to share. The squirrel was only a memory to his stoma
by then.

He made his way around the far side of the ridge
approach with the setting sun behind him. There was i
need to take a chance on their seeing him first, whoever
was. There was always the possibility that a Crow raidi
party had ventured this close to the Sioux camp. Tl
thought crossed his mind that this might not be a ba
thing—maybe he wouldn't have to travel north to find tl
horses he sought for Sleeps Standing. He tied his hor
to a dead cottonwood that had fallen into the edge
the stream and went the rest of the way on foot. Litt
Wolf thought it strange that there was no smoke fro
campfires. This made him even more cautious. Whoev
it was thought it necessary to make a cold camp. He conti
ued in a half trot until he was up under the crown of tl
ridge. Then he dropped to all fours and crawled toward tl
top. He knew they were soldiers before reaching the cre

of the ridge because he could hear their conversation on the wind. He pulled himself up behind a low bush where he could see into the encampment.

They were soldiers all right. From the size of the camp, he estimated several hundred, maybe more. They were not the soldiers he had fought nine days before on the Rosebud. These were all horse soldiers, no infantry. He worked his way around the perimeter of the camp, moving silently, like he had learned to move when he was a boy, when he and his friend Black Feather competed to see who could stalk a deer with nothing more than a knife. He took special care to locate the sentries. There were two on this side of the camp and he waited until they had moved apart. There should be pickets also, soldiers on horseback patroling the outer edges of the camp. The sun slid below the horizon and now the ridge was bathed in twilight. He lay flat behind a dead tree while a picket rode slowly by. Then he jumped up and made his way quickly to a large boulder. From there he could see the entire camp. Scanning the area in the fading light, his gaze stopped on a figure in knee-high officer's boots who was giving orders to two other soldiers. He felt the bile slowly rising inside him. There was no mistaking the thin face with the sharp nose and long hair touching the shoulders of his white shirt. *Custer!*

He fought to hold his emotions in check. His initial impulse was to charge into the camp and attack this hated enemy, kill him where he stood, in the midst of his soldiers. A second and calmer thought told him that would be a foolish sacrifice of his life. Also, he had an obligation to ride to Sitting Bull's village with the news of Custer's soldiers so close to them. There was no choice. Slowly and carefully, he withdrew from the edge of the camp and made his way back to the stream and his horse. Once out of range of the ridge, he urged the Medicine Hat into a gallop.

CHAPTER 26

"What's ailing you, Squint? You look sadder'n a gelding in a pasture full of mares." Andy Coulter came over to squat beside the small fire Squint had built to boil some coffee. He watched as Squint poked the ashes up around the small tin pail he was using for a coffeepot. When Squint did not answer right away, he went on, "Now that I think on it, you been kind of quiet for the last two days."

Squint's only response was a grunt; his attention was entirely on his coffee and he stared at it until it started to boil. When the first bubbles began to stir in the inky black liquid, he quickly removed the pail from the ashes. Only then did he speak, "If you want some of this, you'd best find you some kind of cup."

"How 'bout this'un?" Andy laughed and produced a tin cup from the pocket of his coat. "I knew you couldn't start your day without you had your coffee." He watched intently as Squint swished the dark liquid around a few times to mix it a little before pouring some of it into his cup. "I reckon you just forgot the general ordered a cold camp," he teased as he settled back to let the coffee cool a bit before risking his mouth on the hot tin cup.

"Horse turds," Squint replied with a measure of disgust. "You know as well as I do that ain't nobody gonna see this little fire. Last night might have been different but in the morning light it don't make sense to go without hot coffee." He paused to sip cautiously from the tin pail. "Besides, every redskin in the territory knows we're here already, except maybe the deaf and dumb ones."

Andy just smiled knowingly. "I expect so," he said after a moment. "You still ain't told me what's ailing you."

Squint was hesitant to answer. He looked around him at

the sprawling bivouac, at the troopers looking after their gear in preparation for orders to mount and proceed with the march. "I don't know, Andy. I just got a bad feeling in my craw about this whole campaign."

Andy didn't understand. He knew Squint wasn't afraid of a fight. At least he never had been as long as he had known him. "Bad feeling about what?" he asked. "Hell, we got six hundred seasoned troopers here."

"Andy, you've been looking at the same sign I have. That trail we been following looks like a whole village was on the move."

"Yeah, but like I said, there's over six hundred of us."

Squint seemed perplexed. "That ain't the point. The point is where they're headed. Ever since the spring snows melted, Injuns have been leaving the reservations to join Sittin' Bull. Sittin' Bull's camp is somewhere on the Yellowstone or Little Big Horn and that's where this trail is leading. There ain't no tellin' how many Sioux and Cheyenne and Arapaho there are in these basins."

Andy thought this over for a moment. "I reckon you're probably right, but we're supposed to join up with General Terry in a couple of days. And Tom told me we're supposed to join up with a bunch from Fort Fetterman and another bunch is coming down from Montana. Hell, we're gonna have enough soldiers to clean out the territory before we're through."

"Maybe, but I still think we're awful damn close to a helluva lot of Injuns and I ain't seen none of them other soldiers yet."

Their conversation was interrupted by the sound of one of the Pawnee scouts returning to camp. "He shore is riding that horse hard," Andy observed. "Reckon he found something."

"Looks that way, don't it?"

They were not long in finding out. Before Squint had finished his coffee and put out his fire, they heard the officers barking out commands to prepare to mount. A few minutes later they were joined by Tom, riding toward the rear of the column.

"We're moving out," Tom confirmed. "The scouts spotted some smoke on the far side of the ridge. There's a hostile camp on the river. Colonel Custer wants to catch

'em before they can scatter and disappear into the hills.
Andy, he wants you to ride back with the scouts and look
it over."

Squint stepped up on the Appaloosa and reined back
while Andy galloped off to the head of the column. Andy
called back after him to follow. He was about to do so
when Captain Benteen rode up to them and signaled for
Squint to join him and Tom.

"Tom, your men ready to move?" Benteen asked. "Let's
move smartly, mister. The colonel wants to catch them nap-
ping." He turned to Squint. "You can go ahead with
Coulter, but when you get back, I want you with me. Is
that understood?"

"Yessir," Squint replied quietly. "I'll be back." He rode
off in pursuit of Andy.

The column marched at quick pace toward the Little Big
Horn. Andy and Squint, along with three Pawnee scouts,
were far out in front. When they were about two miles
from the river, Squint held up his hand, motioning for the
scouts to halt.

"What is it?" Andy whispered and, before Squint could
answer, he saw what had stopped him. "I see 'em," he said
softly. On the far side of the river, several tipis could be
seen. "How many you reckon?"

"Don't know. We need to get closer."

They decided to send the Pawnee scouts back to notify
Custer of the Sioux camp while they went on a little closer.
"Tell him, many Injuns ahead," Andy instructed the scouts.
When they had gone, he and Squint rode on another mile
closer. From this point, they could see more lodges along
the west bank of the river.

"Sizable camp," Andy said. "Whaddaya think? Maybe
four, five hundred?"

Squint was not sure. "Don't know. From what we can
see from here, I'd say that was a pretty fair estimate. We
probably oughta come back and scout up the river a'ways
after we report this to Custer."

"Reckon you're right," Andy agreed. "Let's go tell the
general." They mounted up and returned to intercept the
column.

*   *   *

Some five miles from the point where Andy and Squint scouted the Sioux camp, Little Wolf sat cleaning his rifle. Unknown to the two scouts, the great Sioux and Cheyenne camp stretched some four miles along the Little Big Horn. The lodge Little Wolf sat before at that moment was on the northern end of the village. He had been a very busy man since he rode in the night before. It had been dark for several hours when he arrived and he went straight to Two Moon's lodge to report the presence of the soldiers between the Rosebud and the Little Big Horn. Two Moon, the Cheyenne war chief, was surprised to hear of this and he took Little Wolf to report the news to Sitting Bull.

"It is as I promised you," the Sioux spiritual chief told them. He received the news with a calm that indicated the confidence he felt. Sitting Bull had been making medicine for many days and his visions had foretold of the coming of Custer. Only a few days before he had told his war chiefs of a vision sent to him that told of many soldiers coming, and in the vision, he saw the soldiers dying and falling to the ground like hundreds of dead leaves.

"How many are the soldiers?" Sitting Bull asked.

Little Wolf replied that he estimated there to be four or five hundred, maybe more; it was difficult to be sure in the fading light. Sitting Bull called for a council of all the war chiefs to alert them to ready their warriors to repel an attack on the village. Among the leaders, Gall and Crazy Horse urged that a counterforce be mounted to meet the soldiers before they reached the village. Others were not convinced this was the thing to do. Sitting Bull listened to the arguments for a while before speaking.

"Why should we go out to do battle? It is better to wait here and defend our village. We are many more in number than the soldiers. They would be foolish to attack us. They will have to cross the river to get to us. It is better to hide our warriors in the gullies along the riverbanks and in the high grass between the river and the village. We will cut them down as they cross the river. I have seen it this way in my vision."

So confident were the war chiefs in the prophecy of Sitting Bull that they felt invincible. They would heed his advice and see to the readiness of their warriors. It was very late when Little Wolf returned to the tipi of his friend

Sleeps Standing but it mattered little, for everyone in the village was awake and scurrying about to prepare for battle.

Even though the leaders had decided they could defend the village successfully, the women, Rain Song among them, were still busy packing for flight in case it became necessary to abandon the camp. For this reason, Little Wolf had no opportunity to speak to Rain Song alone. He had hoped to hint to her what his dream had told him but it had to be done in the right way. Although he had been unable to rid his mind of her, his ego dictated that he should not tell her this at this point. There was a remote chance that she might have changed her mind about wanting him and he did not want to risk damaging his dignity. So, in the bustle of a camp preparing to fight, there was no time for anything else, other than a glance in her direction as he went about the business of making war.

So now he sat, cleaning his rifle, hoping to have an opportunity to speak to her before the certain chaos that was bound to take place in a matter of hours. But it was not to be. Sleeps Standing rode up at that moment.

"Little Wolf! Come quickly! Two Moon summons you."

He responded without delay. Sliding his rifle in its buckskin saddle sheath and leaping upon the Medicine Hat, Little Wolf followed his friend toward the center of the village where Two Moon was in council with his war chiefs. When they rode up, he interrupted his talk to greet them.

"Little Wolf, we have need of your keen eyes and silent step. The soldiers cannot be far from our village. If they are indeed bent on attacking us, it will be before the sun is directly overhead. We must be sure where they plan to attack us. Time is short and we must be ready. I have been in council with the Sioux chiefs. Since the soldiers are approaching the lower end of the village where the Sioux are camped, Gall's warriors will conceal themselves in the gullies and ravines along the river. Crazy Horse will hide his braves in the tall grass on this side of the river. We will ride to the point of attack to strengthen our brothers. You and Sleeps Standing must cross the river and signal us as soon as you can see where the soldiers are going to try to cross. I will hold my warriors on the rise beyond the Sioux lodges. I can see your signal from there if you take a position on the hill we can see beyond the bluffs." He pointed to a distant hill across the river. "Will you do this?"

"We will go at once," Little Wolf responded. He and Sleeps Standing exchanged brief glances and Little Wolf wondered if his own face reflected the radiance he saw in his friend's. The excitement that he read in Sleeps Standing's eyes told him that his friend was filled with the anticipation of combat and the glory that accompanied it. There was a feeling of tense anticipation throughout the entire village. Maybe it was due to Sitting Bull's prophecies of the victory to come, he wasn't sure. But this day was somehow different from battles he had engaged in in the past and he was caught up in the excitement that flowed through his people on this day.

They galloped through the busy camp and crossed the river. On the far side, Gall's warriors were already positioning themselves in the many gulleys along the water's edge. Painted faces with the same excitement he had seen on Sleeps Standing's face looked up at him at they rode by. This was to be a day of glory for his people.

When they reached the specified hilltop, they hobbled their horses out of sight behind the hill and waited, searching the rolling plains to the south and east for the first signs of cavalry. Looking back across the river, they could see Two Moon and his war council waiting on the rise of ground directly behind the tipis of Lame Dog's band of Lakotas.

"A man can ask for no greater honor than this," Sleeps Standing stated, the excitement in his voice causing it to tremble as he spoke. Little Wolf said nothing but smiled and nodded agreement. "Once again we fight side by side, my friend. Perhaps we will die together, if that is Man Above's wish." His smile broadened. "If it is to be, there is no greater thing for me than to die fighting beside my friend, Little Wolf."

Little Wolf was touched by his friend's words. He reached out and laid his hand on Sleeps Standing's shoulder. "We have traveled many paths together, my friend. We will fight well this day, and when we have defeated the soldiers, we will go back and celebrate our victory." He paused as Sleeps Standing beamed, then added, "Then I will steal ten fine horses to offer you in exchange for Rain Song as my wife."

Sleeps Standing's face fairly shone with the pleasure he could barely contain. "I knew we would be brothers! This is indeed a glorious day!" He clapped his friend on the shoulder several times. "This is the best day of my life!"

The morning sun was high in the sky when Squint and Andy galloped back to meet the column. They rode up to Custer, who had already sent for Reno and Benteen when he saw the two scouts approaching. The colonel said but one word when they pulled up before him.

"Where?"

Andy answered, "General, they's about two miles straight ahead."

"How many?"

"Hard to say. From what we could see, I'd say they was at least five or six hundred. But I couldn't say for shore without we circle around and scout up the river a ways."

Custer was impatient, his eyes flashing as he listened to the report. "But what you saw was maybe five or six hundred?" he insisted.

Squint answered. "Well, yessir. But, like Andy said, we can't say for shore until we scout further upstream."

Custer did not seem to be listening. "We've got them, gentlemen. We've got them right where we want them."

Major Reno interjected, "Sir, aren't we supposed to wait for General Terry's men to join up?"

Custer's eyes flashed in a moment of anger before his face relaxed in a benevolent smile. "Major Reno, thank you for reminding me of my orders but I think you will agree that it is the responsibility of command to seize the opportunity when you have the advantage. I don't intend to let these devils slip out from under us this time. We'll strike them before they have a chance to run." His hand rested on the handle of his pistol as he thought for a moment before continuing. "Major Reno, you will take your battalion and attack directly across the river. I will lead mine along the bluffs of the river and support your attack from the flank. Captain Benteen, your battalion is to break off to the left of this trail and scout the territory to the south, along the river, and cover that route of escape in case any of the hostiles evade my flanking movement. But don't tarry, Captain, you must be ready to come up in support of the main attack." He returned the salutes of both officers. "And gentlemen, the object of this mission, and the order of the day, is annihilation. Is that clear? Women, children, dogs, horses . . . all are hostiles."

Following orders previously given him, Squint followed Captain Benteen back to his battalion. He touched his hat with one finger in a salute to Andy Coulter as he galloped away.

CHAPTER 27

The sun was directly overhead when Sleeps Standing pointed to a small cloud of dust beyond the river bluffs. Within a few minutes' time they were able to pick out the blue uniforms of the troopers advancing toward them in a long line, two abreast. The two warriors watched patiently as the soldiers advanced along a line paralleling the river. When they were about a mile away, some of the soldiers broke off from the others and turned east toward the river below the village. The remaining soldiers continued on toward the village. Little Wolf could see that his estimate of the night before was accurate. There were about five or six hundred troopers in all. A scout rode several hundred yards in front of the soldiers, searching the river for a possible crossing. Little Wolf was amused by the caution the scout, a Pawnee apparently, displayed as he was careful to keep below the bluffs in order not to be seen from the village. Little Wolf knew in advance where the scout would decide to cross. It was the only place suitable for a sizable force to cross en masse, and it was the place where Gall and Crazy Horse were hidden, waiting.

When it was obvious the Pawnee had made his decision and rode back to meet the soldiers, Little Wolf turned and signaled across the river to Two Moon, indicating the point of attack. Then he signaled that the second group of soldiers split off to the south of the village. He and Sleeps Standing stayed until the main body of troopers approached the crossing. There the soldiers split into two groups again. One group continued on along the bluffs while the second prepared to cross the river. The stillness of the day was then pierced by the sharp staccato notes of a bugle and the troopers broke into a gallop and came crashing down into the river. Little Wolf looked back at the village. He could see his people scurrying about the tipis, women and children running, gathering up belongings. Bands of warriors were running toward the river to defend the village. There were thousands of warriors, Sioux, Cheyenne, Arapaho, streaming toward the river like a flood, eddying around the lodges and flowing into the high grass between the village and the river.

"Come!" Sleeps Standing shouted. "Let us join the battle!"

Their job done on the hill, they jumped on their ponies and galloped down the hill. The first ranks of soldiers were charging down the bluffs already and plunging into the river, rifles blazing. They were cut down by a hailstorm of fire from the ravines along the riverbank and the charge was halted before the first soldier reached the midpoint of the river. Another wave of troopers came on behind the first and made it into the middle of the river. They, like the first wave, were met with blistering fire as hundreds of warriors rose up from the grass between the river and the village.

Little Wolf and Sleeps Standing rode at full speed along the riverbank, firing as they rode at the ranks of soldiers now retreating back across the river into the gullies under the bluffs. Some of the soldiers dismounted and began to fight on foot. Little Wolf rode into the swirling water to join hundreds of his brothers who were swarming across the river. The air was alive with the snapping of flying lead and the screaming of men and horses, and thick with the black smoke of gunfire. Little Wolf emptied his rifle and reloaded time and again. The soldiers on foot were taking heavy casualties so they remounted and retreated back up the bluffs until they found a position they were better able to defend.

In the confusion of the battle, Little Wolf searched in vain for the familiar figure in knee-high boots and long hair. He could not see anyone that resembled the hated enemy in this group of retreating soldiers. He looked toward Sleeps Standing who had remained at his side.

"Longhair?" he asked.

Sleeps Standing shook his head no.

He wheeled and galloped off to join the fighting now going on downstream where the second group of soldiers had tried to make their way down through the gullies and across the river. The Sioux, led by Gall, rose up like angry hornets, pushing the soldiers back up into the bluffs. Two Moon's Cheyennes, now joined by Little Wolf and Sleeps Standing, streamed into the river after the demoralized troopers. Through the smoke of black powder, Little Wolf caught a glimpse of an officer behind the retreating troopers. He was mounted on a dirty white horse, his saber in his hand, shouting unheard orders to the men around him. *It was Custer!*

"Mine must be the hand that slays him!" Little Wolf growled. He raised his rifle and fired but his aim was spoiled when the Medicine Hat almost stumbled. There was no opportunity for a second shot, for Custer turned and rode back up the bluffs, his men falling back around him, firing desperately as they retreated. The air was filled with death. Individual rifle shots were indistinguishable as the river basin was engulfed in the enormous roar of battle.

"After them! They are running!" someone yelled off to his right. It sounded like Two Moon but, in the heat of the moment, he could not be sure. With the others, he pushed on after the retreating soldiers, caught up in the bloodletting.

"The hill!" someone else shouted. "They are trying to get to the hill!"

Little Wolf looked around him. The numbers of Sioux and Cheyenne were still increasing as many of the warriors who had pushed the first group of soldiers back had now joined in the pursuit of Custer's group. The soldiers were successful in reaching the hill and prepared to defend it against the Indians now swarming upon them from all sides. They were to find it was not a defensible position. In no more than an hour, they were overwhelmed. Little Wolf, trying to get to Custer, fired three times into the ring of soldiers surrounding their leader. Each time a soldier fell. Now he had a clear shot at the long-haired officer, who was frantically yelling commands and waving his saber in the air. He took careful aim and squeezed the trigger only to hear the empty click of the firing pin on the metal jacket of the bullet. Quickly, he ejected the faulty cartridge and reached for another only to find that he had fired his last round. He immediately looked to his left for Sleeps Stand-

ing but he was no longer by his side. Frantically he looked
right and left, but there was no sign of his friend. They had
become separated in the assault on the hillside. He dropped
his rifle and took his bow from his back. The thought struck
him that it was more proper to put an arrow into Custer's
chest instead of a rifle bullet.

As he advanced toward the rapidly diminishing circle of
blue uniforms, he was aware of the rising frenzy of the
warriors as they sensed the annihilation of their hated
enemy. Several soldiers broke from the circle and attempted to run for their lives but there was noplace to
escape as the warriors now completely surrounded the hill.
Little Wolf's eyes were on Custer alone. Making his way
up the hill, now on foot, he readied his arrow and thoughts
of Morning Sky, Spotted Pony, Buffalo Woman, Black
Feather and Black Kettle flashed through his mind. He
could feel the blood pumping furiously in his heart as he
neared the summit.

Custer fell to one knee. He had been hit! One of the
soldiers quickly went to his fallen commander and struggled
to help him up again. Little Wolf stopped and calmly
sighted his arrow, then released it. The flight was barely a
few seconds but it seemed to him that it was in the air a
long time before it buried deep into the white shirt, and
the man fell back to the ground. Within seconds the final
handful of soldiers were lying dead around their leader.
The air was filled with the victory war whoops of his brothers and the hill was overrun with warriors. Within minutes
women and children, swarming over the fallen soldiers,
scurried up from the river to witness the massacre.

Little Wolf stood over the body of Custer, spellbound by
the lifeless form of the devil who had dwelt in his mind
for so long. He who would annihilate a people had been
annihilated instead. *Custer was dead.* At once a great
weight seemed to disappear from Little Wolf's soul. He
stood motionless, looking down at the insignificant corpse
of one who had been such an evil force in his life, while
the women and children of the village stripped the bodies
of everything useful. Off to the side, he heard a Sioux warrior say to someone, "Look at him. The golden cougar is
no more. Longhair is dead." In that instant Little Wolf
recalled his vision of long ago when the great bear con-

quered the cougar that stalked him. But there was no time
to think about it further, for there was still fighting beyond
the bluffs where the first group of soldiers had taken a
stand. He climbed on his pony to join in the assault. As he
did so, he stepped around the body of one of Custer's
scouts. The man was not a Pawnee. He was a squat stump
of a man, a civilian scout, Little Wolf guessed. If there had
been time to think about it, he might have remembered
him as the third man with Squint Peterson and Tom Allred,
when they trailed Little Wolf that day on the Little
Missouri.

They could hear the gunfire in the distance and, from
the sound of it, there must have been a tremendous battle
taking place. At first, Squint figured Custer's and Reno's
men must evidently be slaughtering all life in the Sioux
camp. But as the gunfire continued and increased in vol-
ume, he began to worry. Turning to Tom, he said, "I don't
like the sound of that. I believe our boys have run into
something they wasn't expecting."

"Peterson! Any way we can get out of these damn gullies
any quicker?" The strain in Benteen's face was evident as
the frustration of being slowed down by the rough terrain
along the bluffs began to wear away his patience. There
was a hell of a lot of action going on up ahead and they
were bogged down in a series of ravines and deep gullies
that slowed the horses to a walk.

"No sir," Squint replied. "I'm leading you the shortest
way out. If we don't head away from the river, we ain't
ever gonna get out of here."

They had not encountered any hostiles on their approach
to the Sioux camp, only rough country. Now, when he could
well imagine his troops were needed in support, Benteen
was forced to be late to join the battle. Even before his
fears were justified, Benteen had an eerie feeling about the
assault on the Sioux camp. He had been in silent agreement
with Major Reno—Custer should have waited for General
Terry as he was ordered to do. Finally reaching the open
prairie again, he ordered the battalion into a canter. They
had not traveled a mile when they were met by Custer's
bugler, riding toward them at a gallop. Benteen halted the
column briefly while he took the message from the wide-

eyed trooper. The message read, *Benteen. Come on. Big village. Be quick. Bring packs. P.S. Bring packs.*

Benteen looked up at the bugler. "What's going on up there, son?"

"Sir," the bugler stammered, his speech broken with a heavy accent. The man was obviously a foreigner. "Major Reno charge across river. Many Indians shoot from other side."

"Has Colonel Custer engaged the enemy yet?"

"I don't know, sir."

Benteen turned to Tom. "All right, Mr. Allred, let's move 'em out."

The scene that greeted Captain Benteen was one he was not expecting. When he arrived at the bluffs of the river, what was left of Reno's battalion was fighting for survival, having been backed up into the ravines. The arrival of Benteen's fresh troopers was enough to cause the hostiles to fall back for a while, but even with the reinforcements, the soldiers were still vastly outnumbered. Benteen gave orders to establish a perimeter defense that stalemated the attacking hordes before them, but it would be only a matter of time before they were overrun. In the chaos of retreating troopers and flying lead, Benteen searched for Major Reno. He found him, frantically issuing commands to his junior officers in an effort to deploy his outnumbered troopers.

"Marc! What happened?"

Reno appeared to be in a daze. He stared at his fellow officer for a long time before answering, the grime and sweat of the battle etched on his face. "We ran into a buzzsaw, Fred. I swear, I don't know if any of us are going to get out of this alive. There's thousands of hostiles out there. I don't know how long we can hold them off. It was suicide! We charged into the river and there was a solid wall of hostiles on the other side. They were in the gullies, in the grass, everywhere. They all had rifles, they just—"

"Where's Custer?" Benteen interrupted.

"Overrun!" Reno almost shouted. He turned and pointed toward a ridge. "He fell back to that hill. We tried to reach him once but there were too many hostiles between us. It was all I could do to save as many of my men as I could."

"Well, we can hold this position for a while longer. Maybe we can try to rescue what's left of Custer's men." He summoned his junior officers around him to come up with a plan. "Gentlemen," he began. "Colonel Custer may already have been completely overrun. We can spare one company of men to try to break through to him. I'm not going to order anyone to do it. I want a volunteer."

There was a moment of silence. Even the constant roar of gunfire around them seemed to pause for a moment. Finally someone broke the silence.

"I'll go." It was Tom Allred.

"Dammit, Tom, I thought you'd been in the army long enough to know not to volunteer for nuthin.'" Squint fussed over his saddle pack in preparation to mount.

"You don't have to go," Tom replied quietly.

"Well, the hell I don't. Somebody's got to look after you. Andy Coulter'd probably take my scalp if I let somethin' happen to you." He filled his pockets with extra cartridges. "Besides, it was mighty damn nice of you to volunteer this whole damn company. I know these boys is pleased to git a chance to stick their fannies out there in the middle of them Injuns."

Tom refused to be riled by the scolding. "Squint, Andy's up there."

"I know it, son." He and Tom exchanged glances and Tom knew Squint had not forgotten that for a moment. "Well, let's git on with it."

When his men were ready and mounted, Benteen stopped him for some last-minute instructions. "Tom, don't push it. If you can work your way through to the ridge, fine. But I'm not calling on you to sacrifice yourself or your men. Understood?"

"Understood. Don't worry, I'm not in any hurry to die."

"Good luck then."

It was the middle of the afternoon when Tom and Squint led the company down along a deep ravine toward the hill where Custer's surviving troopers were last seen. They met only sporadic fire until they reached a point near the head of the ravine, some six hundred yards from Custer's embattled defense. Suddenly they were swarmed upon from three sides by a screaming wave of painted Cheyenne warriors.

Tom's horse was shot out from under him and he barely managed to roll out of the saddle before the beast pinned him to the ground. In less than thirty seconds, Squint was there to pull him up behind him on the Appaloosa. With his men falling on either side of him, Tom yelled for the company to fall back and take cover.

"This ain't gonna work, Tom!" Squint shouted over the roar of gunfire around them. "Them Injuns is thicker'n hairs on a beaver."

"We've got to do something," Tom shouted. "We can't stay here. I want to make one more try to break through."

Both men fired until they emptied their weapons, then reloaded and continued to fire. There were targets everywhere. They hardly took time to aim. Squint was as brave as any man when it came to facing certain death, but he failed to see the logic in getting himself killed when it served no purpose. And he could see no purpose in exposing themselves to all that enemy fire. Meanwhile, a small band of hostiles had managed to work its way around to the side and were now zeroing in on the troopers' exposed left flank. It was time to abandon the mission and save as many as possible.

"Tom, Custer's done for. Ain't nothing nobody can do about that now. And the rest of us is soon gonna be buzzard bait if we don't get the hell out of here." His tone was unmistakably authoritative. It was not a simple suggestion.

"You're right," Tom replied reluctantly. "All right!" he yelled to his men. "Mount up and withdraw. And do it smartly, dammit! Sergeant Porter, your men will form the rear guard. The rest of you men watch your flanks and let's get the hell out of here!"

They withdrew in orderly fashion, retreating gradually, fighting as they went. Halfway back to the battalion, they were suddenly attacked by a small band of Cheyennes that had worked in behind them. Tom dropped off the back of Squint's horse and jumped up on the horse of a fallen trooper. As he did, a rifle ball smacked into the fleshy part of his upper arm, causing him to yell out, more in surprise than pain. When he looked back, Squint's saddle was empty. In a panic, he looked left and right, desperately searching for the big scout. Then he saw him, fighting with two Cheyenne warriors on the ground. Before Tom could

get to him, Squint was successful in freeing his right hand
long enough to pull his pistol and dispatch one of the savages while fending off the knife blows of the other with his
left. Tom pulled his revolver and put a bullet through the
skull of the hostile. Squint looked startled for an instant
as the Indian's face suddenly split, showering his sleeve
with blood.

When he turned to see who had saved him, he froze in
his tracks. Directly behind Tom, a Cheyenne warrior rose
up, rifle raised, poised to shoot. It was too late to save
Tom, as the hostile was ready to pull the trigger, but Squint
could at least kill the bastard who killed Tom. He quickly
raised his pistol, but the hostile did not fire. Instead, he
hesitated. Squint took aim, being careful not to hit Tom.
The hostile was dead in his sights but Squint still did not
pull the trigger. It all happened within a few seconds, time
enough for Tom to react. Seeing Squint raise his pistol and
point directly at him, he could guess he was about to be
attacked from behind. He whirled, firing as he did. The
hostile fell to the ground.

"Jesus!" Tom exclaimed, his heart in his throat. "Why
didn't you shoot?" It appeared to him that Squint had simply frozen.

Moving quickly now, Squint rushed to the fallen Indian.
"Because *he* didn't shoot," he yelled as he turned the hostile over on his back. "It's Little Wolf."

"What?" Tom gasped, still confused. "Little Wolf?"

Squint was hurriedly checking over the prone figure before him. "He's only wounded. You just creased his skull.
He's out colder'n hell though. Here, gimme a hand and
we'll put him on his horse."

Tom, still unable to understand Squint's concern for the
wounded man, pulled at Squint's shoulder. "Come on.
We've got to get out of here. The rest of the company are
getting ahead of us." He cocked his pistol and shoved the
barrel down against Little Wolf's head.

Squint knocked his arm aside and hissed, "He's your
brother!"

"He's a damn Indian!"

"He coulda kilt you but he didn't!" Squint shot back
in anger.

"Leave him then. We're all going to be dead if we don't get out of here."

Squint looked at his young friend, oblivious to the fighting around them. "I can't leave him hurt. Somebody might finish him off."

"Suit yourself. I'm leaving. He's just another damn hostile as far as I'm concerned." He mounted and rode off toward the battalion.

Squint wasn't sure what he should do. He didn't want to leave Little Wolf out there alone, but he couldn't stay with him. For want of a better idea, he lifted him up across his saddle and grabbed the Medicine Hat by the reins and galloped off after Tom.

The reception Squint received when he brought the wounded Cheyenne warrior back to the battalion was one of amazement. Captain Benteen was astonished. "Why in hell did you bring that savage back here? We're fighting for our lives, man! We're in no position to take prisoners. Shoot him!"

"Wait a minute, Captain." Squint had to think fast. "You don't want to shoot this Injun. This here's Little Wolf hisself, one of the biggest Cheyenne war chiefs. Why, Custer hisself put a price on his head for capture. You don't want to shoot Little Wolf. The army druther take him back to Fort Lincoln for trial."

The subject of their discussion was only then beginning to show signs of life. Little Wolf groaned and slowly rolled over on his side, still unable to gather his wits, unaware if he was among friends or enemies. At his first movement, several guns were instantly leveled in his direction.

"Hold on," Squint pleaded. "Don't nobody get excited. He ain't armed. Look at him. He don't even know where he's at."

Benteen gazed at the wounded Cheyenne with a cold eye. He was more concerned with the ring of savages holding his men pinned down. He had no time to worry about one dazed Indian. After thinking about it for a moment longer, he said, "Drag him out of here and shoot him."

Major Reno, who had been a witness to the discussion, raised his hand, stopping the two troopers who moved to carry out Benteen's orders. "Just a minute, Fred. You know, Peterson may be right. This is the bastard Custer put a price on. He's the renegade that's been raiding with the Cheyennes for years." His eyes were wild as he glanced back and forth between Benteen and their captive. "We may not get out of this mess with our lives. But if we do, somebody's going to have to answer for this massacre. I'd just as soon have this bastard to hand over to the brass back at Fort Lincoln."

Benteen reconsidered. "Maybe you're right, I don't know . . ." He was concerned with more important issues, like staying alive. "Just get him out of my way." He paused a moment, then ordered, "Lieutenant Allred, take charge of the prisoner and make sure he doesn't get away. If our position is overrun, shoot him."

Tom flushed. "Sir, I don't think I should . . ."

"Just do it, Tom!" Benteen was rapidly losing his patience. The matter was trivial in the face of their immediate peril. Before returning to the more pressing problems at hand, he paused, just then noticing the blood soaking through Tom's sleeve. "You better get that attended to. Is it bad?"

"No sir," Tom replied. "I think the ball went right through."

Two troopers grabbed Little Wolf by the shoulders and roughly dragged him away. Tom reluctantly followed, giving instructions to tie up the prisoner's hands and feet. His mind was in a turmoil over the unforeseen turn of events that had placed his own brother in his hands. He told his conscious mind that he and Little Wolf were coincidentally birthed by the same woman, but they were not brothers. The man was a savage. He had killed Tom's comrades. He should not feel compassion for this renegade, this Cheyenne war chief, this enemy of his country.

Squint stepped aside to let Tom pass. He said nothing to him, but studied the expression in his eyes. The distress he read there was evidence of the storm raging in Tom's mind.

Together, Reno and Benteen came to a decision. Custer was finished. Of that they were certain. Since darkness was not far off, they decided to fall back to a better position in the hills. There they dug in and prepared to hold out until General Terry's forces could reinforce them.

For two days they held. Even though they were hammered continuously by the hostiles, the embattled troopers dug in and repelled attack after attack. During the afternoon of the second day, one last assault was launched against the encircled cavalry. When it failed, the fighting tapered off to occasional sniper fire. Later in the evening, the entire village of Sioux and Cheyenne left the valley, heading toward the Big Horn Mountains.

Major Reno and Captain Benteen ordered their troops to remain dug in, ready to repell further attacks. But the battle was over. The following morning, Squint was able to boil his coffee in peace, without the threat of a Sioux sharpshooter adding spice to his bacon. That afternoon, General Terry arrived to rescue the remnants of what was once the proud Seventh Cavalry.

CHAPTER 28

Little Wolf sat astride the Medicine Hat, his feet tied under the pony's belly, his hands bound tightly together. He had not spoken a single word in English since his capture. The bandage around his head had fallen off and no one was concerned enough to replace it or even see if the wound was healing. He watched sullenly now as Tom Allred rode toward him. Tom did not speak to him at all, preferring to give instructions to his guards and ignoring the tall savage. Little Wolf understood this. Tom was a soldier. He was his enemy. As far as Little Wolf was concerned, the slate was clean between the two brothers. He looked for no compassion from Tom. Surprising to him, however, was Squint's attitude. Listening to his guards' conversation, he learned that Squint was the one who insisted that his life be spared. Little Wolf was not especially appreciative for the gesture. Death in battle was an honorable way to die. He much preferred it to spending the rest of his life in a white man's prison. And if he was to be hung, as the guards said, he would still be robbed of a warrior's death.

Squint stayed completely away from him. This disappointed him, for he and Squint had parted as friends when they left the Wind River camp. Reflecting on the matter, he decided he couldn't blame Squint for looking out for his own hide. It wouldn't sit well for Squint if the army thought he might be soft in his attitude toward Indians. But it was ironic that he would not be in this predicament had he not hesitated to pull the trigger when he ambushed Squint and Tom. It was only at that instant that he realized who the two men were. He was ready to fire when he recognized Squint, but he just could not pull the trigger. Neither could Squint when he realized it was Little Wolf.

But, he reminded himself, Tom did not hesitate. He would remember that if the opportunity came for escape. It was a long ride to Fort Lincoln—he was constantly guarded but someone might get careless along the way.

A trooper galloped back to Tom. "Sir, Captain Benteen's compliments. He wants to see you right away."

Tom dropped out of the column and rode after the trooper. He found Benteen waiting in the shade of a cottonwood tree where he had been in conference with Major Reno and two staff officers from General Terry's command.

"How's the arm?" he said in greeting when he saw Tom grimace a little when he dismounted.

"It's all right. Sore as hell, but nothing I can't live with."

"Tom, I'm sending you back to Lincoln." He held up his hand to silence Tom. "I know you want to stay with the battalion on this campaign but I'm sending you back with our celebrity back there."

"Sir," Tom pleaded, "is it necessary to send a line officer to escort a prisoner? A damn Cheyenne prisoner at that? I'd be of more use to you with the battalion."

It was obvious the matter was not up for discussion. Benteen's manner was one of impatience. "Like I said, this one's a celebrity. He rates an officer. Besides, that arm could use a little time to heal."

Tom could see there was little use in arguing. "Yessir. Can I take Peterson with me as scout?"

Benteen had to think this over for a moment. He trusted Squint and he felt more comfortable when he was with the battalion. "All right," he finally decided, "take him with you." He paused. "Take three men with you. That ought to be enough to guard one Indian, don't you think? That will give you extra men to split up sentry duty when you camp."

Tom offered a halfhearted salute and returned to his company. So, he thought, he was not to participate in the campaign against the Sioux. It was going to be a major operation. Already they had joined with troops from Fort Fetterman and additional units from the Montana territory. Washington had already authorized the marching orders of thousands more. The massacre of Custer's Seventh Cavalry had sent massive repercussions throughout the government. The Sioux and Cheyenne were to be finished once and for

all. And, at least for the initial campaign, he was to si'
it out.

The orders suited Squint just fine. He allowed as how he
had had enough Indian fighting for a while. In addition, he
wasn't fond of mop-up type operations anyway. He was
getting sick of fighting in general and was spending more
thoughts lately on the Oregon territory. The sight of Little
Wolf tied to his horse was not especially pleasant for him
but, other than that, he was in good spirits when their small
party broke off from the main body early the next morning
and headed east.

A sergeant and two privates were picked to guard Little
Wolf. Tom passed along his orders to them, addressing the
sergeant. "Sergeant Spanner, I want you men to keep a
sharp eye on him. I intend to see this Indian gets delivered
to Fort Lincoln to hang and I don't want anybody to get
careless."

Squint watched from a few yards' distance. Little Wolf
tried to catch his gaze but Squint avoided eye contact. Instead, he turned his horse, the Appaloosa given him by
Little Wolf, and rode out ahead.

On the second day out, they crossed the Rosebud and
followed it north to intercept the Yellowstone. Tom figured
it would take seven days of hard riding to make Fort Lincoln so he didn't permit the detail to linger. They rode each
day until after dark before making camp, rising before
sunup the next morning to start out again. Tied hand and
foot, it was a hard ride for Little Wolf but he did not
complain. The soldiers, on the other hand, were grumbling
about the long hours in the saddle whenever Tom was out
of earshot.

The fading light of the setting sun on the fourth day out
found them trailing single file along a narrow path that
hugged a steep bank of the Yellowstone, where the river
forced its way through a narrow gorge. Heavy rains two
days before had caused the river to swell as it rushed
through the gorge. Some twenty feet below them, the swift
current of the muddy water swirled past boulders and dead
trees that had snagged upon them. Squint signaled a stop
and dismounted. He walked back to talk to Tom. Sergeant
Spanner joined them a few moments later.

"This might not have been a good idea," Squint said,

scratching his head, looking first at the narrow ledge that served as a trail and then at the rushing water below them.

Spanner offered his comments. "Hell, I wondered why we didn't go around this bend of the river anyway. It wouldn't of took two hours more." His expression hinted that he questioned Squint's judgment as a guide.

Squint went on, "It'da been all right if we had got here before the sun went down. I didn't remember this trail being this skinny. We could have swung around and missed this piece of the river, I reckon, but this way is quicker. If we're real careful and don't get in too much of a hurry, we can camp about a quarter of a mile from here in a nice little clearing."

Tom listened attentively. "All right then." He turned to the men behind him. "You men hear that?" When he received murmurs of "Yessir," he turned back to Squint. "You might want to check on the prisoner's ropes. Make sure his feet are tied to that damn horse."

"Yessir, Lieutenant," Squint replied and walked back along the trail to the Indian pony.

Sergeant Spanner stepped up in the saddle again and looked toward the sky. "We best make time. When that there sun dips below the prairie, it's gonna be like somebody blew out the candle."

No one noticed that Squint had pushed his skinning knife up the sleeve of his buckskin shirt. He approached the prisoner and looked up into the eyes glaring back at him. He couldn't help but smile as he loudly remarked, "We want to make shore you're nice and comfortable, Mr. Little Wolf." He reached up and took Little Wolf's hands and pretended to be checking the knots. As an astonished Little Wolf stared in disbelief, the knife slid down from Squint's sleeve and he quickly cut the through the ropes until they were held by little more than a thread. "They ought to hold," he announced and then bent down and repeated the motions on the ropes holding the prisoner's feet. When he straightened up again, he whispered, "I hope you can swim." Back on his horse, Squint called out, "All right, let's go," and the single file of soldiers and prisoner continued cautiously along the narrow path.

They had gone about fifty yards further when Squint pulled aside and waited for the others to catch up. It was rapidly getting darker. When Tom caught up to him, Squint cautioned him. "Sir, this here's a real narrow place. Look like a rock slide took out part of the trail. One slip and you could find your ass in the river. Good place to camp right around the next bend."

Tom pulled his horse over beside Squint's and waited for the rest of the detail to catch up. When the Medicine Hat filed by, Tom reached out and took the bridle and pulled the horse aside on the trail. "Sergeant Spanner, you and the other two cross over by that washout. When you get on the other side, get ready to take the prisoner when he crosses. We'll hold him here and send him over when you get ready. I don't want to take any chances in this place."

Sergeant Spanner paused for a moment as if uncertain whether to proceed or not. Tom motioned for him to pass and he urged his horse forward, the two privates following, carefully guiding their horses over the treacherous piece of trail. What happened in the next instant was over before anyone had time to react. Squint pulled out his big army revolver and fired it three times at the horses' hoofs. At the same time he kicked the Appaloosa hard into the Medicine Hat. The combination of the sudden explosion under the startled horses plus the impact of the Appaloosa on the Medicine Hat caused both horses and their riders to go over the side and plunge twenty feet into the muddy water.

In the following seconds, Tom backed his horse until he had room to turn around. His pistol was out immediately and he fired six quick shots at the rapidly disappearing figures floundering in the swift current. One of the three troopers made his way back down the trail in time to get off several shots at the dark lumps now fading into the evening dusk.

"You got him!" Tom shouted at the startled and confused trooper. "Nice shooting, soldier! You got him!"

The trooper was totally at a loss. "What about Squint, sir?" In the confusion of the moment, he had forgotten that one of the objects in the river was the scout.

Tom was quick to reassure the poor man. "Private, don't trouble your mind about it. You are a soldier. You are trained to react and react you did. As far as I'm concerned, you just saved the government a hanging. The incident is closed. No one has to know you shot Squint. It couldn't be

elped anyway. The light was bad and I'm not sure you
even hit Squint. But you damn sure got the Indian, right
between the shoulder blades."

"Oh my God, sir, I couldn't hardly see what I was shooting at. I didn't think. When I saw you shooting, I just natu-
ally reacted."

"Don't go blaming yourself for this. This is just one of
hose things that happen sometimes in war. Like I said, I'm
not sure you hit Squint. If he doesn't show up in a day or
wo, we'll just assume he drowned. The main thing is that
he Indian is dead for sure. My report will show that the
prisoner was shot while attempting to escape. It will also
how that you acted courageously and professionally." He
urned the poor man around and pushed him back toward
he other two. "By the way, you might be called upon to
ell what happened. It's a good thing you saw the Indian
go under."

"Yessir," the bewildered young man replied, "I saw the
whole thing." No one thought to ask why Squint had fired
his pistol in the first place.

"Make for that bank over there!" Squint shouted as the
wo men struggled to stay with their horses. They had
drifted at least a mile, keeping the horses' heads turned
into the center of the river so they would swim with the
current. Both horses naturally wanted to make for the
hore right away so Squint and Little Wolf had to keep
pulling their heads back toward the middle. Now, far
enough downstream, they let the animals swim to shore.
Once the horses felt sand under their hooves, they scrambled up the bank snorting and shaking. Squint and Little
Wolf staggered up behind them.

"We made it, partner! That there was quite a ride!" He
aughed and whooped, jumping around on one foot in an
effort to jar the water out of his ears. "Yessir, that was
quite a ride." Little Wolf was staring at him in disbelief,
till not sure what to make of his sudden liberation. When
Squint stopped laughing and bouncing long enough to no-
ice puzzlement on his friend's face, he calmed down and
aid, "You didn't think ole Squint was gonna let anybody
hang you, did you?"

Little Wolf spoke for the first time since they had

plunged into the river. "We must leave here. The soldier will be looking for us." He was happy to be free but he was still confused by the way it happened.

"Relax, ain't nobody gonna be lookin' for us. Hell, we're dead as far as the army is concerned. Tom'll see to that."

"Tom? But he shot at us."

Squint laughed. "Tom's a better shot than that." Then he went on to explain how the two of them, Tom and himself, had cooked up the whole scheme. That was the reason they had taken the trail by the river in the first place. When they plunged off the bank into the river, Tom pretended to shoot at them and he would tell the troopers with him that he killed them.

"What if they don't believe him?"

"I ain't worried about that. Neither is Tom. He'll handle it."

Little Wolf was amazed. "I thought he wanted me dead."

"He did for a while but I had a little talk with him and he began to see that you was as much Cheyenne as he is soldier. And looking at it from your side of the fire, you weren't doing nothing but fighting to save your people."

This brought Little Wolf's thoughts back to his village. "Squint, where are my people now? Do you know?"

"Well, I do know that after the fight at the Little Big Horn, most of your people figured there was gonna be hell to pay for the lickin' they put on the army, so the tribe scattered. I heard that Two Moon took his Cheyennes back into the mountains." He studied his friend's expression for a long time, waiting for Little Wolf's reaction to this news. When he was met with nothing but a long thoughtful silence, he prodded. "What do you aim to do? Go find 'em?"

"I have to. There is something I must do."

"Ah, horseshit! I done risked my neck to save you from hanging and you ain't had enough playin' Injun yet? Hell, I'm tard of fightin. I'm headin' out to see that Oregon territory. I swear, I thought you'd be ready to go with me. Can you see there ain't no future left for the Cheyenne or the Sioux now? They ain't stoppin' this time till they wipe 'em out or put 'em on a reservation."

Little Wolf couldn't resist the opportunity to tease his old friend. "Why would I want to go anywhere with you

fter the way you treated me since I was captured? I
hought you were supposed to be my friend."

"Damn your hide," Squint roared. "I had to play like I
vasn't no friend, me and Tom both, else you'd more'n
kely be headed to Fort Lincoln with somebody else right
ow, if they hadn't already shot you."

Little Wolf laughed and gave his friend a big bear hug.
You are right. I am tired of fighting. Now that Longhair
dead, I am ready to go to Oregon with you."

"Hot damn, you mean it? Let's git going then!"

"First I must find Two Moon. There is something I
hust do."

Even with Little Wolf, Squint couldn't help but be a little
ervous as they approached the small circle of tipis tucked
p under the cover of a steep ridge. Trigger fingers were
ertain to be itchy after the Little Big Horn. Little Wolf
topped and studied the forest around them before making
is way down the valley to the stream. Squint stayed close
ehind, leading the horses. Little Wolf could tell they were
art of Two Moon's band by the markings on the lodges.
here was no sound of alarm as they rode out of the trees
nd splashed through the stream. As they approached the
amp, several braves emerged from the tipis to greet them.
he first, a young brave with a wide grin on his face, ran
> grasp Little Wolf's arm.

"Little Wolf! I knew you would return. They said you
ere taken by the soldiers but I told them you would
eturn."

Little Wolf dismounted and hugged Sleeps Standing. "I
as afraid you had been killed. When I last looked for you,
ou were not there."

The two friends laughed and pounded each other on the
ack as a small crowd gathered around them. The men
apped Little Wolf on the back and expressed their joy in
eeing him alive. After a while, Sleeps Standing paused and
odded toward Squint, still in the saddle and more than a
ttle nervous.

"I see you have brought a friend with you." He looked
round Squint at the string of eight ponies. "The signs on
lose ponies look like Crow markings. Are they his?"

"No, my friend." Little Wolf smiled. "One pony is his to

use as a packhorse. One of them is for Rain Song to ri‹
to the far mountains with me. The other six are for you
exchange for Rain Song as my wife.''

Sleeps Standing threw his head back and whooped. H
pounded his friend on the back again. "How do you kn‹
I will trade her for six measly Crow ponies?" he tease‹
then laughed good-naturedly. "I will give her to you f
five of the ponies. You will need a packhorse too if y‹
are going to the far country.''

Rain Song had seen Little Wolf and Squint ride in‹
camp. Although her heart leaped with joy at the sight
the man she loved, a man she had feared dead, she did n
run to greet him. Instead, she remained in the open e
trance of the tipi, where she had been grinding seed for
bread paste. He could not see her but she could hear t‹
men talking. She had thought a great deal about the nig
when she went to Little Wolf's bed. Sleeps Standing h‹
encouraged her to do it, but she knew afterward that it h‹
not been fair to Little Wolf. She had tried to tell hers‹
that she must forget him, but she found it impossible
do. When Sleeps Standing returned from the fighting a‹
told Lark that they must take up the tipi and leave at on‹
Rain Song did not want to leave before Little Wolf r
turned. But Sleeps Standing told her that several of t‹
warriors had seen Little Wolf shot and captured by tv‹
soldiers.

Now he was back. She wanted to run to him and ho‹
him close to her but she was afraid he would be angry if s‹
did so. So she sat, quietly grinding the seeds and listening
the conversation coming from the group of people in fro
of Two Moon's lodge. Suddenly she stopped and strain‹
to hear the words spoken by Little Wolf. At once she re‹
ized what he had just said to Sleeps Standing. At first s‹
couldn't believe it and feared her ears had tricked her. B
no, he was telling Sleeps Standing that the horses were f‹
her! Her heart seemed to stop beating moments befor‹
Now she could feel it pounding in her bosom. She wait‹
no longer.

While he talked with Sleeps Standing, Little Wolf's ey‹
scanned the camp behind his friend in an effort to get
glimpse of Rain Song. He had expected to see her as so‹
as he rode in but she was nowhere in sight. What if s‹

wasn't here? The thought triggered a twinge of panic in his brain but he dared not let it show in his face as he exchanged news of the battle with Sleeps Standing. What if he had already married another, thinking that he did not desire her? But Sleeps Standing said nothing of that. In fact, he accepted the horses Little Wolf offered. So she must be in the village. Maybe she was hiding because she changed her mind and no longer wanted him.

"Little Wolf!"

He turned to see Rain Song running to him, tears of joy running freely down her cheeks. His heart took wings and he ran to meet her. She leaped up into his arms and he rushed her to him and spun her around and around while he showered his face with kisses. Their embrace was met with a loud roar of approval from the people of the camp.

"I think you just wasted five good horses," Squint remarked, laughing. "She'da gone with you for one small muskrat."

Little Wolf turned to Squint and said, "Now, my friend, we will go to Oregon."

The following morning they set out for Oregon but they never actually got that far. After traveling through the mountains for eight days, they came upon a river basin at the foot of a great white wall of mountains, a wall that seemed to rise all the way up into the heavens. The valley before it was green and lush and there were signs of all manner of game everywhere. The river was deep and clear. Just the sight of it held them spellbound. And all at once, Little Wolf remembered. He had been here before, in a vision. It was in his dream, his vision when he was but a boy. This was the place that had appeared to him that night on the mountain when the grizzly watched over him while ___ place he was meant to find.

___ de their home. It wasn't Ore-
___ egon was nothing more than
___ place that suited his fancy.
___ able to find any place
___ get busy

of foolishness. The next most important thing was to ge
Little Wolf and Rain Song busy making some babies. H
had a feeling he was going to need a lot of little young'ur
around to wait on him in his old age.